A DANGEROUS WOMAN

Mark was on his back, and his eyes were closed. Connie's knife was out as she approached the bed. Her hand was steady. She had a mission.

He seemed to sense her presence and opened his eyes. He didn't recognize her in his disguise and there was a puzzled look on his face.

Connie leaned closer so that she could look directly into his eyes. "Do you know who I am?"

"No, but I'd like to. What's your name?"

"I'm your angel."

"Angel, huh? That's a nice name."

"Why don't you ask what kind of angel I am?"

Mark grinned. "What kind of angel are you?"

"I'm your angel of death." Connie pulled off the wig and removed her glasses. "I'm sure you recognize me now."

Mark blinked and then looked bewildered. "What are you talking about? And why did you wear that wig?"

He didn't have time to say anything else as Connie's knife slashed down . . .

Books by Joanne Fluke

Hannah Swensen Mysteries

CHOCOLATE CHIP COOKIE MURDER
STRAWBERRY SHORTCAKE MURDER
BLUEBERRY MUFFIN MURDER
LEMON MERINGUE PIE MURDER
FUDGE CUPCAKE MURDER
SUGAR COOKIE MURDER
PEACH COBBLER MURDER
CHERRY CHEESECAKE MURDER
KEY LIME PIE MURDER
CANDY CANE MURDER
CARROT CAKE MURDER
CREAM PUFF MURDER
PLUM PUDDING MURDER
APPLE TURNOVER MURDER
DEVIL'S FOOD CAKE MURDER
GINGERBREAD COOKIE MURDER
CINNAMON ROLL MURDER
RED VELVET CUPCAKE MURDER
BLACKBERRY PIE MURDER
DOUBLE FUDGE BROWNIE MURDER
WEDDING CAKE MURDER
JOANNE FLUKE'S LAKE EDEN COOKBOOK

Suspense Novels

VIDEO KILL
WINTER CHILL
DEAD GIVEAWAY
THE OTHER CHILD
COLD JUDGMENT
FATAL IDENTITY
FINAL APPEAL
VENGEANCE IS MINE
EYES

Published by Kensington Publishing Corporation

EYES

JOANNE
FLUKE

KENSINGTON BOOKS

http://www.kensingtonbooks.com

KENSINGTON BOOKS are published by

Kensington Publishing Corp.
119 West 40th Street
New York, NY 10018

Copyright © 1996 by Joanne Fluke
Previously published under the pseudonym Chris Hunter. The original year of publication was July 1996.

All Kensington titles, imprints and distributed lines are available at special quantity discounts for bulk purchases for sales promotion, premiums, fund-raising, educational or institutional use. Special book excerpts or customized printings can also be created to fit specific needs. For details, write or phone the office of the Kensington Special Sales Manager: Kensington Publishing Corp., 119 West 40th Street, New York, NY, 10018. Attn. Special Sales Department. Phone: 1-800-221-2647.

Kensington and the K logo Reg. U.S. Pat. & TM Off.

ISBN-13: 978-0-7582-9110-3
ISBN-10: 0-7582-9110-8
First Kensington Mass Market Edition: May 2016

eISBN-13: 978-0-7582-9111-0
eISBN-10: 0-7582-9111-6
First Kensington Electronic Edition: May 2016

10 9 8 7 6 5 4 3 2 1

Printed in the United States of America

PROLOGUE

Alan Stanford's smile disappeared with his last bite of turkey. It had been a pleasant Thanksgiving meal with his parents and his younger sister, but Alan's time was about up. He'd promised his girlfriend, Connie Wilson, he'd make the big announcement when dinner was over, and the traditional dessert was about to be served.

Alan's hands started to shake as the maid carried in the pumpkin pie. It was lightly browned on top and still warm from the oven, the way his father, the senior Mr. Stanford, preferred. When the maid presented it to his mother to slice, just as if she'd baked it herself, a wry smile flickered across Alan's face. It was doubtful that Mrs. Stanford had ever ventured as far as the kitchen, and the thought that his impeccably groomed, silver-haired mother might put on an apron and roll out a pie crust was patently ridiculous.

Rather than think about the words he'd soon have to utter, Alan considered the hypocrisy of etiquette. One praised the hostess for a delicious dinner, even if it had been catered. And one always called the daughter of a colleague a lady, whether she was one or not. The term "gentleman" referred to any man with enough money to make him socially desirable, and an estate was simply a home with enough land to house a condo complex. All the same, etiquette might save him some embarrassment tonight. There would be no scenes, no tears, no recriminations. After Alan had informed the family of his decision, his father would suggest he and Alan retire to the library where they'd discuss the matter in private.

"This is lovely, Mother." Beth, Alan's younger sister, was dutifully complimentary. "And I really do think it's much better warm, with chilled crème fraiche."

Alan's mother smiled. "Yes, dear. Your father prefers it this way. Another piece, Ralph?"

"Just a small one." Alan's father held out his plate. "You know I'm watching my cholesterol."

Alan waited while his mother cut another piece of pie. Nothing ever changed at the Stanford mansion. His father always said he was watching his cholesterol, and he always had a second serving of pie. Every Thanksgiving was exactly the same, but Alan was about to change the order of their lives. By next Thanksgiving, there would be two more guests at the oval table. The rules of etiquette were clear. They'd be obligated to invite his wife and his son.

There were three bites remaining on his father's plate, perhaps four if he ate all the crust. Alan knew how a condemned man felt as his father's fork cut and carried each bite, one by one, to his mouth. The white linen napkin came up, to dab at the corners of his father's lips, and Alan took a deep breath. He'd promised Connie. He couldn't delay any longer.

"I have an announcement to make." Alan's voice was a little too loud because of his effort not to sound tentative. "Connie and I are getting married."

There was complete silence around the table. It lasted for several seconds, and then Beth gave a hesitant smile. "That's wonderful, Alan. Isn't that wonderful, Mother?"

"Oh . . . yes." His mother's voice was strained, and Alan noticed that all the color had left her face. He could see the lines of her makeup, the exact spot where the edge of the blush met the foundation. "Yes, indeed. That's wonderful, dear."

Was it really going to be this easy? Alan turned to look at his father. The older man was frowning as he pushed back his chair. "Superb dinner, Marilyn. Alan, why don't you join me in the library for a cognac?"

It wasn't an invitation; it was an order. Alan slid his chair back and stood up. Then he walked to the end of the table to kiss his mother on the cheek. "Thank you, Mother. Dinner was excellent."

"Coming, Alan?"

His father looked impatient, so Alan followed him to the second-floor library. He accepted a snifter of cognac, even though he wasn't fond of its taste, then waited for all hell to break loose.

"Sit down." Alan's father motioned toward the two wing chairs in front of the fireplace. A fire had been laid. As it burned cheerfully, it gave off the scent of cherry wood. Naturally, the fire was real. The fireplace was made of solid river rock; no expense had been spared when his grandfather had built the Stanford mansion.

Alan's father took a sip of his cognac and set it down on the table. He then turned to Alan, frowning. "Now that we're away from the ladies, suppose you tell me what *that* was all about."

"Connie and I are getting married." It was difficult, but Alan met his father's eyes. "Don't worry, Father. I don't expect you to approve, or even understand, but I love Connie and I want to spend the rest of my life with her."

Ralph Stanford sighed and then shook his head. "Now, son . . . I'm sure she's a fine girl, but you can't be serious about actually bringing her into our family."

"I'm very serious." Alan managed not to drop his eyes. "We're getting married next week, Father. It's all arranged. Of course we'd be delighted if you'd come to the wedding, but Connie doesn't expect it and neither do I."

Alan's father sighed again. "All right, son. I'd hoped I wouldn't have to resort to this, but I see that I have no other choice."

Alan watched as his father walked to the antique desk and opened the center drawer. Ralph Stanford's mouth was set in a grim line as he handed Alan a typed report in a blue binding.

"Read this. There may be some facts about your intended that you don't know."

Alan's hands were steady as he opened the binder and started to read. Everything was here, from Connie's illegitimate birth to her mother's years on welfare. The investigator hadn't mentioned the name of Connie's father. That was too bad. Connie would have liked to know. But the report went into detail about the man Connie's mother had married, how he'd abused her and forced her into prostitution to support his drug habit, how she'd been an alcoholic.

It was a wonder that Connie was so kind and loving, coming from a background like hers. Alan sighed as he read about how her stepfather had repeatedly molested her, had even offered her to his friends.

Alan knew all about Connie's past, how she'd run away the night of her fifteenth birthday, lived with a series of men, worked in a topless club as a dancer, and finally saved enough money to finish a secretarial course. Alan had met Connie at work, when she'd come in as a temporary replacement for one of the secretaries. She'd agreed to move in with him only after she'd told him the story of her life.

When he'd finished the last page and closed the report, Alan handed it back to his father. Then he waited. The ball was in his father's court.

Ralph Stanford cleared his throat. "Well, son?"

"Don't pay him, Father." Alan managed not to grin.

"What?"

"Don't pay this detective. He left out the part about Pete Jones, the truck driver Connie lived with for almost a year.

And he didn't find out about the job Connie took in a massage parlor on lower Hennepin."

"You knew about all this? Still you want to marry this woman?"

Alan smiled. His father looked utterly deflated, the first time Alan had seen him like this. "It's not a question of *wanting* to marry Connie. I'm *going* to marry her. And nothing you can say will stop me!"

"But . . . why?"

"Because we love each other." His father seemed to have aged in the past few minutes, and that made Alan feel bad. But he'd promised Connie he'd tell him everything, so he had another blow to deliver. "Connie's pregnant. We didn't plan it, and she suggested abortion, but I wouldn't agree. She only did it to please me. She wants this baby just as much as I do."

Alan's father swallowed hard. A vein in his forehead was throbbing as he leaned forward to put a hand on Alan's arm. "Listen to me, son. You're falling into the oldest trap in the world!"

Alan shook his head. "It's not a trap. I'm the one who insisted that Connie marry me. She knew you wouldn't approve, and she didn't want to cause trouble in the family. She was willing to leave and raise the baby herself."

As Ralph Stanford remained silent, Alan's hopes rose. Was it possible he'd convinced his father? Would the family accept Connie and the baby?

The library was so quiet Alan could hear the individual flakes of snow as they blew against the windows. It was turning icy as the night approached; the temperature had fallen to single digits. Each gust of wind was followed by sounds like those of a snare drum as snow turned to sleet hit the glass panes.

At last Alan's father nodded. "All right. The two of you will continue to live in the condo, where she'll have every advantage. The family will support her, pay her medical bills, and provide any help she needs. When she gives birth, we'll do a paternity test; then you'll have our permission to marry."

"What!" Alan was so shocked, he stood up. "A paternity test would be an insult to Connie—and to me! I'm telling you, Father, this baby is mine!"

"Perhaps. But we can't take the chance that you're wrong. Just remember, son, it's a wise man who knows the father of his own child."

"You're crazy!" Alan was so upset, he found he was fumbling for words. "Listen to me, Connie would never . . . I can't believe that you'd actually . . ."

Alan's father rose and took his arm. "Calm down. I'm not accusing her of anything. I'm just saying that before you commit yourself, it's best to make certain. If it'll make you feel better, we won't even tell her about the paternity test. Our own doctor will do it in the hospital and will keep it strictly confidential."

"There won't be any paternity test." Alan's eyes were hard as he pulled away. "I'll give you until this time tomorrow to make a decision. You'll accept my wife and my child—welcome them into the family—or you'll never see me again!"

Alan's hands were shaking as he pulled out of the driveway. For the first time in his life, he'd taken a stand. He should feel proud that he hadn't let his father browbeat him into submission, but he didn't, not yet. He was too furious about his father's accusation to experience any emotion but rage.

How dare his father suspect Connie of tricking him into marriage! What gall to say that the baby might not be his!

Alan was so upset he took the curve a little too fast and his Porsche started to skid on the slippery pavement.

He knew better than to stomp on the brakes. He'd grown up in Minnesota and was accustomed to winter driving. He steered in the direction of the skid, gained control of the powerful car, and touched the brakes lightly to slow. The Stanford mansion was up in the hills, overlooking Lake Minnetonka. The downhill road was steep and curving, and the snow had turned to sleet. If he didn't pay attention to his driving, he could skid through the guardrail on his way home.

Connie would be waiting for him at the condo. Thinking about her made Alan's anger begin to subside. He wouldn't tell her about his father's reaction. He'd just say he'd given the family until tomorrow to work things out. And he certainly wouldn't mention the accusations his father had made; Connie would be crushed. It was up to him to protect her from his family.

Alan switched on the car's stereo. Connie's favorite CD started to play, and he smiled. That was when he noticed the lights in his rearview mirror.

A truck was bearing down on him, following much too closely. The driver honked his air horn, several rapid blasts to signify that he wanted to pass, but there was no place to pull over on the narrow, two-lane road.

The truck driver hit his air horn again, one long blast that shattered the stillness of the night. His emergency lights were blinking on and off, and Alan knew what that meant. The driver had lost his brakes and was heading for the escape lane about a mile ahead.

Alan pressed down on the gas pedal. He had no other choice. If the driver had lost control of the truck, he'd be rear-ended.

The next few moments were tense. Alan screeched around the curves, hoping he could out distance the runaway truck. He came out of the curves much too fast for a road partially covered with icy snow, but the exit for the escape lane was just ahead.

Alan watched in his rearview mirror as the truck barreled onto the escape lane. This stretch of roadway climbed gradually uphill, with sand traps to slow the truck. At the end was an absorbent barrier, especially designed to stop a runaway truck with minimal damage.

"Thank God!" Alan reached up to wipe his forehead. Sweat was streaming into his eyes, and he was almost weak with relief. If the truck had rear-ended him, they'd both be dead. But he'd made it through the curves. Now everything was just fine.

There was a sound like a gunshot, and Alan's Porsche swerved sharply, almost wrenching the wheel from his hands. His right front tire had blown. He was heading straight for the ditch!

He fought the wheel with all his strength, struggling to control the skid. It worked, and he was just thanking his lucky stars, when the unexpected happened again. There was another explosion, and his left front tire blew out.

Alan wore an expression of shocked disbelief as his Porsche swerved in the opposite direction. Then he was crashing through the guardrail, hurtling out into space, rolling end over end to the bottom of the hill.

When the Porsche hit the rocks at the bottom of the ravine, it flipped over several times, coming to rest on its back, its racing tires spinning uselessly in the air. Alan was trapped in the expensive shell of his luxury car. He didn't hear a passing motorist call out to him, didn't smell the stench of gasoline or experience the salty, slightly metallic taste of his own blood. He didn't see the paramedics flip open his wallet to discover his organ donor card, didn't feel careful hands pull him from the wreck. The quick action of the well-trained emergency team kept his heart pumping blood and his lungs taking in oxygen, but the brain of the man who had been Alan Stanford showed when checked at the hospital, a flat, unending line on the graph—death.

CHAPTER 1

Connie Wilson frowned as she stared out at the snow-covered courtyard. The condo association had decorated for Christmas, and this was the night they'd turned on the lights. She had watched them from her third-floor windows, draping the tall, stately pines with strings of multicolored bulbs. Now that the lights were on, the gently falling snow reflected all the colors, but Connie was too worried to appreciate the lovely sight. She didn't even smile as she spotted the life-size sleigh nestled under the trees with the illuminated figures of Santa and his elves. It was almost ten, and Alan still wasn't home.

He'd never stayed at his parents this late before. The Thanksgiving dinner had begun at three, and meals at the Stanford mansion were always served on time. Even with all the courses associated with the traditional Thanksgiving feast, they must have been finished by four or four-thirty.

Alan had promised to make his announcement right after dessert. Perhaps that had been as late as five, but there was no way the obligatory snifter of cognac, sipped with his father in the library, could have taken more than an hour. Even if Ralph Stanford had objected to the marriage, as Connie was sure he had, father and son wouldn't have argued this long.

So what was keeping Alan? She paced back and forth across the white carpet, doing her best to think positive thoughts. Alan loved her. She was sure of that. And he was determined to marry her, with or without his parents' permission. He had been ready to slay dragons for her when she'd kissed him good-bye; nothing Alan's parents could say or do would sway him.

And he wasn't the type to stop off for a drink. He always called her when he knew he'd be late. Even if there'd been a terrible family fight, he would come straight home to her. But what if his parents hadn't objected? What if he had convinced them that marriage to her was acceptable? Was it even remotely possible that he was with his family right now, planning the wedding?

Connie thought about that for a moment, then shook her head. Alan had told her all about his family, and she was sure the Stanfords would never approve of her as a prospective daughter-in-law. They were probably laying down the law right now, telling Alan that if he went ahead with this unsuitable marriage, they would disown him.

She pictured Alan coming in the door, his face lined with worry. She'd put on coffee, so it would be ready when he got home. He loved a good cup of coffee. One was bound to make him feel better.

Connie measured out the espresso beans, put them in the electric grinder. She loved coffee, too, and she adored the espresso Alan had taught her to make in his machine. But the doctor had told her that too much caffeine during a pregnancy could cause problems, so she had decided to give up coffee until after the baby was born.

There were so many things to remember. Connie frowned slightly as she glanced at the list she'd tacked up on the kitchen bulletin board. No caffeine, no alcohol, a high-fiber diet, moderate daily exercise, and plenty of rest. She was doing everything her doctor had recommended. Her friends from the past would never believe the fun-loving exotic dancer had stopped drinking, toned down her makeup, and let her bleached blond hair grow out to its natural color. Connie now looked like the girl next door, wholesome, sweet, and totally natural.

When the coffee was ready to brew, she went into the huge living room. She glanced at the clock and sighed again. It was almost ten-thirty. Should she call Alan at his parents' house to make sure everything was all right? She debated for a moment, even going so far as to pick up the phone, but she replaced the receiver in its cradle without punching in the number for the Stanford mansion. A call from her might rock the boat, and that was the last thing she wanted to do.

She sat down on the couch and stared at the snow falling outside. She was just thinking how pretty it was when the telephone rang. She reached out to it, crossing her fingers for luck. It just had to be Alan!

"Mrs. Stanford?"

The voice sounded official, and Connie could hear other voices in the background. "No. I'm not Mrs. Stanford. Is this a sales call?"

"No, this is Central Dispatch, Minneapolis Police. Do you know an Alan Stanford?"

"Yes." Connie swallowed hard. "Alan's my fiancé. Is something wrong?"

"Two officers are on their way to talk to you. They should be there any minute."

"But . . . why? What's happened?"

"Just relax, Miss . . . ?"

Connie clutched the phone so hard, her knuckles were white. "Connie Wilson. But can't you tell me—"

"I'm sorry." The voice interrupted. "I'm just a dispatcher, and I don't know. They just told me to call this number to confirm that someone was home."

Connie's head was spinning. Had Alan been arrested? She was about to ask, even though the dispatcher probably wouldn't know, when she heard a sharp knocking. "Someone's at the door. It must be your officers."

"Please let them in. And thank you, Miss Wilson."

There was a click, and Connie dropped the phone back into its cradle. Her legs were shaking as she rushed across the carpet to answer the door.

"Miss Wilson?" The older officer flashed his badge. "May we come in, please?"

"Yes. Of course." Connie stood to the side so both men could enter. "But . . . how do you know my name?"

"The dispatcher told us. We were in radio contact. Please sit down, Miss Wilson."

Connie had a wild urge to refuse. If she didn't sit down, perhaps they would leave. And then Alan would come in the door, and—

"Miss Wilson? Please."

The older officer gestured toward the couch. Connie sat. "What is it? What's wrong?"

"There's been an accident, Miss Wilson."

The blood rushed from Connie's face, and she swallowed hard. "But . . . Alan's all right, isn't he?"

"I'm afraid not." The older officer shook his head. "Do you have anyone who can come to stay with you, Miss Wilson?"

"No. There's no one. But I don't need anyone to stay here. I have to go to the hospital to see Alan!"

"There's no need for that, Miss Wilson."

"Alan's dead?" Connie's eyes widened. "No! That can't be true!"

"I'm afraid it is. Why don't you let us call someone for you. A friend? Family? You shouldn't be alone at a time like this."

"No!" Connie shook her head so hard, she became dizzy. "You've got the wrong person, that's all. It was someone else. You just thought it was Alan. Alan's alive! I know he is!"

"Calm down, Miss Wilson."

The older officer tried to put an arm around her shoulders, but Connie shrugged it off. "You'll see. It's a mistake, that's all. Alan'll be coming through that door any second, and we'll all have a good laugh."

"Miss Wilson . . . I know how hard this is to accept, but we made positive identification at the scene."

"Nooooo!" Connie started to sob, and tears poured down her face. Alan couldn't be dead! Not Alan! Then she was hit by a terrible cramping. She screamed in pain.

"Miss Wilson . . . Connie. Please." The older officer looked terribly concerned. "Are you ill?"

She opened her mouth to tell him, but nothing came out. She felt so weak she could barely move, and dark spots swirled in front of her eyes. Another cramp struck, as if it were trying to split her in two, and she looked down to see that the couch was wet with blood.

"The . . . the baby! Save the baby!" Connie forced herself to choke out the words. She heard the younger officer radio for an ambulance, but just as he was giving the address, everything went black.

CHAPTER 2

Jill Larkin Bradley paced across the kitchen floor of her childhood home on River Road. They'd moved to the four-bedroom, two-bath home in a rural suburb of Minneapolis when her father had died, two years ago. Jill loved the old house with its wooden floors, large airy rooms, and comfortable, overstuffed furniture. She was the third generation of Larkins to live in this house, and that gave her a sense of continuity. There were memories here of the happy times when she was a child, of her college years when she'd brought friends home for long weekends, and of the holidays she'd shared with her family. There were sad memories, too, of visiting her mother in those last months, of watching the grief that had settled into permanent lines on her father's face, and of seeing his gradual decline until death had taken him, too, less than a year later.

Jill's husband, Neil, hadn't wanted to move. Their single-bedroom, high-rise apartment, adjacent to the University of Minnesota campus, had been perfect for him. He'd been two blocks from his office in the English Literature building, and had walked to work every morning. But Jill's commute had been a killer. She was an assistant DA, and her office was located in downtown Minneapolis, right across from the central police station. The only way for her to get to it was through street traffic. Many mornings it had taken her over an hour to drive to work. Now that they'd moved, they both had a twenty-minute commute, but the fact that their house on River Road was centrally located for both of them didn't seem to matter to Neil. He hated to be inconvenienced, so he complained constantly about the traffic.

Jill sighed as she paced to the counter and then back again. She knew the real reason Neil had resisted their move. His teaching assistant, Lisa Hyland, had lived in their building. And that had been very convenient for him.

Two years ago, Jill had caught them in bed together. She'd wanted to leave Neil, to file for divorce and move back to the home she'd inherited from her father, but her husband had been persuasive. He'd apologized, held her when she'd cried, and told her he loved only her. So Jill had been persuaded to stay with him, but only if they moved across town to her childhood home, where she'd never have to see Lisa again.

Looking back on it now, Jill knew why Neil had agreed to the move. Associate professors barely made enough money to support themselves, and he'd needed her income. The prospect of living in a large house with room for an office was also a factor, since he had decided to write a book.

Neil's book had been published last November. The time had been right for a mystery thriller, and to Jill's delight, it had climbed to the top of the charts. There had even been a publicity tour; that was how Jill had found out that Neil was still involved with Lisa. One of her Chicago cousins had taken a picture at his book signing. She'd sent Jill a print, and there was Lisa, standing right next to Neil.

Jill had called a good divorce attorney, but he'd advised her against filing papers so close to the end of the year. If she could stick it out for a few more weeks, she could avoid some complicated tax problems, he'd said. Of course Jill had stuck it out. She'd been married to Neil for over three years; a month or two more wouldn't make any difference. She'd also followed her attorney's advice in not mentioning that she was planning to seek a divorce.

Christmas had entailed the usual round of social engagements. The district attorney had thrown his annual party, and Jill had attended with Neil. There had been Neil's English department party, a Christmas dance at the chancellor's home, and a Minnesota Bar Association dinner. Neil's brother and his wife had flown in for the holidays; Jill had felt like a hypocrite as she'd served the traditional Christmas Day dinner. They'd gone to a party on New Year's Eve, watched the bowl games with the neighbors on New Year's Day. And then Jill had gone back to the office.

Preparing divorce papers had taken time, ten weeks to be exact. Her lawyer had wanted to wait until Jill and Neil had filed their tax forms before he worked out a financial settlement. When Jill had gone to his office to sign the forms, an urgent call had come in for her. Neil had been taken to the hospital; the doctor attending him had asked her to come immediately.

Jill's hands had been shaking as she'd driven to the hospital. Was this God's way of punishing her for trying to divorce Neil? She was a rational person, she told herself, and she'd refused to believe God kept track of every broken marriage. Neil's hospitalization was a coincidence, nothing more, nothing less. But it had kept her from filing for divorce.

The doctor had explained everything when she'd arrived. Neil would be kept several days for testing and observation, but he was convinced that Neil's eyesight was failing, that he had a rare, degenerative disease called Lompec's Syndrome. There were only five cases in the medical literature. Dr. Varney had seen one case when he'd been an intern, and he believed there was hope if they treated Neil with a combination of powerful drugs to knock out the virus.

Jill had nodded. What was the prognosis? Would the drug therapy restore his sight?

Not entirely, Dr. Varney had told her. The disease had already done considerable muscle damage, but that could be handled surgically. Right now, Neil was experiencing tunnel vision, another symptom of Lompec's Syndrome. His peripheral vision was narrowing quite rapidly, and even with the proper drug therapy, it would take time to improve.

Jill had shuddered. The whole thing sounded horrible— and it had happened so suddenly. Only last week Neil had mentioned that he wasn't seeing well and might have to get glasses, but neither of them had realized he had such a disease.

Dr. Varney had nodded. That was the problem with Lompec's Syndrome. The symptoms came on so gradually, the patient learned to compensate for his impaired vision. Luckily, Neil had come in for testing while there was still time to reverse the process, but they were too late to save his corneas. He would need a double corneal transplant, and Dr. Varney had already put Neil's name on the waiting list.

Jill had asked the obvious question. What if they couldn't find a donor in time? And even if they did, what if the transplant didn't work?

The doctor had told her not to worry, that they'd cross that bridge when, and if, they came to it. Drug therapy would slow and eventually stop the progress of the disease, but even if Neil's eye muscles were repaired and he responded well to the corneal transplant, there was no harm in being prepared. The Institute For The Blind had some excellent programs, and he'd advised Neil to enroll. The Institute would provide a support network to help him through his anxious time.

Of course Jill hadn't filed the divorce papers. She couldn't leave Neil at this time of uncertainty. But he hadn't been easy to live with, and tonight she felt trapped and resentful. She no longer loved him, but she had to stay with him. It wasn't so much the vows she'd taken when they'd married. "In sickness and in health" was definitely a factor, but what trapped her was her own sense of fairness. Neil was in trouble; leaving him now would be wrong.

Today the hospital had done more tests, and the results weren't good. Neil's eyesight had deteriorated drastically in the past eight months. He was still able to distinguish between dark and light, but his peripheral vision had narrowed to the point where he could only see in an arc of twenty degrees in the strongest light.

Neil refused to take classes at the Institute. He said it was beneath his dignity to stumble around with a white cane and a guide dog. He was wallowing in self-pity, which was only natural, but lately he'd begun to take his frustration out on her. Jill understood his anger. Fate had dealt him a cruel blow. But she really didn't know how much more abuse she could take.

Neil's hope for a transplant was fading, too. He'd only be a candidate for a few more weeks. After that, his nerves would have degenerated to the point where a transplant wouldn't restore his sight. Something had to happen soon, and Jill felt like a ghoul every time she called the doctor to see where Neil's name was on the list. It was too much like hoping that someone would die so Neil could have his eyes.

She sat down at the kitchen table and did what she'd gotten in the habit of doing for the past six months; she thought about how she'd feel if their positions were reversed and she was the one losing her sight. She was sure she'd spend her time storing up beautiful memories: the colors of a splendid sunset, the graceful pattern of a single snowflake, the deep black velvet of the winter sky at night, the face of the person she loved. Perhaps Neil was doing all that, but Jill felt fairly certain that her face wasn't the one he was memorizing.

It was almost midnight, time to check on Neil. Jill sighed as she climbed the stairs. The doctor had prescribed a mild sedative, and Neil was sleeping. Jill tucked the blankets around him and sighed again. She'd just been promoted, and the rise in status entitled her to a year's leave. She'd planned to apply for it, but the counselors at the Institute had advised against it. They'd insisted that Neil had to learn to cope on his own, that she would be doing him a terrible disservice if she allowed him to become dependent on her.

Jill reached out to touch her husband's face. Neil was a handsome man with dark hair and finely chiseled features. He was tall, over six feet—that was what had first attracted her to him. They'd met at a college reunion, her fourth, his fifth. At the time he'd been a teaching assistant, and she'd been the youngest lawyer on the district attorney's staff.

The dance was dull. There was no other word for it. Jill was sorry she'd come. Responding to a call from the alumni association, she'd purchased a ticket even though she'd never intended to use it. She'd marked the date on her calendar at the office, and tonight a minor miracle had happened. Her boss had come into the law library and told her that she could leave early. Jill had rushed home, put on the red cocktail dress she hadn't worn since the office Christmas party, and gone to the dance.

The next hour had been depressing as she'd been reunited with the gang from the dorm. Jennifer was married, expecting her first child. All she could talk about was natural childbirth and the pros and cons of breast-feeding. Lauren was engaged, looking radiant and flashing a diamond that must have weighed in at three karats. She talked about going abroad for her month-long honeymoon and about the huge house her fiancé, the doctor, was buying. Marcia was Marcia, nosey as ever, asking why Jill didn't have a boyfriend and offering to set her up with a divorced cousin.

"Jill? Jill Larkin? Is that you?"

Jill swiveled around to see a chubby redhead in a black cocktail dress, holding the arm of a very handsome, very tall man. At first Jill didn't recognize her, but then the redhead smiled and Jill knew it was Adele. Though Adele was forty pounds heavier than she'd been in college, she still had the gap between her teeth she'd sworn she'd have fixed after graduation.

"It's good to see you," Jill said, and she smiled with genuine warmth. Adele had been one of her favorites in the dorm, always cheerful and always urging them all to do what she called "the good, fun things," like going down to the public library on Wednesdays to read to the kids, finding homes for the stray cats who hung around the campus, and delivering home-baked cookies to the local senior citizen homes.

"I know what you're thinking." Adele laughed. "You're wondering why I didn't get my teeth fixed."

Jill nodded. "You're right. Tell the truth, Adele . . . did you spend the money on a home for stray dogs and cats?"

"Not exactly. I spent it on tuition. I'm getting my doctorate in social work." Adele turned to the handsome man beside her. "Professor Neil Bradley meet Jill Larkin."

The man reached out to take Jill's hand. "Hello, Jill. It's not really Professor Bradley, not until next year. And then it's only associate professor. Just call me Neil. It's a lot less complicated."

"Neil's my boss." Adele beamed. "I work part-time at the ESL lab."

Neil noticed Jill's puzzled expression, and he explained.

"English as a Second Language. Adele helps foreign students brush up on their English skills."

"That's a perfect job for her." Jill felt the color rise in her cheeks. Neil was still holding her hand. "What do you teach, Neil?"

"I'm Dr. Brown's teaching assistant for Metaphysical Poets."

Jill smiled. What else could she do? She knew absolutely nothing about Metaphysical Poetry.

"I also fill in for Professor Harris on Fridays. He teaches a class on Sir Thomas Wyatt."

Jill raised her eyebrows. Wyatt had been one of her mother's favorite poets, and she knew one piece of information about him. Perhaps it would be enough to get by and impress this handsome, soon-to-be professor. "Was Wyatt really Anne Boleyn's lover before she married?"

"The jury's still out on that." Neil looked pleased that she knew something about his field. "Let's just say Wyatt was in the right place at the right time, and anything's possible. Would you like to dance?"

"I'd love to!" Jill gave a deep sigh of relief as Neil escorted her to the dance floor. She loved to dance, and she was good at it. Everything would be fine just as long as he didn't expect her to say anything intelligent about poetry.

Neil took her into his arms, and they began to move rhythmically. He was a good dancer, and Jill managed to match his steps perfectly. She searched her mind for something to say, but he was quicker.

"You seem to know something about poetry, Jill. Who's your favorite poet?"

She took a deep breath. Her mother had always said if you could get a man to talk about himself you wouldn't have to say another word all night. "I'm not sure, Neil. How about you?"

"I'm not sure, either. Of course there's Shakespeare. And Keats . . . and Shelly . . . and Byron. And I can't forget Poe."

Jill smiled and nodded. Her mother was right. But Neil didn't begin to rhapsodize about poets in the way she'd expected. Instead, he asked her another question.

"How about favorite poems? Do you have one?"

"Oh . . . well . . ." Jill tried to come up with an answer, but Neil was holding her so close, all she could think about was the way his body was pressing against hers. It was no use trying to dredge up the name of a suitable poem. She decided to be honest, even though she was going to blow her first chance at a handsome, eligible guy in months.

"Look, Neil . . ." She raised her head to meet his gaze, and she almost lost her train of thought. His eyes were a gorgeous, deep brown color, and they were warm, like polished wood in the sun.

"Yes?"

His smile made Jill's knees weak. How would his lips feel pressed tightly against hers? And his hands, with those long, strong fingers, stroking her body?

"Jill? Why are you blushing?"

Embarrassed, she said the first thing that popped into her mind. "I'm not blushing. That's just a reflection from my red dress."

"I see." Neil laughed. "Now what were you trying to tell me?"

Jill dropped her eyes. It was impossible to think when she was looking at him. "I only took one class in poetry, and that was because it was required. I'm not really into poetry, Neil."

"Thank God!"

Jill was shocked when Neil started to laugh. "Why are you laughing?"

"Because I'm not into poetry either."

"But . . . you teach poetry!"

Neil nodded. "That's true, but I'm only a TA. I don't get to choose the subjects that interest me. The department gives me an assignment, and that's what I do."

Jill nodded. That made sense. If she'd thought about it, she would have realized that teaching assistants went wherever they were needed.

"I'm glad you're not into poetry, Jill. Most of the women I meet around here expect me to spend the evening reading them sonnets."

"You mean, 'How do I love thee?'" Jill started to grin.

"You got it! And that gives me a great idea. Why don't we go back to my apartment and actually *count* the ways I can love you."

Jill laughed. "That's got to be the most original pick-up line I've ever heard!"

"Thank you, but I'm serious. I really would like to make love to you."

As her mind started to whirl, Jill took a deep breath. This wasn't some pick-up in a bar by an attractive stranger. He was an alumnus, almost a classmate, and she'd met him through her friend, Adele. She certainly wasn't drunk, no alcohol had been served at the dance. And he couldn't be married, Adele would have told her.

"Well, Jill?"

His brown eyes searched hers, and she felt a flush of passion color her face. Even though she'd never been tempted to have casual sex before, what did she have to lose?

"Why not?" Jill snuggled even closer. "But don't forget that I'm a lawyer. If you make promises you can't keep, I might just sue."

Jill sighed as she remembered how he'd taken her back to his one-room apartment and made love to her. Neil hadn't been her first lover, but after the first time she'd shared his bed, she'd vowed that he'd be her last. He had told her he felt the same way, and after six months of dating, he'd proposed to her. She'd accepted and here she was, living with a man she no longer loved.

"What happened, Neil?" Jill frowned as she looked down at his face. "I loved you. I really did. Why did you push me away?"

But she already knew the answer to that question. They'd grown apart. They hadn't really known each other before they'd married, and they hadn't truly been compatible. Neil was selfish. He wanted everything done his way. He also needed constant reassurance, something Jill was unwilling to give him. Reassuring Neil was a full-time job, and when Jill was busy with her real job, Neil found plenty of attractive female students to feed his ego. Lisa hadn't been the first, Jill knew that now. And she wouldn't be the last.

The phone rang, jarring the stillness of the night, and she rushed down the stairs to answer it. It was almost two o'clock in the morning. Who could it be at this hour?

"Hello?" Jill's voice was shaking slightly, even though she told herself it was probably just a wrong number. A phone call in the middle of the night didn't always mean disaster.

"Mrs. Bradley? It's Dr. Varney at the hospital."

There was a stool by the hallway phone and Jill sat down. Her nerves on edge, she gripped the phone tightly. "Yes, Dr. Varney?"

"I want you to bring Neil in right away. There was a fatal accident tonight, and the victim had filled out a donor card. We'll harvest the corneas for Neil when he gets here."

Jill swallowed hard. "Harvest?"

"It's a medical term. Get here as soon as you can, but don't feel you have to hurry. We're keeping the donor on life support until his organs can be harvested for transplant."

"All right, Doctor. Thank you." Jill hung up the phone and sat there, stunned.

"Jill?" Neil was standing at the top of the stairs, his voice groggy with sleep. "Did I hear the phone ring?"

"Yes, Neil. I'm coming." She rose and took several shaky steps. Her legs were trembling, and she gripped the banister as she climbed up the stairs. The news Dr. Varney had given her was awful and wonderful at the same time. It was a tragedy for the donor's family, an incredible stroke of luck for Neil. Someone had died in a horrible accident, but now Neil could get his life back.

CHAPTER 3

She was in bed in a room with pale blue walls, a room she didn't recognize. Connie tried to focus her eyes, but the objects about her remained hazy and all she could really see was the pretty blue color of the walls. This wasn't her bedroom. She'd painted that herself, and it was green, the ugly, split-pea shade of green that covered the hallways at school.

In fact, Connie had found the can of paint at school and had brought it home to cover the stained plasterboard walls in her room. The school Dumpster held all sorts of wonderful things: stubs of pencils, partially filled notebooks that had blank pages she could use, and the best find of all—old books, thrown out by teachers because they were ready to fall apart. Connie had taken the books home to read. She loved to read even though her stepfather called her lazy for wasting her time with books.

The fog that seemed to fill her mind lifted a bit as Connie blinked her eyes. She didn't live at home with her mother and stepfather any longer. She could remember running away, escaping from the house where she'd been forced to do all those awful things. No, she wasn't at home . . . but where was she?

This wasn't the room she'd rented at the boardinghouse.

Its walls had been a cheery yellow that made the sun seem to shine, even on a rainy day. And it wasn't one of the bedrooms at the condo. They had been hung with expensive wallpaper in beautiful designs she'd chosen herself.

But she *was* in bed. Connie looked down to see that she was covered by a white sheet and blanket. Whose bedroom was this? And how had she gotten here?

"Hello, Connie. I see you're awake."

A tall, black woman wearing a white smock and slacks stepped into the room. Connie struggled to sit up, but could only manage to raise her head slightly. "Please . . . where am I?"

"University Hospital. They brought you in last night. Don't worry, honey. A couple days of rest and you're going to be just fine."

It took a moment for the words to filter through the layer of fog that still clouded her mind. She was in a hospital. They'd brought her in last night, and she needed rest. "Wha . . . what happened to me?"

"I'll ring for the doctor. He'll answer all your questions." The black woman walked to the bed and took a glass of water from a tray. "How about something to drink? You're probably thirsty."

"Yes. Yes, I am." Connie tried to take the glass, but her hands didn't seem to work. She was so tired, she could barely lift them from the white blanket.

"That's okay, honey. I'll hold it for you. You're still a little dizzy from the anesthetic."

Of course. The anesthetic. But why had she needed an anesthetic? Had she been in some kind of accident? "Am I . . . hurt?"

"No. You're all fixed up, thanks to Dr. Peters."

The woman held the glass in front of her lips, and Connie found the straw. The water was lukewarm, but it tasted delicious so she took several swallows.

"There. Now just rest a minute, and I'll get Dr. Peters. He's the resident on call. He told me to beep him the minute you woke up."

"You're a nurse?" Connie blinked and tried to focus on the woman's face. It kept shrinking and expanding before her eyes.

The woman smiled—Connie could see that—and then she nodded and pointed to something pinned to the front of her smock. "Gladys Raft, RN. And you're . . . ?"

"Connie Wilson." Connie tried to smile back. She was sure the nurse knew her name, but they always asked to make sure you hadn't suffered any memory loss.

There was the sound of approaching footsteps, and a moment later, the door opened again. A short man who had brown hair and wore glasses walked to the bed and smiled at her. There must be a course on smiling for employees of this hospital, she thought.

"I'm Dr. Peters. How are you feeling?" The doctor reached out to take her pulse.

"Fine, I think. But everything's still a little foggy, and I can't seem to focus my eyes."

The doctor nodded. "That'll wear off. Just give it time. Do you know why they brought you here?"

"No." Connie tried to shake her head, but it was too heavy to move. It felt like a granite boulder on her shoulders, immobile and huge. "The nurse said you'd tell me."

"I will. But first I want you to answer a few questions for me. What's your name?"

"Connie Wilson."

"Good." Peters looked pleased. "And where do you live, Connie?"

"Three eighty-one Ridgecrest. It's a condo complex in Edina."

"Very good. And you live alone?"

Connie tried to shake her head again, and this time it moved. "I live with my fiancé. It's his condo."

"And his name is . . . ?"

"Alan Stan—" Connie stopped suddenly as memories came rushing back. The telephone call. The two policemen at the door, looking so somber. And the awful news they'd brought.

She must have moaned, or made some kind of sound, because the doctor motioned to the nurse. "Just take it easy, Miss Wilson. Gladys?"

Connie turned to look at the nurse who was handing Dr. Peters a syringe. "No! You've got to tell me the truth! Is Alan . . . dead?"

"I'm afraid so, Miss Wilson. Now just relax, and I'll give you something to help you—"

"No!" Connie struggled to sit up. "The baby! Our baby! Is the baby all right?"

The sympathy on their faces told Connie all she needed to know. She let out a little cry of anguish, then fell back onto the pillows. "The baby's dead, too?"

"We did all we could, Miss Wilson." The doctor reached for her hand again.

And Connie let him take her arm and give her the injection that blanked out the pain of knowing she'd lost everyone who'd ever mattered to her.

The waiting room was pleasant, with comfortable, tweed-covered furniture and carpeted floors, and Jill knew she should sit down and try to get some rest. Her legs were shaking. She couldn't keep pacing much longer. But every time she tried to relax on one of the chairs or the couches, she'd hear footsteps in the hallway and leap back to her feet.

She glanced at the clock on the wall and frowned. It was almost six in the morning. Neil had been in surgery for over two hours. Did corneal transplants usually take this long? Or was something terribly wrong?

It took some self-discipline, but Jill forced herself to sit down in the chair nearest to the door. She wished it were summer and the sun were up. It was always easier to handle your worries in the sunlight. But this was the heart of the winter, the darkest season of the year, and the sun wouldn't peek over the horizon before seven in the morning.

The glare of the fluorescent lights hurt her eyes, and she leaned back and closed them. She hated fluorescent bulbs. They gave everything an overly white, almost antiseptic glow that wasn't duplicated anywhere in nature. Sunlight was warm, fluorescent light was cold. Jill shivered even though the waiting room was well heated.

The trip to the hospital had been tense. She'd tried to make cheerful conversation, but Neil had looked grim every moment of the way. Jill could understand why he'd been so bleak. He was a pessimist, and Dr. Varney had told them if the muscular repair surgery and the transplant failed, there might not be time for a second chance.

Months ago, when Dr. Varney had first diagnosed Neil's disease and had told them he needed a transplant, Jill had used the online service on her office computer to research the statistics. The information she'd gotten wasn't very encouraging. Nationwide, there were over forty-two thousand people on the waiting list for various transplants and five of them died each day for lack of a donor organ.

Jill sighed and covered her eyes with a hand. Even though Neil wasn't facing death, she felt hideously depressed in this last dark hour before daylight. Crying might help, but she wouldn't let herself indulge in the luxury of tears. She had to be strong for Neil, and she had to think positive thoughts. The transplant would work. It had to. It was Neil's last hope for normal life, a life without a seeing eye dog or a white cane—or total darkness even on the sunniest day.

There were hushed voices in the hallway, and Jill looked up to see a couple walk by. The woman's shoulders were shaking silently. She was sobbing in grief, and the man was trying to comfort her. Jill couldn't hear what he was saying, but she knew the words. She'd spoken the very same platitudes to her father, the night her mother had died. *Her suffering's ended and perhaps it's a blessing. No one should be forced to live with constant pain. She wouldn't want to see you like this. You should try to remember only the good times and keep her alive in your heart.*

The man stopped at the nurses' desk and pulled out a handkerchief, handing it to the woman with an old-fashioned, almost gallant gesture. The woman reached up to touch his face, and then she took the clean square of linen to dab at her eyes. They were united in their grief. Both wore the face of sorrow, but it was apparent that their love for each other would be a consolation.

After they'd left, Jill felt very much alone. She wished she had someone to turn to, someone who would sit on the tweed chair next to hers and tell her that everything was going to be all right. Her parents were dead, she had no children, and her friends from college had all gone their separate ways. Her coworkers cared, but they had lives of their own. She had no one.

But Neil wasn't alone. He had her. She'd promised that she wouldn't leave him. He had Lisa, too, and all the other women who seemed to find him so charming. Visitors would come to see him, flowers would arrive, cards and letters would pour in from his students, friends would call to wish him well.

How could she be so alone when Neil had so many people who adored him? Was it her fault for isolating herself from those who might have cared about her? Was her personality defective? Was she unlovable? Or was she simply a loner who'd unconsciously pushed everyone away?

A tear rolled down her cheek, and Jill wiped it away with the back of her hand. Her mother'd had a favorite saying for times like this. SPS Self-Pity Stinks. Jill knew she was indulging in a massive bout of self-pity. Perhaps it was because she hadn't slept. She was exhausted, and the past few hours had been incredibly tense. Here she was, feeling sorry for herself, when all of her sympathy should go to Neil.

"Stop it!" Jill whispered the words, and then she got up to pace the floor again. The activity seemed to help. It made her feel more in control. If Neil's operation wasn't successful, they'd just have to manage. It was like Dr. Varney had said; many other people had learned to cope with the loss of their sight.

But she was being a pessimist, and that wouldn't do. Neil's chance for a complete recovery was very good; corneal transplants were quite routine. She should think of this as a miracle. Her husband might be able to see again. And she should say a little prayer for the unknown person who'd been kind enough to fill out a donor card.

Jill stopped suddenly as she remembered the older couple in the hallway. Could they be the parents of the person who'd given Neil his eyes? Was their grief lessened, knowing that their son might be giving the gift of life to others? Would it be a comfort if she told them how grateful she was?

Before she'd quite realized what she was going to do, Jill rushed out to the nurses' desk. There was a file open on the counter, but the desk was unmanned and the older couple was gone. Just then the doors of the operation room opened and Dr. Varney came out.

"Jill." Varney was smiling. "Neil's doing very well. They've taken him down to the ICU."

Her hopes rose. "Then the operation was a success?"

"Yes. Everything went perfectly. Of course we won't know with any certainty until the bandages come off."

Jill nodded. Dr. Varney had explained that Neil's recovery would take time. "When will you remove them?"

"The day after tomorrow. He'll be sedated until then. We don't want him to make any sudden movements that might strain the stitches."

Jill nodded again. "Should I go down to the Intensive Care Unit and wait?"

"I'll take you there. You can have a quick peek, and then I want you to go home and get some sleep."

"But . . . shouldn't I be there when Neil wakes up?"

Dr. Varney shook his head. "We used a local, Jill. He was groggy from the sedative, but he was awake the entire time. What he needs now is sleep, a full eight hours, and so do you."

They'd been walking toward the end of the hall, and as they approached the elevator, the doors opened. They stepped in. Dr. Varney pressed the button for the third floor, and then he noticed that Jill was giggling. "What's funny?"

"I've been watching people ring for the elevator all night, and it's always taken at least five minutes. You didn't even ring and the doors opened the second you got there."

"Now you know what they mean by doctor's privilege." Varney wore a perfectly deadpan expression.

Jill laughed so hard she had to hold her sides. She knew she was overreacting, but she couldn't seem to help herself.

"Come on. It wasn't that funny." Dr. Varney looked concerned as he patted her on the shoulder. "I know it's been a rough night, but Neil's going to be just fine."

The corridor that led to the ICU was brightly illuminated, and the light glaring off the white tiles made Jill's eyes ache. Varney pressed a buzzer by the door, and a nurse opened it.

"How's he doing, Rina?" The doctor ushered Jill in and stopped at the desk to pick up at a chart.

"Just fine, Doctor. Vital signs are normal, and he understands about the head restraint."

Neil was in a small room right next to the charge nurse's desk. He was flat on his back with his head nestled into something that looked like a huge, hard pillow. There was a padded strap across his forehead, and it was attached to the pillow on both sides with Velcro fasteners.

"Neil? I'm here." Jill was surprised to find that she was whispering. Hospitals seemed to do that to a person. She cleared her throat and took her husband's hand. "How are you feeling?"

His voice was groggy, but he still managed to sound angry. "How do you think I'm feeling? I can't see a damn thing!"

"Neil? It's Dr. Varney. We'll take the bandages off on Sunday for a quick look; then they'll have to go on again. I'm sorry, but you'll have to wear them for at least a week."

"Hi, Doc." Jill noticed that Neil's voice was much warmer. It was clear he hadn't realized the doctor was in the room. "That's okay. I understand. It's just frustrating . . . you know?"

Varney nodded. "I can imagine. Try to be patient. This'll take time to heal."

"Okay. I'll do my best, Doc."

"Good." Dr. Varney smiled at Jill. "You need to sleep, so I'm going to send Jill home. Is there anything you want to tell her before she goes?"

"No. I can't think of . . . Oh, yeah. Call the department and tell them I'm here. And call Lisa at home. She should know."

The color rose in Jill's cheeks and she immediately dropped Neil's hand. "You want me to call *Lisa*?"

"Somebody's got to. She's still scheduled as my TA."

Jill was too embarrassed to meet Dr. Varney's eyes. Had

he guessed that Lisa was much more than Neil's teaching assistant?

"Jill?" Neil's voice was softer, more intimate. Even though he couldn't see her face, he seemed to sense that he'd upset her. "You don't have to call Lisa. Just ask someone at the department to get in touch with her. I want her to know I won't be back for next semester so she can start making other arrangements."

"All right." Jill's voice was shaking slightly. Was it possible that this was purely business, that Neil had actually broken off with Lisa?

"Thanks for being here, Jill." Neil reached out for her, and she gave him her hand again. He squeezed it once; then he smiled. "You've been a tower of strength. I really couldn't have gone through all this without you."

As she headed for the door, Jill began to frown. Neil had thanked her, and he'd called her a tower of strength. That was nice, but one crucial thing was missing. Not once, during this long, lonely night, had her husband told her that he loved her.

CHAPTER 4

It was Saturday morning and Connie was all dressed and ready to go. They'd told her she could leave the hospital at eleven, so she was sitting on the edge of the bed, waiting for Dr. Peters to sign her release papers.

"Okay, Connie. You're all set." Dr. Peters handed her a small paper bag with the name of the hospital pharmacy imprinted on the front. "When you get home, I want you to go straight to bed. Take one of the white pills three times a day, and if you have trouble sleeping tonight, take one of the small, blue pills."

Connie nodded and stood up. "Thank you, Doctor. May I leave now?"

"Just wait for the wheelchair. They'll bring it up in a minute."

"Wheelchair?" Connie was puzzled. "But I can walk."

"It's against hospital regulations. You're still under our care until you're officially released at the front desk. Just ask the orderly to call you a cab, and he'll wheel you right out to the curb."

Connie opened her mouth to protest. She felt just fine, she certainly didn't need a wheelchair. But the doctor seemed to know exactly what she was thinking because he shook his head.

"Sorry. I know it doesn't make much sense, but that's the way we have to do things. Once you've been admitted, you have to be wheeled out. Just enjoy the ride—and call me if you have any problems."

Connie sighed and then nodded. "Okay. Thank you for everything, Doctor."

Peters started to leave, but he turned back at the door. "You've had a terrible shock, Connie. You really shouldn't be alone. I want you to call someone who can stay with you for a few days."

"All right. I'll do that." Connie couldn't quite meet his eyes. If he found out she had no one to call, he might not release her. It was kind of him to worry about her, but there was really no need. Once she got back to the condo and surrounded herself with Alan's things, she'd be perfectly fine.

Jill was at her desk in the Criminal Courts Building, going over a brief. There really hadn't been any reason to come in on a Saturday, but after she'd stopped to see Neil at the hospital, she hadn't felt like going back to the house. There was always work she could do at the office. Her caseload was heavy and that was exactly the way she liked it. Work kept her from thinking about Neil and what her life would be like if the transplant failed.

A familiar voice floated in from the hallway, and Jill began to smile. She recognized the trace of a Texas drawl that had never been completely erased by twelve years in Minnesota.

"Doug? Doug Lake?" Jill got up from the desk and poked her head out the door. And then she saw him, her favorite cop on the Minneapolis force.

"Hey, Jill!" Doug grinned from ear to ear. He was a tall,

lanky man with sandy hair that always looked tousled, more at home in blue jeans and a checkered shirt than in the business suit he was wearing. "Long time no see. How's it going Mrs. Assistant District Attorney?"

"Just fine, Mr. Lead Sergeant Detective." Jill grinned back. She'd met Doug when she'd first come to work at the district attorney's office. He'd been a rookie working crowd control, part of the small equestrian unit, and she'd been the youngest lawyer in the office, at the very bottom of the pecking order. Jill's boss had assigned Doug's case to her. A drunk had thrown a bottle at his horse. The drunk had gotten a fine and a considerable amount of jail time; Doug and Jill had been friends ever since.

"They told me about your husband." Doug's grin disappeared, and he looked very sympathetic. "I'm really sorry, Jill."

Jill nodded. "Me, too. I just hope the transplant works."

"When will they know?"

"At two o'clock tomorrow." Jill clasped her hands behind her back. They were starting to tremble. "The doctor's taking off the bandages to check."

"Do you have someone to go to the hospital with you?" Doug still looked concerned. "I can switch my schedule if you need me."

"Thanks, but I'll be just fine." Jill was surprised by the offer. She knew how difficult it was for him to switch schedules. He would have to call in a favor to get someone to cover his shift.

"Here." Doug scribbled a number on a card and handed it to her. "You shouldn't be alone at a time like this. That's my home number. Call me if you need to talk."

Jill tucked the card into her pocket and nodded. "Thank you. I really appreciate it."

"Hey, no problem. What are friends for? Let me know how it goes, okay?"

"I'll do that." Jill nodded, and just then the receptionist motioned to Doug.

"Gotta go. I've got an appointment with Hayes, and it's not smart to keep the big man waiting." Doug grinned at her. "I get off at eight. Call me anytime after that."

As Jill watched him stride down the hall, she felt much better. She'd shared an occasional lunch with Doug, and they'd worked together on several cases, but she hadn't realized that he thought of her as a friend. She knew very little about his personal life, only a few things about his professional one. He'd left Texas when he'd finished college, and he'd graduated from the Minneapolis Police Academy with honors. He'd risen rapidly in the ranks, everyone including his supervisors liked him, and he'd passed his detective's exam the first time he'd taken it. Jill didn't know whether Doug was married or whether he had a girlfriend, or even where he lived. The only personal thing she knew about him was that he liked his coffee strong, with three sugars and two creams.

When Jill turned around to go back to her desk, she was smiling. Doug Lake was a mystery, and she liked mysteries. Perhaps he was married to a wonderful woman. If so, she could invite them for dinner one night. But would that work? Neil liked to choose his own friends, and he wasn't interested in meeting any of hers.

After her marriage, Jill had stopped inviting coworkers to her home. She never knew when Neil would be sarcastic. At times he'd actually been rude to her friends. There was no way Jill could anticipate, with any degree of certainty, how Neil would treat their guests.

She sat down in her chair and switched on the light. As she picked up her brief and started to read it again, she found herself hoping that Doug wasn't married. It was a lot safer that way. If Neil was in one of his moods, he might try to hit on Doug's wife. Doug would react as the other husbands had, and then she'd lose him as a friend. No, it would be much better if Doug weren't married. And, to be perfectly honest with herself, it would be better if she weren't married.

Connie smiled as she walked down the corridor and approached the door to three eighty-one. She was home and she could hardly wait to take a shower and crawl into the bed she'd shared with Alan. Of course she'd be lonely; she knew that. But she could slip on one of Alan's shirts, smell the aftershave he'd always worn, and for a few hours at least, she could pretend that he was still alive.

There was something wrong with the lock. Her key didn't seem to fit. Connie wiggled it around and tried to force it into the slot, but she couldn't get the door to open. Now she'd have to go down to the office and call for a locksmith.

As she rang for the elevator, Connie glanced at her watch. It was almost one o'clock. She hoped the office hadn't closed for lunch. She could never remember the schedule. Did they take their lunch hour from twelve to one . . . or from one to two? And was it different on Saturdays? The elevator doors opened and Connie stepped in, thankful that it was empty. She didn't want to accept the condolences of the neighbors yet. If anyone said a kind word to her, she was sure she'd break down in tears.

The office manager had just closed up for lunch, but when he saw Connie he unlocked the door. He looked worried, almost nervous at seeing her, and at first Connie was puzzled. In the past he'd always been very friendly. Perhaps he was just one of those people who didn't know what to say when tragedy struck.

"Hello, Harry." Connie stepped into the office and waited for him to speak. Surely he'd offer some sympathetic word, tell her how sorry he was about Alan. But Harry didn't say anything at all. He just sat there silently, avoiding her eyes.

"There's something wrong with my lock." Connie held out her key. "This doesn't go in all the way, and it won't turn at all."

Harry nodded, but he still didn't meet her eyes. "I didn't know you were coming back today, or I would have put a note on your door."

"A note? But why?"

"I've got some bad news." Harry pulled out a chair and motioned for her to sit down. "Please take a seat. This isn't going to be easy, Miss Wilson."

Connie seated herself, and this time Harry met her eyes. He looked very upset, he was frowning. "You'd think they'd have the guts to tell you themselves, but they left it to me!"

"Tell me what, Harry?" Connie's hands started to tremble. "What's wrong?"

"The Stanfords. They sent in a moving crew this morning. There's a whole pile of boxes that belong to you at the back of the office."

"I . . . I don't understand!" Connie was so shocked, she hardly knew what to say. "I know Alan made the mortgage payment this month. How could they do that?"

"That's what I asked them. They said the condo was in Alan's name. Now that he's gone, and he didn't leave a will, it goes to them."

Connie took a deep breath and tried to think. "I guess they're right. I just don't know. I never thought about Alan . . . dying."

"It's a dirty shame, but I checked with the lawyer that lives in three seventeen, and he told me there's nothing you can do. They own the property. You can't even get in."

Connie nodded. It was so much to take in, all at once. "But they left me my things?"

"That's just it. They only left *your* things. I went up there while they were packing. Everything that belonged to Alan went in one set of boxes. They had those hauled to a storage place. Your things went in another set of boxes, and they brought them down here."

"They took the furniture?"

Harry nodded. "I asked the movers if they'd leave your bed and the sofa and one of the chairs. But they said they had their orders from the Stanfords—everything had to go."

"Everything?" Hot tears stung Connie's eyelids.

"They said Alan had paid for everything and now it all belonged to his parents. Even that picture of him on your dresser, and the photo albums and everything in the cupboards. They left you your clothes and some personal things, but that's about it."

"So they took everything away and changed the locks?"

"That's right." Harry nodded. "I'm really sorry, Miss Wilson. I tried to save something for you, but they wouldn't let me come in any farther than the front entry way."

Connie's mind was reeling. She didn't know what to do. She'd lost Alan, their baby, and the home they'd shared in less than twenty-four hours. "Do you think I could use your phone to call the Stanfords? Maybe there's some kind of mistake."

"You can try, but don't get your hopes up. People like the Stanfords don't have hearts. All they've got are rolls of dollar bills in their chests!"

"That's what Alan used to say." Connie gave a small, sad smile. "But I still think I should call them. I want to hear it from them."

Harry nodded and pushed the phone to her side of the desk. "Look, Miss Wilson . . . Connie. Give 'em hell, okay? Alan was crazy about you. He told me you were going to get married. What they did to you is just plain wrong!"

Connie's hands were shaking as she dialed the number. She knew the Stanfords hadn't approved of her, but she hadn't dreamed they hated her quite this much. What could she say to change their minds, to convince them that she was grieving over Alan just as much, or more, than they were?

"Stanford residence. Elsa speaking."

It was the Swedish maid, and Connie immediately felt better. She'd never actually spoken to Elsa, but Alan had told her the woman was very nice. "Hello, Elsa. This is Connie Wilson, Alan's fiancé. May I please talk to Mr. or Mrs. Stanford?"

"I'm sorry, Miss Wilson, they're not taking any calls. They told me to say if you have any questions, you should contact their lawyer, Mr. Quentin Avery."

"Their lawyer? But . . . won't they just talk to me?"

"Could you hold the line for a moment, please?" There was the sound of a door closing softly, and then Elsa's voice came on the line again. "Miss Wilson? I can't talk long, but I want to tell you how sorry I am. Alan told me he loved you, and it's not right what they're doing."

Connie blinked back tears. When she spoke again, her voice was shaking with emotion. "Thank you, Elsa. Alan said you were nice, and he was right."

"Please call their lawyer, Miss Wilson. I'll give you his number. The Stanfords could have arranged for you to have something of Alan's, I just don't know."

As Connie wrote down the lawyer's number, her spirits rose. Perhaps Alan's parents had acted out of grief, packing up his things so quickly and changing the locks on the door. But now that they'd had time to think about what they'd done, they might have reconsidered. Mr. Avery might tell her that it was all a mistake and she could move back into the condo.

"Thank you, Elsa." Commie managed a small smile. "Do you think if I call again, Alan's parents will talk to me?"

It was several moments before Elsa answered, and when she did, she sounded doubtful. "They just told me they weren't taking any calls, except from their lawyer. But he might know, and I think you should call him right away."

CHAPTER 5

It was a gorgeous reception area with soft leather wing chairs and Tiffany lamps, but after almost an hour of staring at the design on the expensive oriental carpet, Connie was feeling much more anxious and much less impressed. When she'd called Mr. Avery, his secretary had given her an appointment at four. The lovely grandfather clock in the corner was only seconds away from chiming five times, and Connie was still waiting.

She didn't like waiting rooms. They'd always meant trouble in her life. She remembered sitting on a cheap plastic chair at the emergency clinic, waiting for the doctor to stitch up her mother's lip; one of her mother's "dates" had split it. And pacing the tile floor at the veterinarian's office, only to find that her stepfather had injured her kitty so badly, the little creature couldn't be saved. Waiting in a small, cramped room on a scratchy sofa for a job that had been filled hours ago. Sitting on a folding chair in the wings until it was time for her to strip for old men with bleary eyes and alcohol-saturated breath, men who reached out to grope her if she ventured too close to the edge of the stage.

"Miss Wilson? Mr. Avery will see you now. Follow me, please."

Connie jumped to her feet as the receptionist beckoned. She was a cold-eyed brunette in her early thirties with an impeccable figure and hair that looked too perfect to be real. She led Connie down a long corridor to a set of double bronze doors.

The receptionist knocked twice, and then she opened the doors to usher Connie in. "Mr. Avery? This is Miss Wilson."

"Thank you, Sheila."

The cold-eyed brunette made a hasty exit, and Connie took several steps forward. Mr. Avery looked imposing behind his huge mahogany desk. He appeared to be in his fifties. There were streaks of silver in his dark hair, but he looked tan and fit, obviously the product of a pampered life.

"Miss Wilson. Sit down."

His voice had the ring of authority, and Connie sat in the leather chair facing his desk. He had gray eyes that reminded her of polished steel. There was no hint of a smile on his face.

"I have some papers for you, Miss Wilson." The lawyer handed her a manila folder with a sheaf of papers inside. "Read them and sign them in duplicate, please."

Connie frowned as she opened the folder and began to read the papers inside. They were standard forms of some sort, but she wasn't sure what they meant. "Excuse me, Mr. Avery. What are these?"

"The first is an agreement not to press suit against any member of the Stanford family. The second is a voluntary restraining order."

Connie glanced down at the papers again, but they still didn't make sense. "I don't understand. Why would I want to sue the Stanfords?"

"For palimony, loss of support, that sort of thing. But I can tell you, Miss Wilson, you would not win."

Connie shivered a bit. Mr. Avery kept his office quite cold. Perhaps he didn't want his clients to stay very long. She remembered reading something about a palimony suit, some famous actor's girlfriend had sued him, and it had been splashed all over the tabloids. But even if she'd wanted to do such a thing, how could she sue Alan? "But Alan is . . . dead. I couldn't sue him for palimony."

"Precisely. You seem to be an intelligent woman, Miss Wilson, and I'm sure you'll want to cooperate. Now if you'll just sign . . ."

"No." The hair on the back of Connie's neck bristled. She hated it when people talked down to her, yet that was exactly what Mr. Avery was doing. "You just told me I couldn't win a palimony suit, so I don't see any reason to sign."

Mr. Avery began to frown. "Look, Miss Wilson. It's just a precaution. Alan's parents need reassurance that you won't bring a lawsuit. You've got to understand their position. They're grieving for their only son."

"They're grieving?" Connie was so angry, she almost jumped up from the chair. "How do you think *I* feel, Mr. Avery? I lost the man I love, I lost our baby, and then I lost my home!"

"Please calm down, Miss Wilson. I appreciate the emotional strain you must be experiencing. I know this could seem odd to you, but people handle grief in various ways. The Stanfords have pulled the wagons in a circle, so to speak. They've gathered all of Alan's belongings, in the hope that these things may provide some comfort to them."

"And they left me out in the cold for the Indians to scalp!" Connie shivered again. "If they're so damned grief-stricken, why don't they talk to me? Why don't they find out what Alan really thought? What Alan was really like? I lived with him. I was a part of his life every day and every night. And now that he's dead, they're . . . they're pushing me away!"

"Believe me, that's not their intention." Mr. Avery looked very sad. "Their grief is too fresh right now. It would be too painful for them to bring anyone into their family circle at this time of sorrow. Perhaps it would have been different if you hadn't lost Alan's baby. Then they might have taken some comfort in the fact that a part of their son would live on."

Despite herself, Connie nodded. What Mr. Avery said had the ring of truth.

"Please sign the papers, Miss Wilson. Give them the peace of mind they need. Do you really believe Alan would have wanted you to cause his parents additional grief?"

Connie sighed. Another point, and it was well taken. "Alan never wanted to hurt his parents. I know that. And I don't want to hurt them, either. Tell me about the papers again, Mr. Avery. The first set promises that I won't sue them?"

"That's correct."

Connie paged through the document and found the line for her signature at the bottom. Her hand was shaking slightly as she signed both copies. "What about the other set?"

"It's a voluntary restraining order. It promises that you won't try to contact them until they're ready. They need time, Miss Wilson. Give Alan's parents time to cope with the loss of their son."

"All right." Connie felt terribly weary as she signed the second set of papers. The Stanfords should have known that she wasn't the type of person to force herself on them. But as she handed the papers back to Mr. Avery, she had a terrible thought. "How about Alan's funeral? Please, Mr. Avery . . . I need to see him again to say good-bye! They won't keep me away from his funeral, will they?"

"Of course not. But you see, Miss Wilson, there won't be a funeral. Alan didn't want one. His wish was that he be cremated and placed in the family mausoleum."

"Alan didn't want a funeral?" Connie frowned slightly. Perhaps it was true. They'd never discussed it.

"Alan thought funerals were much too painful for the survivors. He wanted his family to hold a memorial one year after his death. Alan felt it should be a celebration of his life at a time when everyone could remember him without tears."

Connie nodded. That sounded like Alan. He'd always been very concerned about everyone else's feelings. "So he'll be cremated?"

"That's right." Mr. Avery nodded. "Just as soon as the hospital releases his body."

"His . . . body? But the police told me Alan died at the scene of the accident. Why does the hospital have his body?"

"You didn't know?" Mr. Avery looked surprised. "Several years ago, Alan filled out a donor card. It was on the back of his driver's license."

It took Connie a moment to get over her shock, but then she remembered. She'd seen the pink card on the back of Alan's license. Perhaps that was one of the reasons he'd insisted on cremation. He hadn't wanted anyone to see him after they'd taken his organs.

"This is for you, Miss Wilson." Mr. Avery handed her a small white envelope. "Alan's parents wanted you to have it. The family is leaving the country for a while. Going to Italy, I believe. They have a villa there."

"But . . . do you think they'll call me when they get back?"

"I'm sure they will." Mr. Avery stood up, signifying that her appointment was over. "Good luck, Miss Wilson. I'm very sorry we had to meet at such a distressing time."

Connie rose. Mr. Avery was extending his hand, so she shook it. It was cold and dry, exactly what she'd expected, and Connie shivered as she followed him out of his office, down the long corridor, and past the deserted reception area.

"Good-bye, Miss Wilson." Mr. Avery held open the outer door.

"Good-bye, Mr. Avery." Connie went through the doorway and walked to the elevator. It wasn't a long wait, the building seemed to be deserted, and when the doors slid open she found that she was the only passenger.

Her hands were trembling as she pressed the button for the ground floor. She waited until the doors had closed, then removed the envelope from her purse and held it close to her chest. What was inside? A picture of Alan? A small keepsake of his that they wanted her to have? A handwritten note from Alan's parents, apologizing for changing the locks on the condo and moving her things? A sympathy card that said they were terribly sorry she'd lost the baby?

The envelope was sealed, and Connie was almost afraid to open it. She hoped it would contain something of Alan's. She had nothing of his, and desperately needed a memento that had belonged to the man she'd loved. It would be a comfort to her, something she could keep forever.

The elevator stopped on the ground floor, and Connie got out. She called for a cab at the pay phone in the lobby. Then she stood by the huge plate-glass window, watching snow drift down as her fingers slowly opened the envelope. It had to be something of Alan's. It just had to be!

Connie held her breath as her fingers pulled out what seemed to be sheets of paper, five of them, exactly the same size. Then she took a deep breath and looked down at what she was holding.

"Money!" Connie's eyes widened in shock. There were five crisp hundred-dollar bills, nothing more, not even a note.

Her first instinct was to tear up the bills and throw them in the trash. The Stanfords had decided to buy her off with five hundred dollars. It was a reward for signing the papers and promising not to make trouble. They'd been smart enough to realize she had no income. Much as it rankled, Connie knew she'd have to keep the money.

A horn honked outside, and she looked up. Her cab had arrived. She pushed open the door, ran out to the curb, and climbed into the backseat.

"Where to, lady?"

The driver turned around to look at her, and for a moment Connie wasn't sure. She couldn't go back to the condo. It was no longer her home. But where could she go?

"Lady?"

The driver was frowning. He looked impatient, so Connie gave the first address that popped into her head. It was a dive, a bar on lower Hennepin. She'd gone there with the other strippers when their shift was over.

"You sure you want to go there?" The driver looked surprised when Connie nodded. "It's no place for a lady like you."

Connie almost laughed out loud. She was no lady. All he had to do was ask the Stanfords. They'd paid her off with hundred-dollar bills in a plain white envelope, as if she were some kind of expensive whore!

"Did you hear me, lady?"

"I heard," Connie nodded, bitterly. "Just take me there. I know what it is, and you're wrong. It's exactly my kind of place."

CHAPTER 6

"I'm scared, Jill." Neil reached out for her hand. "What if the disease destroyed too many nerves? If they take off the bandages and I can't see, I . . . I don't know what I'll do!"

Jill gripped his hand tightly. She'd never seen him this vulnerable before, and her heart went out to him. "Don't borrow trouble, honey. Dr. Varney said the operation went perfectly. I'm sure it's going to be all right."

"That's easy for you to say! You have no idea what I'm going through. Let me tell you, it'd be a lot different if *you* were the one who was stuck here with bandages over your eyes! What time is it anyway? And where's that damned doctor?"

"It's almost two." Jill did her best to be patient. Neil had been like a bear all morning, alternating between rage and utter despair. Several minutes ago, she'd gone out to the desk to ask if he could have a tranquilizer, but the nurse had told her they'd have to wait for the doctor to arrive. "I know it's hard, Neil, but try to relax. Dr. Varney will be here any minute."

"And doctors are always on time. Isn't that right, Jill?"

From the tone of his voice, she knew he would have

glared at her if he'd been able. She'd seen that caustic glare many times in the past; she knew it well. She could almost feel it searing the inside of his closed eyelids, making the bandages smolder with his hurtful brand of sarcasm. "Neil . . . please. It's not good for you to get upset."

"I . . . am . . . not . . . upset!"

His voice dripped icicles, and Jill found herself backing away from the bed. Even though he was flat on his back in a head restraint, he still held the power to intimidate her. But today, some crazy instinct made her do something totally unexpected. Influenced by the vampire movie she'd seen the past night, she raised both forefingers in the sign of the cross and stifled a very inappropriate giggle.

"Jill? What was that? What are you doing?"

"It's all right, Neil." She dropped her hands and moved toward the bed again. "I was just . . . uh . . . coughing."

"Well, you'd better not be coming down with a bug. I need you to take care of me!"

The words on the tip of Jill's tongue struggled to be set free. She wanted to tell him that if he wasn't nicer to her, she might very well walk out the door. But she stifled the words and then sighed. Her husband was anxious and frustrated, both entirely understandable reactions. Today he would learn whether he'd ever be able to see again.

There were footsteps in the hall, someone walking quickly and with authority. The steps slowed at the door, and a moment later, Dr. Varney stepped into Neil's room. "Jill . . . Neil. How are you this afternoon?"

Jill glanced at Neil. Would he make some sarcastic retort about how he'd been a hell of a lot better before he'd set foot in this hospital? Would he lash out at the doctor for being late? But Neil didn't do either. He just smiled, the nicest smile that Jill had ever seen.

"I'm fine, Doc." Neil's voice was friendly. "Are you going to let me sit up?"

Dr. Varney shook his head. "Not right away. We'll take off your bandages first, and then we'll see."

"I hope you're right!" Neil actually produced a laugh. "About the seeing part, that is."

The doctor laughed, too, and patted Neil on the shoulder. "I'm glad you're in good spirits. Now let me tell you exactly what I'm going to do."

Jill listened while the doctor explained. They would pull the drapes and turn off the fluorescent lights. After almost forty-eight hours of total darkness, a sudden exposure to light could be painful. Dr. Varney would use a small, specially designed light to examine Neil's eyes. Neil had to be careful not to move his head or open his eyes.

"I don't understand," Jill said, "if Neil isn't supposed to open his eyes, how can you tell whether he can see?"

Dr. Varney turned to her. "I'll check for perceived light through Neil's eyelids. That'll tell us whether the optic nerve is functioning properly."

"Doctor?" A middle-aged nurse with frizzy blond hair entered the room. She was pushing a cart draped with sterile towels.

"Thanks, Mary Ellen." Dr. Varney smiled at her and then turned to Neil. "Mary Ellen's my assistant. She wasn't scheduled to work today, but she came in as a favor to me."

Jill held her breath. Was Neil going to complain that it was a rip-off, an excuse for the hospital to bill their insurance company for Mary Ellen's overtime? But her husband just smiled that same nice smile.

"Thank you, Mary Ellen." Neil sounded very grateful. "I really appreciate it."

The nurse nodded. "No problem. Now don't worry, Mr. Bradley. I've been assisting Dr. Varney for almost ten years, and we haven't lost a patient yet."

Neil chuckled. "That's good enough for me. I'm all yours,

Mary Ellen. And please call me Neil. That way I'll feel I know you."

Jill stared at her husband. He sounded gracious and utterly charming, the way he'd been when she'd first met him. People who met Neil casually, often told her how lucky she was to be married to him. They felt they knew him, but they only knew the witty, amiable professor. Jill knew Neil's dark side, his fits of rage, his biting sarcasm, and his totally demanding nature.

"Jill?" Dr. Varney turned to her. "Could you pull the drapes while Mary Ellen removes Neil's bandages?"

"Of course." Jill hurried to the window. She hadn't noticed it before, but the drapes were lined with a material that completely blocked out the daylight.

"Why don't you sit down in that chair by the wall switch?" Dr. Varney pointed to a chair near the wall. "We'll leave the lights on until the final gauze strip. I'll tell you when to turn them off."

Jill sat down in the chair he'd indicated and tried to relax. She was glad Dr. Varney hadn't suggested she sit by the bed. If she'd held Neil's hand, she might have somehow conveyed the panic she was feeling.

It took several minutes for the nurse to remove the layers of bandages. When there was only one strip of gauze remaining, Dr. Varney flicked on his light and motioned to Jill. "All right. Turn off the lights."

Jill reached up with fingers that trembled and flicked the wall switch. It took her eyes several seconds to adjust to the darkness, and when they did, she saw Dr. Varney's light illuminating the last gauze strip.

"Keep your eyelids closed, Neil." Dr. Varney removed the last strip. "Now, with your eyes closed, I want you to tell me if you perceive any slight indication of light."

Jill held her breath as the doctor moved his light over Neil's eyelids, back and forth, from his right eye to his left.

This was the moment they'd been waiting for. Would Neil be able to see again?

"It's . . . red. I can see a red glow, and it's moving back and forth."

"That's my light." Dr. Varney's voice was loud in the stillness of the room. "Keep your eyes closed, Neil. Mary Ellen's going to cover one of your eyelids with a patch and then I'll use my light, again. I want you to tell me if you still see that red glow."

Mary Ellen covered Neil's left eye with a patch of cloth. Dr. Varney moved his light in the same pattern, from the right eye to the left, and then back again.

"Yes. I can see it." Neil's voice was shaking. "That's good, isn't it?"

"That's very good. Now keep your eyes closed while Mary Ellen moves the patch to your right eye. We're going to do the same thing, in reverse."

This time Neil laughed out loud. "I see it! You're moving it in a circle."

"Very good. Now, keep your eyes closed and concentrate. Sometimes we want things so badly, our minds play tricks on our bodies. We have to make sure that's not happening in your case, and that's why I'm going to run a control. Do you know what that is?"

Jill winced. Of course Neil knew what a control was! Every student who'd ever taken freshman psychology knew about experiments and control groups. Dr. Varney was talking down to Neil, and Neil despised condescending people. She just hoped that her husband would restrain himself and not say something sarcastic.

"I think I know." Neil's voice was even and reasonable. "You're running a blind test, but I can understand why you didn't want to use that term."

Dr. Varney chuckled. "You're absolutely right. Mary Ellen will put a patch over both of your eyes. One patch will have a clear lens which will let in the light. The other lens will be opaque. Since the patches feel exactly the same, you won't be able to tell which of them contains the clear lens. As soon as Mary Ellen gets them in place, I want you to tell me which eye perceives the red glow."

Jill had been relatively calm, but now her hands began to tremble. This was the test that would tell them if Neil's sight had been restored. She shut her own eyes, almost afraid to watch as Dr. Varney conducted the test. She heard the doctor's questions and Neil's answers, and then the test was over.

"Congratulations, Neil." Dr. Varney patted him on the shoulder. "We have every indication that the transplant was a success. Now keep your eyes closed while Mary Ellen puts on a fresh bandage. If you promise not to make any sudden head movements, we'll only use the restraint at night."

"I promise. Thanks, Doc!"

Neil sounded sincerely grateful, and a phrase from "Amazing Grace" floated through Jill's mind. "*I once was lost, but now I'm found. Was blind, but now I see.*" Neil had been lost in a dark world and now he was found. He'd almost been blind, but now he would be able to see again. Was it conceivable that Neil's terrible selfishness and his mood swings had been discarded with the bandages that had covered his eyes? Did she dare to hope that her husband was a changed man?

As soon as Mary Ellen had taped the first pad of gauze in place, Dr. Varney walked over to flick on the lights. Then he went back to the bed and patted Neil's shoulder. "Do you have any questions, Neil?"

"Just one." Neil grinned. "Everyone's been great, but when can I get out of here? I want to go home and have a big slice of Jill's pot roast."

Dr. Varney laughed. "I can understand that. I eat in the

cafeteria occasionally, and I know hospital food isn't exactly gourmet fare. I want to keep you for three more nights, just to be on the safe side. If everything's normal, I'll release you on Wednesday, right after I've made my rounds."

"Okay." Neil started to nod, but he caught himself. "No sudden head movements, right?"

"That's right. I've got to run, Neil. I've got surgery in an hour."

Since Mary Ellen was still bandaging her husband, Jill stepped out into the hall with Dr. Varney. "What time are your rounds on Wednesday, Dr. Varney?"

"Between three and four. Is that a problem for you?"

"I don't think so. I have to be in court at ten, but we should be through by three at the latest."

"I'd forgotten you were a lawyer." Dr. Varney frowned slightly. "Since you work, we'll have to discuss some arrangements for Neil. Your insurance provides a day nurse for the first two weeks, but I think you should start looking for someone after that."

"But . . . Neil will be able to see by then, won't he?"

"Not well enough." Dr. Varney looked very serious. "Your husband will be able to distinguish between dark and light, but I had to do considerable muscle repair. Eye muscles can be retrained. That won't be a problem. But it's only fair to tell you that it'll take time."

Jill nodded. "How much time?"

"It depends on the individual. During the first month, I'll want Neil to come in three times a week for therapy. Once he learns the exercises, he'll be able to do them at home, but he'll experience episodes of double vision for at least six months."

"I see." Jill tried not to frown. Neil's recovery would be a lot slower than either of them had anticipated. "How about an eye patch? Would that help to correct the double vision?"

"Absolutely. But he has to remember to switch it every

four hours. We don't want one set of eye muscles to become lazy, while the other set grows stronger."

"That's it?" Jill's relief was short-lived when the doctor shook his head.

"Do you remember our discussion on tunnel vision?"

"Of course." Jill nodded. "Right before the operation Neil could only see in an arc of twenty degrees. You told us that between one-sixty and one-seventy degrees was normal."

"That's right. For all practical purposes, Neil's back to square one. I wouldn't expect any big changes right away. In time the arc will widen, but it could take a year before his peripheral vision is fully restored."

Jill began to frown. "Neil's not going to be happy about that!"

"I guessed as much. I have patients who manage to cope with this type of visual difficulty, but to be quite frank . . . I don't think your husband is one of them."

Jill's eyes widened. Even though Neil had been perfectly charming, he hadn't fooled Dr. Varney.

"And since we're speaking frankly, I don't think Neil will get along well while you're at work."

"But I can't take time off right now." Jill's frown deepened. "Should I hire a nurse for him?"

"You don't need a nurse. A housekeeper or a companion would do just fine. All she has to do is fix his meals, drive him in for therapy, and make sure he changes his eye patch. The hospital has a list of recommended names if you'd like them."

"I would, thank you." Jill gave a sigh of relief. She didn't know the first thing about hiring a companion or a housekeeper, and she didn't have time to run an ad in the paper and interview applicants.

"Good luck." Dr. Varney reached out to shake her hand. "Just stop at the desk on your way out and ask for the list. And if you don't mind a word of advice . . . you may go through several candidates before you find exactly the right person."

Jill was amused as she turned to go back into Neil's room. Dr. Varney certainly had Neil pegged! But then a new worry surfaced in her mind. She had to come up with some incredibly tactful way to tell Neil that he needed a companion. He hated having people come into their home. He resented the intrusion so much, he'd even forced her to give up the weekly cleaning service. Jill knew if she failed to find exactly the right words to explain the situation to Neil, he'd reject the idea entirely. He might even get so angry, he'd demand that she give up her job and stay home as his personal slave!

Of course, she wouldn't do that. She wasn't about to give up her career. She just hoped the hospital would give her a very long list of names. If Neil's recovery was as slow and as difficult as Dr. Varney had implied, his companion would need the patience of a saint to cope with him.

CHAPTER 7

"I'm really happy for you, Jill. I'll pick you up for lunch tomorrow and we'll celebrate with a couple of greasy hamburgers." Doug Lake hung up the phone, a smile on his face. It always gave him a lift to hear Jill's voice, and he was glad that her husband was going to be all right. Jill was . . . well . . . Jill was Jill. It was difficult for him to think of words to describe her, so he let his mind roam through all the best experiences in his life. Jill was like a cool mountain breeze on a muggy Texas afternoon, a deep swallow of icy well water at the end of a dusty trail, a crackling fire on a bitter winter night, a marshmallow toasted perfectly over a campfire, the outside all golden and crusty and the inside packed chock-full of melted sweetness.

Comparing Jill to a marshmallow made Doug grin. Marshmallows were fluffy, airy little things, and there was nothing fluffy or airy about Jill. She had substance. Furthermore she could be as tough as a linebacker with the Dallas Cowboys. He'd seen her tackle a couple of lying witnesses in court; she'd known exactly how to break them down. But even though Jill was tough, there was nothing remotely masculine about her. She was all woman, and that was what made her so appealing.

As he sat down at the table to eat his microwave dinner, Doug remembered the first time he'd met Jill. He'd been a rookie cop, outraged that someone had thrown a bottle at Tessie, the best horse in the entire police stable. Jill had been a pretty young prosecutor, an incredibly leggy blonde with straight, swinging hair and a figure that suggested she was no stranger to long-distance running. The first question she'd asked was whether Tessie was all right. When he'd told her Tessie's cut wasn't deep and it would heal just fine, her blue eyes had turned darker, the color of cobalt, and as hard and steely as the barrel of his service revolver. Then she'd said, "Good. Now let's make sure we really nail this guy!"

They'd nailed him, but not in the way Doug had expected. Since he hadn't been on his horse when the bottle had been thrown, the man had faced only a drunk and disorderly charge and an attempt to destroy city property. But when Jill had questioned him, Doug had admitted that he'd reached out to try to deflect the bottle and had received a small cut on his thumb.

Jill had then gone after the perp with both barrels blazing, and the defendant had been convicted of not two, but three offenses. She'd nailed him on drunk and disorderly, willful destruction of city property, and assault on a police officer, a much more serious charge.

When they'd left the courtroom, Jill had asked him to take her to the police stable. She'd fed Tessie an apple and then taken Tessie's picture. The next time he'd entered Jill's office, he'd seen Tessie's picture on the wall behind her desk, complete with a label on the frame that named the horse as Jill's first client.

Doug wished he hadn't been involved with someone at the time. If he'd been free, he would have asked Jill for a date. As it turned out, he'd been a fool. Less than a year later, the woman he'd been dating had decided she wasn't cut out to be a cop's wife. She'd married an accountant with a nine to five schedule, and the last Doug had heard, they had a little house in Elk River with a dog and two kids.

When he had finally worked up the nerve to call Jill's office, her secretary had told him she'd flown to Florida to meet her fiancé's brother. Doug had thanked the woman politely, but he'd put his fist through the pantry wall right after he'd hung up the phone. He'd waited too long—he'd blown it. Perfect women like Jill didn't stay single forever. Why hadn't he had the brains to realize she was the only one he'd ever really wanted to marry?

Jill had sent him a wedding invitation, but Doug hadn't had the heart to go. He'd told her he had to work, and he'd sent something that the clerk at Dayton's Department Store had recommended. He'd left instructions to wrap the silver ice bucket in wedding paper, and it had been delivered to Jill's family's home, where the reception had been held.

Doug was sure Jill didn't know how he felt about her. He'd been very careful to keep their relationship friendly and professional. She was his friend, but other, deeper feelings lurked just beneath the surface, like a granddaddy catfish that hid under the mirrored face of a lake, poised and ready to leap up from the depths at precisely the right moment.

Jill rarely talked about her husband. Doug had been surprised when he'd learned that Neil had written a book. He'd picked it up at a discount bookstore and had read it on his vacation. It had been a well-written mystery with a fairly interesting plot, but it hadn't impressed Doug all that much. The lead character was a police detective, but it was obvious that Jill's husband didn't know anything about real police work. If Doug had tried any of the stunts Neil's detective pulled in the book, he would have been up before the disciplinary review board before he'd had time to fill out the paperwork.

So why hadn't Jill caught the obvious errors in her husband's book when she worked with police detectives every day? Doug hadn't wanted to ask her, but one day she'd volunteered the information. Neil had worked alone, sequestered in his office with his computer and his printer. He hadn't wanted Jill to read his book until it was published.

At the time, Doug had wondered what kind of marriage they had. If he wrote a book, he'd want his wife to be the first to read it. It would be something they could share, and he'd certainly value his wife's advice. As far as Doug was concerned, Neil had shot himself in the foot. If he'd asked for Jill's advice, his police detective would have been more believable.

Although there was still some food on his tray, Doug dumped the remainder down the garbage disposal. He hated microwave dinners. The vegetables were mushy, the potatoes were watery, and the meat was so tasteless he felt like retrieving the box from the trash to find out what he'd eaten. But popping a frozen dinner in the microwave was efficient. It seemed like a waste of time to cook from scratch for himself.

Doug had learned how to cook from his grandmother. There were some things he prepared very well, like Tex-Mex tamales that would make your eyes water, fried chicken that was crispy on the outside and juicy on the inside, and mouthwatering barbecued ribs on the grill. Doug enjoyed cooking if he had a guest, but that didn't happen very often. He could count the guests who'd come for dinner on the fingers of one hand.

The night stretched out before him, and he wasn't sure what he wanted to do. There was nothing on television that interested him. There were no movies he wanted to rent. He was always welcome at the cop bar near the precinct, but he didn't feel like lifting a brew with burned-out colleagues who had no life beyond the force. He'd been there, done that, and it was boring, listening to the same old stories again and again. The older guys talked about the big cases they'd had, the cases nobody else had been able to solve. They were desperate to find some pleasure in recalling a time when they were sharp and smart and useful.

The younger guys were even more pathetic, delaying that moment when they'd have to go home to an empty apartment or a marriage that was heading for the rocks. It took a special type of woman to marry a cop, to live with the fear and uncertainty that went with the job. The wives never knew if their husbands would come home injured, or come home at all. It was almost like being a single parent; they could never count on that romantic anniversary dinner or the baby's first birthday party. Telephones and pagers became their enemies. Because nothing took precedence over work, the wives had to take on the responsibilities of both mother and father; it wasn't surprising so many of them bailed out.

Jill could be a cop's wife. She was strong, and she knew how the system worked. She would understand when he was on call, or if he had to work overtime. But she was married, and he really shouldn't be thinking about her. Her husband was a very lucky man; Doug hoped he appreciated how special Jill was.

He walked to the bookcase and took down Neil's book. There was a color portrait on the back cover, and he sat down on the couch to stare at the man who'd married Jill. Neil was handsome, and he looked sophisticated. If Doug had been a movie director, he would have cast Neil Bradley as a distinguished college professor complete with tweed jacket, intense brown eyes, and a pipe that would have cost Doug a week's paycheck. But Neil had money, now that his book was such a success. Jill had married a real winner. Still, it was odd that she never really talked about her husband.

Doug had always been intrigued by puzzles, and he tried to put all the pieces he'd gathered into place. Jill hadn't seen her husband's book before it had been published. That meant they led separate lives; there were things they didn't share. And Jill never mentioned her husband. It wasn't that she kept her private and her professional lives totally separate. She had spoken of her parents on many occasions, and she'd told him stories about the friends she'd had in college. But she never talked about Neil unless someone asked her a direct question.

Two negatives, but that didn't necessarily spell trouble. Was there a third? Doug thought for a moment, and then he remembered that Jill kept a picture of her mother and father on her desk. There was also a picture of a family reunion, with aunts and uncles and cousins. But the last time Doug had been in her office, almost three years after she'd married Neil, he'd noticed that there was no picture of her husband.

There was a fourth negative. Doug sighed as it came to him. Jill's wonderful smile, the smile that had lit up a room in the past, had been missing for the better part of a year. Was her marriage in trouble? Or was he just grasping at straws, hoping that someday she'd be free to start a new life with him?

It was dark and they were in bed. Connie snuggled up to Alan's back and sighed. Her stomach was queasy and her head felt weightless, like a balloon filled with helium on a string. Was she getting another of her headaches?

She hadn't had a migraine since she'd moved in with

Alan. In the past they'd been horrible, keeping her flat on her back in bed for days, unable to eat or even open her eyes. This one seemed coiled, at the very top of her skull, like a rattlesnake ready to strike.

She'd gone to the doctor several years ago, and he'd given her medication. There were warning signs for migraines—Connie knew them all. The doctor had told her to take a pill the moment she started to see the bright patterns of yellow and red start to swirl behind her eyelids.

But the patterns weren't swirling; they were flashing. And they were flashing in a regular rhythm. On, off. On, off. Keeping time like a metronome. Was this really a migraine? Or was it something else?

Cautiously, Connie opened her eyes, but she didn't experience the familiar flash of pain. And then she saw what was making the pattern, a red neon sign that was blinking on and off.

Dew Drop Inn. Connie mouthed the words, but she didn't say them aloud. Alan was a light sleeper and she didn't want to wake him. But there was no place called the Dew Drop Inn near their condo. Where were they?

On a trip. They'd taken a trip and they were in a hotel. But where had they gone? And why? Connie wished she could remember, but she felt completely disoriented, and her stomach was churning alarmingly. She took a deep breath, that seemed to help, and then she moved very slowly to the edge of the bed. Her mouth was dry. She was terribly thirsty. A glass of water might help.

She reached for the light. There were always lamps on both sides of the bed in hotels. But she stopped as she touched the bedside table. A light would wake Alan, and he had trouble getting back to sleep if she woke him in the middle of the night.

Connie's bare feet touched the floor. She was surprised to

feel the linoleum, not carpet. Alan didn't like to stay in cheap hotels, but perhaps he'd been tired after driving all day and this had been the only place he could find.

As she stood up, Connie's head began to whirl. Uncomfortably woozy, she reached out for the wall to steady herself, realizing the source of her problem. This wasn't a migraine. It was a hangover. She'd had too much wine with dinner. Alan must have decided to stop here because she was too sick to go any farther.

Heat rose to Connie's cheeks, and she knew she was blushing. How embarrassing! She hoped Alan wouldn't tease her about this when he woke up. But perhaps he would have a hangover, too. She could hear him snoring; he only snored when he'd had too much to drink. It was a good thing they'd stopped here for the night and not attempted to drive any farther.

As she thought about it, Connie became less embarrassed. At least she wasn't the only one who'd gotten drunk. They'd have a good laugh about this in the morning, and they'd make a pact never to drink too much in the future. Connie knew she'd keep her promise. The way her stomach was rolling and lurching, she didn't think she'd ever be tempted to drink again!

She moved slowly, inching her way across the unfamiliar room. She didn't want to stumble over any furniture and wake Alan. There had to be a bathroom. Every hotel room had a bathroom. All she had to do was find it and she could drink some water and take some aspirin.

As her hand found a doorknob, she resisted the urge to giggle. She hoped it wasn't the outside door! She didn't have on a stitch of clothing, and she didn't want to wander out into the hallway and have the door lock behind her!

Connie pulled the door open and gave a huge sigh of relief as her fingers touched the inside wall. It was tiled.

Definitely a bathroom. She stepped in, pulling the door closed behind her, and flicked on the light.

The bright beam hurt her eyes, and she blinked several times. This was a perfectly nice bathroom, small but clean, with two plastic-wrapped glasses on the counter. Connie unwrapped one, ran some water, and found the complimentary basket of toiletries. It contained a small bottle of hand lotion, a matching bottle of shampoo, a new bar of soap, and a purse-size tin of aspirin.

After she'd taken two tablets and washed her face, Connie felt a little better. She wished she could take a cold shower to clear her head, but that would be sure to wake Alan. It was best to let him sleep. He'd have to drive in the morning.

Connie flicked off the light and opened the bathroom door. Alan was still sleeping; she could hear him snoring softly. She crossed the room very quietly and slid into bed, trying not to jiggle the mattress. She was just preparing to pull up the blanket when she felt Alan reach for her.

"I'm sorry if I woke you." Connie whispered in the darkness. "Go back to sleep, honey."

Alan was silent, and for a moment Connie thought he'd gone back to sleep. But then he chuckled and she felt his fingers on Connie sighed softly. His hand was so warm, and the way he was touching her made her hold her breath in anticipation. It was unusual for Alan to wake up to make love to her, but from all indications, last night must have been an unusual night.

"What do *you* want?" Connie's voice was light and playful. Alan like it when she teased him. And then she reached out for him, under the covers, and gave a little gasp of surprise. Alan was more than ready. He felt huge and hard in her hand.

He groaned when her fingers closed around him, and

Connie giggled. Alan loved it when she played with him. Her fingers circled, touching and then rubbing, and that was when something very unusual happened. Alan lifted her up until she was straddling him on the bed.

"Honey! What are you . . . ?"

But Connie didn't have time to finish her question. Alan pushed on the back of her head and guided her mouth down to him. Connie was shocked and she gave a little giggle of surprise. Alan had never done anything like this before! He'd always preferred what she called "nice" sex, sex with the lights out in the missionary position, fondling and touching but nothing else. Tonight he wanted something more, and Connie was delighted to give it to him.

He groaned as her tongue brushed against him and she giggled deep in her throat. This was going to be fun. She could hardly wait to see Alan's reaction when she really got started.

It was no less than Connie had expected. He almost went ballistic. And that was when Connie got her second shock. He grabbed her quite roughly by the arms and lifted her up in the air, positioning her directly above him and pushing her down.

Connie's mouth opened in a soundless expression of surprise. This wasn't like Alan at all! He'd always been so concerned about her pleasure, asking her whether she was ready for him, and guiding himself inside her so gently. There was nothing gentle about Alan tonight. He'd changed, and Connie wasn't sure she liked it!

But she started to when he moved beneath her, lunging up with his body. He was like a madman, intent on that final pleasure, and Connie gave a little moan in the back of her throat.

"Move, baby. Move it around for me."

His voice was hoarse, so thick with passion that Connie

almost didn't recognize it. Alan sounded like a stranger, and she shivered in excitement. This was a side of him she'd never seen before. The gentle man she loved had turned into an animal, raging with passion.

He guided her hips in tight circles, and Connie moaned again. It felt fantastic. She began to move in wider and wider circles, riding him like a stallion.

"Oh, yeah. That's good! You got it now, baby!"

Connie had the insane urge to laugh. Where had Alan picked up this dialogue? Had he been reading pornographic books, or watching X-rated films?

But she didn't have time to think about that for long. He reached out to grab her breasts, and all other thoughts were driven from Connie's mind as passion began to consume her. There was no sense of time or even of decency. They were two animals, a male and a female, mating in a burst of heated arousal. She cried out. Once. Twice. Strangled little sounds that let him know she was reaching the pinnacle. And then his voice mingled with hers in a full-throated shout as they both gave voice to that crashing completion.

They stayed there, glued together by the memory of what they'd felt, until he broke the spell. He patted her once, a friendly pat, nothing more, nothing less, and then he moved away to his side of the bed. Connie frowned as she heard him begin to snore again. Why hadn't he said anything? Alan always told her he loved her after they'd made love. His silence made her feel bereft, as if she'd been used and then abandoned by the man she loved.

Connie inched her way to his side of the bed. Even though he'd gone back to sleep, she needed to feel close to him. She cuddled up to his back, pressing her body against his and sharing his warmth, but she couldn't seem to go to sleep. It was a reversal that puzzled her. Alan was the one who'd had trouble going back to sleep. She'd always dropped right off the moment she'd closed her eyes.

She stayed there for long minutes, trying to doze, but her thoughts were a jumble of frightening images. Two policemen, their faces solemn, telling her something she couldn't remember. A bed on wheels, traveling down a long, brightly lit corridor. The face of a man she didn't recognize, seated behind a huge mahogany desk.

It was no use. She couldn't sleep. Connie slid to the edge of the bed and sat up. Even though she didn't smoke, her mouth tasted like stale tobacco, and she was terribly thirsty again. She didn't want another glass of lukewarm water. She needed something with bubbles to settle her stomach.

In most hotels you could find a soft drink machine in the hallway. There would be an ice machine, too, and perhaps even some snacks. Now that she thought about it, Connie realized she was very hungry. A soft drink and some crackers would tide her over until it was time to eat breakfast.

Connie explored the room in the darkness until she found her clothes. It wasn't easy. Her skirt was near the dresser, her blouse was under the chair, and her suit jacket was in a heap in the middle of the room. She found her panties and stockings, but she couldn't locate her bra. It didn't really matter. She'd wear her coat and no one would know the difference.

She dressed in the bathroom, where there was light. Her head was still spinning, so she had to sit down several times to keep from losing her balance. She slipped on her coat and her shoes, she'd found those in the bathroom, and at last she was ready to go.

Money. She needed her purse. She just hoped she'd brought it in and not left it behind in Alan's car. She opened the bathroom door a crack, so a little light seeped out into the room, and smiled as she spotted it on the floor. A moment later, after checking to make sure the door wouldn't lock behind her, Connie stepped out of the room.

She was outside! Her eyes widened as she saw a line of cars parked at the snow-covered curb. They'd stopped at a motel. She was very glad she'd found her coat as a blast of winter air made her shiver. She almost ducked back inside the room. But the frigid air seemed to clear her head a bit, and she really needed something to eat and drink.

A sign pointed the way to the office, so Connie followed the arrow. The walkway was covered, and she swayed slightly as she made her way to the front of the building. There were three vending machines in a small, partially enclosed area; Connie smiled as she saw them. One held newspapers, another was a soft drink machine, and the third contained cellophane-wrapped packages of snacks.

Connie opened her purse and unzipped the pocket she used for change. She had enough for a soft drink, but she needed one more nickel to get the crackers she wanted. She fumbled inside the purse, hoping some change had dropped to the bottom. That was when she felt an envelope and drew it out to see what it was.

The envelope was plain white, and she didn't remember seeing it before. She opened the flap and frowned as she saw it contained one crisp hundred-dollar bill. Why did she have a hundred-dollar bill in a plain white envelope?

As she stared at the envelope, a rush of memories bombarded her. The policemen. Alan. Their baby. The way the Stanfords had rejected her. She pressed her hand over her mouth to stifle a scream. Where was she? Why was she here? And who was that man in the motel room?

"Noooooo!" Connie's cry was anguished, the wail of the mortally wounded. The Stanfords were right. She was nothing more than a highly paid whore. But the Stanfords didn't matter. She didn't care if they hated her. The only person who mattered to her was Alan.

She was running then, across the snow-covered parking lot, to the highway that stretched out before her. Someone had to stop. Someone had to help. Someone had to take her to the hospital so that she could find him. She had to see Alan one more time, to gaze into his dear, dead eyes and beg for his forgiveness.

CHAPTER 8

The call had come in at midnight, a disturbance at Universal Hospital. A two-man patrol car had been dispatched, but they'd encountered a burglary in progress and they'd be delayed. The dispatcher had called Doug because he lived quite close to the hospital, asking if he'd drive over and check it out.

Doug had been almost relieved as he'd dressed and hurried to his car. He hadn't been sleeping anyway. Thoughts of Jill had kept him awake. He'd needed something to distract him.

It was a short drive to the hospital, only ten minutes on the deserted streets. Doug parked in a red zone next to the emergency room door, then flipped down the visor so his police identification card would be visible through the windshield.

A starched model of efficiency was manning the desk, tightly curled hair with streaks of gray, thick coke-bottle glasses, and a snow white uniform. She looked up as Doug came through the door and frowned disapprovingly. "Please move your car. You're parked in a red zone."

"Sergeant Lake. Minneapolis PD." Doug flashed his badge. "You reported a disturbance?"

The nurse looked relieved, and she actually smiled. "They've got her cornered down at the morgue. Jimmy? Take Sergeant Lake to the basement."

"I'm coming, Miss Applegate." A tall, black-haired youth rushed up. When he saw Doug, he grinned. "Hey, Sergeant Lake. How's it going?"

At first, Doug didn't recognize him, but then he remembered the collar he'd made two years ago. This was Jimmy Redwing, a young Sioux teenager, who'd fenced a stolen watch for drug money. Jimmy had been a skinny kid back then, with long hair tied back in a greasy ponytail. He'd had a real punk attitude, and Doug had doubted whether the system would work. But it looked as if Jimmy had cleaned up his act.

"Hi, Jimmy." Doug smiled. "I almost didn't recognize you without the hair."

"Yeah. Miss Applegate cut it for me. She's my work-study sponsor, and you have to look neat to get a job here. Come on, Sergeant Lake. I'll take you to the morgue."

On the way to the basement, Doug learned a lot about Jimmy Redwing. He'd been sent to the Bar None Ranch, a juvenile facility in Anoka. It was a real, working ranch, quite a change of environment for an Indian kid who'd grown up in the projects. In addition to three squares a day and four hours of classes, Jimmy had learned to ride and care for his personal horse. At the ranch he'd learned to be responsible, and he was currently living at a halfway house where employer-sponsors interviewed the teenagers for part-time jobs. Miss Applegate had hired Jimmy Redwing; she was his sponsor.

"So how do you like your job?"

"It's great." Jimmy started to grin again. "Miss Applegate runs my tail off, but she lets me do everything. She says I'm a natural, and she's getting me into the paramedic program."

"How about high school?"

"I did that." Jimmy's grin grew wider. "She helped me study and I passed my equivalency test. I get off parole in January. Then I can start taking classes. It's pretty expensive, but the hospital's going to work out a schedule so they can hire me part-time."

"Congratulations, Jimmy. It sounds like you really turned your life around."

Jimmy nodded. "Working here helped a lot. The first day I was here, they brought in a kid. He was only fourteen, but he died of an overdose. It made me think, you know? I decided the next time I saw you I'd thank you for busting me. If you hadn't caught me and sent me away, I could've ended up just like that kid."

"Hey, Jimmy . . . I'm glad everything turned out right." Doug patted the young man on the back. A cop didn't get much appreciation. Most of the people Doug arrested were resentful. They accused him of picking on them even though they were breaking the law. Seeing kids like Jimmy, who'd made it in spite of the odds, was the thing that kept him going.

As Doug and Jimmy stepped off the elevator, they heard someone screaming, a woman, her voice high pitched. She sounded frightened, hysterical. Doug increased his pace.

"You hear that, Sergeant Lake?" Jimmy hurried to keep up with Doug's long strides. "That poor lady's still screaming. She was screaming when I was down here before."

Doug turned to him. He might be a valuable witness. "Do you know why she's screaming?"

"Not exactly. But I heard her say she had to find her boyfriend. She wanted to apologize, or something like that. She started screaming right after we put her in restraints."

"Did she hurt anyone?"

"I don't think so." Jimmy shook his head. "But we're going to have to get a new window for the morgue. When she found out the door was locked, she picked up a big flower pot and heaved it at the glass."

"Did she cut herself?"

Jimmy shook his head. "All the glass went inside. I helped the security guys pull her back before she could jump through the window."

"Good work." Doug nodded. "Who called security?"

"I did. She came in through emergency, and she looked weird. I could tell there was going to be trouble."

"What kind of weird? Describe it for me, Jimmy."

"Well . . ." Jimmy hesitated a moment. "I'd say she was on something. Pupils dilated, rapid breathing, flushed skin. You know what I mean?"

"I know. What do you think it was?"

Jimmy shrugged. "PCP, maybe. She's not very big, but she was super strong. It took all three of us to hold her down."

They rounded the corner and Doug saw the broken window. A heavy brass flower pot, still holding a potted palm tree, lay on the tiled floor of the morgue. Jimmy hadn't been exaggerating when he'd said she was strong. "How much does that flower pot weigh?"

"I don't know, but the janitor can't move it by himself. That's why they got that dolly." Jimmy pointed to the small block of wood with wheels propped up against the wall. "I saw her lift up that tree like it was a feather and toss it through the window."

As Doug rounded another corner, he saw her. She was a slim, brown-haired woman who would have been pretty under any other circumstances. Even though she had on an old-fashioned straitjacket, it still took two security guards to hold her down.

Jimmy ran toward the security guards, and Doug followed him. He tapped the older security guard on the shoulder, then pointed to Doug. "Chuck? This is Sergeant Lake."

"Hi." Doug flashed his badge. "What have you got here?"

"A wildcat." Chuck was an older black man with salt and pepper hair. He looked worried as he turned to Doug. "If we let her go, she tries to kick us. And she won't stop screaming."

The woman looked up at Doug. Her eyes were wide and frightened, and they didn't seem to be focusing properly. She stared at him for a moment, then started screaming again.

Doug motioned for Jimmy to take Chuck's place, and they walked down the hall. Chuck unlocked a door to a vacant office. Then they stepped in and closed the door.

"Tell me what happened." Doug sat on the edge of the desk and pulled out his notebook.

"I don't know, but it's a good thing the kid called us when he did. We got here just in time to keep her from going through that window. I hate to think what might have happened if she'd gotten into the morgue."

Doug nodded. "What time was that?"

"A little after midnight. Tommy and I were just taking our break."

Doug glanced at his watch. It was almost one. "And she's been screaming all this time?"

"That's right. She stops for a couple seconds to catch her breath and then she starts in again."

"Has anyone given her a tranquilizer?"

"Not yet." Chick shook his head. "The doctor said he had to wait until you got here. He doesn't know what she's on, and he can't do a blood test unless you arrest her and sign off on the form."

Doug nodded. It was standard operating procedure. If the woman's condition wasn't life threatening, the hospital couldn't treat her without a signed release form. "Okay,

Chuck. Call him and tell him to bring me the form. I'll arrest her for destruction of property and sign it. And let's have an orderly bring down a gurney with straps."

"Okay. You got it." Chuck used his radio, and a few minutes later an orderly brought a gurney. It took all five of them to strap the woman down, but finally she was rendered immobile. Doug signed the release form. Then the orderly wheeled the woman away, accompanied by Jimmy and the younger security guard.

"What a relief!" Chuck sat down in a chair and stretched his arms. "You wouldn't think a tiny little thing like her could be so strong. I'm going to wake up with a stiff back tomorrow, I can tell you that!"

"Do you think she was trying to hurt you?"

Chuck thought about it for a moment, then shook his head. "She was just trying to get in that morgue. She thought her boyfriend was in there, and she had to see him."

"Do you think she was on some kind of drug?"

"I don't know." Chuck frowned. "She was grieving for her boyfriend, I can tell you that. And she thought we were keeping her from seeing his body. She was crazy, but I don't know if it was drugs."

While he was waiting for the results of the blood test, Doug interviewed everyone who'd come in contact with the woman. He learned that she'd carried no identification and no one knew who she was. Her clothing was expensive and so was her watch, but they provided no clue to her identity. She'd come into the emergency room alone and had followed the signs to the morgue. The cars in the parking lot were all accounted for. Either someone had dropped her off, or she'd arrived by bus or taxi.

It was two in the morning when the blood work came back from the lab, and it was negative. No sign of drugs or disease. Since she was still screaming, the doctor gave her a tranquilizer, and when she was quiet and her vital signs were stable, Doug turned her over to two uniforms for transit to the county jail. Jane Doe, the name they'd given the woman for booking purposes, would be on suicide watch in a private cell. If they were lucky, she'd be able to tell them her real name at her arraignment in the morning.

It was three in the morning when Doug shook Jimmy's hand and headed for the door. But he stopped and turned back when he remembered that Jill's husband was a patient. "Hey, Jimmy. My friend's husband is here. I won't wake him, but do you think I could take a quick peek?"

"No problem, Sergeant Lake." Jimmy sat down at the computer. "What's his name?"

"Neil Bradley."

Jimmy typed the name on the screen and nodded. "He's in room five eighteen. Just take the elevator up to the fifth floor and turn left. If anybody gives you any grief, just flash your badge."

Doug felt a little strange as he rode up in the elevator and walked down the corridor to room five eighteen. He wasn't sure why he wanted to see Jill's husband. Perhaps it was just to look at him, to see if there was something in his sleeping face that would provide an answer to why Jill had chosen him. It couldn't be good looks alone; Jill wasn't that shallow. There had to be some other reason, and perhaps he'd learn it if he saw his rival in the flesh.

The door to Neil's room was open and Doug peered in. Neil was in bed, his eyes bandaged, his head in some sort of restraint. His sleeping face was relaxed and appeared younger than the picture on the book cover. As a matter of fact, Neil Bradley looked vulnerable, almost pathetic, and Doug felt ashamed for spying on him.

He was just about to leave when Neil made a sound. He was trying to talk. Doug stepped into the room. If Neil was awake and needed something, he could help him ring for the nurse.

Neil spoke again, a mumbled word, and Doug moved to the bed. Perhaps he needed something?

"Lisa? Where are you? I need you, Lisa!"

Doug nodded. Lisa must be the name of Neil's nurse. "Just hold on, Neil. I'll get her for you."

Doug hurried out of the room and raced to the nurses' desk. Two nurses were sitting there talking, and the younger one looked up.

"Hi. The patient in five eighteen, Neil Bradley. I just looked in on him, and he's asking for a nurse named Lisa."

The younger nurse nodded. "I know. He does that every night. Mr. Bradley's talking in his sleep."

"Are you sure he doesn't need something?"

"We're sure." The older nurse spoke up. "I just checked on him a couple of minutes ago. He was sleeping like a baby."

Doug raised his eyebrows. "He had me fooled. I really thought he was awake. Is Lisa his day nurse?"

"No." The younger nurse shook her head. "There's no nurse on this floor named Lisa. We think he's asking for his wife."

"But his wife's name is Jill."

The two nurses exchanged surprised glances; then the younger one shrugged. "Lisa could be anyone. He's dreaming."

"Okay." Doug nodded. "Thanks for letting me peek in on him."

The older nurse smiled. "No problem. You said you were a friend of his wife?"

"That's right. Jill's an assistant DA, and I work with her."

"I wouldn't mention this to her, Sergeant." The older nurse looked concerned. "It might hurt her feelings. Lisa could be anyone, a former wife, a sister, a girlfriend. There's just no way of telling."

The younger nurse nodded. "This isn't unusual, Sergeant. Patients say strange things when they're sedated."

"Don't worry. I won't mention it to her. I'll just tell Jill I saw him and he was sleeping."

Doug was thoughtful as he walked to the elevator. Who was Lisa? And why was Neil asking for her, instead of Jill? It was another piece of the puzzle, and he needed to figure out where it fit in.

CHAPTER 9

Connie awoke to a babble of women's voices. At first, they were all mixed together in some great cacophony, one indistinguishable from the other. She listened for a while. The voices were like the white-noise machine Alan had in the bedroom to block out the sounds of the city so he could sleep. One setting sounded like the ocean, with rhythmic waves crashing against the shore. Another made her think of a breeze sighing through the tall grasses of a field. The third setting was her favorite. It sounded like rain falling gently from the sky, a warm summer rain that made sidewalks fresh and clean and caused flowers to give off their scent.

She might have fallen asleep again, but she woke up when the voices got louder. Had Alan forgotten to turn off the television? It was a very noisy program, but by concentrating on tones and inflections, she found she could focus on an individual speaker.

"Should'a killed him when I got the chance, him and that woman in Mama's bed, both of them naked as jaybirds. All's I done was cut him up a little, and they drug me down here. 'S not fair."

Connie frowned. Was this the television, or was she dreaming? And then there was another voice, high pitched like a little girl's.

"I wasn't even working, you know? I was just sitting at the bus stop when this guy in a shiny white Lincoln pulls up. He says he wants to party, and he waves a hundred at me. How am I supposed to know he was setting me up?"

Connie opened her eyes, and she saw the bars. At first she thought they were some sort of gate, but then someone else spoke.

"Just ask if he's a cop. They gotta tell you. If they don't, it's entrapment."

"Oh, yeah?" It was the girlish voice again. "If you're so smart, what are you doing in here?"

"I asked and he didn't tell me. That's why the judge is gonna let me walk. I know my rights. You just watch and see."

Connie shuddered. Those bars weren't part of a gate. She was in jail! But what had she done? Everything was a blank. She sat up on the narrow bench that had served as her bed and looked down at her clothes. Her skirt was filthy, as if she'd been rolling around on the floor, and the sleeve of her green silk blouse was torn.

"So I asks him, why me? He's the one you should take. And he says maybe that's true, but there's a witness that seen me with the knife. It's gotta be that woman. I'm gonna get her just as soon as I get out."

It was difficult to stand, but Connie managed to push herself upright. She was in a small cell, no bigger than her closet at the condo, with a toilet and a sink. There was a piece of polished metal over the sink, and she walked toward it, steadying herself against the wall.

When she caught sight of her reflection, she almost fainted. Her hair was matted with something that smelled horrible. There was a scratch on the side of her face, and her eyes looked puffy, as if she'd been crying. On the inside of her left arm was a small purple bruise.

There was a clang and then heavy footsteps approached her cell. Connie turned around to see a tough-looking woman, dressed in a uniform, unlock her door. "Well, Sleeping Beauty. You don't look so good this morning. What do you say we get you cleaned up?"

Connie didn't know what to say. This woman must be a prison guard, and she didn't want to alienate her. She just nodded and tried to smile.

"They told me you were a wildcat last night. You're not going to try anything, are you, honey?"

Connie swallowed hard and found her voice. "No. I won't. I promise."

"Good." The guard smiled. "You cooperate with me and everything'll be just fine. Turn around and back up toward me. Take it nice and slow."

Connie turned and started to step back, but she lost her balance and had to catch herself against the wall. "I . . . I'm sorry. I'm dizzy."

"That's okay. Just stand right there and I'll come to you."

Connie leaned against the wall while the guard snapped handcuffs around her wrists. She felt sick and very woozy. "What's wrong with me?"

"They gave you a shot in the hospital. I'll get you in the shower and that should help. Just lean on me and walk."

Connie did her best to proceed, but she had to lean heavily on the guard. She was embarrassed when she stumbled, and she tried to apologize. "I'm sorry. My legs don't work right."

"Don't worry about it. I could carry a little thing like you if I had to. Do you remember your name this morning?"

Connie nodded, but that was a big mistake. When she

moved her head, it hurt. "Connie Wilson. I've got my driver's license in my purse."

"Sorry, Connie. You didn't have any personal effects when they brought you in."

Connie frowned. "My purse is gone?"

"That's right. Come with me now. We're going to walk down this hall to the door at the end."

The tiled hallway seemed endless, but somehow they made it. The guard steadied her against the wall and unlocked the door with a key. She helped Connie through and motioned for her to sit down on a bench.

"This isn't the Hilton, but it'll have to do." The guard opened a locker and took out a blue cotton dress. "I'm going to put you under the water so you can wash some of that gunk out of your hair. Then I'll help you dress in these clean clothes. You don't have a problem with that, do you?"

Connie shook her head, and this time it didn't hurt quite as much. "No. Thank you very much."

"That's got to be a first!" The guard actually grinned. "Nobody's ever thanked me before."

Connie tried not to blush as the guard helped her out of her clothes and led her to the shower stall. The woman unlocked Connie's handcuffs, turned on the water, and handed her a bar of soap. "Can you handle it, or do you need help?"

"I think I can do it." Connie nodded.

"Okay. I'll leave the door open. If you need help, just holler for me."

Connie gasped as she stepped under the stream of water. It was cold, but it seemed to clear her head. As memories came rushing back, tears rolled down her cheeks, along with the streams of water. Alan was dead, and she'd lost their baby. But why was she here, in jail?

It hurt to wash her hair, and her arms ached, as if she'd lifted a heavy weight. But Connie managed to get it done.

There was no shampoo, so she used the bar of soap. She noticed other bruises on her body, some on her legs that looked like finger marks and several more on her arms.

When she was through, the guard handed her a towel. Connie shivered as she wrapped it around her body. She was cold and she felt sick, but her mind seemed to be working again.

"Feeling better?" The prison guard led her over to the bench again.

"Yes, thank you."

"Good." The guard smiled again. "Hold out your arms and I'll help you dress."

Connie felt like a child as the woman dressed her in a white cotton bra and panties. The blue prison dress was shapeless and had no belt, but it was clean, which was an improvement over her own dirty clothes. She even got a pair of slippers with rubber soles—a size too large, but Connie could walk in them.

"You're all set. And I got to say, you look a hundred percent better." The prison guard put down the comb she'd used on Connie's hair, then snapped the handcuffs back on. "You're not up for another thirty minutes, but you can wait in the holding area."

"Do you know what I'm waiting for?" Connie was puzzled.

"Your arraignment, honey. You're up before Judge Swensen at ten. You've never been in jail before?"

"No." Connie shook her head. "Do you . . . uh . . . do you know what I did?"

The prison guard nodded and took Connie's arm to lead her back down the hallway again. "Drunk and disorderly, and destruction of property. You don't remember?"

"I don't remember anything. What did I destroy?"

"You smashed a window at the hospital." The prison guard used her key and the elevator doors opened. "Step in here, honey, and I'll take you up. There's a phone in the holding area. You're entitled to make one call, so start thinking about who it's going to be."

As they rode in the elevator, Connie's mind was whirling. Who could she call? Alan was dead, she'd promised not to contact the Stanfords, and she hadn't kept in touch with any of the people she used to know.

The elevator doors opened and they stepped out into a room with only three pieces of furniture, a desk and two chairs. The desk had a metal bar bolted to the top and the guard took the handcuff from Connie's right hand and fastened it to the bar.

"Here's the phone." The guard opened a locked drawer and pulled out a phone. She set it on top of the desk and nodded to Connie. "Go ahead. You can make your call now."

Connie stared at the phone for a moment, then shook her head. "There's nobody I can call."

"Are you sure? Most people call their lawyers."

Connie's fingers touched the phone. The only lawyer she knew was Mr. Avery. It would be a waste of time to call him. He was the Stanfords' attorney; he wouldn't help her. She pushed the phone back across the desk and shook her head, again. "Thank you, but there's no one I can call."

"Okay." The guard put the phone back in the drawer. "If you can't afford to hire a lawyer, Judge Swensen will appoint one for you. Your arraignment will be postponed until you have time to meet with him."

Connie nodded and blinked back tears. If Alan were still alive, she'd have plenty of money for a lawyer. But if Alan were alive, she'd have no need for one. She wouldn't have broken that window, and she wouldn't be here in jail.

"Hey. Buck up." The guard patted Connie on the shoulder. "Judge Swensen's okay. Since this is your first offense, he'll probably make you pay a fine and let you go."

Connie forced a smile. The guard was trying to be nice, but she didn't know that Connie had no money to pay a fine. Even if someone had found her purse, they'd take out the money before they returned it.

The phone rang once, startling Connie, and the guard unlocked the drawer to answer it. "Okay. I'll bring her in."

Connie started to shake as the guard snapped on her handcuffs and led her through a side door to the courtroom. There she found another bench to sit on, and she kept her head down, too ashamed to face anyone.

The guard leaned close to talk to Connie. "There's two ahead of you. Just sit here and listen; then it'll be your turn."

The other two women had lawyers, which made Connie feel very alone as she sat on the bench and waited. When it was her turn, the bailiff read her name and the list of charges.

"Are you represented by council, Miss Wilson?" The judge looked bored, even though the courtroom clock showed that it was only ten-thirty in the morning.

"No, Your Honor." Connie swallowed hard. "I don't have—"

"Excuse me, Your Honor." A short, balding man in an expensive suit rushed up the aisle. "Harvey Green. I'm representing Miss Wilson in this matter."

The judge nodded. "Good morning, Mr. Green. I was under the impression you handled only corporate matters."

"That's true, Your Honor, but this is an unusual case with extenuating circumstances. May I have a few minutes of Your Honor's time in chambers?"

Judge Swensen looked surprised, but he nodded and banged his gavel. "Court is in recess for ten minutes. I'll see counsel in my chambers."

"I thought you didn't have a lawyer." The guard leaned close to talk to Connie again.

"I don't." Connie's face mirrored her shock. "I've never seen Mr. Green before in my life!"

It seemed to take forever for the hands on the courtroom clock to move, but at last the ten minutes were up. Mr. Green and the prosecutor came back into the courtroom, followed by Judge Swensen. They took their places. The bailiff announced that court was again in session, and Mr. Green stood up. "Your Honor, I move that the charges against my client be dismissed. Since this is her first offense, and it was prompted by extreme emotional stress, I ask that the record of her arrest be expunged."

"The people have no objection, Your Honor." The prosecutor nodded and got to the feet.

"The defendant is remanded into the custody of Mr. Green." Judge Swensen banged his gavel. "All records will be expunged, and this case is dismissed."

The next few minutes were a confusing blur. Connie was taken to another room, where she changed into the street clothes Mr. Green had brought for her. After she'd signed the release papers, she was taken out to the lobby to find Mr. Green waiting for her.

"Thank you," she said to him. She felt dazed. "But . . . I don't understand."

Mr. Green smiled at her and opened the door of a car that was parked at the curb. "Come along, Connie. We'll talk about this on the way to my office. I'm Alan's lawyer, and he left something for you."

Connie was silent as Mr. Green drove away from the jail. Her mind was spinning with unanswered questions. If Mr. Avery was right and Alan hadn't drawn up a will, how was it possible that he'd left her something? The whole thing was so confusing, Connie closed her eyes and leaned back against the headrest to think about it.

"That's a good idea. Get some sleep. You've had a rough couple of days."

Connie nodded. Mr. Green was being very nice. And even though she didn't think it was possible, she promptly fell asleep.

CHAPTER 10

Jill was just pouring herself a cup of coffee in the small office kitchen when the newest member of the staff came in. His name was Dave Kramer, and he made Jill feel old. Even though he'd passed the bar last year, he looked much too young to be a lawyer.

"Hi, Mrs. Bradley." Dave gave her a boyish grin and opened the refrigerator to pour himself a glass of milk.

"Hello, Dave." Jill smiled back. Dave was a nice guy. It wasn't his fault he made her feel ancient. "I thought you were scheduled for court this morning."

"I was, but the case was dismissed."

Dave took a sip of milk, and white foam clung to his upper lip. Jill tried not to laugh. He looked like a child with a milk mustache. "Tell me about it," she said.

"A woman broke a window at the morgue last night, trying to get to her boyfriend's body."

"Good heavens!" Jill was shocked. "Was she drunk?"

Dave shook his head. "Grief stricken is more like it. Once her lawyer told me the story, I couldn't help but feel sorry for her. When the police told her her boyfriend was dead, she went into shock and lost their baby. She was in the hospital for a couple of days, and when she got back to their condo, she found out that his parents had changed the locks."

"That's horrible!" Jill began to frown.

"I know, but there wasn't anything she could do. Her boyfriend didn't leave a will so all of his property went to his parents."

Jill's frown deepened. "The poor thing was left out in the cold?"

"Completely." Dave nodded. "His parents wouldn't even speak to her. She went a little crazy. When they arrested her, she was screaming about how she had to see her boyfriend one more time."

"Her lawyer pleaded extenuating circumstances?"

Dave nodded and took another drink. His milk mustache grew whiter, and Jill resisted the urge to hand him a napkin. "Her lawyer put up the money to replace the window, and the judge remanded her into his custody. I'm just glad I didn't have to prosecute her. She'd never been in any trouble before, and she looked like a nice woman."

Jill was thoughtful as she carried her coffee back to her office. Hard-luck stories were a part of their job, but this one sounded genuine. The woman had obviously loved her boyfriend so much she'd gone off the deep end when he'd died. It made her wonder what she'd be like if Neil died. Would they have to carry her off, screaming hysterically in grief? Or would the fact that she didn't love him, that she stayed with him out of a sense of obligation, help her to cope with the loss?

Connie's hands were shaking, and she clutched her purse tightly as she got out of the taxi and walked toward the bank. Someone had found her purse at the hospital, but just as Connie had feared, the envelope with her money was missing. They'd even taken the twenty dollars she'd tucked in the back of her wallet, but she had her driver's license to show to the people at the bank.

As she opened the door and entered the lobby, Connie felt like an impostor, even though Mr. Green had assured her that everything was perfectly legal. Two months ago, when Alan had learned she was pregnant, he'd set up a bank account for the baby with a balance of a hundred thousand dollars. It didn't matter that she'd lost the child. Her name was the only one on the account, so the money was hers.

Of course she'd asked the obvious question. Was it right for her to use the money when Alan had put it in an account for his baby? Mr. Green had nodded. Then he'd said it was not only right, it was exactly what Alan would have wanted her to do.

"Can I help you, ma'am?"

Connie moved forward and approached the teller, an older woman with dark hair and wire-framed glasses. "Yes. I'm Connie Wilson. Mr. Green sent me here. I'm supposed to ask for Mrs. Talbot. He said he'd call, and she'd be expecting me."

"Just a moment, Miss Wilson." The teller picked up a phone and dialed a number. She spoke briefly and then closed her window and opened a locked door, motioning Connie inside. "I'll take you to Mrs. Talbot's office."

They went upstairs in a small elevator, and the teller led Connie down a carpeted hallway. She knocked at a door, then opened it, standing aside so Connie could enter.

"Good afternoon, Miss Wilson." A tall blonde, her hair caught back in a gold barrette, stood up and shook Connie's hand. "Mr. Green called to say you'd be making a withdrawal. My deepest condolences for your loss."

"Thank you." Connie's voice was little more than a whisper.

"I have your checkbook ready." Mrs. Talbot pushed

a folder and a checkbook across the desk. "There's also a bank credit card with an initial limit of twenty thousand dollars, and a copy of your latest bank statement. All you have to do is sign the green signature card and fill out the withdrawal slip."

Connie opened the folder. Everything was there and she nodded.

"I've marked the signature block." Mrs. Talbot pointed to the signature card. Connie signed it. "If you'll just tell me the amount you wish to withdraw, I'll send for one of our runners."

Connie felt dazed. This morning she'd been broke. Now she had a hundred thousand dollars at her disposal. This whole day had been mind-boggling. "I'm not really sure how much I'll need."

"Let's discuss it then." Mrs. Talbot opened the center drawer of her desk and pulled out a leather-covered note pad. "Mr. Green said you'd want to rent a furnished apartment, but I'd advise you to draft a check for that. It's not wise to carry too much cash—your landlord can call me to verify your assets. You can use the credit card for any big-ticket items, but you'll need some cash for immediate purchases. Does a thousand in twenties sound about right?"

Connie nodded. "Yes. That's fine."

"All right." Mrs. Talbot filled out the withdrawal slip and handed it to Connie to sign. Then she picked up the phone and punched out a number. "Allison? Please have Mr. Cox put a thousand in twenties in an envelope and bring it up to my office. I have the signed withdrawal slip and my client is waiting."

Connie frowned slightly. She'd never received this kind of service in a bank before. Of course, she'd never had an account with a balance of a hundred thousand dollars, either.

Mrs. Talbot smiled at Connie again. "Have you given some thought about where you'd like to relocate?"

"Uh . . . no, not really." Connie's mind was spinning. Everything was going so fast, she hadn't had a chance to catch her breath.

"I'd suggest a hotel then, until you have time to contact a rental agent. The Radisson is nice. We use it occasionally for conferences. And there's always the Marriott. They're both centrally located."

Connie nodded. A hotel made sense, but she wasn't about to blow her money on an expensive room. "That's a good idea. Thank you very much."

"You'll need transportation. There's a Hertz office two blocks from here, and Avis is right across the street."

Connie nodded again. Mrs. Talbot was right. She'd need a car, but renting wasn't smart. It was money thrown away, with nothing to show for it. She'd buy a used car tomorrow.

Before Mrs. Talbot could make any more suggestions, a young woman in a ponytail stepped into the office. She handed Mrs. Talbot an envelope and then just stood there while Mrs. Talbot counted the money.

"Thank you, Allison." Mrs. Talbot handed her the withdrawal slip. "This goes straight down to Mr. Cox."

"Yes, Mrs. Talbot. I'll make sure he gets it." The girl nodded, gave Connie a shy grin, and hurried out of the office.

"Thank you for your help, Mrs. Talbot." Connie took the envelope and stood up. She wanted to leave before Mrs. Talbot gave her any more advice.

"Thank *you*, Miss Wilson." Mrs. Talbot came around the desk to show Connie to the door. "If you have any problems, please feel free to call. My card is stapled to the inside of your folder."

* * *

An hour later, Connie was in her hotel room. It was in a little place on a side street called the Lexington Arms. Her room wasn't large, but it had a separate bathroom, a color television, and a view of the park below.

After she'd showered and washed her hair with the shampoo the hotel provided, Connie sat down on the bed and went through her purse again. She'd been so excited when Mr. Green had told her that Alan had left her something. She'd desperately wanted some personal item, a photograph of Alan or his college ring. But he hadn't known that he was going to die. Even if he had, he would never have suspected that his parents would take his things and leave her with nothing.

There was nothing of Alan's in her purse, and Connie wiped away a tear. She still felt guilty about using Alan's money to pay her court costs and to rent this hotel room. Mr. Green was right; Alan would have wanted her to have it. But the money had really been intended for their child. Now Alan was dead, and so was his baby. She'd lost the only part of him that had been left alive.

But was that true? Connie took a sip of coffee she'd ordered from room service, and thought about it. Alan had been an organ donor. There must be some stranger out there who had a part of Alan in his body. More than one, she'd bet. If she could just find them, she might not feel this horrible sense of loss. But how could she do that? Hospital records were confidential. She would have to get access to those records and locate the people who'd received Alan's organs.

Connie had chosen the bar deliberately. It was filled with lowlifes, its red plastic booths, cracked and faded. Tabletops scarred with cigarette burns and scratches. Blinking beer signs over the bar, and a bartender who could not have cared less about his customers' approval. It had been close to midnight when Connie had slid onto a stool. She'd smiled at the bartender, ordered a ginger ale, and tipped outrageously when he'd brought it. Then she'd asked him for advice.

The bartender hadn't even bothered to play it coy. He'd just pocketed the second twenty-dollar bill and pointed to a guy in a striped polo shirt. Now she was sitting across the booth from him, watching him guzzle the beer she'd bought.

The beer disappeared without a word. He set down the bottle, then shrugged. "Sure, lady. I can do it, but it'll cost you."

"How much?" Connie stared at him as he thought about it. He was tall and thin, with stringy black hair, and his clothes hadn't seen the inside of a Laundromat in recent history. He didn't look trustworthy, but this was the third bar she'd tried that night.

"Five hundred. In cash."

Connie's eyes narrowed. She had to be careful. "I'll give you a hundred, the rest when you hand me the list."

"Hey . . ." The man looked hurt. "You think I'm gonna rip you off?"

Connie met his eyes and gave him the tough look she'd used when guys had groped her at the club. "I wouldn't try it if I were you."

"Okay, okay." The man held up his hands. "You want it tonight?"

"The sooner the better. I'll give you a bonus if you produce."

"Come with me." The man stood up. "If you're that spooked, I'll even let you watch. Ralph's got a modem in the back room."

Connie followed the man through a door and into a tiny office. Against one wall was a table that held a computer and a printer.

"Pull up that chair and be quiet." The man pointed to a folding chair that looked as if it might collapse. "This could be a little tricky. Just let me get online, and I'll take a whack at it."

Connie pulled up the chair and watched as he typed several commands on the keyboard. A moment later the screen lit up and there was the sound of a dial tone. He typed in a number and it rang twice. There was a high-pitched beep.

He nodded. "Okay. I got 'em. Now all I have to do is crack their password."

It took several minutes of trial and error, but at last the computer screen started to scroll. He stopped it on the date she'd given him and began to go through the entries.

"There he is!" Connie pointed as Alan's name flashed on the screen. It was followed by a series of numbers. The man stopped the scroll to print them out. "Do you know what those numbers mean?"

"Sure. They're identification codes from the National Organ Bank. Each one represents an organ recipient."

Connie's eyes widened. When she'd met the hacker, he hadn't seemed very bright, but she was rapidly changing her mind. "Numbers won't do me any good. How do we get their names?"

"I have to tap into the national files. They're protected so it's gonna be a little harder." The screen went blank and he punched in another number. "I'm accessing the eight hundred directory."

Connie nodded and watched the screen. It was scrolling through a list of eight hundred numbers. The words NATIONAL ORGAN BANK flashed on the screen, and he scribbled the number on a pad.

"Okay. This one's gonna take a while. If you want to help, get me another beer."

Connie jumped up from her chair and hurried back into

the bar. She was back in less than a minute, setting the beer on the table, where he could reach it. "Any luck?"

"I'm getting it. There're only a couple of permutations left."

Connie held her breath as he typed in a code and the words LIMITED ACCESS flashed across the screen. A loud beep sounded, and the line disconnected.

"Shit!" He took a sip of beer. "I really thought I had it that time. Let me try again."

Connie shut her eyes and prayed that he'd be successful. She just had to have those names!

"All right! We're in!"

"We are?" Connie opened her eyes. The screen was scrolling again.

"Get me that printout, will you?"

Connie snatched it up and handed it to him. Her hands were trembling so, she almost dropped it. He froze the screen, typed in the first code from the printout, and a name appeared on the screen.

"Here's the first one. I'll print it out."

Connie was smiling as the printer activated and a name appeared on the paper. William Rossini, with an address and a telephone number.

"Here's the next one."

A second name came on the screen, a third and a fourth. When he was through, she had seven names, complete with addresses and telephone numbers.

"That's it." He shut off the computer and raised his arms to stretch. "You satisfied, lady?"

"I am." Connie reached in her purse and handed him a roll of bills. "Here's the five hundred I promised you, and an extra hundred for doing it tonight. Thanks . . . uh . . . I don't even know your name."

"That's okay. I don't know yours, either. Let's keep it that way and we'll both stay out of trouble."

Connie nodded. It made perfect sense. "Is there a back door?"

"Right through there." He pointed to a hallway that led to a door. "Go down the alley, turn left, and you can catch a cab at the corner. Unless you want to stick around for a while. You're a good-looking woman, and I might be up for a party tonight."

"Thanks, but no thanks." Connie hurried down the hallway and through the door. She ran down the alley and out to the sidewalk, where a group of people were standing at the bus stop. A few seconds later, a taxi cruised by and Connie waved it down. She gave the driver her address, the Lexington Arms, and she didn't relax until she was back in her room with the door locked securely behind her.

Suddenly ravenous, Connie ordered two sandwiches from room service. When they came, she wolfed them down and then spread out the list on the bed. Seven names. Seven strangers. Seven chances to be close to Alan again. She'd start with the first name and work her way through to the last. It might take a while, but Connie had finally found a way to have a part of Alan with her forever.

CHAPTER 11

Almost three weeks had passed since Neil had been released from the hospital, and Jill was running on empty. She'd hired a companion from the hospital's list, but the woman had quit after only a week. The second had stuck it out for ten days, but the third had left in tears at the end of her first day. The fourth companion, Mrs. Helen Burns, was due to arrive this morning. Jill hoped she would work out. Dr. Varney had been right when he'd told her she might go through several names on the list. Neil was a difficult patient, and it took a special type of person to cope with him.

A blue Honda drove up and parked in front of the house. A moment later, the driver's door opened and a heavyset, black woman got out. Jill took heart. Perhaps this woman would be able to hold her own with Neil. He prided himself on being a liberal, and he might not be so quick to insult a member of a minority.

Jill opened the door, a smile on her face. "Mrs. Burns?"

"Just call me Helen." The woman smiled. "And you must be Mrs. Bradley."

Jill nodded. "Jill. Come in and I'll show you around."

Neil was still sleeping, so after a quick tour of the house,

Jill poured cups of coffee. When they were seated at the kitchen table, sipping the brew and eating some of the Danish she'd picked up at the bakery, Jill broached the delicate subject of Neil's temper.

"I have to be completely honest with you." Jill frowned slightly. "I'm afraid this job won't be easy. My husband has a nasty temper, and he's gone through three other companions in the past month."

Helen nodded. "I heard. But you don't have to worry. I'm used to dealing with cantankerous people."

"That's good." Jill smiled in relief. "Just don't take anything he says personally. He snaps at everybody, including me. He doesn't really mean it. I think he's just frustrated because he can't see."

Helen nodded and got up to get the coffeepot. She poured second cups and then smiled reassuringly. "It'll work out. I've got a real thick skin. Your husband and I are going to get along just fine."

"In case you have any problems, my work number's on speed dial. Just dial eleven and the call will go through automatically."

Helen shook her head. "We won't have any problems. Did you leave me a list of instructions?"

"They're on the bulletin board in the pantry." Jill opened the door so it was visible. "Neil's eye patch has to be switched every four hours, and he has a two o'clock appointment for therapy at the hospital."

"How about food? Does he have any restrictions?"

Jill shook her head. "Not really. But you don't have to cook, Helen. There's a little café about a mile from here and I've made arrangements with them. Just tell them it's for us and they'll deliver."

"But cooking's usually part of the job." Helen started to frown. "Don't you want me to cook for your husband?"

"Of course I do. But the last three companions tried to cook for him and it didn't work out. Neil's very picky."

"Aren't they all!" Helen laughed. "Why don't I try it for a couple of days and see what happens? If he won't eat what I fix, I'll call the café and order in."

"That's all right with me." Jill glanced at her watch and stood up. "If you don't have any other questions, I really should get to work."

"Go ahead. And don't worry. Your husband and I'll get along. I've never been fired from a job yet."

Jill laughed. "I can practically guarantee you won't be fired from this one. My only worry is that you'll quit."

"Not a chance." Helen shook her head. "This is real convenient for me. I only live ten minutes away, and the hours are perfect. You're going to be stuck with me until your husband can see again."

Connie hung up the phone and sighed. William Rossini was still in the hospital, and his visitor list was restricted to immediate family only. She'd just have to wait until he was released, but there was cause for celebration.

She'd told the man on the switchboard that she was a friend, and he'd put her through to the head nurse. Connie had learned that William Rossini preferred to be called Willy, he was recovering nicely from his transplant, and he was in stable condition. The nurse hadn't known exactly how long Willy would be hospitalized, but she'd told Connie that he'd probably be released in time to spend Christmas at home.

Connie glanced out the window at the park below. She was still staying at the Lexington Arms, but she'd found a car. It was a black Nissan Sentra with a small dent on the passenger's door, five years old and in good running condition. The upholstery was wearing out, but they'd thrown in seat covers and a set of tires, so she'd bought it for three thousand dollars.

She flipped open the ledger she'd purchased and frowned. The money was disappearing so fast it scared her. Six hundred to the hacker who'd gotten the transplant list, a thousand to Mr. Green to pay her court costs, a hundred and forty a week for her hotel room, and all those other things that added up so quickly, like auto insurance and phone bills and food. She'd gone through over six thousand dollars, and there was no money coming in.

Should she get a job? Connie thought about it for a moment, then shook her head. A secretarial position would take up too much of her time. She had to be free to contact the people on her list. She could always work a couple of shifts at the club, but she didn't want to go back to topless dancing unless she absolutely had to. It was better to live frugally and wait to see what would happen. She'd look for a job when her plan succeeded and she had a connection with Alan again.

"How's the companion thing working out?" Doug passed Jill the catsup and mustard. It was one of his infrequent lunches with her and they were sitting in a wooden booth at The Beef Barrel.

"We're on our fourth. Today's her first day." Jill took the precaution of tucking a napkin under her chin. The burgers at The Beef Barrel were messy, and she had to go back to work. "She seems nice, but so did the others. I'm just hoping she lasts."

"What's the problem?" Doug dipped a crisp french fry into the pool of mustard on his plate and popped it into his mouth.

"Neil."

It was the first time Jill had mentioned her husband since he'd come home from the hospital, and Doug smiled to encourage her. "Neil didn't like the other three?"

"I don't know if he liked them or not. They quit before I could ask him. Neil's not the easiest guy to get along with."

Doug filed that comment away for future reference. It was another piece of the puzzle, but he didn't dare ask Jill for more information. She always clammed up when he questioned her about Neil. "How about Christmas? Are you all ready?"

"I haven't even thought about it!" Jill gave a little laugh. "We're not having any company, and Neil doesn't want to go out. I guess we'll just treat it like any other day."

"No Christmas tree?" Doug started to frown. He loved Christmas trees. He trimmed one every year, even when he planned to spend Christmas alone.

Jill looked thoughtful. "Maybe I'll get one. It won't seem like Christmas without a tree. But it seems silly to decorate it just for myself."

"But it wouldn't be just for you. Even if Neil can't see how pretty it is, he can enjoy the smell of fresh pine needles."

"That'd be true for another person, but you don't know my husband." Jill smiled wryly. "He'd probably take one sniff and tell me not to use so much Pine-Sol when I wash the floor!"

Doug cracked up. It was good to see that Jill hadn't lost her sense of humor. "How about the department party? Are you going?"

"I almost have to." Jill nodded. "They'll expect me to put in an appearance, but I think everyone'll understand if I leave early."

"Of course they will. Did you draw your name yet?"

Jill nodded. "They passed them around this morning. I got Captain Pierce. You know him pretty well, don't you?"

"Sure."

"Tell me what I can buy for him." Jill started to frown. "The limit's five dollars, and I don't have a clue."

Doug shook his head. "He's going to be tough. He smokes cigars, but the kind he likes are over the limit. And there's no way you can get a bottle of good scotch for under five dollars. He's always reading. How about a book?"

"Okay. What does he like to read?"

Doug laughed. "Detective stories, what else? But you probably won't be able to find one he hasn't got."

"Any other suggestions?"

Doug thought about it for a moment, then nodded. "How about a Harley key chain? He's always talking about the hog he's going to buy when he retires."

"Great idea!" Jill began to smile. "The kiosk in the lobby sells things like that. I'll pick one up today and have it gift wrapped."

"Okay. I thought of yours. Now you have to help me with mine."

"It's a deal." Jill grinned. "Who did you get?"

"Maggie Peterson."

"Oh, murder!" Jill made a face. "Maggie's impossible. I got her last year and had to settle for a box of scented soaps."

Doug nodded and hoped he didn't look guilty. He'd already bought Maggie's gift, a little dried-flower arrangement for her desk. He really wanted to get something for Jill, and this was a ruse to find out what she wanted.

"Let's approach this from another angle." Doug leaned across the table. "You've done these Christmas-gift drawings before. What's the gift you never got but always wanted?"

Jill didn't even take time to think about it. She just blurted out the words. "Chocolate-covered cherries in a gold box with a red and green plaid bow."

"Really?"

"Really." Jill nodded. "When I was in high school, we drew names for Christmas. I got a nice notebook from Ethan Johnson, but my best friend got a box of chocolate-covered cherries from the captain of the football team."

"In a gold box with a red and green plaid ribbon?"

"That's right." Jill grinned. "She let me have one, and it was the best candy I ever tasted!"

Doug started to laugh. "Are you sure that wasn't just because it was from the captain of the football team?"

"Well . . . you could be right." Jill started to blush, even though it had happened years ago. "I wanted to date him, so that might have had something to do with it. But don't get candy for Maggie, Doug. I happen to know she's on a diet."

"Okay, I won't."

"Turnaround's fair play." Jill picked up her hamburger again. "What's the best gift you never got?"

Doug shook his head. "I don't know."

"Sure, you do. Think about it."

They both ate their hamburgers in silence for a minute, then Doug nodded. "A picture. My buddy was on the basketball team, and he was going out with the head cheerleader. She gave him a picture for Christmas."

"What kind of picture was it?" Jill did her best to sound casual. She wanted to get Doug something, and she needed to know what he liked.

"It was a picture of her in a silver frame. She was wearing her outfit, a short little skirt and a letter sweater, and holding her pom-poms. She even signed it in silver ink and wrote a personal message. 'You're a real winner, Caroline.'"

Jill nodded. If she knew who Caroline was, she could call and ask for one of her old cheerleader pictures. That would be a real surprise for Doug. "What happened to Caroline? Did she marry your buddy?"

"No. They broke up right before the senior prom. The last I heard she was somewhere in New York with her fourth husband."

Jill tried not to look disappointed. She'd gotten nowhere fast. But before she could ask any more questions, a pager beeped.

Doug reached into his pocket and pulled one out. He pressed the button for messages, but there were none. "That's not for me. Is it yours, Jill?"

"I don't know." Jill opened her purse and took out her beeper, but the screen was blank. "It's not mine, either."

The pager was still beeping, and Doug glanced around at the other booths. At least ten other people were scrambling for their pagers, but after they'd checked them, they all wore puzzled expressions.

"It's okay, folks. It's mine." A waitress hurried past the booths, carrying a tray laden with food. "They just put in a new system. The kitchen beeps us when our orders come up."

Doug and Jill laughed, along with everyone else. But then another beeper sounded, and this time it was Doug's pager.

"Sorry, Jill. I've got to go." He took a last bite of his hamburger and slid out of the booth. "Take your time. I'll pay the tab on my way out."

She shook her head. "That's okay. I need to get back early, and it's my turn to pay. Do you want a doggy bag?"

"No time. I've got to rush. See you next week, same time, same place?"

Jill nodded and watched him rush out the door. She called for the check and had the waitress pack up Doug's food in a carton. She'd drop it off on her way to the office.

It made her feel good to do something nice for Doug. Perhaps he didn't know it, but every time she saw him, he lifted her spirits and made her forget her problems. He was funny and kind, and he made her feel attractive. It would be a cold, dreary world, Jill decided, without her friend, Doug Lake.

CHAPTER 12

It was the Friday before Christmas, the day of the department Christmas party. Jill took one last look in the mirror and slipped into her coat, belting it tightly around her waist. Helen was in the kitchen, and she didn't want to answer any questions. She wasn't sure how she'd explain the outfit she was wearing.

"Good morning, Jill." Helen looked up from the stove as Jill entered the room. "I know you're running late this morning, so I fixed you some breakfast for the road."

Jill smiled as she saw the biscuits Helen was wrapping in foil. Neil's newest companion was a gem. She kept the house neat, made sure Neil kept all his appointments, and even started dinner if Jill had to work late. And so far, to Jill's complete amazement, Neil actually seemed to like her. "Thanks, Helen. Those biscuits smell wonderful!"

"It's my mother's recipe. She made the best biscuits in Georgia. And the jam's homemade blueberry. I picked the berries and put them up last fall."

Jill shook her head. "You're amazing. I don't know what we ever did without you."

Helen smiled and waved away the compliment. "You'd

better get on the road. It's still snowing, and the freeway's going to be a mess."

"You're right." Jill pulled on her gloves, took the package Helen handed her, and headed for the door. "I should be back around four. Today's the Christmas party, but I'm not staying long."

"Stay as late as you want. I don't have to be home at any particular time. It'll do you good to have a little fun."

"Thanks." Jill was smiling as she went out the door, but she gave a little yelp as she slid into the driver's seat of her car. Bare legs were definitely not advisable during winter in Minnesota!

The freeway was a mess, exactly as Helen had predicted, and Jill bailed out as soon as she could. She took surface streets until she came to Hennepin Avenue, then she turned east. Her appointment was at nine, and she had only five minutes to spare as she turned into the alley and parked behind the building.

Jill pulled her coat tightly around her as she rushed inside. Thank goodness she wouldn't have to wear this outfit much longer! When she rang the buzzer, the outside door clicked open. She'd explained what she needed on the phone last week, and Myron Sawyer, a friend of her father's, had promised her that he could deliver a print by noon.

"Jilly! It's been too long!"

"I know." Jill laughed as Myron engulfed her in a bear hug. He was a small man, thin and wiry, with snow white hair, but he'd always been strong. He'd carried her around on his shoulders when she was a child, and he'd been the family photographer for as long as she could remember.

"Come in here, Jilly, and let's get started."

Myron ushered her into his studio, a large room with drapes, various backdrops, and cameras of all shapes and sizes. He'd started in the business by shooting modeling portfolios, but the last time she'd spoken with him, he had told her he was going to go into something less demanding.

Jill frowned slightly as she gazed around the studio. There were props in every corner, feather boas in variety of colors, fake palm trees with beach backdrops, champagne bottles with crystal glasses, and painted oriental fans. "What's this, Myron? I thought you were getting out of the modeling business."

"Believe me, I tried." Myron sighed. "I started by doubling my prices, but the girls kept right on coming. I doubled them again, and would you believe? My business increased! I guess they figure I must be the best because I charge so much. As of last week, I'm the most expensive photographer in town, and they're practically breaking down the door to get an appointment."

"Now you can't afford to quit . . . right?"

Myron nodded. "Every time I tell them I'm getting out of the business, they offer me more money. I'm stuck, Jilly, but at least my bank account's growing. I figure if I stay in for another year or so, I can put all the grandkids through college."

"I'm sorry, Myron." Jill started to frown. "If I'd known you were this busy, I'd never have asked you for a favor."

Myron patted her on the back. "No problem, Jilly. It's always good to see you, and you don't want a modeling portfolio, do you?"

"Hardly. But I do want something unusual. Promise me you won't laugh, Myron."

Myron nodded. "Okay. I won't. What do you want, Jilly?"

"A picture of me in this outfit." Jill blushed as she slipped off her coat. She knew she looked silly in the short, red pleated skirt and the tight, white sweater with the huge red letter on the front.

Myron struggled not to laugh, then snorted, instead. "You're a cheerleader, Jilly?"

"That's what I'm *supposed* to be. I know I look ridiculous, but it's for a joke Christmas present."

"Okay." Myron nodded. "Did you rent that outfit?"

"No. I borrowed it from the high school girl down the street. The only things she didn't have were the pom-poms."

"I think I've got pom-poms around here someplace." Myron pointed to a huge steamer chest. "Check in that trunk, Jilly. I'll see what I can find in the back."

Jill located the pom-poms in the trunk, under a pile of gold and silver scarves. She was just shaking them out when Myron came back. He was carrying a roll of backdrop paper, and was grinning from ear to ear.

"You're going to love this." He picked up a stepladder and carried it over to the far wall. "Go put your hair in a ponytail while I hang the backdrop."

Jill shook her head. "My hair's too short for a ponytail. I tried it at home. It wouldn't work."

"Then use a wig. There's one in the dressing room that'll match your hair."

In less than five minutes, Jill was ready, complete with white socks and tennis shoes. She smiled as she saw the backdrop Myron had hung. It was a football field with fans and bleachers.

"Stand right here, Jilly." Myron pointed to a mark on the floor. "And give me a cheerleader pose."

Jill did her best, and it didn't take long for Myron to shoot a roll of film. She then used the dressing room to put on the dress she was wearing to the office. When she came out, Myron was waiting for her.

"It's in the tank." He grinned, "I'll blow up the best shot and have my assistant deliver it to your office by noon."

Jill opened her purse and took out her checkbook. "Thanks, Myron. What do I owe you?"

"Lunch. Two weeks from Tuesday, unless you're in court. I want a greasy hamburger, dripping with onions, and an update on everything that's happening in your life."

"It's a date." Jill nodded. "I'll pick you up at one o'clock, and we'll go to The Beef Barrel."

As Jill said good-bye and hurried back out to her car, she wondered what she should tell Myron. He'd said he wanted to know what was happening, but he had been her father's friend. She was too embarrassed to tell him how dismal her life really was.

"Oh, great! Just what I needed!" Jill frowned as she pulled the cardboard parking ticket from her windshield wiper. She'd parked in a loading zone; the fine was twenty-five dollars. Of course she'd pay it, but it was just another irritation in a life already filled with inconveniences. If this was any indication of what the remainder of the day would bring, she felt like turning around and going back home!

Jill sighed as she unlocked her car and brushed the snow from the windshield. She couldn't go home. Neil was there, and she just couldn't cope with him for a whole day. He was fine when Helen was around, but the moment she left for the evening, he began to complain.

Of course Neil had problems. Jill was the first to admit that his limited eyesight was a terrible burden for him to bear. But he accused her of being unsympathetic and demanded that she wait on him until it was time for bed. That wouldn't have bothered her if he hadn't criticized everything she did. The coffee was too weak, the house was too hot or too cold, the cookies she baked weren't as good as the ones from the bakery, the television programs she watched were insipid.

Jill had tried to bring her work home, hoping that he would understand if she had briefs to prepare or court transcripts to read. But Neil resented her work and expected her to spend every moment with him. She wasn't allowed to have any time for herself. He accused her of being selfish if she spent twenty minutes in the shower. He wanted her to be his personal slave, so going to the office was her only means of escape.

No, she definitely didn't want to go home. Jill drove down the alley and turned onto the street. What would Myron say if she told him she'd made a terrible mistake when she'd married Neil? What if she admitted that her husband had been unfaithful and she'd been about to divorce him when the doctor had discovered Neil needed a transplant? Myron thought she had a good marriage, and Jill didn't want to disappoint him. It would be almost like disappointing her parents.

Should she lie and say everything was fine? Jill sighed and shook her head. Myron had known her since she was a child. He'd realize that she wasn't telling the truth. It would be safer to talk about her job, to tell Myron about her clients and the judges she faced in court. If he asked any questions about her marriage, she'd change the subject as fast as she could. Myron was old-fashioned, just as her parents had been. People of their generation believed that a marriage should last a lifetime. When they'd exchanged their vows and spoken the line, "'Til death do us part," they'd taken the commitment literally. But did a bad marriage really have to be a life sentence?

The parking garage was on her left. Jill flicked on the signal, waited until the oncoming traffic had passed, and then pulled into the entrance. Her spot was on the third level underground. She entered the narrow, corkscrew ramp that led into the bowels of the building. As she drove around and around, circling down to the subbasement, Jill laughed bitterly. This ramp was like her life, spiraling around, descending into the depths. She was stuck in a circle of her own making, an endless coil she'd entered into the day she'd married Neil. Her path had been set then, and she was headed for rock bottom, but there didn't seem to be any way to break free.

It was the Friday before Christmas, and Connie was lonely. In this time for relatives and immediate family, she had no one. She'd heard that the Christmas season was the most dangerous time for people who were alone. Depression could set in, so there was an abnormally high suicide rate over the holidays. Connie could understand why. Others had parties to attend, preparations to make, and gifts to buy for loved ones. If you were alone, Christmas only deepened your sense of abandonment.

Only one thing saved Connie from severe depression. She had a mission in life, one last obligation to the man she'd loved. It was almost time to put her plan into action, and she was counting the days.

"Be patient, Alan. It won't be long now." Connie smiled at the picture of him she'd hung over her bed. It was a newspaper photo taken on the day Alan had gone to work for his father. The photographer had kept the negative on file, and Connie had paid him to make her a print.

Connie called the hospital. When she hung up, she was smiling. Willy Rossini had been released, and he was home with his family. It was time for the first step of her plan.

"I'll be back later, honey." Connie blew a kiss to Alan. "I have to spend some of the baby's money, but it's the only way."

Twenty minutes later, she was in a beauty parlor just down the street from Dayton's Department Store. She knew it was expensive, but she needed the best beautician money could buy.

"Do you have an appointment?" The receptionist frowned

as Connie shook her head. "I'm sorry, but we can't do walk-ins today. Everybody's booked solid."

Connie nodded and reached into her purse. She'd expected this and had planned her approach. "I know I should have made an appointment, but it just slipped my mind. Isn't there any way you could work me in?"

"It's the week before Christmas. Normally, it wouldn't be a problem, but . . ." The receptionist's eyes widened as Connie put a twenty-dollar bill on her appointment book.

"I know you're busy, but this is terribly important." Connie laid out a second twenty-dollar bill. "It's the governor's dinner, and I simply have to look my best."

The receptionist nodded and reached for the bills. "I could probably work you in between Roland's next two appointments. Mrs. Adamczak just wants a blow dry and Miss Murphy is always late. What did you need?"

"Everything." Connie gave a little laugh. "Tell Roland I'm tired of being me. I need a totally new look."

It took over two hours and it cost a small fortune, but Connie was smiling as she went out the door. She was now a redhead with soft, curly hair, and she was carrying a large bag of the makeup Roland had taught her how to use.

Clothes were next. Connie headed straight for Dayton's side entrance. She wouldn't go up to the Oval Room. Their clothes were stylish, but much too matronly. She wanted a younger, sexier look, so she'd have better luck at the ground-floor boutique.

Music was blaring from the speakers as Connie entered the boutique. The noise was deafening, but she managed to smile when a salesgirl came over the help her.

"Yes, ma'am. We do have designer originals." The salesgirl's eyes began to sparkle at the prospect of a big commission. "What did you have in mind?"

"I need a full outfit. Dress, shoes, coat, and accessories. It's got to be fabulous, but I don't have much time."

Within moments, it seemed, Connie was standing in front of a tall mirror in a dark green cashmere dress that hugged her figure and a pair of high-heeled leather boots that were the exact color of butterscotch candy.

"That looks great on you!" The salesgirl nodded. "We carry a leather coat that matches the boots, but it's on the expensive side."

"How expensive?"

The salesgirl winced. "Over eight hundred dollars. I know that's a lot of money, but it's high-grade leather."

Fifteen minutes later, Connie had loaded her purchases into the trunk and she was on her way back to the Lexington Arms. Alan was waiting for her; she could hardly wait to show him her new look. He'd be impatient. She'd been gone for a long while. But he was understanding and knew she had things to do.

She parked in the lot, then juggled her bags as she took the elevator to the second floor. She'd put on her new clothes for Alan, he was bound to like them, and then they'd have a nice romantic dinner that she'd order from room service. After dinner was over and they were cuddling in bed, she'd tell him exactly what she had to do to keep him alive forever.

CHAPTER 13

As she hopped on the freeway, Jill was singing Christmas carols along with the radio. The department party had been fun, and Captain Pierce had loved his Harley Davidson key chain. One of the young detectives had drawn her name. It was obvious that his wife had helped him shop, for Jill had opened her package to find a lovely wool scarf in her favorite shades of blue and purple.

Although she loved the scarf, it was the other gift she had received that was responsible for her good spirits. That was from Doug, and she'd giggled like a schoolgirl when she'd opened it. It was a five-pound box of chocolate-covered cherries in a gold box with a red and green plaid bow on top.

Jill had been embarrassed when she'd seen the photo Myron's assistant had delivered. Myron had caught her in profile with her head to one side, holding the red-and-white pom-poms in outstretched arms. Her skirt was too short and her sweater was too tight. She wondered how she could possibly give a gift like that to Doug.

But there hadn't been time for another photo session, so Jill had decided to make the best of it. She'd written her message on the front of the print with a silver felt-tipped pen, "You're a real winner, Jill." Then she'd mounted the photograph in the silver frame she'd bought that morning, and she handed it to Doug, blushing.

He had been surprised and pleased when he'd seen the photograph. He'd even hugged her and told her he'd never feel deprived again, now that he had his own cheerleader photo. And he'd said that Jill was much prettier than Caroline had ever been!

Jill took the exit for River Road, stopping at the red light at the bottom of the ramp. While she was waiting for it to turn green, she reached down to lift the lid from her box of candy.

With the sweet taste of chocolate and a cherry in her mouth, Jill turned left and drove the last six blocks. She was smiling as she approached her house, but her smile turned to a frown when she noticed that Helen's blue Honda wasn't parked in its usual place. Neil hadn't had any therapy appointments scheduled for today. Where could they have gone?

Jill pulled into the garage and unlocked the door to the house. There was no need to worry. Helen was a responsible person. If she'd taken Neil somewhere in her car, she would have left a note. But there was no note on the pantry bulletin board or under the refrigerator magnets. Had there been some medical emergency so serious that Helen hadn't had time to call or even scribble a message?

"Helen? Are you here?" Jill's pulse was racing as she rushed into the living room. And then she saw it, a beautiful Christmas tree decorated with all her favorite ornaments.

"Hi, Jill. Surprise!"

Jill whirled around, and her eyes widened as she saw Neil. He was sitting on the couch, all dressed up, in a white shirt, tie, and his favorite tweed jacket. "Neil! Where's Helen?"

"I let her go a couple of minutes ago. We had your secretary call when you left the party, and we figured you'd be home about now." Neil grinned and patted the couch next to him. "If you hand me that champagne bottle before you sit down, I think I can open it. You might have to pour, though."

Jill lifted her eyebrows as she spotted the champagne chilling in a silver ice bucket on a stand. "Champagne? But . . . why?"

"It's our anniversary. Did you forget?"

Jill winced. She'd forgotten all about it. "I'm sorry, Neil. I did forget. But *you* remembered!"

"That's quite a switch, isn't it?" Neil laughed. "Maybe it's because I'm not working and I've got plenty of time to think about the important things in my life . . . like you, Jill. You're very important to me."

Jill winced again. He was obviously waiting for a response, and she didn't want to hurt his feelings when he was being so thoughtful. "Thank you, Neil. You're very important to me, too."

"How do you like the Christmas tree? We had it delivered this afternoon. I told Helen where you kept the decorations, and she trimmed it."

"It's beautiful!" Jill sat down on the couch and gazed at the tree. Helen had done a marvelous job.

Neil popped the cork on the champagne and covered the mouth of the bottle with a clean, white towel. "I hope I didn't spill any."

"Not a drop." Jill reached out to take the bottle. She poured two glasses. "Thank you, Neil. I really wanted a Christmas tree. This was a lovely surprise."

Neil grinned. "But that's not all. Helen set the table in the dining room, and we're eating in style tonight. The caterers will be here at six."

Jill blinked and took a sip of her champagne. "Caterers?"

"That's right." Neil seemed pleased that she was surprised. "We're having a smoked Norwegian salmon appetizer with capers and toast points, and an endive salad. The main course is filet with Bearnaise sauce. It comes with fresh asparagus and Lyonnaise potatoes. After that, we'll have coffee and strawberries Romanoff for dessert."

Jill was so surprised, she almost dropped her glass of champagne. "But, Neil . . . that's exactly what we had for our wedding reception!"

"And you thought I didn't remember." Neil reached out to hug her. "I remember every moment, Jill, and I love you even more than I did then."

"I . . . I . . ." Jill was so flustered, she wasn't sure what to say. "I just can't believe you planned all this!"

"I didn't do it alone. Helen helped a lot. She even took me shopping. I've got an anniversary gift for you."

Jill's mind was spinning as Neil reached under the cushion and took out a small gold box,

"Open it now, honey." He handed it to her. "I can't wait to see if you like it."

Jill's hands were trembling as she lifted the lid and drew out a beautiful heart pendant. A diamond was set in its center, and it hung from a delicate gold chain. "Neil! It's . . . it's gorgeous!"

"I thought you'd like it. Helen took me to a jeweler. I told him exactly what I wanted, and he made it for me. It's an original, honey. No one else has anything like it."

Jill blinked back the tears of happiness that threatened to spill from her eyes. Neil was being so sweet. If things could only stay this way, they'd have a chance to make their marriage work.

* * *

The dinner was absolutely delicious, and after the caterers had left, Jill curled up on the couch with Neil. With the stereo turned to a classical station, she sipped the fine brandy the caterers had poured and smiled in contentment.

"Are you happy, honey?" Neil slipped an arm around her shoulders.

"Yes." Jill nodded and snuggled a little closer, "Thank you for a wonderful evening, Neil."

He began to grin. "But it's not over yet. Finish your brandy and let's go up to bed. I've got another surprise for you. I think Helen was a little embarrassed, but I bought something else for you at the mall."

Jill's mind was whirling as they climbed the stairs, Neil's hand warm in hers. If only this moment could last forever, she could forget the mistakes of the past. Neil seemed to love her. He really did. Could she love him again if she let the painful memories go? Was it possible that they could start over and make their marriage work?

"Look under the pillow, honey." Neil smiled at her as they entered the bedroom. "I think you're really going to like it."

Jill walked to the bed and lifted the pillow to find a tissue wrapped package. She held it in her hand for a moment, regretting that she didn't have anything to give him in return.

"Go on, honey. Open it."

Jill opened the package and gasped. Nestled inside the tissue paper was a lovely blue silk negligee trimmed with soft, fine lace.

"Do you like it?"

He sounded anxious, and Jill reached out to hug him. "I love it, Neil! But I really wish I'd remembered our anniversary. I didn't give you anything at all."

"I can think of something you could give me." Neil chuckled as he unzipped her dress and slipped it off on her shoulders. "And you wouldn't even have to go out shopping."

Jill laughed. Then she kissed him. Neil wanted to make love to her, and it felt almost like their wedding night. He'd planned the perfect dinner, given her the perfect presents. He seemed like the old Neil, the Neil she'd married, and her body began to respond to him.

"It's been too long, honey." Neil kissed her neck; then his lips traveled lower as he began to undress her. "I may not be able to see you, but I remember how lovely you are."

Tears began to gather in Jill's eyes, and she reached out for him. Neil needed to know that she still loved him. What kind of wife would she be if she refused him?

And then they were on the bed, bodies pressing together. His fingers stroked her lovingly, and Jill felt the first warm flush of passion color her skin. His hands were gentle as they moved her to the center of the bed, and she moaned in pleasure as familiar caresses ignited the fire deep within her.

"I missed you, Jill." Neil's voice was low, and it trembled slightly. "Did you miss me?"

"Yes. I missed you, too." Jill's voice was choked with emotion. She'd missed the way things had been at the beginning, when she couldn't wait to be alone with Neil. She'd missed his kisses and the way they'd played on the rumpled sheets in his apartment. She'd missed the sense of belonging with him and knowing that he belonged with her, the assurance that came with love and passion.

And then he was inside her, the man she'd loved with all her heart. Jill cried out and lifted her hips, clasping him tightly and moaning deep in her throat. "Yes, Neil . . . yes!"

Time seemed to stand still as they merged and separated, merged and separated, in a rhythm as old as humanity. He followed, she led. She led, he followed. Their lips merged, their breath mingled. It was a dance of lust, their bodies sliding and pressing and swiveling and pounding until passion faded away and they were left with an exquisite memory.

They didn't speak. There was no need. Jill stroked his shoulders and sighed softly. It was a new beginning, and all her bitterness was washed away in a flood of love and passion.

She must have slept then, because daylight was beginning to color the horizon when she opened her eyes. She turned to Neil with a sigh, and he reached out for her again.

"Are you awake, honey?" Neil's voice was soft and caring.

"Yes." Jill smiled at him in the dim gray light of dawn. "I'm awake."

His hands were gentle, rubbing her back, and Jill snuggled closer. Then they were making love again, sleepy soft love in the early morning.

When it was over, they slept again until the sun came through the bedroom curtains. Another hug, another kiss, and Jill glanced at the clock on the dresser. "I'd better get up, honey. Helen'll be here soon. Do you want to get up now? Or would you rather sleep for a while?"

"Sleep. Tell Helen not to wake me before ten."

Neil rolled over onto his side, and then he started to laugh. Jill stared at him for a moment, but his laugh was contagious and she joined in. "What's so funny?"

"Your new nightgown. You didn't even get to try it on."

"You're right." Jill grinned as she reached down to pick up the negligee. "But there's always tonight. I'll try to beat the traffic and get home early."

"Okay, honey. See you tonight."

Jill gathered up her clothes. So she wouldn't disturb Neil, she took them to the guest room to shower and dress. She felt wonderful, like a bride on her honeymoon, and she was smiling as she hurried down the stairs, got her heart pendant from the box by the couch, and clasped it around her neck.

By the time Helen rang the doorbell, Jill had the coffee ready. She opened the door, smiling. "Hi," she said.

"Hello, Jill. Did you have a nice dinner last night?"

"It was wonderful!" Jill led the way to the kitchen. "Thanks for helping Neil shop. I just love my heart pendant and the negligee."

Helen nodded. "I didn't do much. I just drove him around. He knew exactly what he wanted to buy."

"Isn't it beautiful?" Jill touched the pendant. "He was so proud of himself for getting me something original. He told me he had the jeweler make it up and no one else has anything like it."

Helen nodded, but she started to frown. "Does Mr. Bradley have a sister?"

"No, he's an only child." Jill noticed Helen's frown. "What's wrong, Helen?"

"Nothing a little coffee won't fix. What time does Mr. Bradley want to get up?"

Jill began to feel anxious. Helen usually called Neil by his first name, but today she'd called him Mr. Bradley. "Are you sure there's nothing wrong?"

"The traffic was brutal this morning." Helen walked to the counter and poured herself a cup of coffee. "You'd better allow some extra time. Every snowplow in the city is out."

Jill nodded. "I'm glad I've got a flexible schedule today. It doesn't matter if I'm a little late, and I'll try to get home early."

"Good." Helen nodded. "I'll start dinner if you want me to. There's a nice ham, and you can have the leftovers for sandwiches over the weekend."

Jill smiled. "Ham sounds wonderful. Thank you, Helen. I really don't know what I'd do without you."

"Me, neither!"

Helen laughed and that made Jill feel much better. Perhaps

she'd just been reading too much into Helen's expression. It really wasn't that unusual for Helen to refer to Neil as Mr. Bradley. She might have done it before; Jill just hadn't noticed.

It was cold, and there were several inches of snow on the ground. Jill opened the garage door, then frowned as she started the car. She let it warm up for several minutes and then backed out onto the street. She had a good relationship with Helen. She thought of her as a friend. Surely Helen would have told her if something was wrong, wouldn't she?

CHAPTER 14

"Look at me, Alan." Connie twirled in front of the mirror. "Do you think Mr. Rossini will be able to resist me?"

There was a silence, and then she laughed, a light flirtatious giggle. "Alan! You shouldn't say things like that! But you're right. I do look fantastic."

Connie listened for a moment; then a frown spread across her face. It was clear she didn't like what Alan was saying.

"Do I really have to tell him?" She picked up Alan's picture to stare into his eyes. "I know it's only fair, but . . . what if he says no?"

There was another long silence, and then Connie sighed. "All right, Alan. You win. I know Mr. Rossini's going to be a nice man. It'll be almost like seeing you again. He's got a part of you inside him."

Connie stepped closer to kiss Alan's picture, her lips brushing lightly against the glass. Then she cast one last look at the mirror and smiled as she went out the door.

The office had been a madhouse, and Jill was tired when she got off the freeway. Crime rates always rose during the holiday season. The crowded malls brought out the muggers, purse snatchers, and pickpockets in full force. When people were filled with the joy of the season, they sometimes forgot to take the usual precautions. They walked around with open purses, left their credit cards on the counters of stores, and neglected to lock their car doors. Good will toward men translated into easy targets for criminals, and there had been over thirty arrests at the SouthDale Mall last night.

The house looked beautiful as Jill approached it. The curtains were open in the living room, and the lights from the Christmas tree reflected on the fresh blanket of snow outside the window. It looked as if someone had opened the door to scatter handfuls of brightly colored jewels on the snow-covered lawn. It was a lovely sight, but Jill had the real jewel, the one that counted, hanging from the thin, gold chain around her neck, tangible proof that Neil loved her. Last night had been wonderful. Her husband was back. And for the first time in months, she was glad to be coming home to him.

She pulled into the garage and unlocked the door, a smile on her face. "I'm home! Where is everybody?"

"I'm in here," Helen called out.

Jill hung up her coat, placed her boots on the rug by the door, and hurried to the kitchen. She could smell the ham in the oven, and the scent of apple pie was in the air. "Hi. It smells wonderful in here! Where's Neil?"

"He's resting upstairs." Helen poured her a cup of coffee and motioned to one of the oak chairs by the round kitchen table. "Sit down, Jill. I have to talk to you."

Jill pulled out a chair and sat. Helen didn't look happy. "What's wrong?"

"I really hate to do this." Helen sighed as she, too, sat down. "But I like you, and I just can't ignore what happened today."

Jill took a deep breath. This sounded serious. "What happened, Helen? Tell me."

"It's Mr. Bradley. He doesn't have a sister."

Jill nodded. "That's right, but what does that have to do with—"

"He lied to me," Helen interrupted. "When he ordered that pendant for you, he had the jeweler make two. He told me one was for you and the other was for his sister."

Jill sighed. She should have known last night was too good to be true. But perhaps Neil had given the second pendant to his sister-in-law and Helen had just misunderstood. "Did he tell you his sister's name?"

"No. But he gave it to someone today. Mr. Bradley had a visitor, a woman named Lisa. He said she was his teaching assistant, and I saw him give her the pendant."

Jill swallowed hard. The pendant was suddenly heavy on her neck, and she reached up to unclasp it. She put it down on the table, then took a deep breath. "There's something else, isn't there?"

"Yes. It's not my place to tell you, but I think you should know. Mr. Bradley took her into the bedroom and locked the door. They didn't come out for two hours."

"I see." Jill nodded. "Thank you for telling me, Helen."

Helen looked worried. "I didn't want to. You were so happy this morning, I wasn't going to say anything. But when I saw him give her the pendant, and they went into *your* bedroom—"

"I understand," Jill said. "It's all right, Helen. You did the right thing."

"That's what I thought, but I've been worrying about it all day. I have to give notice, Jill. I just can't stay and take care of him, now that I know what's going on. I like you too much and I don't think I can be halfway civil to him."

Jill put a hand over her eyes. Thanks to Neil she'd just lost the best housekeeper and companion they'd ever had.

"All right, Helen. I understand. Could you give me time to find someone to replace you?"

"Of course." Helen reached out to touch Jill's shoulder. "I'll interview people if you want me to. I'm sure I can find someone. And . . . I'm sorry, Jill. I don't want to leave you in a bind, but I just can't stay."

Jill picked up the pendant and then she rose. "Thank you, Helen. Why don't you take this and give it so someone for Christmas? I . . . I don't want it."

"But it was expensive!" Helen's eyes widened. "Are you sure?"

Jill nodded. "I'm positive. Consider it a parting gift from Neil and an apology from me for being the one who was blind."

"All right." Helen gathered up her things and headed for the door. "I'll see you in the morning, Jill. And I'll get started on those interviews right away."

The kitchen was silent when Helen had left. Jill sat back down at the table and sipped her lukewarm coffee. How could she have been such a fool? She'd actually believed last night had been a new beginning. She'd been so happy, so eager to trust Neil again. But now she knew the truth. Tears rolled down Jill's cheeks, and she sobbed quietly. Nothing had changed, nothing at all. Neil couldn't be trusted. She'd let him hurt her again.

"Way to go, Champ!" Willy Rossini's boss punched him on the shoulder. "See that redhead out there in the showroom? She asked for you, personally!"

Willy stood up and glanced out at the showroom. They didn't have regular offices in the dealership, only thin partitions of fiberboard that were barely five feet high and only large enough to hold a small desk with two straight-backed chairs.

"She's a real looker, huh?"

Willy nodded. The redhead was gorgeous and she was standing by the newest model in the showroom, a silver Mercedes loaded with expensive options.

"What are you waiting for, Willy? Get out there and sell her a car!"

"Right." Willy nodded, again. He was sure he didn't know the redhead. If he'd seen her before, he wouldn't have forgotten her. Perhaps a former client had recommended him and given her his card. He put a welcoming smile on his face and walked onto the showroom floor. "Hello. I'm Willy Rossini. You asked for me?"

The redhead turned, and Willy's breath caught in his throat. She was even more gorgeous up close.

"Hello, Willy." The redhead smiled. "What time do you get off for dinner?"

Willy tried not to show how surprised he was. "Uh . . . well . . . I can take my break anytime."

"Good. I don't know this area very well. Is there someplace private where we could meet?"

Willy frowned slightly. The redhead wasn't acting like a client. But if she didn't want to buy a car, what could she possibly want with him? "Well . . . there's the Lamplighter. It's about a mile south of here on the corner."

"Great!" The redhead smiled again. "I'll leave right now and get us a booth. What do you want to drink?"

Suddenly, Willy had a flash of insight. He'd been top salesman three months running. The redhead must be checking him out for a rival dealership. "Coffee's fine. I have to go back to work."

"You don't drink then?"

The redhead put a hand on his arm, and Willy went weak in the knees. "Sure, but never on the job. I need a clear head to sell these beautiful babies."

"Of course you do." The redhead looked pleased. "I can

tell you take your work very seriously. Will it bother you if I have a glass of wine?"

Willy gulped. The redhead's eyes were incredible, a lovely emerald green. "It won't bother me at all."

"I'll be waiting. Just ask for Cherie White when you come in."

"Cherie." Willy breathed out the name and stared after her as she left. What a body! What a smile! What a woman!

"That didn't take long." Willy's boss came rushing up. "Is she a hot prospect?"

Willy nodded. What else could he do? He didn't want to tell his boss that he was being recruited by another dealership. "She wants me to meet her for dinner. I'll bring some brochures and see what I can do."

"Take as long as you need." Willy's boss clapped him on the shoulder. "She smells like money, so go in for the kill!"

Willy was grinning as he headed to his cubicle to pick up some brochures. What his boss didn't know wouldn't hurt him, and the other dealership might pay a lot better. Even if he didn't get the new job, dinner with such a gorgeous babe was something he wouldn't pass up on a bet.

Doug grinned as he walked through the Christmas tree lot. Carols were blasting from a portable CD player inside the heated kiosk, and he wondered how many times the heavyset blonde manning the counter had been forced to listen to "Rudolph the Red-Nosed Reindeer." The trees, arranged in bundles according to length, were tied tightly with twine so their frozen branches wouldn't snap off in the cold.

"Can I help you, sir?" A teenage boy emerged from the kiosk. As he hurried to Doug, he zipped up his parka and pulled on heavy gloves.

"I'm looking for a six-foot blue spruce." Doug smiled at the boy. "I need a fresh tree that hasn't been shaped."

The boy nodded. "There's a load in the back. It came in last night, but it's not sorted."

"That's okay." Doug followed the teenager to the back of the lot, where trees were stacked against a fence. The fence was marked at intervals of one foot with painted lines.

"The green line's six feet." The boy pointed to a green line that ran along the fence. "If you find one you like, I can tag it for you."

Doug walked past the trees until he found a blue spruce. "How about this one?"

"I think it's over six feet." The boy stood the tree next to the fence and nodded. The top was well over the green line. "I can top it for you, but you'll have to pay the seven foot price."

"That's okay. Turn it around so I can see the back."

The boy turned the tree while Doug watched. It was difficult to judge a Christmas tree that was tied into a bundle and resembled a carrot, but Doug had learned the hard way. The first year he'd spent in Minnesota, he'd taken home a tree, set it up in the stand, and come into the living room the next morning to find gaping holes where branches should have been. He was much wiser now, and he surveyed the tree carefully to make sure it was uniformly shaped.

"That one's fine. Don't bother to top it though. I'll do it in the morning, when it warms up."

The boy nodded and looked hopeful. "Do you want me to tie it on top of your car?"

"No. It'll fit inside." Doug pointed to his ford Explorer, the only extravagance he'd allowed himself since he'd joined the police force. He knew the boy probably worked for tips so he handed him the keys. "Just back it up here, and load it for me. I'll go up to the counter and pay."

"Yes, sir."

The boy was grinning as he handed Doug a red tag and raced off to get the Explorer. Doug paid for his tree, declined the opportunity to buy a tree stand, a wreath, or an evergreen garland, and got back to his Explorer just as the boy had finished loading his tree.

"I wrapped it in plastic before I put it in." The boy turned to Doug. "I didn't want any needles to fall off."

"Good." Doug smiled and handed the boy a five-dollar bill.

"Thank you, sir!" The boy's eyes widened as he saw the size of his tip. "When you get it in the stand, drop a couple of aspirin in the water. It'll keep longer that way. Have a great Christmas, and here . . . this is from me."

Doug smiled as the boy handed him a small package wrapped in brown paper. "Thanks. Merry Christmas to you, too."

The traffic was heavy as Doug pulled out of the lot, and he didn't get a chance to look at the package the boy had given him until he'd parked in his spot at the apartment building. Then he unwrapped it and pulled out a sprig of mistletoe.

Doug started to grin. Mistletoe was a Christmas tradition. He'd hang it over his doorway, and it would give him license to kiss any woman who came through his door. Of course, the possibility that any woman would ring his bell was very unlikely.

As he carried his tree to the garage elevator and rode up to his floor, Doug found himself wondering if mistletoe was still a Christmas tradition. Kissing a woman just because she was standing under a sprig of mistletoe was probably politically incorrect. It could even be grounds for a sexual harassment suit. Perhaps it would be wiser to dump the mistletoe in his kitchen wastebasket and not take any chances.

"The hell with it! I'm putting it up!" Doug set his tree in the stand, dropped two aspirin in the bowl, and filled it with water. Then he got out his stepladder and tacked the mistletoe over his door.

Five minutes later, Doug was relaxing on the couch, enjoying another Christmas tradition—hot chocolate with a splash of brandy, a drink his family had always enjoyed after they'd brought home their Christmas tree. The room smelled good as the frozen tree began to warm up and its pine fragrance filled the air. He'd trim it tomorrow, with the decorations he'd brought from the ranch in Texas, ornaments that had been on Lake family Christmas trees for three generations. There were the blown-glass strawberries that had belonged to his grandmother, the strings of old-fashioned bubble lights that looked like candles, and the brightly painted elves and other wooden Christmas figures his grandfather had whittled on the porch by the light of a kerosene lantern on quiet summer nights.

Doug sighed. His family was gone now, and he missed them. He'd lost his mother first, when he was a boy, of a heart defect no one had known she had. Then his grandparents had died while Doug was still in high school, and his father had passed away three years ago. Doug had sold the Lake family ranch when he'd gone back to Texas for his father's funeral. A former ranch hand had bought it. Although Doug knew he'd be welcome to visit, seeing his old boyhood home, newly renovated, didn't appeal to him. He had his memories, and trimming the Christmas tree with all the old ornaments made him feel as if his family were all out there somewhere, pleased that he was keeping some of the Lake family traditions alive.

The branches of the blue spruce were starting to thaw and spread slightly, so Doug got up to walk around the tree. There didn't seem to be any bare spots. He'd made a good choice. The mistletoe, hanging over the doorway, caught Doug's eye, and he smiled as he imagined a beautiful woman walking through his door, a woman who would welcome his kisses and come in to help him trim the Christmas tree.

If he could share the season with any woman in the world, who would she be? Doug sat down and thought about famous actresses, beautiful models, and former girl-friends, but none of their faces stayed in his mind. The woman he wanted had hair the color of morning sunlight, eyes so blue you could drink in their color like a cool, re-freshing swallow of water, and the perfectly shaped legs you might find on a runway model. Her smile was pure joy, and he knew her lips would be soft and sweet like the petals of an exotic flower. She would fit into his arms as if they'd been created for each other, laugh at his jokes even if they weren't funny, and cry with him when he was feeling sad. Her face was always there, hovering at the very back of his mind. No other woman could erase her image. The one he wanted with him was Jill.

CHAPTER 15

They were sitting in the back room at the Lamplighter, and they'd talked throughout dinner. Since only one other booth was occupied, it was almost as if they had the room to themselves.

"Take a look at this. It's one of my favorites." Willy handed Cherie his Swiss Army Knife. He'd just finished telling her about his knife collection, and she'd seemed very interested.

"Why do you need all these blades?'

She stared down at the knife in fascination, and Willy laughed. "They're not all blades. Most of them are tools for survival. There's a pair of scissors, a bottle opener, screwdrivers, a file, and a magnifying glass. There's even silverware. See the fork and the spoon?"

"This is incredible!" She looked up with a smile. "How many things are there?"

"A hundred and eighteen. You can do anything with this knife, from field dressing a deer to building a temporary shelter in the woods."

"You really seem to love knives, Willy."

She reached out to touch his hand, and Willy began to

feel slightly uncomfortable. Of course he was flattered by her interest, but she was staring at him with such intensity it was almost spooky. He couldn't help feeling that she must know him from somewhere, but he'd thought about it all during dinner and he just couldn't place her. Who was she? A former client? Someone he'd met at a convention or a party? It seemed impossible that he could forget such a beautiful woman.

"You look uncomfortable. What's the matter, Willy?"

God, she was perceptive! Willy shivered under her intense gaze. "Well . . . I was just wondering if I know you from someplace."

"Not really." Her laugh was like quicksilver, dissolving into beads that skittered away. "You don't know me, Willy . . . but you have something that used to belong to me."

Willy raised his eyebrows. "I do? What's that?"

"Your kidney."

"My . . . kidney?" Willy made a conscious effort to stay calm. What the hell was she talking about?

"You had a kidney transplant, didn't you?"

Willy nodded. "Yeah, but . . . that came from a donor. A dead donor. There's no way my kidney belonged to you."

"Oh, but it did." She laughed again, a light carefree kind of laugh. "You see, Willy, your kidney came from the man I love, the man I was going to marry."

Willy swallowed hard. He was beginning to understand. "Okay. I get it. And believe me, I'm sorry about your boyfriend. But . . . what does that have to do with me?"

"I need something from you, Willy." Her voice was low and intimate, and she leaned forward to touch his hand again. "It's something that only you can give me."

He resisted the urge to pull away. Was she some kind of fruitcake? "Uh . . . well . . . sure! It must have been rough for you, losing your boyfriend and all. If there's any way I can help—"

"I just knew you'd say that!" She smiled and closed her fingers around his hand. "It's very sad, Willy. I was pregnant when Alan died. When they told me about his accident, I lost the baby."

Willy nodded. He'd always been a sucker for a sad story, and he felt really bad for her. "That must have been awful for you, Cherie. I'm really sorry."

"Thanks, Willy." She gave him a sad little smile. "Losing the baby was horrible, but that's not all. While I was in the hospital, Alan's parents closed up the condo and they took all his things. Now I don't have anything of Alan's to remember him by."

Willy shook his head. "The bastards! Can't you call 'em and ask for a picture or something?"

"They won't speak to me. They didn't want Alan to marry me in the first place. But you have something of Alan's. You have his kidney."

"Hey . . . wait a second." A chill ran down Willy's back. Was she a nutcase who wanted her boyfriend's kidney back?

He must have looked scared, because she started to laugh. "Relax, Willy. I know what you're thinking, but this isn't a scene from a horror movie. Alan wanted to donate his organs, and I'm glad you have his kidney."

"That's a relief!" Willy laughed, too. "For a second there I was beginning to get nervous. But . . . you said you want something from me. What is it?"

"I want a baby."

The expression on her face was soft and pretty, but beads of sweat popped out on Willy's forehead. What the hell was she talking about? "You want . . . a baby?"

"I want your baby. Make me pregnant, Willy."

Willy knew he was staring at her, but he couldn't seem to help it. Normally, he would have killed for the chance to get a woman like Cherie in the sack, but this was weird!

"Just think about it, Willy. You have Alan's genes in your body. He's alive, and he's a part of you. If I have your baby, it'll be like having a part of Alan back with me again."

She was still holding his hand, and Willy jerked away. "Hey, Cherie. You're kidding me . . . right?"

"No. I'm very serious. You'll make me pregnant, won't you Willy?"

Willy shivered. The expression in her eyes was so determined, it scared him. He swallowed once, then shook his head. "No way. Look, Cherie, I can understand why you're so upset. What you've been through is enough to drive anybody a little bit crazy. But you're on the wrong track here."

"You won't make me pregnant?"

Her voice was a little too loud, and Willy put his finger to his lips. "Keep it down, Cherie. I told you before, you're talking crazy. Why don't you go home and get a good night's rest? Things'll look better in the morning."

"Let me get this straight, Willy. You're refusing to make me pregnant?"

Her voice was softer, but it scared Willy all the same. Even more frightening was the way she was handling his Swiss Army Knife. She kept pulling out the biggest, sharpest blade and then flipping it back, over and over.

"Answer me, Willy." She looked up from the table and met his eyes. Her stare was cold, chilling.

Willy swallowed again and reached for his knife, but she pulled it back, out of his reach. He knew he had to be firm with her. She was really flipped out. Humoring her wouldn't do any good. "No, Cherie. I won't make you pregnant. You're crazy. What you need is some professional help."

"I'm crazy?" Her eyes began to smolder. "You're the one who's crazy, Willy. Alan promised me that you'd cooperate. He said he'd make you understand!"

Willy began to frown. "Alan? But you told me Alan was dead."

"He's inside you, Willy. Listen to him. He'll tell you what he wants you to do."

Willy shivered, though the restaurant was warm. She was getting crazier and crazier. Was she on some kind of drug? "Get this straight, Cherie. I'm not going to sleep with you, I'm not going to get you pregnant, and I'm not going to listen to somebody that's dead. You must have had a little too much of something—drugs, booze, whatever. Why don't you head on home and sleep it off?"

"You don't understand, Willy." She reached out for his hand again. "Please . . . you just have to do it! It's the only way I can keep Alan alive!"

"No way." Willy shook his head. She looked ready to cry, but he hardened his heart. She was crazy, and he had to get rid of her. She could make all sorts of trouble for him if she followed him around, begging him to get her pregnant. "Go home, Cherie. There's got to be a law against this kind of thing. You're harassing me, and you'd better get out of here right now or . . . I'll just have to call the cops!"

"You're a nasty man, Willy Rossini! You don't deserve to have a part of Alan!"

She slid out of the booth so quickly, she knocked over his cup of coffee. Willy mopped up the mess with a napkin and breathed a sigh of relief as he watched her go out the door. That was the last he'd see of her, thank God!

But she still had his Swiss Army Knife! He frowned. It was one of his favorites, but he guessed it was a small price to pay to get rid of her. He could always order another from one of his catalogs.

But what would she do with his knife? She was crazy and now she was armed. Should he call the cops and tell them that there was a crazy woman out there somewhere, wandering the streets with his knife?

Willy thought about it for a moment and then rejected the idea. She hadn't actually done anything illegal, and if he reported her to the police, he'd have to tell them the whole crazy story. His boss was bound to hear about it. They'd joke about it at the dealership for the next twenty years. It would be smarter to keep this to himself. He'd just tell his boss he'd given her the brochures and she'd promised to contact him when she was ready to buy.

The waitress stopped by his booth and smiled. "Will that be all, sir?"

"Yes. Thanks a lot." Willy handed her a tip and stood up. He was thinking about Cherie as he paid the cashier and headed out the door. Did he actually have her boyfriend's kidney? The doctor had told him the donor's name was confidential, so he had no way of knowing whether that part of her story was true. It could be a figment of her imagination, and she could be out there right now, trying her story out on another guy.

But she had known about his transplant. Willy shivered as he zipped up his parka and stepped out into the cold. She must have asked questions about him because she'd even found out where he worked. Did she know his home address? Would she knock on his door and try to force her way in?

It was dark as he headed across the parking lot, and he shivered slightly. He wasn't exactly afraid, but it gave him a very uneasy feeling to walk past the rows of deserted, snow-covered cars. He felt naked without his knife, and he wondered if he should start carrying some kind of weapon. She was crazy. And she was angry with him. It was impossible to guess what she might do.

His car was parked in the back row. Willy's hands were shaking slightly as he unlocked the driver's door. He glanced around carefully as he slid in behind the wheel, checking the backseat to make sure that she wasn't hiding there. Nothing was moving in the parking lot, but Willy didn't relax until he'd slammed his door and locked it. Was she out there somewhere, watching him start his car and turn on his headlights?

Willy backed carefully out of the parking spot and drove toward the exit. Just as he turned onto the street, a dreadful possibility occurred to him. She'd told him he didn't deserve to have her boyfriend's kidney. Was she crazy enough to try to kill him to get it back?

She'd watched him as he'd come out of the restaurant and scurried across the parking lot. He had moved very fast and he'd glanced around constantly, his eyes searching the dark shadows. His behavior had given Connie a feeling of satisfaction. At least she'd managed to make him nervous. But Willy Rossini deserved a lot worse than a few sleepless nights.

It wasn't that he'd refused her. Connie had prepared herself to cope with that. But when he'd called her crazy and had threatened to call the police, she had known that she had no choice but to act. She wasn't afraid of the police. She'd done nothing wrong. But if Willy managed to convince them that she was crazy, they might lock her up and stop her from contacting the other candidates on the transplant list.

Connie stared down at the knife she still clutched in her hand. She wasn't a violent person, but there was no other alternative. She had to silence Willy before he could tell anyone else what had happened in the back room at the Lamplighter. She'd used a fake name as a precaution, but he could describe her. He could also describe the car she was driving, and someone at the dealership might even remember her license plate. Alan was depending on her. She couldn't take chances. That meant Willy Rossini had to die.

She put her car in gear and followed as Willy drove out of the parking lot. She'd made a dreadful mistake by telling him about Alan's kidney. Alan had assured her that Willy would understand, but he hadn't.

"I'm sorry." Connie shook her head sadly. "I tried to do things your way, Alan, but it didn't work. People just don't understand us, honey. They think we're crazy, so we can't make this kind of mistake again."

At least this was a good area for what she had to do. Connie glanced around and smiled as she saw that most of the factories were closed for the night. If she remembered correctly, there was a perfect street for it about three blocks up. When she forced him to turn right, he'd be stuck at the dead end with nothing but deserted warehouses around him.

Connie stepped on the accelerator and pulled up behind him. He couldn't see her. The interior of her car was dark, and her headlights were practically blinding him. All she had to do was stay right on his bumper and make him so nervous, he'd turn onto the dead end to get away from the driver that was following him too closely.

"Jesus!" Willy swore softly as he noticed the headlights behind him. The driver was right on his tail, and the streets were icy. Willy tried to speed up, but the other driver kept pace with him. The lunatic couldn't pass. This was a two-lane road, and there was a solid line of oncoming traffic.

"Okay, mister. Go ahead and kill yourself. I'll just get out of your way." There was a street coming up, and Willy turned on his signal. He was going pretty fast, but he didn't dare slow down or the guy might hit him from behind. It was probably some idiot from Florida or California—where they didn't have snow. Minnesota drivers knew how treacherous icy roads could be.

The street was only a few feet away. Willy gripped the

wheel tightly, and made a skidding turn, fishtailing to a stop at the side of the street. Mr. Lunatic could drive on his merry way and kill someone else on the road.

Willy took a deep breath. It had been a close call. Then he glanced in his rearview mirror and saw that the other driver had made the turn, too! What was going on here?

Suddenly he had a terrible suspicion. Perhaps the other driver wasn't from out of state. It could be Cherie.

Willy didn't take the time to find out. He just put his car in gear and roared off down the street. She was right behind him, practically running him off the road. And then he saw the sign at the end of the block. DEAD END.

"Oh, my God!" Willy hit the brakes and swerved. He almost managed to make the U-turn at the end of the street, but his right rear tire slipped off the pavement. He was stuck! And Cherie was right in back of him, preventing him from backing up!

Frantically, Willy revved his motor. If he could just get a little traction, he could jump the curb and pull forward. But his tire dug in deeper and deeper.

That was when he saw her coming toward him, a tire iron in her hand. Willy's mouth opened in a terrified scream as his window shattered. And then, in the space of only a few seconds, he was no longer capable of screaming . . . or even breathing.

CHAPTER 16

Jill was watching the last of the evening news when the telephone rang. She reached out for the remote control, pushed the button that muted the sound, and picked up the phone.

"Jill? It's Doug. Did I wake you?"

"No." She flicked off the television. The news was over anyway. "I just finished watching the news."

"What's your route home from the office?"

She was frowning as she told him. It was a strange question to ask.

"Did you pass Baylor Street tonight?"

Jill's frown deepened. Doug sounded worried. "Yes. I pass it every night. What's wrong, Doug?"

"Plenty. What time?"

"I'm not sure. I got home at seven, so it must have been about five forty-five."

"That's what I thought." Doug sounded even more worried. "You might have been there."

"I might have been *where*?"

"Passing Baylor Street. There was a homicide tonight. The victim left the Lamplighter Restaurant at six thirty-five. That put him on Baylor about ten minutes later. You must have been driving by when it happened. Can you see the dead end from the road?"

"Not really. It's around the bend." Jill shivered slightly. Even though she'd worked on hundreds of homicides, there was a quality in Doug's voice that made her feel uneasy. "Tell me about it, Doug."

"We found the victim's car at the dead end. His right rear wheel was stuck. The killer smashed in the driver's window to get to him."

"Was it gang related?" Jill asked, though she'd never heard of gangs in that area.

"I don't think so. The victim was a white male in his late thirties with no history of gang affiliation. No record, either. He was a salesman at Froelich Motors."

Jill nodded. She passed the dealership every day, and Neil had bought his Mercedes there. "Suspects?"

"Not yet."

Doug still sounded worried, and Jill knew there was something he wasn't telling her. "It was a bad one?"

"Yeah. Bad." Doug paused for a moment. "I'll tell you about it tomorrow, but take another route to work. That whole area is going to be crawling with cops."

Jill shivered. She'd never come quite this close to a murder before. "Okay, Doug. Thanks for the tip. Was it a shooting?"

"No. Are you free for lunch tomorrow?"

"Just a second. I'll check." Jill flicked open the small appointment book on the table and turned to tomorrow's date. "I have an arraignment at ten, but I'm coming straight back to the office. What time?"

"Meet me at The Beef Barrel at noon. Do you have a cell phone, Jill?"

"No." She began to frown again. Doug still sounded worried, and she wasn't sure why.

"Okay. I've got to get back to work. Make sure you lock your car doors."

"I'll do that. Good night, Doug." There was a bemused expression on Jill's face as she hung up. Doug was worried about her safety. It was clear he cared about her, and that made Jill feel warm inside for the first time since Helen had told her about Neil and Lisa.

It was a new day, and Connie was ready. She was wearing a midnight blue cashmere sweater and skirt. Around her neck was a long rope of cultured pearls. She'd done her hair in a French twist, secured at the nape of her neck, and she wore tiny pearl earrings that matched her pearls. She looked elegant and sophisticated, the perfect match for the next candidate on her list.

Ian Perkins had received Alan's liver, and Connie knew where he lived. She'd told the hospital she wanted to send a card to his home, so they'd given her his address on Forestview Lane. Connie had driven past and had discovered that it was an exclusive area with expensive homes on huge, wooded lots. If Ian Perkins owned a home on Forestview Lane, he had to be rich.

"Don't worry, Alan. We'll be successful this time." Connie pulled on her new calfskin gloves and slipped on her white wool coat. She touched her lips to Alan's picture, then went out the door. She wasn't going to make the mistake of telling Ian Perkins the real reason for her visit. She'd just say she was a volunteer from the hospital and had come to see if there was anything she could do for him.

As she climbed into her car, Connie was smiling. She even had a new identity for the occasion. She was Camille Ward, a recent Vassar graduate, doing volunteer work for the hospital until she decided what she wanted to do with her life.

Traffic was light, so Connie practiced her prepared speech as she drove toward Forestview Lane. "Hello, Mr. Perkins. My name is Camille Ward, and I'm a volunteer from the hospital. I've been assigned to help you with your recovery. There's no charge, and I'll be at your disposal for the next four weeks. I'll be happy to run errands, prepare your meals, or do anything else you might want."

Connie said the speech three times, and then she laughed. "And by the way, Mr. Perkins . . . in return for my services, I'd like you to service me in bed just as soon as you're able."

Of course she wouldn't say that! She giggled as she turned on to Forestview Lane. He'd get the idea, all by himself. And once she was sure she was pregnant, she'd disappear. When Mr. Perkins called the hospital to ask where she was, they'd tell him they'd never heard of Camille Ward.

The house was definitely imposing. Connie parked at the curb and got out. She locked her car, a precaution she probably didn't have to take in this area, and put a bright, eager smile on her face as she walked up the brick steps to the Colonial-style home.

A wreath of pinecones decorated the door, brightened by a gigantic red bow. On its steamers was the phrase HAPPY HOLIDAYS in fancy gold letters. Connie stared at it for a moment, then sighed. Tonight was Christmas Eve. She'd forgotten all about it. Alan had always loved Christmas, and they'd planned to decorate the condo this year. Now the condo was gone, but she'd do something special with Alan when she got back to the hotel. Perhaps she'd even pick up a small tree for the dresser, one that was already decorated and strung with lights. They could have dinner in their room and listen to some Christmas music before they went to bed. It wouldn't be like the huge Christmas party they'd planned to have, but it would be a nice intimate evening for just the two of them.

Connie rang the doorbell and almost immediately, a maid in a starched, black uniform responded. "May I help you, ma'am?"

"Yes." Connie smiled her broadest smile. "I'm Camille Ward—a volunteer from the hospital. I'd like to see Mr. Perkins."

The maid looked surprised. "But he's not here. Mr. Ian is still at Fairdale Convalescent. He won't be home until next week."

"I'm sorry I disturbed you." Connie looked very apologetic. "The hospital must have given me the wrong address. Could you tell me how to get to Fairdale Convalescent?"

The maid nodded. "It's on Seventh and Gillette, right next to the park. Mr. Ian is in room one-fourteen. You say you're from the hospital?"

"Yes." Connie was smiling as she nodded. "I'm a volunteer. I was assigned to visit Mr. Perkins to see if he needed any help."

The maid smiled back. "He'll be glad to see you. His parents visit in the evenings, but he gets lonely all day by himself. Tell him I said hello, will you?"

"Of course. And your name is . . . ?"

"Gretchen. And since you're going there, would you mind taking his mail?"

"I'd be happy to." Connie was grinning as she took the stack of cards the maid handed her and hurried back to her car. This was a lucky break! If anyone at the convalescent home asked her why she was visiting, she could tell them she stopped by to bring Mr. Perkins his mail.

Connie glanced down at the envelopes as she started her car. Several were from children. She could tell by the youthful handwriting. Perhaps Mr. Perkins was a teacher. It didn't seem likely that a public school teacher could afford a home in the area, and a maid, but he might have inherited money.

It really didn't make any difference to Connie. Rich or poor, teacher or highly paid executive, Mr. Ian Perkins had exactly what Connie needed. Alan's liver was alive in his body, which made him the perfect candidate to father their child.

They were sitting in the booth Jill had come to think of as theirs. A giant Christmas tree stood in the center of the restaurant, and Christmas carols were playing over the speakers. It was perfect weather for the day before Christmas—snowflakes were falling lazily outside—and Jill knew she would have enjoyed this holiday lunch with Doug if he hadn't just told her about the homicide.

"Are you all right?" he asked.

"I'm fine." She took a sip of her coffee and tried to hide how upset she was. "What do you mean, he was . . . gutted?"

"You don't want a description while you're eating." Doug looked a little sick himself.

"And you don't have any suspects?"

He shook his head. "Zip. Everyone said he was a nice guy with no enemies."

"That could be a cover. Do you think it was a professional hit?"

"No way." Doug took a bite of his burger. "Professional hits are . . . professional. They're usually not this bloody, even when they're trying to send someone a message."

"An inept hit man?"

Doug shrugged. "I guess that's possible, but I saw the crime-scene photos this morning. There was no reason for the multiple stab wounds. The coroner says the first blow was lethal and the others were just window dressing."

"Then you think this was a crime of passion?"

"That's what it looked like to me. The killer was completely out of control with that knife."

"You said he'd just finished having dinner at the Lamplighter?" Jill reached for an onion ring, even though she didn't feel much like eating.

Doug nodded. "He was with a client, a gorgeous redhead dressed in expensive clothing. The waitress said they talked a lot during dinner, and she saw him give her some brochures. We know her name is Cherie White. She told it to the hostess because she got to the restaurant first. And she left first, several minutes before the victim."

"She's not a suspect?"

"Everybody's a suspect, but nothing points to her directly. Women don't usually smash car windows with tire irons, and they seldom use knives. This killing was unusually violent."

"That rules out a woman?"

"Not necessarily. It's just unusual, that's all."

Jill forced herself to take a bite of her patty melt. She didn't want Doug to know this conversation was upsetting her stomach. "Have you located her for questioning?"

"It's not up to me. I'm not the lead on this case. But they'll locate her. Channel four is doing an appeal. If she hears it, she'll come in to clear herself."

"Maybe." Jill nodded. "Unless she's guilty. Then she'll head out of town."

"You're not eating." Doug reached out to pat her hand. "Let's change the subject. This is a pretty gruesome topic for lunch."

Jill shook her head and reached for another onion ring. "I don't have a problem with that. I'm just a little off my feed today, that's all."

"Okay."

Doug nodded, but Jill knew he didn't believe her. Why could he read her so well? He seemed to be in tune with her, to know exactly how she was feeling, though she'd made an effort to hide the fact that this homicide upset her.

"I've got something for you." Doug reached into his briefcase and pulled out a package. "This is a present."

She was surprised. "For me? But . . . you already gave me a Christmas present."

"I know. This isn't for Christmas, and it's not really a present for you. It's a present for me."

"Uh . . . okay." She wasn't sure she understood, but she unwrapped the package. Inside the box was a cell phone. "Doug! Why in the world . . . ?"

"It's so I won't have to worry. What if you'd been stuck on Baylor last night? You could have ended up right in the middle of this thing. It was only luck that you weren't the one forced off the road."

"Forced off the road?" Jill raised her eyebrows in surprise. "You didn't mention that."

"Do me a favor and forget I said that. It's just a theory. There's no evidence to substantiate it. But think about it. What if someone forced you off the road when you were driving home? What would you do in a situation like that?"

Jill said the first thing that popped into her head. "I'd lock all my doors."

"You should lock them every time you get into your car. But that wouldn't have protected you last night. The driver's window was smashed in."

Jill nodded. "I see where you're going. Last night's victim didn't have a cell phone?"

"That's right, and one could have saved his life. If he'd been on the line, giving a description of the other car, the killer might have decided not to approach him."

"I see." Jill nodded again. "That makes sense, Doug."

"Your cell phone is activated and ready to go. I even programmed the numbers. My home's number one, my office is number two, and my beeper's number three."

"Thank you, Doug." Jill was a little embarrassed. She

should have gotten a cell phone for herself. "But you really shouldn't have—"

"I wanted to. This phone holds nine speed-dial numbers. You've got six left. I'll show you how to program them. And don't forget nine-one-one. I didn't bother to grogram it, since it's only three numbers."

"Right." Jill smiled at him. He was really very sweet. "But please, Doug. At least let me pay you back for—"

Doug shook his head. "No way! I told you, this is a present for me. I just want you to promise that you'll keep it charged and carry it in your purse."

"I promise." Jill felt warm inside. No one had ever been so concerned about her before. Neil hadn't ever suggested that she get a cell phone, not even at the beginning when she'd thought he was in love with her.

Connie's hands were shaking slightly as she approached the door to room one-fourteen. She could see him. He was in a wheelchair by the window, staring out at the park below.

"Mr. Perkins?" She kept her voice soft. His back was to her, and she didn't want to startle him. When he turned around in his wheelchair, she was the one who was startled.

Ian Perkins was a boy! He looked to be about eleven years old, with a round face and dark hair.

"Hi!" The boy smiled. "Who are you?"

Connie was so flustered she almost forgot the name she was using. "I'm . . . uh . . . Camille Ward. And you're . . . ?"

"Ian Perkins. But most of my friends call me Spud."

Connie smiled. She couldn't help it. Ian Perkins had a very infectious grin. "Why do they call you Spud?"

"Because I love french fires. They're my favorite food. Hey, Camille . . . have you ever had a french fry sandwich?"

"No." Connie sat down on the edge of his bed. "How do you make a french fry sandwich?"

"You order a super scoop of fries and a bun with nothing but mustard and catsup and pickles on it. Then you put the fries in the bun and eat it. I know it sounds gross, but it's not."

Connie nodded. "It sounds interesting. I'll have to try it sometime. Which place has the best fries?"

"Fast-food chain, coffee shop, or regular restaurant?"

Connie shrugged. "Tell me about all three, the fast-food first."

"Okay. Fast-food is McDonald's, hands down. Tell them you want to wait for a fresh batch, and don't let them give you the ones under the warmer."

Connie nodded. "That's good advice. How about the coffee shops?"

"Embers. Definitely Embers, especially the one on the way to the airport. Their french fries are so good you don't have to douse them with catsup. And for regular restaurants, the winner's got to be the one in the downtown Hilton. They serve curly fires, but they're really crispy and they don't leave any grease on the plate."

"Thanks for the tip." Connie grinned at him as she handed him the stack of envelopes. "Here's your mail. Gretchen sent it, and she said to tell you hello."

Ian's face lit up in a smile. "Gretchen makes super fries. Are you a friend of hers?"

"Not exactly. I just met her a couple of minutes ago. I'm a volunteer from the hospital. I just stopped in to visit you."

"Cool!" Ian grinned at her. "That must be how you got past the dragon lady at the desk. She doesn't let any of my friends visit me. They've got some kind of rule about minors. You have to be eighteen or a member of the immediate family to get in."

Connie nodded. "I know. So how old are you, Spud?"

"I'm eleven, but I'm big for my age. That's why they could give me the liver. It came from a man, but you probably know that since you're from the hospital. I just wish I could thank him, but he's dead. If he wasn't, I wouldn't have his liver."

"Very true." Connie nodded. "Would you like to know more about the man who gave you his liver?"

Ian nodded. "You bet! Did you know him, or what?"

"Yes, but you've got to promise not to tell. The hospital wouldn't let me visit you if they knew."

"Okay, I promise." Ian looked solemn. "I guess that would be a conflict of interest, huh?"

"I guess it would. How do you know about conflict of interest?"

Ian shrugged. "My uncle's a lawyer. I hear stuff like that all the time. So tell me about the man . . . please?"

"All right." Connie smiled at him. He was a very nice boy, and she was glad he had Alan's liver. "His name was Alan, and he was very handsome. We loved each other. We were going to be married."

"Oh, bummer! I'm sorry, Camille."

"So am I." Connie sighed, then forced herself to smile again. It took almost an hour for her to tell Ian about Alan, and when she was through, there were tears in Ian's eyes.

"I wish I could've known him." Ian gave her a lopsided smile. "You really loved him, huh?"

Connie nodded. "I really loved him. And, Spud, I'm really glad he gave you his liver. Take good care of it, and think about him once in a while. You would have liked him a lot."

"I will. Thanks for telling me, Camille. I'll never forget what you said."

"That's good enough for me. And it's good enough for Alan, too." Connie was smiling as she went out the door. She liked Ian Perkins. He would take good care of Alan's liver, but he was too young for their purposes. It was time to go back to her hotel room and tell Alan exactly what had happened. They could rejoice for tonight, celebrating the fact that his liver had found a good home. First thing tomorrow, she would start researching the next name on the transplant list, the next candidate for fathering their baby.

CHAPTER 17

It seemed everyone was going somewhere for Christmas Eve. Traffic was heavy, and to complicate matters, a light snow had started to fall around three in the afternoon. Though Jill had left the office early, her twenty-minute commute had stretched into an hour.

It was dark when she turned onto River Road and headed toward her house. As usual, the homes in this area were decorated for the holidays. She passed one with a life-size manger scene on the front lawn, another with a family of lighted, plastic snowmen.

As she approached her block, Jill noticed that the house lights were on. Since they weren't on a timer, and Neil wasn't in the habit of turning them on, the new companion Helen had hired must have flicked the switch.

Christmas Eve. Jill sighed as she turned into the driveway. Her parents had always had a party, and all the neighbors had come. She remembered her father's dressing up as Santa, long after she'd stopped believing that Santa climbed down the chimney every Christmas Eve. He'd done it for the neighborhood children, and Jill had helped him pass out the presents.

This was the time of year she missed her family the most.

Her mother had baked for a solid two weeks before Christmas: frosted cookies of various shapes, date cakes with chocolate frosting, gingerbread men with red and green icing, fruitcakes, and five kinds of pie including mincemeat which no one seemed to like. She'd also made rum balls.

There were cars lining the street in front of her house. One of their neighbors must be having a Christmas Eve party. Jill opened the garage door to drive inside, and at that moment she realized that the laughter and music were coming from her house!

"Hey, Jill! It's about time you got home!" Tom Hawthorne, one of Neil's colleagues at the university, caught her up in a giant hug the moment she stepped inside.

"Hi." Jill smiled at him. She'd always liked Tom. He had a good heart and was always trying to help people, though sometimes he hindered more than he helped. "What's going on?"

"A little surprise for your hubby. When he said he couldn't make it to my Christmas Eve party, we just packed up everything and brought it over here. Name your poison, Jill. I'm mixing drinks."

"I see that." Jill managed to keep the smile on her face as she caught sight of the kitchen. There were times when Tom resembled an exuberant but very clumsy bear. He had every glass in her cupboard out on the counter, along with a half-dozen varieties of liquor. Her blender was sitting in a sticky puddle at the edge of the sink, and several nearly empty juice cartons lay on their sides, leaking pink and orange and white liquid. It was clear that Tom was mixing his favorite tropical concoctions. "That was . . . uh . . . very thoughtful, Tom."

He stared at her for a moment, then sighed. "I'm sorry. I know I made a mess, but I'll clean everything up. We just thought the old man needed cheering up on Christmas Eve, that's all."

"You were right. He does." Jill took a deep breath and tried to ignore the water dripping from a bag of ice onto the floor and the dirty dishes that were stacked in her sink. "You don't have to worry about cleaning up. We're not having any company tomorrow; I'll take care of it. Who's here?"

"Everybody who showed up at my party. We brought food. There's a table set up in the living room."

Jill nodded. Tom always invited all the single professors and secretaries from the department, everyone who had nowhere to go for the holidays, "Just let me change out of my work clothes and I'll go in to say hello."

"Great!" Tom looked relieved. "I've got your favorite white wine, a whole case of Pinot Grigio. Do you want a chilled glass?"

Jill nodded and held her breath as Tom opened the freezer. When he took out one of her inexpensive wine-glasses, she let out a sigh of relief. Thank goodness he hadn't found the antique, pink crystal goblets that had belonged to her grandmother!

"Here you go, Jill." Tom poured the wine and handed it to her. "How is it?"

Jill took a sip and smiled. "Very good, Tom. I'll just change clothes, then I'll join the party."

As she hurried up the stairs, she was frowning. Why hadn't Neil called to tell her there was a party in progress? She flipped the lock on the bedroom door, in case one of the revelers wandered in, and put on the beaded sweater and matching skirt she'd worn to Tom's party last year. Since they'd arrived late and everyone had been too bombed to notice what she was wearing, Jill thought she might as well give it another try.

As she descended the stairs, she heard a high-pitched giggle and an accompanying burst of male laughter. It was clear that everyone was already quite full of Christmas cheer. If the partygoers were as drunk as they sounded, she might be able to wear this sweater and skirt to Tom's party next year, too!

"Jill!" Another of Neil's colleagues, a female professor who held graduate seminars on poetry, came rushing up to Jill as she started to enter the living room. "How's the lawyer business?"

"Just fine, Norma. Merry Christmas." Jill tried to step around her, but Norma was a big woman and she effectively blocked Jill's view of the living room.

"Don't go in there," she said.

She looked very serious, and Jill started to frown. "Why not?"

"They're . . . uh . . . they're dancing."

Jill nodded. "That's okay. Why shouldn't I go in?"

"Because I don't think you want to see who Neil's partner is."

"Lisa?" Jill took a deep breath as Norma nodded. "Who invited *her*?"

"Tom did. But he invited her before he knew we were coming here. I tried to tell Lisa it wasn't a good idea, but she came along anyway."

Jill laughed bitterly. "That's Lisa. All hormones and no brains. Please don't concern yourself, Norma. I'm aware of what's going on between Neil and Lisa. I just haven't decided what to do about it yet."

"But . . . Lisa's acting almost as if she's the hostess. It's an insult to you, Jill! There are those of us who still believe in the sanctity of marriage."

"Unfortunately, my husband's not one of them" Jill sighed. "But thanks for warning me. I know you were just trying to keep me from being hurt."

"That's true. And that's *all* I was doing. I don't want you to think for a second that I approve of—"

"I know you don't." Jill smiled at her. "Now . . . please. Just let me go in."

"Do you really think you should?"

"Yes," Jill said. "I have to see for myself."

Norma looked as if she still wanted to object, but one glance at Jill's determined expression and she stepped to the side. "Okay. But the party started three hours ago, and you know how strong Tom mixes his drinks."

"I do know." Jill sighed as she stepped into the living room. Tom's party was big this year. There were over thirty people in various stages of intoxication. The guests who were still working on their first drinks were holding animated conversations, their words only slightly slurred. Those who had gone to the kitchen for refills were dancing, though struggling to keep their balance. Any guests who'd had three of Tom's lethal concoctions were stretched out on the couches or the floor pillows, too drunk to even try to move.

"See what I mean?" Norma put a hand on Jill's arm. "You can always tell when Tom's mixing the drinks. There's a ton of food on that table, but nobody's eating."

Jill nodded. "You're right. But I don't see Neil."

"They were here a couple of minutes ago. I saw them dancing by that circular stairway."

"Then I know where they've gone." Jill frowned as she stared at the staircase. It let to her father's old office, over the garage. Since it hadn't been large enough for Neil's new office, they'd converted it to a small guest bedroom.

"Don't go up there. Sit down on the couch and I'll bring you a drink."

"Thanks, but I don't want one." Jill smiled at Norma and patted her arm. "Stay here. I'll be back in a minute."

Jill crossed the room, stopping several times to greet Neil's friends. At last she reached the circular stairway. No one seemed to notice as she climbed it. Jill was relieved. If Neil and Lisa were in the guest bedroom, that would be embarrassing enough.

It was very quiet at the top of the stairs, so quiet that Jill found herself holding her breath as she pushed open the door. A dim light was on and she saw them there, on the small, twin bed. Neither one had noticed her. They were too intent on the pleasure they were seeking. Neil was on his back, and Lisa was astride him, riding him as if he were a stallion.

She kept to the shadows and inched closer. There was only one more thing she needed to see, the thin gold chain around Lisa's neck, holding the heart pendant that Neil had claimed was an original.

Jill retraced her steps and backed out the door, closing it softly behind her. This wasn't the time for an ugly scene that everyone would witness. She took a deep breath and forced her lips into a smile as she descended the staircase. What Helen had told her was true. Neil had given Lisa a copy of her pendant. Or perhaps her pendant had been a copy of Lisa's.

"Are they up there?" Norma was waiting for her at the base of the staircase, and her eyes grew wide as Jill nodded. "You poor darling! What are you going to do?"

Jill shrugged. "Nothing, now. And I'm trusting you not to tell anyone. Can you stay until midnight, Norma? Just in case Neil needs something and Lisa leaves?"

"Of course." Norma nodded quickly. "But, Jill . . . are you going to leave him?"

"I'm not sure. But I have to talk to a friend of mine, and I'd like to do it now."

"I understand." Norma looked very sympathetic. "Go ahead, Jill. It might make you feel better. And don't worry about a thing. I'll stay right here and watch him like a hawk until you get back."

* * *

Doug sat in his apartment, staring at the Christmas tree. He'd mixed a batch of eggnog, following his grandmother's recipe. They'd had it every Christmas Eve at the ranch, but it didn't taste quite as delicious when there was no one to share it.

"To Christmas!" Doug raised his glass toward Jill's picture. He'd placed it on the center shelf of his bookcase, and it had quickly become his favorite possession. It was the most thoughtful gift he'd ever received. Besides, she really looked good in that silly outfit.

What was she doing tonight? Doug took another sip of his drink and imagined her at home with Neil. They were probably sitting on the couch, enjoying a quiet moment and exchanging Christmas gifts. Perhaps they were giving a party. Jill had told him Neil's relatives weren't coming to visit this year, but they could have invited friends.

Although Doug didn't know that much about Jill, he guessed she'd be a good hostess. She'd mentioned a recipe for stuffed mushrooms once; she might have made those for appetizers. She wasn't the type to go into a deli and buy a party platter. If Jill had a table with food, it would be filled with things she'd made herself.

Did she have a fire in the fireplace? She'd asked him where to buy wood, and he'd given her the number of a service that delivered. He'd even told her which type burned best, and she'd thanked him for his advice.

Doug got up and turned on his fireplace. It wasn't real, just a gas log that was supposed to look authentic. Still, it created a nice illusion. Even though he didn't need them, he'd bought fireplace tools to place on the hearth. The only things missing were Christmas stockings hanging from the mantel.

It was so quiet in his apartment, Doug could hear the hiss of the gas log. He remembered how noisy the Christmas

Eve parties used to be, with all the ranch hands from the bunkhouse, folks from neighboring ranches, and a gaggle of excited children waiting for Santa Claus to arrive. Christmas Eve wasn't supposed to be quiet. It should be filled with laughter and music.

Doug got up to turn on the stereo. One of the local stations was playing Christmas carols and that made him feel much better. He cranked up the volume and grinned as he heard a male voice sing "Up on the housetop . . ." It used to be his favorite Christmas carols. When he was a kid, he'd begged his father to let him climb up to the roof and watch for Santa, but wiser heads had prevailed. His dad had brought out a sleeping bag and tucked him in by the fireplace, promising him he'd be sure to wake him up when Santa came down the chimney. Of course he hadn't. But the cookies and milk he'd set out for Santa were gone in the morning, and Santa had even left him a note:

*Thanks for the cookies and milk. You've been a good
boy and your presents are under the tree.
See you next year.*

Love, Santa.

The chorus of the carol was so loud, the knock at the door so soft and tentative, Doug almost didn't hear it. He went to the door, peeked out the fish-eye lens, and his heart skipped a beat as he saw Jill.

Doug pulled the door open so wide it banged against the opposite wall. "What are you doing here?"

Jill looked just as startled as he did. "Oh . . . I . . . I'm sorry, Doug. I didn't mean to interrupt. If you've got company, I can come back another time."

"There's nobody here but me." Doug took her arm and drew her inside. "What's up, Jill?"

"I . . . I just needed to get out, that's all. And I hoped you wouldn't be doing anything on Christmas Eve."

"I'm not." Doug smiled at her. "And it's always nice to get a surprise visit. Come in. Give me your coat and sit down on the couch. I just mixed up a batch of eggnog."

"With brandy?"

Doug nodded. "Remy Martin."

"That's good in eggnog."

Jill was sitting on the couch when Doug came back with her drink. Since he didn't have the proper glassware, he'd poured it into a beer mug on which was printed FROM THE LAND OF SKY BLUE WATERS. HAMMS. THE BEER THAT REFRESHES. "Sorry about the mug. I'm not really set up for entertaining."

"That's okay." Jill laughed. "I'm not really set up for entertaining, either. As a matter of fact, my house will probably be wrecked before I get back."

As she took a sip of the eggnog, Doug studied her face. She looked tense and disappointed. Something had happened to upset her, and she needed to get it off her chest. He sat down in the chair across from her and gave her an encouraging smile. "What's happening at your house—to wreck it?"

"A party. It was going on when I got home, and I . . . I left."

Doug nodded. "Then you weren't the hostess?"

"No. I didn't know anything about it until I walked in. Some of his friends from the department brought the party to him."

Doug raised his eyebrows. It was clear that Jill was talking about Neil, but she'd taken pains not to mention his name. There was definitely trouble in paradise.

"He didn't even call to tell me." Jill took another sip of eggnog. "This is good, Doug. You made it yourself?"

"It's my grandmother's recipe. Do you want to tell me why

you're so upset, or would you rather talk about something else?"

"Something else." Jill didn't meet his eyes. "I'll tell you, but . . . not right now. Your Christmas tree looks beautiful."

"Thanks. See those little handblown glass strawberries? They've been in my family for generations."

"That gives you a nice sense of continuity." Jill looked up at him, then lowered her eyes. "When I got home, he was with Lisa."

Doug struggled to remember, but he was sure that she had never mentioned anyone named Lisa. "Who's Lisa?"

"She's his TA. At least, she was. And now she's his . . . his mistress. He told me it was over, but it's not."

Doug nodded and kept his mouth firmly closed. Jill would tell him if he didn't prompt her.

"I almost divorced him when I found out about it. I caught them together at our old apartment, but he promised me he'd never see her again. Then we moved and everything was going to be all right, but she was with him on his Chicago book tour. I almost divorced him again, right before Christmas last year."

"But you didn't." Doug wasn't questioning her. He was just stating a fact.

"I couldn't. My attorney advised me to wait until we'd done our taxes, because there'd be all sorts of tax liabilities if I filed before the end of the year. So I waited. And then, the morning I was going to file the papers, he . . . he ended up at the hospital."

Doug clenched his hands together. He wanted to strangle the bastard who'd hurt Jill so badly, but that wouldn't help her. "You stuck with him because you felt sorry for him?"

Jill dipped her head in a nod. "That's part of it. I did feel sorry for him, but I had another selfish reason. I knew I couldn't live with myself if I kicked him when he was down."

"The old sense of fair play?"

Jill nodded again. "I guess that was it. And I really wanted to be a good wife, like my mother was to my father. But my father never . . . He wasn't like that at all. He *loved* my mother!"

Doug heard the undertone of anguish in Jill's voice, and he knew that she was sure Neil didn't love her.

"Do you remember Helen?"

Doug nodded and resisted the urge to wipe away the tears he saw in her eyes. "I think so. Isn't she the companion you hired?"

"That's right. She was the best. She quit right after she found out he was sleeping with Lisa. He gave me a pendant, a little gold heart with a diamond. He told me he'd designed it himself, and it was an original."

Doug nodded. "I saw it the day you wore it to the office. It wasn't an original?"

"No." Jill's voice was choked with emotion. "He had one made for Lisa, too. She was wearing it tonight."

"That's why you left the party?"

"That's one reason." Jill took another sip of her eggnog. "The other is . . . I went up to the room my father used for an office and I . . . I found them in bed."

Doug couldn't stand it any longer. Jill looked so miserable he sat down on the couch and put an arm around her shoulders. "Why don't you go ahead and cry? I've got a full box of Kleenex, and it'll make you feel better."

"No, it won't!" Jill shook her head. "I'm all cried out, Doug. I cried the first time I caught them together, and I cried when I found out she was with him at his Chicago book signing. I'm sick of crying, Doug. It's . . . it's so fucking female!"

Doug couldn't help it. He started to laugh. Then Jill was laughing, too, holding him the way he'd always hoped she would, her arms clamped around his neck and her face pressed against the front of his shirt.

They stayed like that for several minutes, laughing at something that wasn't really funny. Doug wanted it to last forever, but at last Jill pulled back and wiped her eyes.

"Sorry, Doug. I ruined your Christmas Eve. I really didn't mean to barge in here and dump on you, but I guess you're my only friend."

"I know that's not true." Doug handed her a tissue. "You have lots of friends, Jill. Still, I'd like to think that I'm your best friend."

"You are. Am I your best friend?"

"Definitely." Doug nodded solemnly. "And since we're best friends, I want you to join me in a Lake family tradition. Just get up, shut your eyes, and follow me."

Jill began to smile. "All right. Where are we going?"

"To the bedroom."

"The bedroom?" Jill began to look a little nervous. "But . . . why?"

"That's a secret. Do you trust me?"

"Yes." Jill nodded and got up from the couch. "Okay. I'm shutting my eyes."

Doug took her hand and led her into the bedroom. He walked her over to the edge of the bed and sighed as he told her to sit down. Jill was finally in his bedroom, but this wasn't the time to indulge any of his fantasies. It was time for a Lake family tradition, just as he'd told her.

"Stay right there and keep your eyes closed." There was a hint of laughter in Doug's voice as he walked over to the dresser and got the two, foil-wrapped packages on top. "Hold out your hand, palm up."

Jill held out her hand. "Okay."

Doug put one of the foil-wrapped packages in her hand and pulled her up from the edge of the bed. "We're going back to the living room. Keep your eyes closed and I'll lead you."

Jill was grinning as they retraced their steps, and Doug

was glad that he'd restrained himself. He knew he'd always remember the way she'd looked, sitting on the edge of his bed. His buddies would say he was a fool for passing up such a golden opportunity. Jill might have slept with him if he'd pushed it. But he was playing for much higher stakes than a one-night stand with a woman who was disillusioned with her husband.

When Jill was seated on the couch again, Doug couldn't resist staring at her for a moment. Even though there were traces of tears on her cheeks, she looked so beautiful she almost took his breath away. "Okay, Jill. You can open your eyes now."

She did and stared down at the object in her hand. Then she started to smile. "It's a chocolate Santa!"

"That's right. We got them from See's Candies when I lived in Texas, but Fanny Farmer's are just as good. Now peel down the foil so his head is exposed."

"Okay." Jill peeled down the foil. "Now what?"

"Now bite it off!"

"You want me to bite off Santa's head?" Jill tried to look outraged, but she laughed instead.

"Absolutely! It's a family tradition. You've got to do it."

"Oh, yeah?" Jill's eyes were sparkling. "I'm not object-ing on moral grounds, but what good does it do?"

"It's very simple. You're sending Santa a message that he'd better bring you what you want for Christmas . . . or else!"

Jill shrugged. "It's too late for me. I already opened all my presents at the office Christmas party. Will it work for next year?"

"Sure." Doug managed to hide his surprise. Didn't Neil and Jill exchange Christmas presents? "Santa's got excellent long-term memory. Just think about what you want for Christmas next year and then bite off his head."

"Okay, but you have to do it, too. Are you ready?"

Doug nodded and they both bit down. As the sweet, dark taste of chocolate filled his mouth, he knew exactly what he wanted. He was hoping Jill would stop feeling guilty about Neil's eyesight and divorce him. Even more important, he was wishing that she would fall in love with him.

"There!" Jill's eyes were warm as they met his. "I did it, and it was delicious. I just hope our wishes come true."

Doug nodded. "So do I."

As they finished their chocolate Santas, Doug was deep in thought. Jill had seemed very serious about her wish. Was it even remotely possible that they were wishing for the same thing?

CHAPTER 18

The party was over and Neil knew he had some apologizing to do. He'd sent Norma home, and he was sitting on the couch, waiting for Jill to come back. Norma had told him what had happened, and although he'd tried to charm her, she hadn't even cracked a smile. If she was so angry at him, Jill would be spitting bullets by the time she got home.

According to Norma, Jill had gone to see a friend. Neil was mildly curious, but he was sure it wasn't a male friend. Jill was probably out there somewhere, driving around and crying over his indiscretion. It was a pattern he knew all too well. She'd sniffle for a while, and then she'd start feeling like a victim. After that had passed, she'd head for home to confront him, fighting mad.

Norma hadn't wanted to leave. She'd said she'd promised to stay until Jill got home and she never broke a promise. It had taken all Neil's powers of persuasion, but at last she had gone. He sipped the ice water she'd brought him and rehearsed what he'd say when Jill came through the door.

I'm sorry, honey. He'd look terribly contrite. *I had two of Tom's drinks before I realized how strong they were, and I started to get depressed. You know how it is. Everyone else was having such a good time, but you weren't here with me. I missed you, Jill.*

She wouldn't give an inch, but she'd be thinking about what he'd said. *If you missed me that much, you should have called.*

I tried to. I couldn't find the remote phone, so I asked her to use the one in the kitchen.

Who? Jill's eyes would narrow.

Lisa. I asked her to call your office and tell you about the party. I really thought you'd come home right away.

Jill's voice would be tight. *I didn't get the message. Are you sure she called?*

She said she did. Then, when a couple of hours went by and you didn't come home, I thought . . . well . . . I thought you didn't care.

That's no excuse for sleeping with her! Jill would glare at him. *You broke your promise to me!*

I know. It's just that Christmas is so depressing. You're supposed to be with your family and friends, but I sit here every day with a paid babysitter who really doesn't give a damn about me. She was here the other day, too. But I swear I didn't sleep with her. I tried to end it, Jill. I gave her a heart pendant just like yours. I thought that would please her and get her off my back. Then I told her it was over.

Jill wouldn't say anything. She'd be too busy thinking, buying part of his excuse.

It's just . . . I can't see! Do you know how awful that is for me? I can't dial the phone, and I can't read. I can't do anything except sit here! And I can't see your face, Jill. That's what really drives me crazy!

That would get to her. Jill was a romantic, and his plaintive words would tug at her heartstrings. She wouldn't forgive him right away. It might take a week or so, but eventually she would. And when she'd forgiven him, things would go back to the old status quo.

Neil sighed deeply. He actually felt a little guilty about what he'd done. He hadn't meant to embarrass Jill, and he knew she shouldn't have taken Lisa up to the guest room in front of their friends. Unfortunately, he had. Now Jill would make him do penance before she granted him absolution.

Neil began to grin as he realized he was comparing his wife to a priest. That wasn't surprising. Jill followed the rules. She was one of life's innately good people. When he'd married her, he'd really thought he could be a good husband, but that dream had gone down the tubes the first day Lisa had walked into his office.

He'd always been a sucker for blondes, and Lisa had been no exception. She was prettier than most graduate students, with a figure a lingerie model could envy. With her sexy, sleepy-eyed look, it seemed she'd just climbed out of bed and was dying to get back there. Lisa had been ripe for the plucking, and he'd known it.

"I really need to raise my grade, Professor Bradley." Her voice had been soft and seductive. "Is there any way you could give me some extra help?"

He'd only been married to Jill for a year, and he'd struggled to resist temptation. He'd given Lisa his standard speech, telling her to reread the material and study every night.

"But it's so hard to study alone. I was hoping you could give me an hour or two, every week. I know you're busy, but it could be anytime you're free . . . even midnight."

The invitation had been very clear, written in her eyes as well as her words. Neil had given it one more shot, the attempt to remain faithful. He'd offered to give her the name of a tutor.

"I tried that, but he doesn't explain things the way you do in class. Please, Professor Bradley . . . I really need you."

He'd reminded himself that he loved Jill and she expected

him to be a devoted husband. He'd offered to tutor Lisa in his office, when there would be other people present.

"Oh, thank you!" Lisa had given him a radiant smile. "But . . . I'm afraid that won't work. I'm taking a full load this semester, so I don't have any free time during the day. I know it's an imposition, but could you possibly tutor me after hours?"

She'd leaned forward then, and he'd caught a glimpse of her perfectly rounded breasts. No bra, and they thrust forward against the silken material of her blouse.

"We live in the same apartment building, Professor. I've seen you by the elevator. I could come to your place . . . or you could come to mine."

That had done it. She was luscious and convenient. And he'd been so bored after his classes were over. Jill was working long hours, trying to climb up the ladder in the DA's office. She'd never have to know.

"Give me your number and I'll call you." He'd taken the number and tucked it into his pocket.

"Oh, thank you, Professor!" She'd reached out to take his hand, her fingers lingering a little longer than was necessary. "You really don't know what this means to me."

He'd glanced at the number several times that week. He'd almost decided to throw it away when Jill had called and said she had to work late.

It had been the hottest night of the year, and the air conditioning in the building had broken down. Lisa had greeted him in a tight pair of white shorts that left nothing to the imagination and a short, pink tank top that had barely covered her breasts. Only a monk could have resisted that kind of temptation.

Once he'd started with Lisa, she hadn't been the only one. It was like the dam of fidelity had broken and he was a free man once more. He'd always enjoyed women, and he'd loved them often and well. It might have been different if Jill hadn't been so wrapped up in her career, but she worked late most nights and all day on Saturdays.

Neil had never been able to stand being alone. Now he wasn't. There had been wives of colleagues, several students, and a secretary who'd worked in the history department. He'd managed to keep those affairs a secret, but the day of reckoning had come when Jill had caught him with Lisa.

Jill had cried and asked him how he'd feel if she were the one having an affair. He'd thought about it for a moment, and then he'd given her the answer she'd wanted to hear. He'd be devastated, of course. The thought of her in another man's arms was so painful he couldn't bear to imagine it. But he'd known that Jill was just playing tricks with words. Jill would never have an affair. She wouldn't even consider sleeping with another man. Why should she when they were so good together and he gave her everything she needed in bed?

If only she could be more flexible! Neil shook his head and sighed. In all other ways she was a perfect wife, but she did have one major fault. Jill assumed that by marrying him she'd earned the right to inflict her puritanical values on him. She was incapable of understanding that Lisa was nothing but a diversion, a pleasant way to pass the time when Jill wasn't home.

His hands were clenched. Neil took a deep breath and relaxed them. This wasn't the time to give vent to his anger. He had to pretend to be remorseful, to beg Jill's forgiveness for his momentary lapse.

He might actually have to give up Lisa. Jill would be more suspicious this time around, so it might be wise to call it quits. Of course he'd miss Lisa, but there were always pretty women on the campus. He wouldn't be alone for long.

* * *

Connie was seated at a corner booth in the bar, nursing a vodka gimlet. She didn't like vodka gimlets, but they had been Alan's favorite drinks and she'd hoped she might feel closer to him by ordering one.

The day had not gone well at all. Connie had left Ian at the convalescent center and gone straight to the next address on her list. Kathy Miller had received Alan's spleen. Though Connie knew another woman couldn't possibly help her, she'd wanted to meet Kathy to see what kind of person she was.

The Miller home was in North Minneapolis, so Connie locked her doors and kept her car windows rolled up as she'd turned off Lincoln Avenue and driven past boarded-up buildings and graffiti-scarred block walls. Several times, when she'd been forced to stop at red lights, groups of black teenagers had stared at her, suspicious of a white face in their neighborhood. Connie had wanted to shout out that she was just passing through, but she'd been afraid her words might arouse anger. Instead, she'd kept a determined smile on her face and she'd avoided all eye contact with anyone who looked like a gang member.

There had been no Christmas decorations in this neighborhood. The only concession to the season had been a hand-painted sign in a liquor-store window, advertising a Christmas special on Bud Lite. She'd seen a dope deal going down, folded money exchanged for a plastic envelope; but she had looked away, pretending not to notice.

Connie's hands had been shaking as she'd turned down Morgan Avenue. This had once been a nice residential area, but now all the houses had wrought-iron security bars on the doors and windows.

She'd pulled over to the curb in front of Kathy Miller's house, a well-kept older home with a shoveled walkway and a Christmas wreath on the door. It also had security bars.

Connie had pressed the buzzer, armed with the bouquet of flowers she'd brought.

"Yes?" A young black woman had opened the inner door to peer out through the security bars.

Connie had smiled. The woman had seemed distracted, but she hadn't appeared unfriendly. "My name is Chloe White, and I have a delivery, a bouquet for Kathy Miller."

"For Kathy?" The woman had looked startled for a moment; then she'd blinked back tears. "Thank you. It must be for her funeral. Kathy died yesterday."

Connie had felt a rush of sympathy. "I'm so terribly sorry. They should have told me before they sent me out here."

"That's okay, hon." The woman opened the door to take the bouquet. "I'll put these in water. It'll give Mama a lift when she comes home from the funeral parlor."

Connie was halfway to her car when the woman called her back. "Hold on, hon. There's no card. Do you know who these are from?"

"Uh . . . yes, I do." Connie said the first name that popped into her head. "They're from her friend, Alan."

Connie's mind hadn't been on the traffic as she'd driven back to her hotel room. She'd been thinking about Kathy Miller and wishing she knew what had caused her death. Connie had spent weeks reading about organ transplants, and she knew there were risks. Patients could die from the surgery itself, or the anesthesia. After the surgery was completed, there was the possibility of infection. Patients who needed transplants were sometimes weakened by disease; they could lack the stamina to recuperate. And even if the patient lived through all those risks, there was always the rejection factor. A recipient's body could refuse to accept the donor's organ, despite treatment with antirejection drugs. Learning of Kathy Miller's death had sobered Connie. She realized she had to get to the other names on her list as quickly as possible.

The cocktail waitress, a hard-eyed brunette who was wearing a ridiculously short, green velvet skirt and a red satin blouse that exposed her cleavage, stopped by Connie's booth. "Do you want a refill?"

"No." Connie motioned toward her glass. "You can take this away."

The waitress looked worried as she picked up the glass. "Is something wrong with your drink?"

"It's fine." Connie smiled to reassure her. "I'm just not in the mood for a gimlet."

"How about a Brandy Alexander? We make 'em in the blender with chocolate ice cream, and they really pack a wallop."

"That sounds great." Connie watched her walk away and then she started to grin. She loved chocolate ice cream, but she hadn't eaten it since she'd met Alan. He liked chocolate, but it gave him hives. She hadn't wanted to tempt him by having it in the house.

Connie's grin disappeared as she thought about Alan. She knew he was still with her, but remembering his face without looking at his picture was getting more difficult with each passing day. At first, his image had been clear. She'd been able to remember the special smile he'd had for her, how his eyes would turn warm when she came into the room, the way his hair curled right above his ears when it was wet from a shower. She'd remembered the feel of his arms around her, the touch of his lips on her skin. All that was fading now, and Connie knew she had to do something to bring it back before Alan was lost to her, forever.

She reached into her purse and pulled out her list. She had to have Alan's baby. It was the only way to keep him alive. But the next name was Shelly Devore's. She'd received Alan's pancreas. Although a woman couldn't help her in her quest for Alan's child, Connie decided to take flowers to Miss Devore tomorrow. She felt an obligation to meet everyone who had received a part of Alan to see if they were worthy of the honor.

The next name on the list made Connie's heart race faster. Mark Turner. He had Alan's second kidney. She'd seek him out right after Christmas to see if he was the right candidate to father Alan's baby.

CHAPTER 19

Somehow, the holiday season had passed. It was the third Tuesday in January when Jill walked into The Beef Barrel, slid into the booth she thought of as theirs, and waited for Doug to join her. She'd poured out her heart on Christmas Eve. She'd been avoiding him ever since. Doug would want to know what had happened, and Jill wasn't sure she could explain it.

When she had gone home, after the party, Neil had been waiting with an apology. She'd expected that, but her reaction to her husband's remorse had surprised even Jill. She hadn't shouted at him or accused him of breaking his promise by sleeping with Lisa. She hadn't stormed upstairs to pack her bags or cried or even been upset. She'd just sighed and uttered four words in a flat, tired voice. "Fine, Neil. Apology accepted."

He hadn't been willing to let it go at that. Perhaps he'd needed the usual fireworks, followed by recriminations and tears. But the whole evening had been a roller coaster of emotions, and Jill had been too drained to fall into the usual pattern. She'd just told Neil that they'd talk about it in the morning and had climbed up the stairs to bed.

The next morning, Neil had offered to call Lisa to tell her their affair was over for good. He'd even asked her to listen in on the extension so she'd know he was serious.

"I don't need to listen." Jill had headed for the kitchen to prepare breakfast. "Just do whatever you think is right."

She hadn't expected Neil to actually call, but he must have gone through with it. A week later, Norma had dropped by her office to ask what she'd said to Lisa.

"What do you mean?" Jill had been surprised. "I haven't seen Lisa since that night at the party, and I certainly haven't called her."

"Well, someone must have. She packed up and left her apartment two days ago. And she's having her transcript sent to the University of Oregon."

"Are you sure?" Jill had been suspicious. Neil had told her he'd broken off with Lisa before and he hadn't.

"I'm positive. I just got a note in my box this morning, asking for her records."

After Norma had left, Jill had found herself feeling strangely detached. She was glad Lisa was gone, but Lisa had been only a symptom of their marital problems, not the cause.

Jill looked up to see Doug approaching the booth. He slid in with a smile and Jill smiled back. "Hi. What's new with you?" she said.

"Rape, murder, and muggings. But that's not exactly new. How about you? Are you okay?"

"I'm fine." Jill realized that her heart was beating at a much faster than normal rate. She'd felt totally insulated the past few weeks, as if nothing could touch her. But the moment Doug had walked into the restaurant, a startling change had occurred. Suddenly, she felt alive again.

"Have you decided what you're going to do?"

Jill knew exactly what he was asking, and she winced

slightly. She'd always been reticent when it came to discussing personal problems, but Doug was her friend. He was also the only person she could confide in.

"Yes." Jill straightened her shoulders. She'd been thinking about her marriage for weeks, and she'd come to a conclusion. "Just as soon as Neil's eyesight tests normal, I'm going to divorce him. I can't think of one single reason for us to stay together."

"Okay. Have you ordered?"

"Not yet." Jill released a deep sigh of relief. Doug seemed to sense that she didn't want to talk about Neil, so he'd changed the subject. "I just asked for a pot of coffee and two cups. I'm not really hungry."

Doug began to frown. "You've lost weight, Jill. Are you getting the flu bug that's going around?"

"I don't think so. I don't feel sick. I'm just . . . not hungry."

"Not hungry is not good. If you don't eat, you'll get sick." Doug motioned for the waitress. "We'll have two specials with a large order of onion rings."

Jill was frowning slightly as the waitress hurried away. "But, Doug, I'm really not hungry."

"See here, lady." He put on his tough look. "If you don't cooperate, I'll just have to force-feed you chocolate Santas."

Jill laughed. "That's no threat. I love chocolate Santas. I just wish you could get them all year long."

"Me, too." Doug reached down to check his pager. Then he stood up. "Sorry, Jill. I've got to call in. I'll be right back."

As he headed toward the pay phone on the wall, Jill felt slightly guilty. The cell phone he'd given her was in her purse. She'd almost offered it to him, but then she'd remembered that she hadn't charged the batteries since he'd given it to her, and she hadn't wanted him to know she'd forgotten.

When the waitress arrived with their food, Jill reached out for a crispy onion ring. Suddenly, she was ravenous. When was the last time she'd eaten? She hadn't bothered with breakfast. She seldom ate in the mornings. And she'd passed up dinner last night. She'd worked through lunch yesterday. That meant she hadn't eaten for almost two days!

No wonder the onion rings tasted so good! Jill reached for another and popped it into her mouth. She followed it with three french fries and a big bite of the daily special, a hamburger covered with cheese and mushrooms.

"Atta girl!" Doug smiled as he slid back into his side of the booth. "I'm glad to see you're eating."

"I guess I just didn't realize I was hungry. This is a delicious burger."

He nodded. "They're good here. When was the last time you ate?"

"Uh . . . well . . . a couple of days ago, to be honest." Jill blushed. "Yesterday was hectic. I never eat breakfast, and I worked through lunch. By the time I got home, I was just too tired to eat."

"Have you had your annual checkup yet?"

She glanced up, startled by the question. Then she remembered that all city employees, including those on the police force and the district attorneys, were required to have an annual physical exam. "No. I haven't gotten around to making an appointment."

"I understand." Doug smiled at her. "You've had a lot on your mind."

"That's true, but I'm glad you reminded me. I'll arrange to have one the minute I get back to the office."

He nodded. "Good. Now have another bite of your burger. I don't want you to starve to death right in front of me."

"Don't worry, I won't. Not when food is this delicious. Do you think we could get a side order of pickles and slices of chocolate cake for dessert?"

"Sure. I can see you're making up for lost—" Doug stopped suddenly. "Jill? Your face is really white. Is something wrong?"

"Be back in a minute." She slid out of the booth as fast as she could and raced for the ladies' room. Perhaps it was thinking of pickles and chocolate cake, but she suddenly felt very sick.

Luckily, the ladies' room was deserted. Jill barged into one of the stalls. It was a good five minutes before she came out again, wiping her mouth with a tissue.

"Is everything okay?" Doug looked sympathetic when she returned to the booth.

"Yes. I guess I shouldn't have gobbled down all that food on an empty stomach."

He didn't say anything, but she knew exactly what he was thinking. "Okay, Doug. You don't have to remind me. I'll see the doctor tomorrow morning."

Shelly Devore had been very nice. Connie had said she was Charlotte West, a volunteer from the hospital, and Shelly's mother had invited her in. Shelly, still recuperating, had been in bed, but she'd seemed to be in good spirits. Connie had learned that she was a kindergarten teacher in her early thirties who could hardly wait to get back to the classroom. Alan's pancreas had found a good home, and Connie had been glad.

It had taken three weeks, but she had managed to locate Mark Turner. And now here she was, at The Palms Apartments, a pink stucco building without a palm in sight. Connie walked past the spa area, a glassed-in enclosure with a pool and a jacuzzi, and followed the signs to the office.

"Turner?" The woman in the office raised her eyebrows. She was an older lady with gray hair and glasses who identified herself as Mrs. Henley, the manager and rental agent. "Are you one of his girlfriends?"

Connie shook her head. "No. I've never met Mr. Turner before. My name is Cheryl Walton, and I'm doing a survey on transplant recipients. I just stopped by to see how Mr. Turner is feeling."

"I can tell you how he's feeling." Mrs. Henley winked at Connie. "Mark's feeling everything in sight . . . with a skirt."

Connie burst into laughter. "Then Mr. Turner's a . . . a ladies' man?"

"You could say that. He's also a real jock. He's a weight lifter, and he swims fifty laps in the pool every day. On weekends, every girl in the building watches him."

Connie smiled. This was good news. "He's recovered from his operation?"

"I guess! Let me tell you, that new kidney didn't slow him down for more than a week! His apartment is right next to mine, and I hear what goes on . . . not that I listen, of course. I can't really help it. It's the walls. They're very thin."

"I'm glad to hear he's doing well." Connie did her best to keep her composure, but she felt like shouting for joy. Mark Turner was in good physical shape, and he liked women. The more Mrs. Henley told her, the more he sounded like the perfect candidate. "Do you know if he's at home right now?"

Mrs. Henley shook her head. "He's working an early shift today. He'll be home by six, though. I've got an appointment to show his apartment at six-thirty."

"Then he's moving?" Connie's heart started to race. She had to find out where he was going.

"It's an intercomplex move. The woman in the two-bedroom right below him is leaving on the fifteenth. Mark's transferring to her place. He needs a second bedroom for all those girlfriends of his."

Connie laughed, but her mind was going a million miles a minute. "Is Mark's apartment for rent?"

"That's right. It's a one-bedroom, with a balcony facing the street. Are you interested?"

"Actually . . . I am." Connie gave the woman an innocent smile. "I'm living in a hotel right now, but I've been looking for an apartment in this area. Your building is one of the best."

"We like to think so." Mrs. Henley looked proud. "I can show you Mark's place right now if you want to see it."

On the way up the stairs, Connie learned that the rent for Mark's apartment was high but not outrageous. Mark had lived there for two years. He was an ideal tenant, with the exception of several loud parties.

Connie did her best to reassure Mrs. Henley. "I don't give parties. I'm very quiet. If I'm home in the evening, I read or watch television."

"No boyfriends?" Mrs. Henley looked slightly suspicious when Connie shook her head. "If you don't mind my asking, why not?"

"My fiancé died in a car accident, and I'm not ready to date anyone else yet."

"Oh, dear! That's too bad." Mrs. Henley looked very sympathetic. "Well, we do have quite a few single men. There's a young dentist and a CPA, and a couple of computer programmers. And then there's Mark. You might meet someone you like right here at The Palms."

Connie nodded. It was clear that Mrs. Henley was trying to play matchmaker. She didn't want to disappoint her. "I guess that's possible."

"Here it is." Mrs. Henley stopped and unlocked a door, motioning for Connie to follow her inside. "This is the living room. The kitchen is right through that arch."

Connie pretended to be impressed as Mrs. Henley showed her the built-in microwave and the special, water-saving head on the shower, but she almost lost it when they stepped into the bedroom and she caught sight of Mark's bed. It was a king-sized waterbed covered with red silk sheets. There were red candles on the bed tables, a faint scent of marijuana still lingered in the air, and the walls and ceiling were completely covered with mirrored glass.

"Quite a showplace, huh?" Mrs. Henley laughed at Connie's startled reaction. "If you don't want the mirrors, I can have them removed."

Connie nodded. "Good! I don't think I want to see my reflection first thing in the morning—especially on the ceiling."

"Then we'll take down the mirrors and repaint the walls. What color would you like?"

"Anything but green." Connie shuddered as she remembered the institutional-green walls in her bedroom at home and what had happened there, so long ago.

"We ask our new tenants to sign a three-month lease. After that, it's month to month. Will that be a problem for you?"

Connie shook her head. Then the full impact of what Mrs. Henley had said struck her. "You mean . . . I've got the apartment? Just like that?"

"Of course." Mrs. Henley nodded. "Mark will be out on the sixteenth. You'll have to give us a few days to repaint, but it'll be ready for you on the twentieth."

Connie was puzzled. "But don't you need references, bank statements, things like that?"

"That's not necessary." Mrs. Henley smiled at her. "I pride myself on being a good judge of character. I can tell you're not the type to cause any trouble. Just give me the first month's rent and a hundred-dollar damage deposit. That's fully refundable if the apartment passes inspection when you leave."

Connie smiled as she opened her purse and counted out

the money. Mrs. Henley thought she was a good judge of character. What would she think if she knew about Willy Rossini and how Connie had been forced to eliminate him from her list of candidates? And what would she say if she knew that Connie's reason for renting an apartment was to seduce Mark Turner?

CHAPTER 20

Jill had kept her promise to Doug, but she hadn't been able to get a doctor's appointment right away. Her family doctor had been on a three-week vacation, so the earliest appointment she'd been able to get was for the twentieth of February. Since this was the twentieth and her appointment was at one o'clock, she had slept late. She wasn't going to the office, and it felt like she was having a vacation.

Neil's conciliatory mood had passed. He'd already exchanged angry words with Sarah, the older woman Helen had hired. Sarah had stormed out in a huff, telling Jill she refused to work for a man who didn't respect her, and Jill had hired Neil's sixth companion, a pretty young farm wife named Bonnie.

There was a giggle from downstairs, and Jill began to frown. Neil was flirting with Bonnie. That meant she wouldn't last long, either. It was practically a given that he would try to get Bonnie into bed. Then one of two things would happen. Either Bonnie would refuse and Neil would fire her, or she would accept and her husband would find out and make her quit.

Jill ignored the giggles and took a quick shower. She'd already chosen the outfit she wanted to wear. She'd bought it last year at an after-Christmas sale, a hand-knit, pale pink sweater with wool slacks to match.

The sweater had been a little loose last year, but it seemed to fit her now. As a matter of fact, it was quite snug. Jill frowned slightly as she pulled on the slacks. They were so tight she had to struggle to zip them up.

It was silly to wear something uncomfortable. She hung the outfit back on its hanger and chose a blue sweater dress instead. That seemed to be much tighter, too, but the material stretched.

Jill sighed as she remembered that day in The Beef Barrel and how worried Doug had been when she'd told him she'd hadn't eaten for several days. He certainly didn't have to worry any longer. Jill's aversion to food had passed. She'd been snacking with a vengeance. She'd even stocked up on all the foods she knew she shouldn't eat like potato chips, Twinkies, and candy bars.

Her overeating could be a symptom of anxiety. She frowned as she considered it. There were days when she was hideously depressed at the thought of leaving Neil, other days when she could hardly wait to file for divorce. Her emotions seemed to change like the wind, whipping her from one extreme to the other. She'd get up in the morning feeling wonderful, invincible and on top of the world, but depression would set in on the way to work, and she'd end up weeping in the car.

She didn't think she was having a mental breakdown. Although she was sometimes distracted, she could still do her job. The DA and the opposing counsel had both complimented her on her last closing argument, and she'd won her last five cases.

Perhaps it was just a touch of the flu. Jill found herself almost looking forward to her physical. She was hoping that the doctor could diagnose her problem, write a prescription, and have her back to normal in a couple of days.

She went downstairs and slipped on her coat and boots. Bonnie and Neil were in the kitchen, but she didn't bother to go in to say good-bye. She'd told them earlier that she was leaving, and the way she felt right now, she could hardly wait to get out of the house.

Her spirits seemed to lift as she backed out of the garage and pulled out into the street. She felt better and better with each mile she drove, and by the time she pulled into the clinic parking lot, she was actually smiling. If this was a case of simple depression, she should definitely get out more. Going to work didn't count. It was something she *had* to do. She should make a point to do something she *wanted* to do, for the sheer fun of it, at least once a week.

"Hello." The receptionist, a friendly gray-haired woman who'd been working for Jill's doctor since he'd first opened his practice, greeted Jill with a smile.

Jill smiled back. "Hi, Delores. How are the grandkids?"

"Just fine, but they're not exactly kids anymore. The youngest just started college this year."

Jill knew she looked surprised. It seemed like just yesterday Delores had shown her baby pictures.

"You're looking good, Jill. Have you put on a little weight?"

"I'm afraid so. I couldn't get my favorite pair of slacks zipped up this morning." Jill knew she was blushing. She must have gained more than she'd thought if Delores had noticed.

"Well, you carry it well. These modern girls are too thin, all skin and bones. It's like my daddy used to say. What kind of man likes to hug a washboard?"

Jill laughed, but she wondered if anyone under sixty even remembered washboards. They'd become obsolete when automatic washers and dryers had come on the market.

"Come with me and I'll weigh you in." Delores picked

up a chart, then led Jill into one of the small examining rooms. "Take off your boots and hop up on the scale."

After pulling off her boots, Jill stepped on the scale. Then she watched, in shock, as Delores moved the metal weight to a spot near the end of the bar. "My God, Delores! I've gained fifteen pounds!"

"Sixteen, but who's counting?" Delores jotted down Jill's weight on her chart. "You're still not overweight, Jill . . . not for your height."

"Maybe not, but I think I'd better go on a diet before I have to buy a whole new wardrobe."

Delores gave her a sympathetic smile. "It'll be easier to diet, now that the holidays are over."

"I hope so."

"Take my word for it. I have to lose ten pounds every January. I just can't resist those Christmas cookies." Delores opened the closet and took a paper gown from the shelf. "Take off your clothes, Jill, and put on this gown. Doctor will be with you in just a few moments."

As Jill undressed and put on the paper gown, she was frowning. No wonder her slacks hadn't fit! She'd go on a diet immediately. There was no time like the present to get back in shape. The minute she got home from the doctor's office, she'd toss out all the chips and candy, and if she felt the need for a late-night snack, she'd eat healthy things like carrot sticks and celery.

Connie smiled as the movers carried in her couch. Since Alan's parents had taken all of the furniture, she had arranged to rent everything she needed, including bedding and dishes. It had been Alan's suggestion, and it made good sense. Connie knew she'd only be staying at The Palms long enough to accomplish her goal, and owning heavy pieces of furniture would present a problem when it was time to leave.

"Where do you want it, lady?"

"Right over there, under the windows." Connie smiled at the two movers. "Put the two round tables on either side with the blue glass lamps on top."

"Where do you want the TV?" Another mover brought in the console television that Connie had rented.

"I'm not sure, but the manager told me this building has cable. Do you see the jack?"

The mover nodded and pointed to the wall opposite the couch. "It's right over here. Do you want me to set it up for you?"

"That would be wonderful!" Connie gave him a smile. If he hooked it up, she'd have to tip him, but she'd been planning to do that anyway.

"How about the bed?"

The first two movers came back in with the bed frame and mattress, and Connie shrugged. "I don't know. Where do you think it should go?"

"As far away from the window as you can get it." The older mover grinned at her. "There's nothing worse than sun in your eyes when you want to sleep."

"That's true. You've set up a lot of places, haven't you?"

The older mover nodded. "Too many. I've been on this same job for fifteen years."

"Then you're the expert, not me. Just set it up the way you'd want it, and it'll be fine with me."

"Hey, lady." The older man gave her a thumbs-up signal. "If you want to get married, I'll ditch my wife for you. She makes me rearrange our furniture every couple of weeks."

It didn't take long to get everything in place. The older mover supervised, and the two younger men moved the furniture. When they were through, Connie gave the younger movers ten dollars apiece, and the older mover got a twenty.

After they'd left, she walked through the rooms, a smile on her face. The apartment looked like a furnished rental, but she didn't care. It was larger than the hotel room, and she didn't plan to spend many nights here. If she had her way, she'd be a frequent overnight guest in Mark Turner's apartment.

"Will you be all right alone here, Alan?" Connie addressed the picture she'd placed on the mantel. She listened for a moment, and then she smiled a soft smile. "I know. But I won't be sleeping with Mark Turner. I'll be sleeping with a part of you."

"Are you sure?" Jill felt faint, and she gripped the arms of the chair tightly.

"You tested positive, Jill." The doctor smiled at her. "Didn't you suspect you might be pregnant?"

She shook her head. "Not really. I've never been regular, and I just thought I had a touch of the flu."

"Well, this touch of the flu will be due in September. Congratulations."

"Thank you." Jill tried to look happy as she stood and picked up her purse. She was about to leave the room when the doctor called her back.

"Jill? Is this pregnancy a problem for you?"

"A problem?" She turned to look at him. There was no way she wanted her family doctor to know that her world had just turned upside down. "Of course not. I'm just surprised, that's all."

"Good. Make an appointment for next month. We'll do monthly checkups, and I'll write you a prescription for prenatal vitamins. You know the rest, don't you?"

Jill's mind went blank. "The what?"

"Get plenty of rest, exercise regularly, eat right, and be happy. That's the prescription for a healthy baby."

"Yes." Jill nodded. "I won't have to stop working, will I?"

"Of course not. You're young and healthy, and I don't

anticipate any problems. Just don't overdo it. Keep a regular schedule and make sure you don't wear yourself out."

Jill kept a smile on her face as she picked up her prescription and accepted Delores' congratulations, but her smile disappeared and her emotional state bordered on panic when she got into her car. How could she be pregnant? She hadn't slept with Neil since . . .

"Our anniversary!" Jill groaned as she remembered that night. She'd been so surprised by the catered dinner and the gift Neil had given her she'd forgotten to use her diaphragm. Now she was pregnant, at the worst possible time. The last thing she needed right now was the added responsibility of a baby!

She started the car and pulled out of the lot. What was she going to do? She believed in a woman's right to choose, but she didn't want an abortion. This was her baby; she couldn't bear the thought of losing it. It was a part of her. But it was also a part of Neil. Did she have the right to leave him now, when she was pregnant with their child?

A horn honked behind her, and Jill realized that she had stopped at a green light. The winter streets were icy; she had to concentrate on her driving. As she pulled forward and turned onto the ramp that led to the freeway, she shivered slightly. She didn't want to stay with Neil, but was it right to divorce him now and deprive him of the chance to be a full-time father to his child? And how about their baby? Was it fair to raise a child without a father?

Jill sighed. It was a real dilemma. She knew that children from broken homes had problems. She encountered them almost daily in court. But children whose parents stayed together and fought constantly also developed problems. Which way was best? Could anyone say for certain?

The truck she was following swerved slightly, and Jill dropped back another car length. The Department of Motor Vehicles put out a traffic safely manual, and she had read the rule for following other vehicles. Drivers were advised to drop back one car length for every ten miles of speed. Since Jill was doing fifty miles an hour, she should be five car lengths behind the truck. There was only one problem with this rule. She'd found that if she dropped back five car lengths, at least four other cars attempted to squeeze into the space ahead of her.

Life was complicated when people refused to follow the rules. Jill sighed and moved over to the slow lane where the traffic was lighter. If Neil had followed the rules, he'd be a faithful husband and if that were the case, she'd be delighted about the baby.

But was Neil the only one who'd broken the rules? Jill frowned deeply as she thought about it. There were rules for wives, too. A wife was expected to love her husband, but she didn't love Neil. Though she hadn't been unfaithful to him in the strictest sense of the word, she'd given her heart to another man. Could anything get more complicated than this? Here she was, pregnant with her husband's baby, and she was in love with Doug Lake.

CHAPTER 21

Connie turned around slowly, in front of Alan's picture. She'd made another purchase, a black satin bikini that was so tiny she almost felt she'd gone back to her job as a stripper.

"How do I look, honey?" She listened for a moment, and then she giggled. "Really? I just hope Mark Turner agrees with you!"

It was always nice to receive a compliment, especially when it came from the man she loved. Connie rushed over to press her lips against Alan's picture. The glass was warm against her lips, as if a living, breathing person stood just on the other side of it. She replaced the picture and picked up a white cotton robe to wear to the pool. "I'll be back later, Alan. And if I'm not, you'll know exactly where I am."

She turned at the door and looked back once more, blowing Alan's picture a kiss. He seemed to be frowning slightly, and she raced back to see what was wrong.

"What is it, honey?" Connie picked up the picture and stared into his eyes. Then she nodded, the smile returning to her face. "Thanks for reminding me. I'd almost forgotten I used a fake name on the lease. It's Cheryl, not Connie. I'll remember."

The hallway was deserted as Connie walked toward the

elevator. Mrs. Henley had been right. This was a quiet building, especially during the day when most people worked. The pool would be deserted, too, and it was a perfect setting for meeting Mark Turner.

Connie pushed open the double, glass doors and entered the pool area. It was in the center of the building, patterned after a Spanish courtyard, completely enclosed by stucco walls. The domed glass roof let in the sun, so the area was always warm. Made of thermal glass, the dome effectively shut out the cold air.

Just as she'd expected, the pool was deserted. Connie took off her robe and stretched out on one of the lounge chairs arranged around the pool. Mrs. Henley had told her that Mark was a bartender who worked the night shift at the Odyssey Club, an expensive bar and restaurant at the top of the Marquette Hotel. He usually came home at three or four in the morning, slept until noon, and swam laps in the pool when he woke up. On some mornings, a girlfriend accompanied him to the pool, but usually his lady friends left long before noon.

Connie glanced at her watch. It was noon now. Mark should be here at any minute. He'd probably be surprised to see her. No one used the pool on weekdays. If he seemed interested in talking to her, she'd give him the same story she'd given Mrs. Henley. Her name was Cheryl Walton, and she did freelance work for a research company. One of her clients was an insurance company who was interested in the survival rates for transplant recipients. She'd only come to The Palms Apartments to interview him for her survey, but she'd liked the place so much, she'd decided to move in.

The glass doors opened, and a man walked in. Connie felt her heart race as she watched him approach. He moved like an athlete, his muscles rippling in the sunlight. His physique was perfect, that of a modern Adonis, and he was so handsome he could have been a superstar.

Connie stared as he stopped at the end of the pool and stretched. No wonder the girls in the apartment complex turned out to watch him swim on the weekends. He still hadn't seen her and she held her breath. Her heart was racing, she suddenly felt weak, and on top of all that, she experienced a twinge of guilt. When she'd decided to have Alan's baby, she'd never anticipated that one of the transplant recipients might actually turn her on.

Mark spotted her lounging on the chair, and he gave a friendly wave. Connie waved back, but tried not to look too eager as he walked toward her.

"Hi." Mark smiled, showing perfectly white, evenly spaced teeth. "I haven't seen you before."

Connie assumed the sexy look she'd used when she was stripping. "I just moved in today. I'm in apartment two twenty-three."

"That's my old place!"

"I know. Mrs. Henley told me." She did her best to stay calm. She hadn't reacted to a man this strongly since she'd met Alan.

"Hey . . ." He started to grin. "Did you leave up the mirrors in the bedroom?"

Connie laughed. "I'm afraid not. I think you lead a much more interesting life than I do."

"Oh?" Mark raised his eyebrows. "Do I detect a note of envy in your voice?"

Connie shrugged and leaned forward a little so he could see her cleavage. "Maybe. I'm new in town, and I don't know many people. It gets lonesome, all by myself."

"I could fix that." Mark looked interested. "What kind of people do you want to meet?"

"Fun people. People like your friends, the kind that spent time in your mirrored bedroom. I'm not into girls, but guys like you . . . that's another story."

"Guys like me, huh?" Mark's eyes traveled up and down

her body. "What's your name? And what are you doing tonight?"

"I'm Cheryl Walton, and I'm doing the same thing I do every night—reading, watching television, being bored."

"What do you say we go out? I know a couple of hot clubs."

"That sounds like fun, but I don't think anyplace could be as hot as your old bedroom." Connie licked her lips suggestively. "Those mirrors definitely gave me ideas."

Mark's eyes began to gleam. "I've got mirrors in my new place. Do you want to check them out?"

"I'd love to. When?"

He held out his hand. "How about right now? I've got a couple of hours before I have to go to work."

Connie was smiling as she took his hand and let him pull her up. She looked into his eyes, saw that he was just as eager as she was, then gave a sexy giggle. "A couple of hours. If you feel the way I feel, I'm not sure that'll be enough time."

"You're kidding!" Neil looked so shocked Jill would have laughed if the situation hadn't been so tense. "But . . . when did it happen?"

"On our anniversary. The baby's due in September."

"Jill. That's . . . great!" He hugged her. "I mean . . . it is, isn't it?"

Jill sighed as she hugged him back. "The timing could have been a lot better, but I guess we'll just have to deal with it. Do you want me to stay, Neil?"

"Stay?" He looked shocked. "Of course I want you to stay! You're my wife!"

"Sometimes I think you have trouble remembering that." Jill frowned slightly. "I'll stay. It's the right thing to do, under the circumstances. But we both have to try harder to make our marriage work."

Neil hugged her a little more tightly. "Jill . . . honey . . . I'll do anything, I promise. You know I love you, don't you?"

"I know." Jill nodded. "But you've loved other women, too. I want that to stop, Neil. I won't stay if it doesn't."

"But how about the baby? You wouldn't leave with the baby, would you?"

"I wouldn't want to." She was doing her best to be very honest. "I want our baby to have two loving parents, but I don't think I can stand watching you have another affair."

Neil shook his head. "Jill . . . I won't! I promise you I won't even look at another woman. I love you, and you don't know what this baby means to me. I've always wanted a son."

"It could be a daughter. It's too early to tell."

"A daughter's good, too. A little girl who looks just like you would be perfect. Boy or girl, it doesn't make any difference. My God! Wait until my brother hears about this! A new baby. They'll be almost as excited as I am!"

Jill stared at Neil in astonishment. He really did seem to be excited. Sometimes children brought a family together. Could it be happening with them?

"I promise I'll be a good father, Jill. And I'll be a good husband, too. Just give me a chance to prove it to you. Let's start over, from the beginning. I know we can make it work."

Jill nodded. Neil looked very serious, and he was trembling slightly as he held her, overcome with emotion. "Okay. I'm willing to put the past behind us and start over."

"Thank you, honey." Neil kissed her cheek. "Now what about the nursery? Should we paint it pink or blue, or maybe a shade of yellow?"

Jill laughed. Neil's excitement was contagious. "We have

to decide where the nursery is to be first. Should we use the guest bedroom at the end of the hall?"

"We could, I guess . . . But how about my office? It's right next to our bedroom, and it'd be more convenient for you. I'll move my office to a smaller room. I don't need all that space anyway."

Jill shook her head. "You don't have to do that. We could put in a connecting door. The other guest room is right next to ours, and it's certainly large enough for a child's room."

"Are you sure? I really wouldn't mind moving."

Jill smiled at him. She was pleased that Neil had offered to give up the office he liked so much. "You don't have to move, honey. I'll call a carpenter tomorrow and ask him about a connecting door."

"You don't have to do that. I'll call. I'll take care of it." Neil sounded a little wistful. "I always wanted to learn how to fix things around the house, but my eyesight isn't good enough yet."

Jill nodded, although that was a total surprise to her. He had never mentioned wanting to be a handyman.

"I'll find somebody who can start right away. We have to put in the door, paint the nursery, and get some furniture for the baby. How do you feel about putting in an intercom system?"

"An intercom?" Jill was puzzled.

"You know, the kind with a receiver in the baby's room. I'll make some calls and check on it tomorrow. Maybe we'll have the house rewired and put a speaker in every room. Then you wouldn't have to climb the stairs to my office every time you wanted to talk to me."

"That would be nice." Jill felt warm inside. Finding out that he was going to be a father had really changed Neil. "What do you want for dinner, honey? It's getting late and you must be hungry."

"Why don't you let me take you out tonight? We should celebrate. I want to show off my beautiful pregnant wife."

"You do?" Jill's spirits rose. Neil hadn't wanted to go out to eat since his operation, and she'd missed doing it. "Where would you like to go?"

"Monty's would be good. You always liked their prime rib. Are you supposed to be careful about eating red meat?"

"I don't think so." Jill shook her head. "The doctor just said to eat a balanced diet. I can't drink more than one glass of wine though."

"Monty's has premium wines by the glass, so that's no problem. I don't want you driving. We'll take a cab."

"I can drive." Jill came close to laughing out loud. He was being so solicitous she felt like a priceless porcelain doll. "Really, Neil, the doctor says I can carry on with my regular schedule. I'm not sick. I'm just having a baby."

He didn't look convinced, but he nodded. "Okay. Do you want to rest up a little before we go? Monty's is open until eleven."

"I don't need to rest. The only thing I want to do is change out of this dress. I noticed it was a little tight when I put it on this morning."

Neil began to grin. "I'll have to get you some maternity clothes. The new companion can help with that. I'll have her drive me out to the mall tomorrow."

"You're going to buy maternity clothes?" Jill couldn't help feeling shocked. Neil had always claimed that shopping for clothing was boring.

"It'll be fun to shop for you. You don't mind, do you, Jill?"

She shook her head. "No. I don't. But . . . are you sure you want to go to all that trouble?"

"I'm sure." Neil hugged her again. "Just write out a list of your sizes. I want to help you, Jill. You work hard, and I know you don't have much free time."

Jill was smiling as she went up the stairs to put on another dress. Talk about a changed man! In the past, Neil had been filled with resentment when she'd asked him to run a simple errand for her, like picking up the cleaning or returning a videotape they'd rented. Now he couldn't seem to find enough things to do for her.

In less than ten minutes, she was dressed in a green wool suit. The skirt had a stretch waistband, and it was still large enough to be comfortable.

"Do you need any help, honey?"

At the base of the stairs, Neil sounded worried. He really was overly concerned about her, but it was a welcome change from his former indifference.

"I'm almost ready." Jill called out to him. "I'll be down in just a minute."

When she came out of the bedroom, she found him waiting on the top step of the staircase. He looked worried, and she frowned slightly ."What's the matter?"

"I'm wondering about these stairs. I'm going to tell the carpenter to put a railing on the other side, too."

"Why?" Jill was puzzled.

"Just in case. You could lose the baby if you fell down them."

"I'm not going to fall down the stairs." Jill smiled at him.

"Maybe not, but you'd better let me help you."

Jill took his arm and let him lead her down. She liked the way they'd reversed roles. She'd been concerned about him when he'd begun to lose his eyesight, and she'd helped him down the stairs. Now that she was pregnant and his eyesight was improving, he was helping her. Perhaps having this baby right now wasn't bad timing after all.

"Do you want to try something new?"

Connie nodded. She didn't have the energy to speak.

They were stretched out on Mark's satin sheets, and she felt gloriously exhausted.

"Spread your legs and close your eyes. I'm going to give you a big surprise."

"You mean . . . now?" Connie raised her eyebrows. They'd just finished making love twice. "I thought you had to go to work."

"I called in and told them my car wouldn't start. The afternoon guy's taking half my shift."

Connie started to grin. As she glanced at his athletic body, her eyes widened in appreciation. Mark had the stamina of a teenager, and recalling the wild things they'd done gave her a new burst of energy. "How long do we have?"

"Another three hours. And I know just how to spend it."

"You do?" Connie started to grin. Mark was insatiable, and that was just fine with her. Each time they made love was a chance for her to get pregnant.

"You're a beautiful woman, you know? And you're very, very sexy."

"Thank you, Mark." Connie managed to hide her grin. He was doing his best to sound sincere. It was obvious that his other girlfriends expected compliments and reassurances in bed. Connie didn't need that sort of thing, but she couldn't tell him that. It might turn him off if he knew the reason she'd become his newest sexual partner.

As he rolled over to hug her, Connie let her fingertips touch the scar from his operation. It wasn't a large scar, and it was fading, but just being this close to a part of Alan made her shiver in delight.

"I'm ready, Mark," Connie whispered in his ear. "Let's do it again, any way you want."

"Any way?"

Connie almost changed her mind when she saw the interest on Mark's face, but she reminded herself of why she was here in his bed. "Any way, just as long as it doesn't involve pain. I'm not into pain."

"Okay. No pain." Mark grinned at her. "Close your eyes, babe. You're gonna love this."

Connie shut her eyes, but she opened them again when she felt something slip around her ankle. "What are you doing?"

"It's silk." Mark reached out to thumb her nipple. "Don't worry, babe. It'll be fun."

"You're sure?" Connie shivered, but it wasn't from pleasure. Mrs. Henley had seemed to think Mark was a decent guy, but how much did the apartment manager know about his personal life?

"Hey . . . relax, babe. I guarantee you're gonna love this."

"I'm going to love what?" Connie kept her voice light and teasing, but she was beginning to be a bit nervous. She wanted to know what Mark had in mind.

"A little light bondage, that's all. Silk scarves around your ankles. I'll leave your arms free. Come on, babe . . . If you don't like it, I'll stop."

Connie thought about it for a moment, and then she nodded. If her arms were free, how dangerous could it be?

"Pretty lady." Mark's voice was trembling with excitement as he tied one scarf to something under the bed. "Give me your other leg, babe. This is going to be fantastic."

"Connie let him tie the scarf around her other ankle and secure it to the bed, but she didn't like this one bit.

It'll be all right. He can't hurt me. He's got a part of Alan in his body, and Alan won't let him hurt me.

CHAPTER 22

Usually a hot shower helped, but this morning it had no effect. Connie groaned as she toweled off and put on a pair of warm-up pants and a matching sweatshirt. She was too sore to wear a bra. Mark had been in one of his rough moods last night, so it was only a matter of time before the bruises would start to appear.

Was it worth it? She frowned as she considered the wisdom of her involvement with Mark. Two months ago, when she'd first gone to his apartment, he'd been kinky but not violent. Lately, the violence had been escalating and so had the bondage. With Connie as his willing partner, Mark had graduated from silk scarves to whips and leather restraints. Connie knew his appetites could lead to something dangerous, particularly since he'd admitted to using several types of recreational drugs. How long would she have to risk her safety?

Alan's picture seemed to be frowning, and Connie walked over to pat the glass. "Don't worry, honey. I won't have to do it much longer, just until I get pregnant with our baby. And I'll be very careful, I promise."

But how could she be? Mark had been holding back on her lately, not giving her what she needed until she'd submitted to his kinky demands. There was no way to protect herself when she was strapped to the bed, no way she could stop him if he decided to strangle her—or smother her or cut her open with a knife.

"What was that, honey?" Connie picked up Alan's picture and held it close to her ear. His voice had once been very clear, but now it was growing fainter with each passing day. "Say it again, Alan. I didn't quite hear you."

Connie listened for a moment, and then she began to smile. "You're right, Alan! It's been over a month since I checked. I'd better look at the calendar."

There was a small calendar by the bed, and she counted off the days. Alan was right. She was three days late and her breasts were tender, the way they'd been the last time she'd been pregnant. Her clothes seemed a bit tighter, too. She'd assumed that the waistband on her jeans had shrunk when she'd washed them, but perhaps there was another reason shy she'd had difficulty zipping them up.

"It's possible, Alan!" Connie's voice quivered with excitement. "And if I'm pregnant, I'll never have to sleep with that bastard again!"

She said a little prayer as she hurried to the bathroom medicine cabinet to get the pregnancy tests she'd bought. She hadn't been sure which one was best, so she'd purchased three different types. If she got a positive reading from one of them, they'd move out of the complex tonight. It would be a relief to get away from Mark Turner and his preoccupation with kinky and dangerous sex.

Jill glanced at the clock. It was ten minutes past one. No wonder her stomach was growling. Unfortunately, she was working through lunch, and she hadn't had time to pack a sandwich this morning. She'd been too busy, questioning Neil.

Bonnie had given notice that morning. She'd lasted much longer than Jill had anticipated, over two full months. A record. She'd told Jill that her husband didn't want her to work, but Jill had known that was just an excuse.

When she'd spoken to Neil, he'd sworn that he hadn't touched Bonnie. Jill wanted to believe him, but she had her suspicions. Bonnie hadn't been able to meet Jill's eyes; she'd been the very picture of guilt. Perhaps she hadn't actually slept with Neil, but something had happened to upset her enough to cause her to give notice.

Jill sighed. There was no use speculating about what had happened. Bonnie wouldn't tell her, and Neil wasn't about to admit to any wrongdoing. Even if he had slipped and made a pass at Bonnie, Jill had to admit that her marriage was still a lot better than it had been. Neil was doing his best to be considerate. He tried to help her around the house, and he kept his temper firmly in check. Jill hadn't been the target of his sarcasm since she'd told him about the baby, and best of all, his excitement about becoming a father hadn't faded since the day she'd told him she was pregnant.

On the drive to work that morning, Jill had faced facts. Her marriage wasn't perfect, but it was working and she was determined to stick with it. She'd also accepted the truth about her husband. Neil loved her, she was convinced of that, but he'd always have problems with being faithful. It was often said that marriage was a series of compromises, and Jill was doing her best to compromise on the issue that meant the most to her, fidelity.

"Hey, Jill. You're looking good. And I really like that dress."

Jill looked up and smiled as Doug poked his head in her office doorway. Although she was only four months pregnant, her waistline had expanded to the point where only a few outfits from her regular wardrobe fit her properly. Today she was wearing a royal blue maternity suit that Neil had picked out at the mall. "Thanks. What are you doing down here?"

"Just dropping off some paperwork. Did you eat lunch yet?"

Jill shook her head. "I've got a doctor's appointment at three so I'm working though lunch. I'll pick up a sandwich on the way there."

"That's exactly what I was afraid of. You said your doctor told you to eat regular meals. How about this morning? I'll bet you didn't have breakfast, either."

Jill winced. "You're right, but I didn't have time. I got a late start this morning."

"So all you've had is coffee?"

"Guilty as charged." Jill sighed. "But the coffee was decaffeinated. That should count for something."

Doug began to frown. "It's a good thing you have me. Somebody's got to make sure you eat right. Clear off your desk and prepare to chow down."

"Chow down on what?" Jill smiled as Doug held up a large white bag, and she hurried to shove her papers to one side.

"It's a chicken and broccoli pasta salad." He plunked the bag on the center of her desk top. "If I know you, you're probably not eating your vegetables."

Jill nodded. "You're right. Thank you, Doug. It was sweet of you to bring me lunch."

"I brought enough for me, too." He took two Tupperware bowls out of the bag and popped off the tops. Then he handed Jill a fork and sat down on the chair in front of her desk. "I'm joining you. It's the only way I can make sure you eat some of that broccoli."

"Yes, Officer." Jill's eyes widened as she saw the huge

portion of salad. She would have been intimidated by the sheer volume of food if it hadn't looked so delicious.

"Go ahead. Start eating." Doug waited until she had taken her first bite. "Do you like it?"

"It's great! Honey-Dijon dressing is my favorite."

"I know. You ordered it on your salad the last time we went out to lunch. How about the broccoli?"

Jill speared a piece and popped it into her mouth. "It's tender, but it's not overcooked."

"The pasta?"

Jill ate a piece and a wedge of chicken. "Very good! The pasta still has some texture. It's cooked just right. And the chicken really tastes fresh."

Doug nodded. "I'm glad you like it. It's got something from every food group. That's supposed to make it nutritious."

"It's not only good, it's good for you, too?" Jill grinned as Doug nodded. "I could eat this for lunch every day. Where did you buy it?"

"I didn't. I made it."

"You made it?" Jill raised her eyebrows. "I had no idea you were such a good cook. But you took a real chance, Doug. What if I'd gone out for lunch?"

"I checked with your secretary, and she said you were working through lunch. That's not right, Jill. It's not good for the baby if you skip meals."

"You're right. I won't do it again." Jill nodded solemnly. Then she said the first thing that came to her mine. "You're taking such good care of me, you'd think *you* were the father of my baby!"

"I wish! I really love kids, Jill." Doug grinned, and she dropped her eyes. She was glad he didn't know what she was thinking. If she were married to Doug, life would be a lot different. He'd be a good husband and father, and she was

willing to bet she wouldn't have to compromise to make
their marriage work.

There was no plus sign! Connie stared down at the test
strip in disbelief, but the minus didn't change to a plus.
She'd been so sure. Still, this was the third home pregnancy
test she'd tried, and all three had come out negative.

"Damn!" Connie was frowning as she dropped the
package into the bathroom wastebasket to join the circle
that hadn't changed to pink and the liquid that had refused
to turn blue. There was no baby, not this month. And God
knew it wasn't for lack of trying!

She scowled as she picked up the trash bag and carried
it to the door. She'd throw it down the incinerator. That
would make her feel better. It was just a pity she couldn't
throw Mark Turner down there, too. He deserved it, but she
still needed him to give her Alan's baby.

"What was that, Alan?" Connie dropped the trash bag
and hurried to Alan's picture. He was frowning, and that
meant something was wrong. She leaned close, listened to
what he had to say, then shook her head. "No. Mark doesn't
use any kind of birth control."

Alan was still talking as Connie carried his picture to the
couch, where they could sit down. "I know he doesn't,
honey. I watch him."

Connie leaned back against the couch cushions, wishing
she could remember how Alan's arms had felt around her
shoulders. She held his picture up to her ear again, concentrated on making out the words he was saying.

"That's true. I know about the shot and the implant. But
I don't think he's the type to . . ."

Alan was talking again and Connie listened carefully.
"That's a good idea. I'll think of a way to ask him. And

you're right. We don't want to waste our time on him if he can't give us our baby."

When the doorbell rang, Connie placed Alan's picture on the coffee table. A change of scene would be good for him. She usually kept him on the mantel during the day, and he spent all night on her bed table.

"Hi, Mark!" she forced a smile as she opened the door. "What's up?"

"I just got the word. There's a party tonight!"

"What kind of party?" Connie's smile turned genuine. If they went to a party, she wouldn't have to spend all night in Mark's bed. When they got back to his apartment, he might be too tired to do anything except make love to her the normal way.

"It's that group I was telling you about. It'll be wild, babe, and I think you're ready to party with them. You'll have the experience of a lifetime."

"Oh, *that* kind of party." Connie began to frown. Mark had been telling her about the crazy parties his friends threw, and she really didn't want to go. "I don't know. I'm not really sure . . ."

"Come on, babe. You've got to learn to live a little! It'll be fun."

"I'd love to go." Connie did her best to sound enthusiastic. This was a perfect chance to ask him about birth control. "But the timing's all wrong for me. I forgot to take my birth-control pill yesterday morning, and I wouldn't want to get pregnant."

He laughed. "You don't have to worry about that. All the guys in my group take precautions. No one wants a kid to slow him down."

"But you don't, do you?" Connie held her breath as she asked the question. "I mean . . . you've never used anything with me."

"I don't have to. I've got built-in birth control. I had a vasectomy three years ago."

"You . . . had a vasectomy?" Connie clenched her hands tightly at her sides. "Why didn't you tell me?!"

"Because you never asked. Come on, babe. It's perfectly safe. What do you say I pick you up at eight?"

Connie's mind spun in circles. She wanted to kill the kinky bastard for leading her on, but she couldn't let him know how she felt. She had to stall him so she could talk to Alan. He'd know what to do.

"I made some plans, but I could cancel." Connie gave him an eager smile. "Let me make a few calls, and I'll let you know in less than an hour."

Mark grinned at her, then tipped her face up for a kiss. "Okay, babe. Come down to my place the minute you know. And try real hard to cancel your plans. This party's going to be the best one yet!"

"Yes. I'm sure it will be." Connie's smile disappeared the moment she'd closed the door behind him. He was a bastard, and now that she knew he couldn't give her Alan's baby, she had no further use for him.

She sat down on the couch and picked up Alan's picture again. "You heard him. He doesn't deserve to have your kidney. What do you want me to do?"

This time Alan's voice was much clearer. He was every bit as angry as she was. They discussed it for a moment, but it didn't take long to make their plans. Connie would go to the party but she'd arrive late, after everyone was too stoned to remember her. The party was the perfect place to steal Alan's gift of life from Mark Turner.

CHAPTER 23

"An ex-hooker, huh?" Mark grinned at the phone as his buddy told him about the woman he was bringing to the party. "Come on, Jerry. There's no way she can do all that!"

But Jerry went right on talking, swearing that everything he said was the gospel truth. "Okay, Jerry. If she's half as good as you say, I want first crack at her."

Mark began to frown as they negotiated. Jerry was willing to let him have the ex-hooker first, but he wanted first crack at Mark's date. That might just present a problem. Jerry was a little rough around the edges, and it took an experienced woman to handle him.

"That'd be okay with me, Jerry." Mark tried to be tactful. "But I don't know how she'll feel about it. She's never been to one of our parties before, and I thought we'd break her in easy."

When Jerry started to argue, Mark's frown deepened. Jerry had a hair-trigger temper, and he didn't want to get the big guy mad.

"Okay. You can have her. But you've got to promise to give her a couple lines of coke before you take her back to the playroom. A drink couldn't hurt, either. Get her bombed and she'll loosen right up. And no rough stuff, huh? You don't want her to go off screaming to the cops."

Jerry seemed willing to listen to reason, and Mark was relieved. "Sure, she's coming. I wouldn't shit you, man. She's gonna be late, but I gave her the address and she said she'd be there before ten."

Mark was grinning as he hung up. His friends were eager to meet his newest discovery, and he'd promised to share her. She might not like it at first. Some of his buddies were into some pretty weird stuff, but Jerry had promised to get her bombed out of her mind. By the time the party was in full swing, she'd be ready for anything anyone suggested.

Mark popped the top on a cold brew and stretched out on the couch to watch the sports channel. They were showing a figure-skating competition, and that really wasn't his thing. The guys looked gay, and the women were skinny, with no tits. Some of the positions they got into were interesting though; Mark wondered how it would be to screw a woman who could bend over backward until her hair touched the ice. Maybe he ought to try to pick up a figure skater. She might have some special talents that would come in handy at one of their parties.

There was a knock on the door, and he got up to answer it. She'd told him she'd drop by to pick up the address before she left for her job interview. He handed over the slip of paper, told her he'd be waiting for her at the party, and closed the door, frowning. It was always risky, sleeping with someone who lived in the same apartment complex, especially because she had his key. If she got mad at him for loaning her out at the party, she might try to get even with him by trashing his place. He'd have the locks changed tomorrow and conveniently forget to give her the new key.

She wouldn't go to the cops. Mark was sure of that. And if she threatened to turn him in for gang rape or some other trumped-up charge, he'd just show her the tape he'd made of her and that would keep her quiet.

Just thinking about the tape made Mark smile. She hadn't suspected he had a hidden video camera in the closet. Women never did. They were much too willing to trust the guy that was banging them. He'd recorded their last session, and it was the best tape he'd ever made. All he had to do was show her a copy and she'd do whatever he wanted.

Pregnancy definitely had its benefits. Neil grinned as he rolled over and hugged Jill. She probably would have left him over that incident with Lisa, but she'd convinced herself it wasn't right to deprive him of fatherhood. He was happy about the baby. It was another tie that would bind Jill to him. And he really hadn't meant to get it on with Bonnie. She was the one who'd come into his room and surprised him when he'd been dressing.

Bonnie had been good, a little on the dull side, but good nonetheless. Some women were better than others, but he'd never met one who'd been bad. It was a shame Bonnie had suffered an attack of the guilts. They could have gone on for several more weeks. A little love in the afternoon was the ticket to fight off his depression.

Of course there was always Jill. Neil reached out to fondle her breast. She was filling out now, getting the kind of figure that really turned him on.

"Honey? Are you sleeping?" He massaged the back of her neck, just where she liked it the most. They'd gone to bed ridiculously early because she'd told him she was tired.

"No, I'm awake."

Her voice was breathless, and Neil felt a rush of power. Although it wasn't as exciting as exploring new territories, there was an advantage in knowing precisely what turned her on. "What did the doctor say about making love? It's all right, isn't it?"

"It's fine." Jill snuggled a little closer, rubbing her body against his. "We only have to be careful the last couple of weeks."

"And you're not too tired?" He congratulated himself for being so considerate. Except for the error in judgment he'd made with Bonnie, he'd been a model husband.

"I'm not too tired."

Jill rolled over, granting him better access to the part of her he wanted most, and Neil stroked her lightly with his fingers. It didn't take more than a minute or two before she made the little purring noise that told him she was ready.

"You'd better get on top." Neil moved her gently so that she was straddling him. "I don't want to hurt you."

To his surprise, she accepted his excuse without protest. That was something new. She'd always preferred having him on top. As she started to move her hips and ride him, Neil gave a groan of pleasure. They said you couldn't teach an old dog new tricks, but Jill was trying so hard to make their marriage work, she might just be successful.

Doug bought the woman another drink, but his heart wasn't in it. Why hadn't he told Jill that he loved her on Christmas Eve? If he'd admitted his true feelings and asked her to leave Neil for him, she might have been with him tonight. But he hadn't thought it fair to take advantage of her when she was so vulnerable, and now he was alone and she was still with her husband.

It was all his grandmother's fault for raising him to be a gentleman. Doug frowned as he took another sip of his drink.

"I love this place." The woman smiled at him. "Everybody here is in the same line of work."

Doug nodded. She was pretty, with short blond hair and a trim figure. "So you like cop bars?"

"They're comfortable. I used to go to regular bars, but the guys would freak when I told them I was a cop."

"I guess that's understandable." Doug tried to think of something to say. He'd forgotten her name. It was Trixie, or Trisha, or something like that, and she'd already told him twice. "I haven't seen you around before. Where do you work?"

"Anyplace they need me. I'm with the school police."

"The school police?" Doug was surprised. "That's a new one for me. I've never heard of the school police."

"Most people haven't. We're a branch of the MPD, but we've got our own station. You've probably seen our cars. They're maroon and white, just like the highway patrol, but they don't have the state symbol on the door."

Doug began to get interested. "So you're like a truant officer?"

"That and a lot of other things. We have full arrest powers on any campus. We can bust drug dealers and vandals, anybody who breaks the law. The only thing we can't do is off-campus pursuit. That's when we have to call you."

Doug nodded. "It sounds like an interesting job."

"Not really." She shrugged. "Most of the time we just provide a presence so the kids won't act up. The only bust I made this month was a ten-year-old tagger, and he was released to his mother's custody. How about you? Have you solved any interesting cases?"

"Not lately." Doug managed to hide his surprise. He must have told her he was a detective.

"Let's not talk about work." She reached out to take his hand. "Let's talk about you and me, and what we're going to do tonight."

This time Doug couldn't hide his surprise. He blinked

and stared at the hand on his. "Uh . . . okay. What do you think we should do?"

"We should go to your place and light a fire. And then we should take off our clothes and see what comes up . . . Unless you're married. You're not married, are you?"

"Uh . . . no. I'm not." Doug stared at her. She seemed serious, and she was very attractive. What was wrong with him? A year ago, he would have jumped at the chance. Now he felt like turning her down and walking out the door.

"Don't tell me. Let me guess." She looked disappointed at his lack of response. "I picked the wrong guy. You're gay?"

Doug shook his head. "No, I'm not. I just can't take you to my place, that's all."

"Then you're living with someone?"

"No." Doug shook his head again. "And don't get me wrong. You're very attractive. But I'm just not looking for someone right now."

She sighed and managed a smile. "Okay. I guess it's true. All the best ones are taken."

"Here. Have another drink on me." Doug left some bills on the bar and slid off his stool. As he buttoned his jacket and went out the door, he realized that she was right. All the best ones were taken. Jill was married, and he wished to hell that he were Neil!

Connie could hear the party three houses away. The windows were closed, but the laughter and the loud music seemed to seep out through the walls. She'd parked around the corner, in front of a house that was up for sale. The windows were dark, and there was no furniture inside. The owners had already moved. That meant there would be no one to give a description of her or her car.

She looked very different tonight. Her hair was tucked up under a brunette wig, and she was wearing tortoise-shell glasses. Her clothing was casual, a pair of jeans and a dark sweater, which she planned to throw out the moment she returned to her apartment. She was carrying a canvas tote bag with several items inside. A change of clothes, a towel in a garbage bag, and Willy Rossini's Swiss Army Knife.

The front door was locked, and Connie didn't ring the bell. She walked around the house, stepping over the patches of deep snow, then tried the back door. It was locked, but there was enough room between the door and the jamb to slip in one of the sturdier blades and pop the latch open. Willy had been right. His Swiss Army Knife came in handy for a lot of different things.

The kitchen was empty. There was an open bag of chips on the counter, but no other food. Mark had told her about these parties; it was clear no one came to eat. Liquor bottles were lined up on the counter, though, and a bag of ice from the supermarket was in the sink. Connie considered having a shot of vodka for courage, but she decided against it. She wanted a clear head for the task she'd promised to perform for Alan.

The acrid scent of burning pot hung in the air. That was good. If they were drugged out, they wouldn't even notice her. She stepped into the main part of the house, moving slowly and carefully as she approached the living room.

A ring of candles flickered on the coffee table, but there was no other light. In the semidarkness Connie could make out a man and two women on the floor. She didn't recognize the man. They were all so stoned, they didn't even notice she'd come into the room.

Connie ducked back into the hallway. She had to locate Mark. She made her way to the dining room, but he wasn't there, either. Two naked women were sitting at the table, snorting lines of coke. They were so intent on what they were doing, they didn't notice her, either.

A stairway let to the upstairs, and Connie climbed it, into

the darkness. She stepped around the couple on the landing and opened the door to the first bedroom.

A large-screen television set up in the corner was showing a porno flick. The couple on the bed wasn't watching. They were too busy indulging in the kind of action on the screen. Connie glanced at the faces of the other men in the room. There were two of them. Neither man was Mark as she backed out of the room and shut the door behind her.

The scene in the second bedroom made Connie flinch. A woman was tied to the bed, and another woman was whipping her. Two men were watching, but neither man was Mark. Connie's hands were shaking as she shut the door and went on to the third bedroom.

The man's face was turned away from her, but Connie recognized him. It was Mark, and he was spread-eagled on the bed. His partner, a blonde with breasts too huge and firm to be natural, was on her hands and knees, straddling him. Mark gave a groan and let his head fall back against the pillows.

They were silent for a moment, then Mark laughed. "Hey, babe. How about untying me now?"

"Not quite yet." The blonde gave him an impish grin. "I think I'll let you think about me for a while and see what comes up."

Mark laughed again, and that was when Connie noticed that he was tied to the bed. It was a reversal of what he'd always done to her, and that made Connie feel glad. She stepped out of the room quickly, before Mark could turn her way, and watched through the partially opened door. After a few moments the woman got up and started to leave.

"Hey, babe. Where are you going?" Marks' words were slurred, and Connie knew he was stoned.

"I need another line. You wore me out, big boy."

"Bring me a hit. Hell . . . bring me two!" Mark started to laugh. "I know a couple of new places we can put it."

"Okey dokey."

The blonde was weaving a bit as she headed for the door. Connie stepped back, into the shadows. The blonde didn't glance her way as she started down the stairs, and Connie slipped into the bedroom unnoticed, locking the door behind her.

Mark was on his back, and his eyes were closed. Connie's knife was out as she approached the bed; her hand was steady. She had a mission. She was here to take away the gift of life that Alan had given him. She'd right the wrong the doctors had done when they'd given Alan's kidney to Mark.

He seemed to sense her presence, and he opened his eyes.

He didn't recognize her in her disguise. A puzzled look appeared on his face. "Hey, babe. Did she send you up to untie me?"

Connie shook her head, and then she leaned closer so that he could look directly into her eyes. "Do you know who I am?"

"No, but I'd like to." Mark's grin came out slightly lop-sided. "What's your name, babe?"

"I'm your angel."

"Angel, huh? That's a nice name. Why don't you take off your clothes and climb on."

Connie shook her head. "Not this time. Why don't you ask what kind of angel I am."

"Okay." Mark grinned again. "What kind of angel are you, babe?"

"I'm your angel of death." Connie pulled off her wig and removed her glasses. "I'm sure you recognize me now."

Mark blinked, then looked bewildered. "Hey, babe . . . What are you talking about? And why did you wear that wig?"

Connie didn't say anything. She just held up the knife and watched the puzzled look on his face turn to fear.

"Hey, babe. What the hell—"

He didn't have time to say any more. Connie's knife slashed down and took his words away. The rest of his question turned into a gurgle. Then he was silent.

"Good-bye, Mark." Connie's voice was cold and emotionless as she slashed him again and again. "You never deserved to have a part of Alan. He was a good man."

When she was through, she looked at him for a long moment. His gift of life was gone. She'd taken Alan's revenge. She unfolded the blanket from the foot of the bed and tossed it up to cover his body. Then she went into the connecting bathroom to take off her bloody clothes.

It didn't take long to shower and then dress in the extra slacks and sweater she'd brought. Connie checked the mirror to make sure she'd washed off all the blood before she stepped out into the bedroom again. The body under the blanket wasn't moving. Mark Turner was stone dead.

The lock on the door was the push-button type. Connie released it and left the room, closing the door and automatically locking it behind her. They wouldn't find him until morning. The blonde might came back, but she'd assume he was with someone else and go on to her next encounter. No one would guess there was a body behind the locked door until the party was over and they got ready to leave.

The couple on the landing had moved, so no one saw Connie go down the stairs. She peeked into the dining room and smiled when she saw the blonde at the table, her head bent low over the line of coke she was snorting. There was no one in the kitchen when Connie slipped out the back door.

Thirty minutes later, she was unlocking the door to her own apartment. Tomorrow was garbage day and she'd thrown the bag containing the bloody clothes and the wig in a nearby Dumpster. It would be emptied in the morning and its contents on the way to the dump before Mark's body was discovered. Since no one at the apartment building had known she was sleeping with Mark Turner, there was nothing to tie her to his murder.

But Alan's picture was frowning again. Connie picked it up and held it close to her ear. "What's wrong? Did I forget something you told me to do?"

She listened and then she nodded. Alan was right. The police would be sure to search Mark's apartment and they'd find her fingerprints. There was also the possibility she'd left some personal item there that would link her with him.

"What should I do, Alan?" Panic rushed over Connie in waves. No one had seen her at the party, but the police might still suspect her. If they put her under surveillance, they would interfere with her plans to contact the next candidate on the transplant list.

But Alan had the solution. He was so wise. Connie pressed her lips to the glass that covered his picture and thanked God he was still with her. "You're absolutely right, Alan. I'll go through his apartment and wipe everything clean. Wait right here. I'll be back just as soon as I can."

It was past midnight, and no one was in the halls. Connie took the stairs. Several moments later, she was unlocking the door to Mark's apartment. It was strange to step inside without Mark there to greet her. She'd never gone to his place when he wasn't there. But knowing she'd never have to endure his strange and painful sexual practices again made Connie smile with relief.

She didn't bother going to the kitchen. She'd never been in there. But she did wipe off all the doorknobs and every flat surface in the bedroom. The dresser was safe. She hadn't pulled out any drawers. But the bathroom was another matter.

Connie wiped the knobs on the shower and the handles on the glass doors. She even wiped down the medicine cabinet because she'd once looked inside for an aspirin. She was about to leave the apartment when she remembered wearing one of Mark's robes. The police probably wouldn't check it for hair or fibers, but it would be smart to find it and take it back to her own apartment.

She opened the closet and flicked on the light. The robe she'd worn was hanging in the back. She shoved some of Mark's clothes out of the way so that she could reach it. That was when she noticed a video camera on a shelf attached to the inside wall of the closet. The shelf was high, almost to the ceiling of the closet. Connie began to frown. There was a similar shelf in her own closet, much too high for her to use. Mark must have built it when he'd lived there, but why did he store his video camera in such a strange place?

There was a three-step kitchen stool in the corner of the closet, and Connie unfolded it and climbed up to look at the camera. When she leaned close and looked through the viewfinder, what she saw made her gasp. Mark had drilled a hole through the wall, and the video camera was aimed directly at his bed!

The implication was so clear Connie shuddered as she climbed down. Her hands were trembling, and she felt ill; but she managed to wipe off the step stool and put it back where it had been. Mark had videotaped someone in his bed, and that someone could very well be her.

Connie searched the bedroom, but the tapes were nowhere to be found. Where would he keep them? She remembered seeing a collection of videotapes at his entertainment center in the living room, and she rushed out to look.

The tapes were all commercially labeled. There were quite a few action-adventure movies, but some of the other titles didn't make sense. They weren't the kinds of movies Mark would have watched. One title in particular caught Connie's eye, Disney's *Cinderella*. Why would Mark buy a Disney film when he didn't have any children?

Connie took down the tape and pulled it out of its sleeve. The tape wasn't a Disney movie. It had a hand-printed label. On it were a date, a time, and two initials—A.J.

There was a frown on Connie's face as she examined several other tapes. Some were real movies, but there was another A.J. label inside the jacket for *Laura*, and she found a T.M. label in the sleeve that should have contained *Anne of Green Gables*.

Mark had been clever, hiding his tapes in plain sight, but Connie now knew his filing system. *Cinderella, Laura,* and *Anne of Green Gables* were all women's names. She pulled out all the other movies with women's names, and every one had a hand-printed label inside. E.V. was in the sleeve for *Tess*, L.R. was hidden in *Sabrina*, and *Anastasia* contained a D.P. label. Connie's initials, which had remained the same even though she'd used the name Cheryl, were inside three jackets. One was *Scarlett,* the second was *Forever Amber,* and the third was *Catherine the Great.*

Just to make sure she was right, Connie checked every tape. Seeing that there were no more hand-printed labels, she gave a sigh of relief. She knew what to do with the tapes of her. She'd take them back to her own apartment and destroy them. But how about the tapes Mark had made of other women?

Put them back on the shelf. The faint, beloved voice spoke directly into her ear. *No one saw you with Mark and you're safe. Keep the police busy, questioning all those other women. It'll take so much time, they won't even look for other suspects.*

"You're right, Alan." Connie smiled as she wiped off the tapes and replaced them. It was the first time Alan had ever spoken to her outside the privacy of their apartment, and she was delighted. Then Alan's voice came to her again.

Hurry home, Connie, and don't forget to wipe the outside

*of the door when you leave. I want to watch the tapes that
bastard made of you.*

"But why?" Connie frowned slightly. She was embarrassed
about showing the tapes to Alan. "You shouldn't watch them,
honey. They're so . . . so awful!"

*You don't have to be embarrassed about anything, darling.
I know you did it for me.*

"That's true." Connie nodded. "But why do you want to
watch them?"

*I need to know exactly what he did to you, so we can celebrate
the fact that he's dead.*

CHAPTER 24

Jill was in her office, sipping her first cup of decaffeinated coffee of the day. She'd bought the morning paper with her since she hadn't had time to read it at home, and she'd just learned about the gruesome murder that had occurred last night.

There was a knock on her door, and she looked up to see Doug standing there. "Hey, there. What are you doing here?"

"You beeped me, didn't you?"

Jill nodded. "Yes, but I expected you to call, not come to my office."

"It's okay. I was talking to the chief, right across the street. What's up?"

"I just read about last night's homicide." Jill handed him the paper. "This article doesn't say much, but I figured you might have the inside scoop."

Doug nodded and sat down on the chair in front of Jill's desk. "It's not my case. They called me in, unofficially, and I was at the scene for a couple of hours. It was bad."

"How bad?" She was concerned. "This isn't just idle curiosity, Doug. Norma Jenkins, one of Neil's colleagues, just made an offer on a house right around the corner from the crime scene. I think I should warn her if the neighborhood's going downhill."

Doug nodded. "That's a good idea. Call her. I checked the stats, and we've had trouble in that neighborhood before."

"What kind of trouble?"

"Loud parties, a couple of drug busts, and three muggings. Two cars were stolen in the past six months, and there were five B. and E.s."

"That doesn't sound good." Jill began to frown.

"It's predictable. Most of the houses are rentals, and groups of singles move in. They're usually young. They pool their resources because they can't afford to rent apartments on their own."

Jill sighed. "The real-estate agent told Norma it was a family neighborhood."

"They'll say anything to get their commission. Last night was the first homicide on record, but I'd tell your friend the area's definitely borderline."

"Thanks, Doug." Jill picked up the phone. "I'll leave a message for Norma asking her to call me."

Doug waited while Jill placed her call. When she'd finished, he gave her an approving smile. "You're a good friend."

"Thanks." She smiled back. "Now tell me about the victim. Who was he?"

"Mark Raymond Turner. He was a bartender at the Odyssey. Twenty-eight years old, athletic, lots of girlfriends, a good-looking guy."

"Do you have any leads?" Jill picked up her pen and began to jot down notes on a yellow legal pad.

"Not yet, but I've got a theory. There were multiple stab wounds."

"And they were the cause of death?" She began to frown.

"No. The victim's throat was slit, severing his carotid arteries. The other wounds were inflicted after death."

"Was the victim . . . uh . . . gutted?" Jill swallowed hard when Doug nodded. "Then you think there's a connection to the Rossini case?"

He nodded again. "It's the same MO with one exception. But don't mention that to anyone else. It's just my theory, and we don't want any publicity about a serial killer."

"Of course I'll keep it quiet," Jill reassured him. "You said there was an exception. What is it?"

"There were no defense wounds."

Jill was surprised. "The victim didn't try to defend himself?"

"He didn't have the opportunity. His hands and legs were tied to the bed."

"But why did he let someone . . . ?" Jill stopped in mid-sentence as the obvious answer occurred to her. "It was some kind of sexual thing?"

Doug nodded. "Sex, booze, and drugs. The victim was attending a party. There's a group—about a dozen people— that gets together every month. We questioned the woman who admitted she tied him up. She's got a couple of priors for prostitution, but she came clean with us. She left him in the room and went downstairs. When she came back, the door was locked. That's a signal they have when they want privacy, but she was curious and peeked through the keyhole."

"That must have been a shock." Jill's stomach lurched. Hearing about the murder made her feel queasy, but she wanted to know exactly what had happened. "Were they good friends?"

"No. She met him that night. It was the first time she'd gone to one of those parties."

"And it'll probably be the last." Jill shivered. "Did you find any evidence?"

"Hair and fiber. The hair's acrylic."

"From a wig?" Jill raised her eyebrows when Doug nodded. "Was it long, or short?"

"Long."

"Then it was probably a woman." Jill jotted down that bit of information. "Did you find anything else?"

"No. We tossed the house, but we didn't come up with a thing except a couple of interesting footprints on the walkway. Female, size six."

Jill nodded. "And no female at the party wore a size six?"

"You got it. So what does all this sound like to you?"

Jill looked down at the notes she'd taken. "A female killer who knew the victim. She followed him to the party, slipped in through the back door and murdered him."

"That's good, so far." Doug gave her an encouraging grin. "Did she know about the party in advance?"

Jill glanced down at her notes and nodded. "I think so. She wore a wig, and she didn't come in through the front door. She wouldn't have taken the trouble to disguise herself and sneak in the back way if she hadn't planned to kill him."

"Maybe, maybe not. She might have worn the wig so he wouldn't recognize her when she followed him."

Jill looked disappointed. "I didn't think of that. But no one saw her, right?"

"That's right."

"Then she couldn't have been at the party for very long. What time did the victim arrive?"

"Eight o'clock." Doug began to smile. Jill was putting the pieces together exactly as he had done.

"And what was his approximate time of death?"

"The coroner says midnight with an hour window, either way. The liver hadn't cooled very much."

Jill was so excited she clapped her hands together. "I knew it! She *did* plan to kill him!"

"What makes you think that?"

"It's simple." She grinned at him. "It was ten degrees

below zero last night. If she followed him to the party, she would have arrived at the crime scene at approximately eight o'clock. No way would she sit out in her car for three or four hours and take the chance of being spotted."

"That's true, but she could have gone somewhere else, come back later."

Jill nodded. "That's possible, but why did she come back if it wasn't to kill him? You didn't find the murder weapon, did you?"

"No. And it wasn't one of the knives from the house. According to the woman who rented the place, she kept all her knives in a knife block. She checked it, and none were missing."

"Then she brought the murder weapon with her. That's premeditation, Doug. They can get her for murder one!"

"If we catch her." Doug looked grim. "They're tossing the victim's apartment right now. If we're lucky, we'll pick up a lead."

As if on cue, Doug's beeper went off. Jill handed him her phone with a grin. "Go ahead. Maybe they found something."

The phone call didn't take long. Jill listened to the one-sided conversation, but she didn't learn anything new. When Doug hung up and turned to her, she leaned forward eagerly.

"They found a bunch of videotapes with initials on the inside labels. His camera was hidden in a closet with a hole drilled through the wall. It was focused directly on his bed."

"Blackmail?" Jill was really interested now.

"It looks like it. They're hoping the people at the party can identify the women in the tapes."

"How about his coworkers?" Jill glanced down at her legal pad. "Someone at the Odyssey might have seen him with one of the women."

"They're taking the tapes to the lab to make stills of the women's faces. They'll show them around at the Odyssey and they'll interview his neighbors. It's possible they'll come up with a lead."

Something about Doug's expression made Jill doubt that. "But you don't think they will, do you?"

"No."

She nodded. "I agree with you. If he was blackmailing her, killing him wouldn't get her the tape."

"Exactly!" Doug gave her the high sign. "This was a well-planned murder. She's smart, Jill. She must have known we'd search his apartment and find her tape."

"But you wouldn't find it if she got to it first. And she would have had plenty of time to do that. How about finger-prints?"

"Very good, Jill." Doug grinned at her. "There weren't any except his. And all the doorknobs were wiped clean."

"That proves she was there! He wouldn't wipe off his own doorknob when he left for the party. They're wasting their time with the tapes, Doug. I don't think they had any-thing to do with the murder."

Doug raised his eyebrows. "Why's that?"

"If she was after a tape, she didn't have to murder him. All she had to do was make sure he was at the party, go into his apartment, and get it. The killing just doesn't make sense with blackmail as a motive."

"Very good." Doug looked proud. "So why do you think she killed him?"

"I don't know. For some reason she hated him. You don't stab someone that many times if you don't hate them . . . especially after they're already dead. I think he did some-thing else to her, something horrible. That's why she killed him."

"My thoughts, exactly." Doug stood up and headed for the door. "Thanks, Jill. You've helped a lot. I don't know what I'd do without you."

She was surprised. "But I didn't do anything."

"Yes, you did. It really helps to run things past you. It's like a reality check."

"It is?" Jill was pleased, but she wasn't exactly sure what he meant.

"Look, Jill," Doug said. "If you agree with me, I know I'm on the right track. See you later, okay?"

"Anytime." Jill smiled, and the smile stayed on her face long after Doug had left. He needed her. He'd practically said as much. And that made her feel very, very good.

"Okay, Alan. I'm calling Harold Woodard." Connie's hands were shaking as she dialed the number. This man just had to be alive! Her heart was pounding so hard she could barely hear the pleasant-voiced woman who answered the phone.

"Hello." Connie tried to sound just as pleasant. "Is this the Harold Woodard residence?"

"Yes, it is."

"Mrs. Woodard?" Connie crossed her fingers for luck. If Harold Woodard was married, it would make matters much simpler for her. At least she wouldn't be dealing with a swinging bachelor like Mark Turner.

"Yes, this is Mrs. Woodard."

Mrs. Woodard sounded a little suspicious. She obviously thought this was a sales call. Connie went into her prepared speech to set her at ease. "I do volunteer work for the hospital, and we're updating our records on transplant recipients. I hope your husband is doing well?"

"Yes, he is." Mrs. Woodard sounded friendly again. "He's completely recovered, and he's back at work."

"That's wonderful news! I'd like to ask him some questions if it's not too much trouble."

"Oh, dear!" Mrs. Woodard sounded apologetic. "I'm sure he'd be glad to help you, but he's next door, in his office."

"Will he be home soon?"

"I'm afraid not." Mrs. Woodard gave a little laugh. "Harold keeps long hours. I won't see him until dinner at six. The phone's not working in his office, but if it's important, I can run over to get him."

Connie thought fast. If Harold Woodard had an office next door, that would be a perfect meeting place. "You don't have to do that, Mrs. Woodard. As a matter of fact, you could probably answer the questions for him. I just need to confirm his age, his marital status, and his blood type."

"Harold's forty-one." Mrs. Woodard seemed glad to answer. "We've been married for fifteen years, and his blood type is A positive."

Connie paused just long enough to give Mrs. Woodard the impression that she was writing down the information. "I'm glad he's married, Mrs. Woodard. We've found that married recipients recover much faster from their transplants. This is just my opinion, but perhaps it's because they have loving support at home. Do you and your husband have children?"

"We have four, two sons and two daughters. Does that make a difference, too?"

"It seems to." Connie began to grin. Harold Woodard had already fathered four children. That boded well for her. "Would you say your husband is happy in his work?"

"Oh my, yes! Harold has a true calling. Even when he was a little boy, he always knew what he wanted to be when he grew up. He enjoys helping people achieve their full potential. Everyone says he's a marvelous counselor."

"I'm sure he is." Connie did her best to sound sincere. "Thank you, Mrs. Woodard. You've been very helpful. And please give your husband my regards."

When Connie hung up the phone, she rushed straight to

Alan's picture. "It won't be long now," she said. "Harold Woodard sounds perfect!"

As she dressed in a demure suit that was tight enough to hug her excellent figure, Connie was smiling. Since Harold Woodard was a counselor, she had the perfect way to meet him. She'd go to his office with a phony problem and ask him to help her. She knew all the tricks, and she'd make sure he was attracted to her. Then all she'd have to do was let nature take its course.

CHAPTER 25

Connie glanced at the address she'd written on her notepad. Harold Woodard's home was supposed to be located at 225 Hiawatha Lane, but she must have written it down wrong. The entire two hundred block of Hiawatha Lane consisted of two buildings. One was a single-family dwelling, a nice, unpretentious residence that appeared to be in excellent repair. The other was a huge church with a spire and a bell tower. A breezeway connected to an addition that housed classrooms.

There was a frown on Connie's face as she checked the numbers on the front of the house. If her address was correct, this was definitely Harold Woodard's home. But his wife had said that he was working in his office next door, and the only adjacent building was the church.

Connie drove around the block and slowed in front of the church. There was a sign on the snow-covered lawn. She stopped at the curb to read it: OUR SAVIOR EVANGELICAL CHURCH. Beneath this, in italics, the sign read *With God's help, all things are possible.* In smaller letters, under the quotation, was additional information: Sunday Services at 9 A.M. & 11 A.M. Reverend H. Woodard, Pastor.

"Oh, no!" Connie sighed in utter defeat. Harold Woodard

had seemed so perfect. He had Alan's heart, he'd recovered completely from his transplant, and he had four children. But he was a minister.

"I'm sorry." Connie reached into the tote bag on the passenger seat and pulled out Alan's picture. "Harold Woodard's a minister. There's no way he'll father our baby."

The picture seemed to frown, and Connie held it close. Alan was arguing with her. He urged her to read the quote again and take it to heart.

"All right, Alan. It says, 'With God's help, all things are possible.' But do you really think God will help me to seduce a minister?"

Connie listened for a moment, then laughed. "You're absolutely right, darling. 'God helps those who help themselves.' But how am I going to help myself to Reverend Harold Woodard?"

Again, Connie listened. It took several minutes for Alan to explain, but when he finished she started smile. Alan was a genius, and he'd come up with a perfect way for her to achieve their goal.

"Oh, my! The poor dear!" Miriam Woodard set the tuna casscrole on the table and sat down in her chair. "Do you think you can help her?"

Reverend Woodard nodded. He'd just told his wife about the young woman who'd come to ask for his help. "I counseled her for over an hour this afternoon, and I don't believe she's suicidal any longer. It's a pity to see a young woman so depressed."

"Did you find out why she's so down?" Miriam passed her husband the bread.

"Yes, I did." Reverend Woodard suddenly noticed how quiet it was. "Where are the children, Miriam? I don't want to discuss the details in front of them."

Miriam frowned slightly. "They're gone, Harold. I told you this morning. They're spending some time with your parents."

"Without us?"

"Yes, dear." Miriam smiled at her husband. "They're going to an ice-skating party. I really didn't think you'd be interested."

Reverend Woodard nodded. "You're right. The last time I put on skates, I almost broke my neck. So . . . we have an evening alone?"

"Only until ten. Tell me about this woman, Harold. She sounds very interesting."

"It's a sad story. She was married on Thanksgiving Day to a man she thought was a God-fearing Christian . . . but she found out otherwise."

"Oh, my!" Miriam raised her eyebrows. "How?"

"He asked her to do certain things she thought were immoral."

"Like what?"

Miriam leaned forward, her breasts brushing the edge of the table. She was clearly intrigued, and Reverend Woodard patted her hand. Perhaps, if they went upstairs early, they could have some time alone before the children came home. "He wanted her to share their bed with another woman."

Miriam was so shocked, her mouth dropped open. "Dear heavens, Harold! That's horrible! What did the poor thing do?"

"She refused, of course." Reverend Woodard managed to hide his amusement. He'd seen some of the wilder side of life before he'd taken his vows. He'd even attended several parties at a friend's fraternity house and tasted the fruits of forbidden lust. But Miriam was the daughter of a minister, and she'd always been sheltered. The concept of a threesome had probably never occurred to her.

"And *that's* why he left her?"

His wife was clearly outraged, and Reverend Woodard

took her hand. "Calm down. She's better off without him, wouldn't you say?"

"I certainly would!" Miriam nodded quickly. "He didn't hurt her physically, did he?"

"No, but there's definitely a case for mental cruelty. He accused her of being a bad wife because she wouldn't obey him. Then he left her on the day before Christmas."

Miriam set her fork down on her plate with a clatter. "How terrible! That man ought to be drawn and quartered!"

"I tend to agree with you. He destroyed her self-confidence, and now she feels she has nothing to offer to any man. She actually asked me if she should have done what her husband wanted."

"The poor dear must be horribly confused." Miriam sighed. "And you told her she'd done the right thing by refusing him?"

"Of course. But I'm afraid my opinion doesn't count for much. After all, I'm a minister. I'm supposed to say that."

Miriam looked thoughtful. "Do you think it would help if she talked to another woman? I could—"

"No, dear." Reverend Woodard interrupted his wife. "You see, she's terribly embarrassed about what happened, and she asked me not to tell anyone. I'm sharing this with you in the strictest confidence."

Miriam nodded. "You know you can trust me not to talk about it. But what can you do for her, Harold?"

"I don't know. That's one of the reasons I told you about her. You're a woman, and you're a wife. I thought you might have some suggestions for me."

"Is she . . . attractive?" Miriam looked thoughtful.

"I think so. I'm no judge of that, but she looks a bit like Mrs. Hampton."

"Mrs. Lester Hampton?" Miriam seemed surprised. "She's a beautiful woman, Harold!"

Reverend Woodard shrugged. "If you say so. I've always

been attracted to women with dark hair and full figures . . . like you, dear."

"Why, thank you, Harold." Miriam was clearly flattered.

"That's beside the point. Now that you know what she looks like, do you think I should try to introduce her to some of the single men in the church?"

"No." Miriam shook her head emphatically. "If she's vulnerable, you shouldn't try to push her into a new relationship. She needs to build up her confidence first."

Reverend Woodard reached across the table to take his wife's hand. "You are an amazing woman, Miriam. So wise. And so very beautiful."

"That was a lovely thing to say, Harold!"

"It comes from the heart." Reverend Woodard got up from his chair to give his wife a hug. "Let's go upstairs, Miriam. We don't have much time alone anymore."

"But the casserole—"

Reverend Woodard laughed. "It can be reheated . . . Can't it, Miriam?"

"Well . . ." She considered for a moment, and then she nodded. "Tuna casserole is very good reheated. Some say it's even better that way."

There was a smile on Reverend Woodard's face as he led his wife up the stairs. Miriam was a good woman. She never refused him. Of course, he didn't ask her to do anything that would offend her sensibilities, as that poor woman's husband had done.

Their bedroom was dark, and Reverend Woodard couldn't help but think of the woman he'd counseled and how attractive she'd been. Without even thinking, he pushed Miriam down on the bed and reached out for her breasts.

"Why . . . Harold!" Miriam gave a startled gasp. "What in the world has gotten into you?"

"I'm not sure. Perhaps it's because you looked so pretty

when I came home tonight. You're irresistible, and I love you very much."

As Reverend Harold Woodard entered the body of his wife, he wasn't thinking about her or their successful but frequently boring marriage. He was thinking about the beautiful woman who'd come into his office that afternoon and pretending that she was beneath him on the bed. Although it would be sinful of him to even consider such a thing, it would be one way to build up her self-confidence!

Jill sat on a swivel chair in one corner of the examination room. Dr. Varney was checking Neil's eyes, and he'd told them that this would be a very important test. Her fingers were crossed in an attempt to bring good luck. If she'd brought a rabbit's foot, she would have rubbed it. Or she'd gladly have thrown salt over her shoulder or clutched a four-leaf clover. Neil just had to be all right!

"Follow the light." Dr. Varney moved the circle of light from the left to the right. "All right. Now close your left eye."

Jill took a deep breath and prayed for good news. Dr. Varney had darkened the room and turned off the overhead lights. The space seemed small and terribly stuffy, but perhaps that was because she was so anxious.

"Hmmm. All right, Neil. Close your right eye and follow the light."

It seemed to take forever to finish the examination, but at last Dr. Varney opened the drapes. Jill blinked as he turned on the overhead lights, and she turned to him with a question in her eyes.

"It went well."

"How well?" She didn't uncross her fingers.

"Very well." Dr. Varney scribbled some numbers on Neil's chart. "There's a thirty percent improvement in your peripheral vision, Neil. It's too early to say for certain, but the therapy appears to be working."

Jill clapped her hands. "That's great! Neil told me he thought he was seeing a little more clearly."

"You were right." Dr. Varney patted Neil on the back. "I want you to continue with the exercises, and I'll see you in four weeks."

Neil nodded. "I will, but I've got a question. Do you think I can go back to work?"

"I don't see any problem with that, as long as you keep the reading down to an hour a day. You won't be able to drive, of course."

Neil looked very excited. "That's no problem. I can find someone to drive me, and I can hire a student reader. I can still lecture and give oral exams, right?"

"Right." Dr. Varney scribbled another note on the chart. Then he looked up to smile at Neil. "Getting a little stir-crazy?"

Neil laughed. "You could say that. And Jill can tell you, I'm going through that list of companions like wildfire. I think it's because I feel cooped up."

"That could be." Dr. Varney winked at Jill. "What do you think? Is he ready to go back to work?"

She nodded. "It's that or a straitjacket. Neil's been like a caged bear the last couple of weeks. I think it'll do him good to get out."

"It's settled then." Dr. Varney turned to Neil. "I'm going to prescribe a pair of sun-sensitive lenses. They'll lighten automatically when you're in the classroom and darken when you're exposed to bright light. Put them on when you leave the house in the morning, and don't take them off until you come home at night. And don't forget to do your exercises. They're critical to your full recovery."

"Full recovery?" Jill leaned forward. Dr. Varney hadn't

mentioned a full recovery since she'd first spoken to him in the hospital.

"It may be a bit early to hope for perfect vision, but given the improvement I've seen today, Neil's prognosis is excellent."

"Hey . . . that's great!" Neil's face lit up in a smile. "You can thank Jill for the improvement. I was slacking off on my exercises before, but she convinced me to buckle down and do everything you said." Jill was surprised. "I did?"

"Sure. You gave me a perfect incentive, honey. I want to be able to see my baby when he's born in September."

"September?" Dr. Varney glanced down at Neil's chart again. "Yes . . . That should be possible. If you keep on improving at the rate I've seen today, you may not even need corrective lenses by then."

Jill was grinning as they made another appointment, took the prescription for the sun-sensitive lenses, and walked out into the parking lot. The sun was shining brightly, and she felt happy. Neil could hardly wait to see their baby. He'd even told Dr. Varney about it. What she'd thought was bad timing when she'd discovered she was pregnant had turned out to be the perfect way to save their marriage.

CHAPTER 26

"Yes, Reverend. I do believe that birth control is a sin."
Connie hid a smile as she answered Woodard. She'd studied
the catechism he'd given her and gone in for counseling
once a day for the past three weeks. If she answered his
questions correctly, and if the reverend believed she was
worthy, she'd be baptized and become a member of the
Evangelical Church this afternoon.

It was all going according to Alan's plan, and Connie
knew exactly what she had to do. Since the Evangelical
Church believed in total immersion in the natural state,
she'd be wearing only a thin white sheet for modesty. Connie
had insisted on a private baptism, claiming that she was
much too shy to appear in church before all the parishioners.
She and the reverend would be alone in the baptismal pool
behind the altar. And by the time Woodard knew what had
hit him, she'd be pregnant with Alan's baby.

"Yes, Reverend. I accept the tenets of the church and the
glory and power of the Almighty and His Son, Jesus."
Connie bowed her head and clasped her hands together as
the reverend began to recite a lengthy prayer for the salva-
tion of her soul. His hand was on her head, and she could

feel his fingers trembling slightly. Would he back out at the last minute, ask someone else to be a witness? Connie didn't think so. Reverend Woodard was a man of his word, and he'd promised her a completely private baptism.

The prayer seemed to go on forever, but at last Reverend Woodard ended with the traditional "Amen." Then he stood up and extended his hand. "Come, my child. You must change to your robes of glory."

"Yes, Reverend." Connie managed to look demure as Woodard led her to a dressing room at the side of the altar. There were two, one for men and one for women. Since Reverend Woodard would be wearing a robe of glory just like Connie's, he went to the dressing room at the other side of the altar.

"It's almost time, Alan." Connie whispered the words as she took off her clothes and hung them on the hooks inside the dressing room. There were no mirrors. She hadn't expected any. The Evangelical Church believed that vanity was a sin. It also insisted on strict modesty. The human body was to be hidden from view to everyone except a spouse.

Connie slipped the gown over her head and bit back a giggle. It was terribly unbecoming with its high round neck that fastened with a button so that no extra skin would be exposed. Floor-length, the gown had sleeves of a raglan cut that came all the way down to the tips of Connie's fingers. With the exception of her head, the robe of glory covered her like a shroud.

"What do you think, Alan?" She twirled around so he could see. She hadn't brought his picture, but she knew that he was with her and that there was an amused smile on his face. "What was that? Say it again, darling. I didn't quite hear you."

Connie listened carefully as Alan whispered in her ear.

"Yes. I'll take it with me. It's the only way I'll be able to get this silly robe off in the water."

The knife was in the pocket of her dress, and she held it in the palm of her hand. The sleeve of the robe covered it completely; Reverend Woodard wouldn't even know that she had it. After she'd slashed open her robe and pretended to drown, he'd carry her back to his office. She'd drop the knife there and retrieve it later, after she had succeeded in seducing him.

"In the name of the Father . . ."

Connie gasped as Reverend Woodard pushed her under the water. Thank God the baptismal pool was heated! He lifted her up again, and she grinned as she saw that his eyes were closed. He always closed his eyes when he prayed. That would give her plenty of time to slash open her robe.

". . . and the Son . . ."

Connie was wise enough to hold her breath this time. She even had time to snap open the blade of the knife before he pulled her up again.

". . . and the Holy Ghost . . ."

The moment she was under the surface, Connie slashed open her robe. Then she closed the knife, crumpled to the bottom of the baptismal pool, and waited for Reverend Woodard to reach for her. It took several moments, but at last she felt arms lift her up to the surface. She took a stealthy breath and held it so he'd think she wasn't breathing.

"Oh, my God!"

Connie resisted the urge to laugh out loud. Was the reverend swearing or praying? She took another furtive breath and made herself go completely limp in his arms."

"Sister? Are you all right, Sister?"

Connie didn't move a muscle or say a word. He knew CPR.

She'd seen the certificate on his office wall. He'd give her mouth-to-mouth resuscitation and, gradually, she would revive enough to kiss him. She'd act confused and frightened, and he wouldn't be able to resist the sight of her naked in his arms. It would be exactly the way Alan had told her. Reverend Woodard was a minister, but he was also a man. He'd seize this opportunity and take full advantage of her.

He was carrying her, and Connie opened her eyes slightly. He was taking her to his office. She felt a smooth cushioned surface beneath her bare body and knew she was on his old leather couch. And then his mouth came down on hers, forcing the breath of life into her body.

It was agony to lie there immobile when she wanted to get on with the action. She forced herself to count to thirty before she took a small breath on her own. Then, with her eyes still closed, she reached up and pulled him down, fastening her lips to his in a kiss that would scorch his propriety away and make him her slave.

He was kissing her back! Connie squirmed beneath him and managed to push up his wet robe. Then she smiled a secret smile as she felt the extent of his arousal.

It was working. He was going to do it. She opened her legs and gave him access to everything he so clearly wanted. But at the last moment, he pulled back with a hoarse, anguished cry.

"Sister! You don't know what you're doing!"

Connie made her voice low and seductive. "Yes, I do. Let's not think about anything except us and how much we want each other."

"No! You were baptized, Sister! You're a child of God now, and I must protect you from yourself!"

She reached for him again, but he was gone and her eyes opened with a snap. He was running from his office as if the dogs of hell were chasing him.

"Shit!" Connie whispered the word, even though she felt like shouting it. Their plan had failed. Reverend Woodard had resisted temptation.

"What should I do, Alan?" She sat up and shivered slightly. The church was cold, she was dripping wet, and she felt utterly defeated. "Do you think I should try again?"

She listened to the faint voice in her head and then nodded. Alan was right. Reverend Woodard wouldn't father their child. It was a waste of their time to even consider it. He'd be on his guard around her from this day forward, and he'd certainly refuse to see her alone.

"Do you think he might tell someone?" Connie shivered with anxiety as she heard Alan's answer. When she looked down at the knife in her hand, she knew what she had to do.

"Oh, Great and Heavenly Father. I am but a poor, miserable sinner, seeking the solace of Thy blessed forgiveness. I am not worthy to look upon Thy holy face, and I beseech Thee to cleanse my mind of impure thoughts so that I may again be cast in Thy image."

Reverend Woodard's voice was hoarse with emotion, and he had to stop to wipe his eyes. Just thinking about what had almost happened made him quake with fright like the shepherds of old. If the new Sister had been sent here by the devil to tempt him, he had come much too close to succumbing.

It was time for him to do penance, to prove to his Holy Father that he was truly sorry. Reverend Woodard's brow was furrowed with thought as he tried to devise an adequate act of contrition. He wanted to atone for his unclean thoughts, but what sort of restitution would his Creator accept?

The moment he thought of it, he knew it was right. He

would become celibate. The priests had been celibate, and so had The Almighty's beloved Son. From this day forth, he would not touch a woman, not even his wife.

Part of Reverend Woodard's mind objected to his hasty conclusion. Did The Almighty really want such a sacrifice? Perhaps he could come to some sort of middle ground, some promise that wouldn't be so difficult to live with.

"Reverend?"

Reverend Woodard whirled around as he heard a soft voice. The newest Sister was standing directly behind him and there was a strange and terrible expression on her face. "Please leave me now, Sister. I'm praying to God for our forgiveness."

"A lot of good that'll do."

Reverend Woodard started to frown. The Sister was obviously ridden with guilt. What other reason would she have for the hysterical laughter that poured from her lips? "Please listen to me, Sister. I know your actions were not deliberate. I intend to intercede for your soul, and I assure you that our Heavenly Father will forgive you."

"But will He forgive *you*?"

"Yes." Reverend Woodard reached out for the Sister's hand. "Our Savior is merciful and kind. He will look into our hearts and see that we love Him and are willing to obey His laws."

"Speak for yourself, Reverend. You weren't so ready to obey those laws a couple of minutes ago."

Reverend Woodard stared at the Sister with alarm. Her face was set in an expression he'd never seen before. She looked hard and dangerous and evil. Had her near brush with death unhinged her mind? Or was there some truth to the ancient stories of devils that could take on human form to tempt holy men of the cloth?

There was a knife in her hand! But that could be an illusion, a figment of his imagination. Reverend Woodard struggled to his feet and made the sign of the cross. "Devil! Get thee behind me Satan!"

"Very good, Reverend."

The smile on her face made the blood drain from Reverend Woodard's. Then her knife slashed down and he was no longer capable of thought or reason or life itself.

CHAPTER 27

Jill was just thinking about what to have for dinner when the telephone rang. She picked it up and smiled as she recognized the voice on the other end of the line. "Hi, Doug."

"I just called to see how your husband's eye exam went."

She could hear the concern in Doug's voice, and she felt a rush of warmth. It was sweet of him to worry about a man he'd never even met. "It went very well. Dr. Varney said Neil should recover his eyesight in time to see the baby when he's born."

"He? Then you know it's a boy?"

Jill started to grin. "No. I guess I should say he or she, but that gets awkward. I don't want to know ahead of time. I may be old-fashioned, but I'd rather wait."

"I can understand that. Knowing would take away the element of surprise. I'm glad your husband is doing better, Jill. I know it's been a strain for you."

"And how!" she laughed. "But it's much better now . . . really. Dr. Varney has allowed Neil to go back to work. That'll help a lot."

"That's good news. I know how I felt when I was down with the flu last year. It was only for a week, but being cooped up really got to me. It's a good thing I live alone. I was so crabby, I could barely stand myself."

Jill nodded, but she had her doubts. Doug didn't seem like the crabby type. She was sure he was exaggerating.

"Okay. I was just checking in. I'm off tonight, so if you need anything, all you have to do is call."

"Doug?" Jill spoke quickly before he could hang up. "What are you doing for dinner tonight?"

"Not much. I thought I'd head down to The Midtown Deli and pick up a Reuben."

"Do you feel like company?" She held her breath, hoping that he would say yes. Neil had called the university the moment he'd come back from Varney's office, and he'd arranged a dinner meeting with the department head. Norma had volunteered to pick him up, so Jill was free for the evening. "Neil's not going to be home. I was just going to heat up a can of soup. A Reuben sounds much better."

"Company would be great! Do you want to meet me there? Or shall I pick you up? The Midtown isn't far from your house."

"Pick me up and I'll show you the house." Jill made her decision quickly. "You've never seen it before."

"Okay. I'll be there in twenty minutes."

Jill was smiling as she hurried up the stairs to dress. She'd wear a pair of maternity jeans and the blue sweat shirt printed with teddy bears that one of the secretaries had given her at the office baby shower. It was too casual for a court appearance, and she'd been wanting to wear it.

Five minutes later she was ready, and she sat back down on the couch to wait for the doorbell to ring. Doug must know where she lived. He'd mentioned that The Midtown Deli was close to her house. But she couldn't remember ever having given him her address.

Jill thought about it for a moment and then realized that he hadn't given her his address, either. She'd looked it up in the personnel records because she'd wanted to know where he lived. Perhaps he'd done the same thing, impelled by the same kind of curiosity. She'd wanted to know everything about him, and he might have felt the same way about her.

Instead of feeling that her privacy had been invaded, the fact he had sought out her address made Jill smile with pleasure. It could mean nothing at all, but perhaps, at one time, he'd truly wanted to be part of her life.

They'd just finished splitting one of The Midtown's giant éclairs when Doug's beeper went off. He pulled it out of his pocket to glance at the number, and then he frowned. "Sorry. It's the station. I've got to call in."

"Here, Doug. Use this." Jill pulled her cell phone out of her purse and handed it to him, glad that she'd remembered to charge the battery last night.

"I'll pay for the call when it comes in on your bill. It's a toll charge from here."

Jill laughed. "Don't be silly, Doug. How much can it be? Just go ahead and use it."

"Okay. It's probably nothing. I'm not on call tonight."

As Doug dialed the phone, Jill held her breath and hoped it wasn't some kind of emergency. But as she listened to his side of the conversation, she motioned for the bill.

"That's okay." Doug scribbled an address on the paper napkin. "I'll just drop off my date and come right over."

His date? The woman in the adjacent booth was staring at her, and Jill couldn't hold back the amused smile that spread across her face. She was obviously pregnant, yet Doug had called her his date.

"Sorry." Doug shut off the phone and handed it back to her. "It's a homicide. I have to go in."

Jill nodded. "That's all right. I already asked for the bill. Is it . . . another one?"

"It looks like it." Doug caught her meaning immediately. "I told them I'd drop you off first."

"I'll go along. It'll save time that way."

"Are you sure?" Doug looked concerned. "They said it was pretty bloody. You won't get upset, with the baby and all, will you?"

"No, I'll be fine. I've been at crime scenes before."

"Okay." Doug nodded. "I may be there for a while, but after things have calmed down a little, one of my team can drive you home."

The waitress rushed over with the bill, and Doug glanced at it. He handed her some money, told her to keep the change, and then helped Jill out of the booth.

Jill glanced at the woman in the next booth. She was still staring at Jill's rounded stomach, and she wore a very disapproving look.

"It was a lovely *date*, Doug." Jill took his arm and smiled at the woman. "In my condition, I don't get asked out very often."

Doug had laughed when Jill had explained about the disapproving woman in the next booth. When he'd apologized for calling her his date, Jill hadn't told him that she'd been secretly pleased by the term he'd used. And of course she hadn't mentioned that if her situation were different, if she hadn't been married to Neil, she would have loved being referred to as Doug Lake's date.

As they approached the scene of the homicide, they were stopped at the corner by a uniformed patrolman. Doug flashed his badge, the yellow crime tape was lifted, and they were allowed to drive through. Doug parked in front of the church and turned to her. "Are you sure you want to go in?"

"I'm sure." Jill unbuckled her seat belt. "There won't be a problem with clearance, will there?"

"No. I might have a problem if I brought you in as a civilian, but you're with the DA's office. Just stick close to me and don't touch anything."

Jill nodded and followed Doug as he climbed the steps of the church. On the drive over, he had told her the victim was a minister, a Harold Woodard. His carotid arteries had been severed, and he had a series of multiple stab wounds. Reverend Woodard's wife had found him when he hadn't come to the rectory for dinner, and she had called the police. Mrs. Woodard had been hysterical when the officers had arrived; the family doctor had sedated her.

The sight that greeted them as they walked up the center aisle was bloody. Jill felt like turning around and running back to Doug's car, but she forced herself to look at the body on the altar. Someone had covered Reverend Woodard with a sheet, and she was grateful for that.

While Doug questioned the first pair of detectives who'd arrived on the scene, Jill glanced around the church. At seeing that a trail of wet footprints led to the altar, she began to frown. Although she was careful not to touch the footprints, she leaned over to examine them closely. Not blood. It looked more like water, as if someone had come out of a swimming pool without a towel.

"Water." Doug arrived at her side so silently, Jill almost jumped. "The reverend had a baptism scheduled for late this afternoon."

"Do you know who was baptized?"

Doug nodded. "His wife said it was a woman named Crystal, but she couldn't give a description because she'd never met her."

"Did you check the register?"

"The register?" Doug's eyebrows shot up in surprise. "What's that?"

"It's where they record the names of new parishioners. I

had a friend who joined this church, and she said that the reverend wrote her name and address in the book."

"Thanks, Jill." Doug turned to one of his men. "Check with the doctor. He's still next door with the reverend's wife, and he's a member of this church. Ask him where they keep the church register."

Jill waited until the detective had rushed off. "There's something else. My friend told me this church believes in total immersion and there's a pool behind the altar. I think she said there were two dressing rooms, one for the women and one for the men."

"They checked that out. There's nothing in the women's dressing room, but the reverend's clothes are still in the men's."

"Of course. After she murdered him, she got dressed and left. I don't suppose there were any witnesses to the baptism?" Doug shook his head, and Jill sighed. "Where do these footsteps lead?"

"From the pool to the reverend's office. And then back here to the altar. But there's only one set of footprints coming from the pool."

Jill thought for a moment. Then she shrugged. "The reverend wouldn't have gone into the pool if he hadn't had anyone to baptize. But there's only one set of footsteps?"

Doug nodded. "That's right."

"Then he must have carried her from the pool to his office."

"Right." Doug seemed pleased by her reasoning. "Why do you think he'd do that?"

Jill shrugged. "She could have gotten sick during the baptism. Or maybe she hurt herself in the pool. It's possible she swallowed some water and started choking. Total immersion, remember?"

"Greg?" Doug motioned to one of his team. "Check out the office. We're looking for a woman's fingerprints. The couch would be a natural, but dust everything in the office and the women's dressing room."

When Greg had left, Jill turned to Doug with a frown. "How about the murder weapon?"

Doug shook his head. "They didn't find it."

"Then it's just like the last time. She must have taken it with her."

There was the sound of a siren outside and Doug put his arm around Jill's shoulders. "That's the coroner's team. I'm going to be busy. Is it all right if I have someone take you home?"

"That's fine."

Doug walked her to the front of the church, where two uniformed patrolmen were guarding the door. "I don't need two men here. Would one of you take Mrs. Bradley home? She'll give you her address."

"I'll do it." One of the officers motioned to Jill. "Come with me, ma'am."

Jill started to leave, but Doug took her arm. He leaned close, so the two officers couldn't hear, and whispered in her ear. "Thanks. You've been a big help. And just in case you have any doubts, you're the best date I ever had!"

Connie was snuggled under the covers, holding Alan's picture close to her heart. She'd just finished telling him about what she'd done, and she gazed at his face a bit apprehensively. "Was that all right?'

Alan seemed to smile, and Connie drew a big breath of relief. Then she held the picture to her ear and listened while he talked to her.

"Of course, darling." Connie hopped out of bed and turned on the bedroom television. "You're absolutely right. They must have found him by now."

The ten o'clock news had just started, and she and Alan

watched as the music swelled and the logo flashed on the screen. The anchorman was handsome and his woman colleague was beautiful, but they both looked very serious as they faced the camera.

"Murder in the place you'd least expect it." The anchorman shook his head. "Police were called to the Evangelical Church located on the two hundred block of Hiawatha Street, the site of a violent homicide."

The camera moved in to show his woman colleague, who took up the story. "The body of Reverend Harold Woodard, forty-one years old and leader of the Evangelical Church, was discovered by his wife, Miriam, at shortly after seven this evening. The motive and identity of Reverend Woodard's assailant or assailants is unknown at this time. Police have launched a citywide search, and they are asking for your assistance.

"If you have any information about any person or persons who may be involved in the murder of Reverend Woodard, please call the number on your screen."

The anchorman took over again as the number flashed on the screen. "We have a reporter live at the scene, and later in the broadcast we hope to bring you interviews with several members of Reverend Woodard's church."

As the station went to a commercial, Connie sighed and snuggled a little closer to Alan's picture. Alan had told her she'd done everything right. There were no clues to link her with the murders, there was no way for the police to find her.

"There's one name left, darling." Connie reached for the list on the bedside table and glanced at it. "He should be a perfect candidate. He's a professor at the university, and I'm going to try to contact him tomorrow. He's the man who got your eyes."

Connie listened as Alan spoke, and then she nodded. "You're right. I wasn't being completely accurate. He received your corneas. "What was that, darling?" Connie listened again, and then she smiled. "I remember. I've heard you say that before, and I believe it. The eyes are the windows to the soul. That's the reason I'm so excited about this. Right now there's a man who's walking around, looking at the world through a part of your eyes."

As Connie settled down to watch the news, she made a vow to herself. This time she'd be very careful, and she would succeed. It was their last chance, Alan was counting on her. She was young enough to fit in on the university campus. There was nothing to set her apart from the other coeds. She'd have her hair colored, a shade of dark blond would be nice. She'd wear it pulled back very casually, and pick up a pair of studious-looking glasses. She would blend in beautifully. No one would suspect that she had an ulterior purpose for contacting the professor.

"I'm going to do it, Alan. You'll see." Connie clutched his picture to her chest and smiled self-confidently. The first thing tomorrow, she'd drive to the campus and get a copy of the class schedule. Then, when she'd perfected her role of serious student, she'd enroll in a class taught by Professor Neil Bradley.

CHAPTER 28

There was a smile on Connie's face as she rushed across the quad. She was going to the campus café to get Professor Bradley a sandwich for lunch. Over the past six weeks she'd made herself indispensable, running errands, reading to the professor, and attending every one of his lectures.

When she had gone to the admissions office, she'd discovered that she was ineligible to enroll. Since she'd left home at sixteen, she hadn't finished high school and the college entrance exam wouldn't be given again until the fall semester.

That hadn't stopped Connie. She'd gone straight to Professor Bradley's office and told him that she was testing the waters, trying to decide if she should take her entrance exam and enroll as a full-time student. He'd been kind enough to let her sit in on his class as an observer, and because she wasn't being graded, Connie had become his unofficial assistant.

The professor taught only one class a day. That was fine with Connie. She was attending only one class, and that class was his. She'd told Professor Bradley that she'd saved enough money from her secretarial job to spend several months on campus, but he'd pulled some strings and now she was earning a small stipend for reading to him and helping him correct his exams.

She'd made sure to stand in strong sunlight so he could see how attractive she was, but so far Professor Bradley hadn't even suggested that they become more than student helper and teacher. That wasn't surprising. She was only with him four hours a day and an hour of that time was spent in a classroom with twenty other students. The other three hours were spent in his office, but they weren't alone then, either. Professor Bradley kept his door open so his students could drop by to ask for advice, and the other professors in the department were always sticking their heads in the doorway.

"Don't worry, Alan. It'll happen, sooner or later," Connie whispered. "I just need to arrange more time alone with him."

A student she'd never seen before was manning the take-out counter. Connie smiled at him as she approached, and his face began to turn red. She knew she looked good in her tight green sweater because he seemed unable to take his eyes off her chest.

"I need a club sandwich for Professor Bradley." Connie managed to keep from laughing at the flustered student. "He wants mayo instead of thousand island dressing, and a side of coleslaw."

"Sure. It'll be up in a minute. Uh . . . do you want anything for yourself?"

His voice cracked and Connie leaned over the counter, deliberately brushing her breasts against his hand. He pulled back as if he'd been burned, and his face turned even redder.

"I mean . . . to eat. You know. Did you want to order any more food?"

"Not for me." Connie shook her head. "I'm dieting today. Gotta watch the figure, you know?"

"Yeah. Uh . . . sure."

He was so embarrassed Connie was afraid he'd get the

order wrong. "I'll be waiting outside. Just wave at me when it's ready. Club sandwich, mayo instead of thousand, and a side of slaw."

"Got it!"

He scribbled the order on a pad, and Connie watched to make sure it was right. Then she walked outside and drew a deep breath of the sweet spring air.

It was beautiful weather. Early May was usually quite chilly in Minnesota, but today she was almost too warm in her sweater. Two girls walked past her in shorts, and Connie grinned as she noticed that one of them was shivering. Professor Bradley had told her that last February, when the thermometer had climbed to the high twenties, several bikini-clad girls from the dorm had stretched out on reflective blankets on top of a snowbank to work on their suntans.

The student at the counter was beckoning to her, and Connie went back inside. She picked up the sandwich, paid for it with the money the professor had given her, and hurried across the quad to his office.

The door was closed, so she knocked softly. She heard a giggle, and then Professor Bradley called out to her.

"Just leave it outside the door, Connie. I'll pick it up later. I'm having a . . . uh . . . a student conference."

"I see." The professor had sounded out of breath, and as Connie set down the sandwich, she heard another giggle. If Professor Bradley was counseling a student, they were certainly having a lot of fun! "Do you want me to come back, Professor Bradley?"

"Yes. In an hour. I should be through by then."

Connie was amused as she walked away. It hadn't taken long for her to hear the gossip about Professor Bradley. He was married, but he'd had several well-known affairs with his graduate students. Even more encouraging was the news that his wife was pregnant. It meant that he was capable of fathering Alan's child. But now it seemed she had a rival for the professor's affections. She had to find a way to monopolize his time.

The coffee room was deserted, and Connie hurried in. She shut the door, then sat down on a chair, pulling Alan's picture from her purse. A whispered conversation in her head wouldn't do. She needed Alan's advice, and it was best to speak with him directly.

"What shall I do, Alan? I need to spend more time with him, and now there's another woman on the scene."

Connie listened, then smiled as the faint, beloved voice told her exactly what to do. Alan had a plan, and it was brilliant. She'd follow his instructions to the letter. They would be bound to work.

Less than a minute later, Connie knocked on Professor Jenkins's open door. "Hi, Norma. I just stopped in to see if I could do anything to help you."

"Come in." Norma motioned to her. "Your timing is perfect. I'm so tired of correcting these miserable exams, my eyes are blurring."

"Relax. I'll do it." Connie pulled up a chair and reached out for the answer sheet. She'd made friends with Professor Norma Jenkins her first day on campus. Now they were on a first-name basis. Norma knew everything that happened in the department, and she wasn't above a little gossip.

"So why aren't you working for Neil?" Norma looked curious.

"Professor Bradley has a student conference. I don't have to be back until two."

Norma raised her eyebrows. "A student conference?"

"That's what he said. It was one of the girls. I heard her giggle . . . twice."

"But you didn't see her?" Norma began to frown.

"No. The door was closed when I brought his lunch, and he said to leave it in the hall. He told me he'd be through in an hour."

A full minute of silence passed while Connie busied herself, correcting exams. She knew that Norma wouldn't be able to stand the silence for much longer.

"Connie?"

"Yes." Connie stacked another corrected exam on the pile of completed tests.

"If I tell you something, will you promise not to repeat it to anyone?"

"Of course." Connie nodded. "What is it, Norma?"

"Neil's not having a student conference. I saw who went into his office, and she's not a student. I guess it shouldn't surprise me that she's still there."

"Oh. I get it!" Connie made herself blush. "I should have known it was Mrs. Bradley. He sounded . . . uh . . . very out of breath. I probably interrupted a romantic lunch."

There was another moment of silence, then Norma sighed. "It wasn't Mrs. Bradley. Lisa Hyland is back in town. She used to be Neil's teaching assistant. He was having an affair with her. Lisa almost broke up his marriage."

Connie's mouth dropped open in pretended surprise. "I promise I won't say anything, Norma. I wouldn't want Mrs. Bradley to hear about this, especially in her condition."

"Good girl! Poor Jill's got enough to worry about— with her job and the baby and the problem with the house-keeper."

"I knew she was pregnant." Connie nodded. "Professor Bradley told me. And Mrs. Bradley is a lawyer, isn't she?"

"She's not just any lawyer. She's the youngest Assistant DA the city's ever had. Jill's very bright, and she's a dear."

"You mentioned something about a housekeeper?" Connie seized the opportunity to pump Norma for information.

"Yes. I talked to Jill on the phone last night, and she said their housekeeper quit. This is the seventh one they've gone through in less than six months."

"But why?" Connie managed to look perfectly innocent as she asked the question. Professor Bradley was probably screwing them as fast as his wife could hire them. "Is Mrs. Bradley difficult to work for?"

Norma shook her head. "Not at all. Jill's just as sweet as she can be. Neil's the problem. You've probably noticed that he can be very demanding. And quite frankly, he has a problem keeping his hands off attractive women."

"I've noticed." Connie laughed slightly. "But I really don't have a problem with that. I've learned plenty of ways to discourage those kinds of advances without hurting anyone's feelings."

Norma raised her eyebrows. "Then he's made a pass at you?"

"Not yet. But if he does, I know how to handle it. And I like Professor Bradley. He's very demanding, but I'm learning a lot. I don't usually get along with men, but Professor Bradley reminds me of my father."

"You don't get along with men?" Norma took the bait that Connie had thrown out. "What do you mean?"

Connie looked worried, and she leaned forward slightly. "If I tell you, you won't say anything, will you, Norma? It could get me into a lot of trouble with my family."

"Of course I won't! What is it, Connie?"

"I'm . . . well . . . I'm gay. And my family doesn't know." Connie lowered her voice. "I'm involved with someone, but she's out of the country. She earned a year's scholarship to Oxford, and she won't be back until Christmas. I promised I'd wait for her. We're going to live together when she comes back, and that's when we'll tell our families."

"I see." Norma nodded. Then she began to smile. "You may not know it, but you're the perfect assistant for Neil. He can't pick up on you."

Connie laughed. "You're right. Maybe Mrs. Bradley should hire a gay housekeeper. That might solve her problem."

"It might." Norma looked thoughtful. "It would have to be a gay woman, though. Neil couldn't stand to have another man in the house. And it would be impossible to advertise a position like that. You'd get slapped with a lawsuit if you even tried."

"I guess that's true." Connie sighed. "It's a pity, though. If I saw an ad like that, I'd jump at the chance to work for the Bradleys."

There was another moment of silence, and Connie held her breath. Would Norma fall into her trap?

"Connie?" Norma cleared her throat. "Did you mean that?"

"Mean what?" Connie finished correcting another exam.

"That you'd like to work for the Bradleys?"

"Of course I would." Connie looked up, having assumed her most sincere expression. "Mrs. Bradley sounds nice, and I already work for Professor Bradley part-time. I could even live in and drive him to work. And to tell the truth, Norma, I could really use the money."

Norma began to smile. "Good! I think you just got a job. Do you mind if I tell Jill that you're gay? It would help to relieve her mind."

"You can tell her." Connie nodded quickly. "But I don't want Professor Bradley to know. He'd probably fire me if he knew that he couldn't . . . well . . . you know what I mean."

Norma clapped her hands. "That's brilliant, Connie! And you're absolutely right. It'll be a secret between you and me and Jill."

"I'm looking forward to meeting Mrs. Bradley." Connie prompted. "I hope she'll like me enough to hire me."

"Of course she will! What's not to like? I'll call Jill this afternoon and find out when the three of us can get together."

"Thank you, Norma." Connie gave her a sweet smile. Alan's plan was working out perfectly. If she landed the position as the Bradleys' new housekeeper, she'd have plenty of opportunities to sleep with Neil. And best of all, Mrs. Bradley would never suspect a thing!

CHAPTER 29

"She's an absolute gem!" Jill was smiling as she faced Doug across the table. They were having lunch at The Beef Barrel again, and Doug had just asked about Connie Walters, their new housekeeper. "I really don't know how I got along without her, Doug. She drives Neil to work, brings him home, and makes all the meals. She even cleans the house and does the laundry and all the shopping."

Doug looked impressed. "She sounds terrific. Did you hire her through an agency?"

"No. Neil found her on campus. She's sitting in on one of his classes, and she's been helping him in his office. One of Neil's colleagues recommended her, and when I met her, I hired her on the spot."

Doug nodded and handed Jill the mustard. "You said she's living in?"

"That's right. We gave her the small guest room above the garage. I showed it to you, didn't I?"

"Yes, you did." Doug smiled. "I'm glad she's working out so well, Jill. Is she an older woman?"

"No. Connie's in her late twenties, and she's very attractive. She's bright, too, and she's got a marvelous personality."

Doug frowned slightly. "Maybe I shouldn't mention this, but I thought you said you'd never hire another attractive young housekeeper."

"I did.' Jill leaned closer so she couldn't be overheard. "This is strictly between us, but Connie is gay. Her lover is in England. They have a monogamous relationship. They're going to live together when she comes home at Christmas."

Doug raised his eyebrows. "It sounds like you found a perfect solution. Congratulations, Jill. And Neil agreed to hire a gay housekeeper?"

"He doesn't know. Connie told me in the strictest confidence. She doesn't want to take the chance that her parents will find out before she's ready to tell them. She's really very considerate, Doug. And she helps me so much. If I forget to take my vitamins in the morning, Connie reminds me. She makes sure I eat right, and she's always talking about the baby. I think she's even more excited than I am."

"She sounds almost too good to be true." Doug frowned slightly. "What was her name again?"

Jill started to grin. She knew exactly what Doug was thinking. "Connie Walters. And she doesn't have a record. I checked before I even met her."

"Good for you." Doug looked pleased. "Do you know much about her background?"

"I know enough. Her parents live on a farm, and they barely manage to get by. Connie dropped out of high school when she was sixteen to help them out financially. She worked as a waitress for over three years, and she finished a two-year secretarial course at night."

Doug nodded. "Then she's qualified to be a secretary?"

"A very high-level secretary. They call them administrative assistants now. She takes shorthand like a dream, and she types over ninety words a minute."

"She sounds overqualified to be a housekeeper." Doug

began to frown. "Couldn't she make more money as an administrative assistant?"

"I'm sure she could, but she really wants to go to college and she can't do both."

"I can understand that. I had to work and go to college at the same time. It was tough to find time to study. What is she? A freshman?"

"Not yet." Jill shook her head. "She didn't graduate from high school. That means she can't enroll as a regular student until she takes the entrance exam at the end of the summer."

"Do you think she'll be able to pass it?"

"Hands down." Jill looked very confident. "Neil says she's one of the brightest students he's ever taught, but naturally there are big gaps in her education. We're tutoring her for an hour every night, and she's already caught up in every subject except algebra."

Doug gave a wry smile. "Algebra was hard for me, too. It's not on my list of favorite subjects."

"Not on mine, either!" Jill laughed. "But Neil's always been a whiz at math, and Connie's studying hard. She'll make it, Doug. I'm sure of it."

"But can she afford to go to college?"

Jill nodded. "She's managed to save quite a bit, and Neil's checking around for on-campus work. She doesn't have any expenses since she's living with us. That means she's saving every penny of her salary for tuition."

"You like her a lot, don't you, Jill?"

"Yes, I do." Jill smiled. "If I have a daughter, I hope she grows up to be just as nice as Connie Walters."

"Connie. You're really an incredible woman!" Neil reached up to squeeze Connie's breasts, then pulled her to him again.

"I've got to get dressed." Connie glanced at the clock and frowned. "It's already two, and I still have to do the laundry before Jill gets home. Hold that thought until tonight. After she's asleep, you can come to my room."

Neil looked disappointed, but he nodded. "You're right. I don't want to do anything to make her suspicious. If the laundry's not done, she might think we were up to something."

"No, she won't. Your wife will never suspect that you're sleeping with me."

Neil laughed. "Then you don't know Jill very well! She's very suspicious."

"I wonder what made her that way?" Connie raised her eyebrows. "I'm sure you've never given her any reason to doubt you."

Neil laughed, but he looked a little sheepish. "Okay, okay. I've given her plenty of reasons. To tell the truth, I still don't understand why she was so hot to hire you. You're young, you're smart, and you're beautiful. Jill must have guessed what would happen if you moved in with us."

"You're wrong." Connie leaned close and nibbled at Neil's ear. "I told you before . . . Jill will never suspect a thing."

"Why not? Did you put her under some sort of spell?"

Connie nodded. "I guess I did, in a way. You see, Neil, your wife is convinced that I'm gay."

"Gay?" Neil looked shocked. "But why would she believe a ridiculous thing like that?"

"Because Norma thinks I'm gay. I told her so, and she told Jill."

"Wait a minute." Neil started to frown. "Why did you tell Norma you're gay?"

"Because I thought it would be great cover for us."

"You were right." He nodded. "But how did you know I was going to sleep with you? I didn't even make a pass until you moved in with us."

"It was inevitable. I knew it would happen, sooner or later."

"And just how did you know that?"

Connie gave him a seductive grin. "Because I wanted to sleep with you. I always get what I want, Neil. If you hadn't suggested it, I would have used every trick I knew to get you into bed."

"Every trick, huh?" Neil thought about it for a moment, and then he began to grin. "I've got a great idea."

"What's that?"

"I'll help you with the laundry. We'll go to a Laundromat, and we can do it in half the time. That should free you up for at least another hour."

"That's true." Connie nodded. "A Laundromat would be a lot faster."

"That's what I thought. And since we've got an extra hour, I have something I want you to do."

"Okay." Connie nodded. "What is it?"

Neil grinned devilishly. "I want you to pretend that we're not lovers. And then I want you to show me exactly what tricks you would have pulled to get me into bed."

"You look tired, Jill." Connie seemed very concerned as Jill stifled a yawn. "Didn't you get enough sleep last night?"

Jill shrugged. "I thought I did, but I couldn't seem to find a comfortable position. I guess it's because I'm getting so big."

"I've got the perfect solution for you." Connie stacked the last of the dishes in the dishwasher and turned to Jill with a smile. "One of my friends recommended it, and I bought it this afternoon. Come with me. I put it in your room."

Jill was curious as she followed Connie up the stairs. The young woman loved to surprise her with little gifts, and they were always things she liked.

"Open it." Connie was smiling as she pointed to the gift-wrapped package on the bed. "My friend said it helped her to sleep when she was pregnant."

The package was wrapped with teddy bear paper, and it was so pretty Jill almost hated to open it. She ran a fingernail under the tape and pulled off the paper carefully.

"So? What do you think?"

Jill stared down at her present, a puzzled expression on her face. It was big and soft, like a feather pillow, but it was shaped so strangely, she wasn't sure exactly what it was supposed to do.

"It's very pretty." Jill stroked the fabric with her fingers. It was printed with blue and pink flowers, and it was very attractive. "But . . . exactly what is it?"

"They call it a preggie pillow. It's really two pillows sewn together with this flat strip in the middle. Do you want me to show you how it works?"

"I think you'd better." Jill gave a little laugh. "I've never seen anything quite like it before."

Connie placed the pillow on the bed horizontally, halfway between the head and the foot of the bed. She smoothed out the flat strip of cloth and turned to Jill. "Stretch out right here on your back. This flat place should be positioned at your waistline."

"I'll try." Jill got on the bed. "But there's a problem, Connie. I'm so big, I don't have a waistline!"

"That's true. Just try to remember where it used to be and that'll be fine."

"This is . . . very comfortable!" Jill was amazed as the two pillows hugged her, one on either side of her body.

"I know. My friend said it was the best shower gift she ever got. Try rolling on your side, Jill. It'll work that way, too."

Jill rolled onto her side, and one pillow cradled her stomach. The other was positioned perfectly, right in the small of her back. She rolled over to the other side, and the pillow was perfect that way, too. "This preggie pillow is a godsend, Connie! I can get into almost any position and still be comfortable."

"That's right. And since the pillows are sewn to the flat piece, they'll stay in place."

Jill smiled. "That's a relief! I've tried using two pillows before, but one of them always falls off the bed in the middle of the night. You don't know how many times I've turned on the light to look for a missing pillow."

"You won't have to do that anymore." Connie looked very proud. "I knew you'd like it. My friend said this pillow practically saved her life in the last three months before her baby was born."

"I can see why she said that. Thank you, Connie. I'm so comfortable, I think I could go to sleep right now."

"That's a good idea." Connie walked to the foot of the bed and removed Jill's shoes. "I'll help you into your night-gown. You'll feel much better in the morning if you get a good night's sleep."

Jill nodded and let Connie help her get ready for bed. She was so sleepy she could barely keep her eyes open. "I should go downstairs and say good night to Neil, but I just don't have the energy."

"Don't worry. He'll understand. I'll tell him you were exhausted and you fell asleep."

"But . . . I was going to help you study for your test." Jill began to feel a little guilty. "And it's only a little past eight."

"Don't worry about me. I'll concentrate on algebra tonight, and if I have questions, I'll ask Neil. Just get some sleep, Jill. And don't worry about us. I'll take care of every-thing."

"I never worry when you're here." Jill smiled at her. "I hope you know how much I appreciate you, Connie. You're such a good friend, and you help so much."

Connie pulled up the blankets and tucked Jill in. Then she turned off the light. "That's why I'm here. It's wonderful to be part of a family again. Good night and sleep well."

"I will. Good night, Connie." Jill's eyes closed the moment Connie left the room. Her last thought, before she fell asleep, was about Connie, about how thankful she was that Neil had agreed to let her sit in on his class. She was a perfect housekeeper and a truly caring friend. She seemed like a member of their family already, though she'd only been with them for six weeks. And best of all, Jill didn't have to lose a moment's sleep in worrying about Neil and Connie.

CHAPTER 30

Connie frowned as she stared down at the circle on her home pregnancy test. She'd been sleeping with Neil at every opportunity, and she still wasn't pregnant.

"Damn!" She threw the package in the garbage and sighed deeply. It had been eight weeks. If frequency was any indication, she should have come up with a positive result long before this.

"What's wrong, Alan?" Connie picked up Alan's picture and held it close to her ear. His voice had been growing fainter lately, and she could barely hear it.

The faint words he spoke made Connie shake her head. "No. I'm sure he's not using any birth control. Jill got pregnant, so I know he's capable of fathering our child."

Alan was speaking again, and Connie strained to make out his words. How long would she be able to hear him? And what would she do if she lost the benefit of his advice?

"Absolutely not!" Connie managed to hear the faint whisper, and she shook her head again. "Jill's not the type to sleep around. I'm sure the baby is Neil's."

Connie listened again and then her eyes widened. "But, Alan! It can't be my fault! I was pregnant before, remember?

The doctor at the hospital told me nothing was wrong. He promised that I could have other babies."

Alan's voice was a little louder, and Connie could hear him more clearly now. She listened. Then a shocked expression appeared on her face.

"I didn't think of that! Mark Turner played around a lot, and I know Neil's done his share of sleeping around. I guess I could have picked up an infection that's keeping me from getting pregnant. Do you think I should go to the doctor and see?"

Alan's response was emphatic. His words were much clearer when he was upset, and now he was definitely upset. "Calm down, darling. I'll call for an appointment and say it's an emergency. I'm sure they'll take me right in."

"I'm sorry, Doug. There's just no connection."

Greg Raleigh, one of the detectives on Doug's team, placed the case file on Doug's desk. Doug paged through it, then sighed. Greg had explored every possibility that he'd suggested, but they'd come up with zip.

"How about college? Or high school?"

"I tried that." Greg nodded. "Woodard's the only one who went to college, and all three victims come from different high schools."

"A sports connection?" Doug doubted that even as he posed the question. He wasn't surprised when Greg shook his head.

"Woodard wasn't interested in sports. He didn't even attend his kids' T-Ball games. Turner was on a soccer team, but Rossini never attended any matches. There's just no common thread."

Doug started to frown. He wasn't willing to let his theory go without checking every possibility. "There has to be a connection. We just haven't found it yet. Clubs?"

"Just some kind of church leadership group for the reverend 'men of Christ' . . . or something like that. His wife said there was a yearly conference in Baltimore." Doug lifted his eyebrows, but Greg shook his head. "I know what you're thinking, but neither of the other two victims ever set foot in Maryland."

Doug sighed. "There's got to be something. How about Rossini? He must have belonged to a couple of clubs. Car salesmen always join everything in sight. It's a way to make contacts."

"You're right. He was in Rotary, Lions, Toastmasters, all the big ones. But the only club Turner ever came close to was that swinging sex thing with his friends."

"How about that sex thing?" Doug looked thoughtful. "Rossini was a bachelor, and he didn't live that far away."

"Nope. There's no connection there, Doug. Believe me, I checked."

"Self-help groups?" Doug brightened as he thought of it. "Turner had a substance-abuse problem."

"That's true, but the other two didn't. And Mrs. Woodard said the reverend didn't do substance-abuse counseling. He referred anybody with a drug problem to a shrink he knew."

Doug nodded. "And you checked with the shrink?"

"Of course I did. He didn't recognize Turner's picture, but he went through all his patient files. Nobody matched the description."

"How about the church itself?" Doug shook two aspirins out of the bottle on his desk. "Did Turner or Rossini ever go there?"

Greg shook his head. "I went to both services on Sunday, and I showed the pictures to everyone there. Nobody remembered seeing them."

"We've got to be overlooking something." Doug popped the aspirins into his mouth and swallowed them with a swig of cold coffee. "Any ideas?"

"No. I tried everything I could think of, but I came up with nothing to show for it. Are you sure these weren't random killings?"

"I don't think so." Doug shook his head. "Still, it's always possible the connection is only in the killer's mind."

Greg thought about that for a minute, but he still looked puzzled. "I don't get it. What do you mean?"

"Maybe they all looked like members of her family . . . or her former boyfriends . . . or neighbors she had. She'd see the connection, but we'd never find it."

"I think I get it now." Greg gave a nod. "If she was a waitress, the victims could have looked like former customers who stiffed her on the tip."

"Exactly. And that gives me an idea. Did any of the victims go to the same restaurants?"

"I don't know." Greg jotted "restaurants" down on his pad. "I'll check it out. We haven't tried that angle before."

"Get right on it. And while you're doing that, I'm going to talk to a friend of mine to see if she's got any fresh ideas."

Greg started to grin. "A woman friend with *fresh* ideas? That sounds interesting."

"She's not that kind of a friend." Doug shook his head. There were times when Greg's adolescent humor got to him, but his colleague was young. With a little more experience, he'd make a good detective. "My friend is married, and she's seven months pregnant. Before you bother to ask, the baby's not mine."

Greg shrugged and got to his feet. "Too bad. I think you'd make a great father. I'll catch you later, boss. I'm going to check on those restaurants."

After Greg had left, Doug stared at the door without seeing it for a long thoughtful moment. Then he straightened his shoulders and sighed. Greg was right. He'd do his best to be a good father, especially if Jill were the woman carrying his child.

* * *

Connie sat there in a daze for a moment. Then she asked the important question. "Are you sure?"

"I'm certain, Mrs. Webster." The doctor used the fake name that Connie had given him. "We can prescribe antibiotics to clear up the infection, but the damage is already done. I'm sorry to have to tell you this, but I'm afraid you'll never be able to conceive another child."

Somehow, Connie managed to listen to his lecture on safe sex. After picking up her prescription at the pharmacy, she drove back to Jill's house. She gripped the wheel tightly and fought to stifle her scream of outrage. Mark Turner hadn't given her the infection that had left her barren. The doctor had told her she'd contracted the infection approximately six weeks ago. That meant Neil had infected her.

"He's a rotten bastard!" Connie was so angry she almost missed seeing the brake lights flash on in front of her, and she narrowly avoided slamming into the car ahead. "He cheated on me!"

There was the sound of a chuckle, and Connie's eyes widened as she heard a familiar voice.

Calm down, Connie. I don't want you to have an accident. And what did you expect? Neil cheated on his wife with you. It's only natural for him to cheat on you with someone else.

"Alan!" Connie's hands began to shake. His voice was clear in her ear, and she hadn't even brought along his picture! "Are you mad at me, Alan? I tried my best. I really did. I slept with him every chance I got."

Don't worry, Connie. It's not your fault. You had no way of knowing he was having a second affair.

"Maybe not." Connie sighed deeply. "But he ruined

everything for us. How can I have your baby if I can't get pregnant?"

You could have Jill's baby. Count back, darling. Count back to when Jill conceived, and you'll see what I mean.

Connie pulled over to the side of the road, even though she knew she'd have trouble getting back out in the heavy, rush-hour traffic. Jill was seven months pregnant and this was July. She had conceived sometime in December.

That's right, Connie. Alan sounded very excited. *It was December. And Neil had his transplant the day after Thanksgiving. What does that mean to us?*

"She's carrying your baby!" Connie's mouth dropped open in surprise. "But what can I do? I can't just take Jill's baby . . . can I?"

It's not Jill's baby, it's ours. Of course you can take it. Listen to me and I'll tell you exactly what to do.

Connie heard him out, and then she nodded. Alan was right. Part of him was alive in Neil's body the night Neil impregnated his wife. Jill was carrying the child that should have been Connie's. And since Jill was pregnant with Alan's baby, they were entitled to take it. Just as soon as Jill gave birth, the baby would be theirs.

Be very careful, Connie. You've got to make sure Jill trusts you completely. If she suspects you, she'll call that detective friend of hers, and that would spoil everything.

"Don't worry, darling. She'll never guess." Connie smiled confidently as she waited for a break in traffic. But then her smile turned to a frown as she thought of another problem. "What will I do about Neil? He'll be at the hospital when Jill has our baby."

Alan had another answer that made Connie's frown disappear. *He won't be around to cause a problem. Just listen to me, and I'll tell you exactly what to do.*

As Connie listened to her beloved's voice, she gave a

huge sigh of relief. Alan's plan would work perfectly. She had no doubt about that.

"Alan? Are you still there?" But his voice had faded away to less than a whisper. He was gone, but she knew exactly what she had to do to bring him back. Once she'd taken Jill's baby, Alan would be with her again. And then he and Connie and their darling baby could live together forever.

Jill jotted some notes on a pad as Doug told her what his detectives had done. "How about barbers? They could have gone to the same barber shop. Or bank. They might have had checking or savings accounts at the same branch. Maybe they even used the same ATM."

"Thanks, Jill." Doug grinned at her. "Anything else?"

She was smiling as she glanced at her notes again. Doug really wanted her advice, and that made her feel good. "All three men owned cars, didn't they? They might have used the same service station or the same mechanic. And you told me Turner had a closet full of silk shirts. They have to be dry cleaned. These men might have used the same place. And don't forget dentists and doctors. You might find something there."

"Okay. I'll give Greg your ideas." Doug's voice was warm. "If you think of anything else, will you write it down for me?"

Jill nodded. "I'd be glad to. I'm leaving early today so drop by before four to pick it up. Neil and I are going to a baby class at the hospital."

"A baby class?" Doug looked puzzled. "What's that?"

"It's a class for new mothers. They teach us breathing techniques to use when we're in labor, and they take us through the whole process, step by step. Tonight's graduation, so we're supposed to bring our husbands. We're going on a tour of the delivery room and the nursery. And they're going to show the husbands what to do if they want to be present during the delivery."

"Is Neil going to be in the delivery room?"

"No way!" Jill gave a little laugh. "He's always been squeamish. He'd probably faint. Some husbands do, you know. He says he'd rather wait until the baby's in the nursery and I'm back in a regular room."

Doug nodded. "Are you disappointed?"

"A little, I guess. But it doesn't really matter. Connie says she'll be with me if I want her. How about you, Doug? If you were married and your wife was having a baby, would you want to be in the delivery room?"

"Absolutely." Doug looked very sure. "I'd want to be with her every minute."

"It wouldn't bother you, seeing your wife like that?'

Doug looked shocked. "Of course it would! But if she wanted me, I'd be there."

Jill was thoughtful as he left her office. He'd make a great husband for some lucky woman—considerate and loving. And he'd make a wonderful father.

A frown crossed Jill's face as she thought about Neil's reaction to the baby class. Although husbands were encouraged to come with their wives, he hadn't gone to a single meeting. He'd already told her that he felt uncomfortable around infants because they were so small and you had to be careful how you held them. Since he didn't feel confident enough to change a diaper or feed their baby a bottle, he'd offered to hire a nanny to help her.

Jill guessed that was better than nothing. Neil had admitted his faults, and he was trying to compensate for them. But she was almost sure that he wouldn't have much to do with the baby for the first year or so. He'd be fine once the child was walking and talking, but she couldn't help comparing Neil's attitude to Doug's.

Doug would change the baby's diapers. Jill was almost sure of it. And he'd take turns feeding the baby and getting up in the middle of the night. He wouldn't hire a nanny to take over for him. He'd enjoy helping out and getting to know his child.

Jill smiled as she imagined life as Doug's wife. He'd hold her hand in the labor room and rub her back between contractions. He'd help her with her breathing exercises and encourage her when she was tired. And he'd be at her side in the delivery room, telling her how much he loved her.

After the baby was born, Doug would spend hours on the phone, calling everyone with the good news. He'd pass out cigars at work and take so many snapshots, the nurses would probably confiscate his camera. He'd bring her flowers. He might even sleep in so that he could hold the baby for the night feeding. And once they got home, it would be even better.

Jill began to dream about how wonderful their life would be. Doug would enjoy spending time with the baby so much, he'd urge her to go shopping or take in a movie so that he could stay home and babysit. He'd learn all the nursery rhymes and the silly little songs babies loved to hear, and he'd buy every toy and gadget on the market for the baby's room.

But he wouldn't ignore Jill. He'd love her even more than he had before. He'd tell her she was beautiful, even though she hadn't lost all the weight she'd gained during her pregnancy. He'd smile at her every time she walked into the room, and he'd never miss an opportunity to touch her. There would be a gentle hand on her shoulder when she was cooking dinner, or a loving caress when she brushed past him. And he'd make love to her passionately and tenderly when they were alone in their bedroom at night.

Jill was lost in her happy dream as she glanced out the

window. The sky was overcast, but the grass was bright green and the leaves on the trees were glistening. The flower beds in front of the building were vivid with red and purple and pink blooms. The brick window ledge was a lovely shade of deep red.

"What are you smiling about?" Jill's secretary stuck her head in the doorway.

"Why shouldn't I smile? It's a beautiful day!" Jill's voice was soft.

"I guess it is, if you're a duck." Her secretary frowned as the first few drops of rain splattered against the window-pane. "Personally, I hate weather like this. Do you want me to type up your notes on the Foxworthy case?"

"Yes, Mary. Thanks." Jill waited until her secretary had left and then glanced out the window again. Mary was right. It was cold and rainy, now that she was no longer imagining life as Doug's wife.

CHAPTER 31

Jill turned to Neil with a frown. "But, honey . . . You know tonight's class is important. We're doing the countdown to delivery and the tour of the hospital. It's our last meeting. We're supposed to bring our husbands."

"I'm sorry, Jill." Neil looked a little guilty. "I feel really rotten, springing this on you at the last minute, but I have to present the budget. Everybody in the department is counting on me to get more money for next year."

Jill couldn't help being disappointed, but she nodded anyway. "Okay. I understand. But it's Connie's night off, and you're not supposed to drive yet. How will you get there?"

"That's no problem. I'll take a cab. Harris says the department will pay for it. Are you terribly upset with me, honey?"

Jill debated for a moment, then decided to be perfectly honest. "Not terribly, but I *am* upset. I really wanted you there tonight. What happened to Professor Harris? I thought he was supposed to present the budget."

"He was, but his wife's sick. When he called to tell me, I offered to do it. Since I worked on it with him, I'm the only one who's prepared to answer their questions."

Jill looked concerned. "Is Harris's wife all right?"

"She'll be fine in a couple of days. The doctor says it's a

bad case of the flu. He put her on antibiotics, but she's still running a fever and she's flat on her back in bed."

"That's too bad." Although Jill had never met Mrs. Harris, she couldn't help feeling sympathetic.

"Look, Jill. I didn't realize this class was so important to you or I never would have told Harris I'd do it. Do you want me to call him back and tell him I can't?"

"Of course not." Jill sighed again. She really wanted Neil to go with her, but if she insisted, she'd feel like a bitch for dragging Professor Harris away from his sick wife. "What time do you have to be there?"

"At seven. Would you call a cab while I get dressed?"

Jill nodded and picked up the phone. "Your tweed jacket's at the cleaner's, but you can wear your blazer."

"Good idea." Neil nodded and started up the stairs. "What time do you have to leave?"

"I don't have to be there until eight. Do you want me to help you dress?"

"No, I can handle it." Neil turned around to smile at her. "Connie put a halogen bulb in my closet, and now I can see just fine."

Jill nodded and dialed the number for the cab company. She'd never thought of putting a halogen bulb in Neil's closet, but it made good sense. Connie was an absolute marvel. She did all sorts of things to make their lives easier. Sometimes Jill wondered how they'd ever managed to exist without her.

"What's the matter, Jill? You sound kind of down." Doug frowned as he paced the floor in his small living room.

"My car won't start, and Neil's gone off to a meeting. He took a cab, so his Mercedes is here, but I can't find the extra set of keys."

Doug nodded. "And tonight's that baby class you were telling me about?"

"That's right. I guess I'll just have to miss it."

Doug reached for his jacket and started to put it on. "No, you won't. I'm off tonight. I'll pick you up in twenty minutes."

"You will?" Jill sounded delighted. "But, Doug . . . it's really out of your way. And you'd have to come to pick me up again—unless you want to sit in."

"That sounds good to me."

"Are you sure you're interested?" Jill sounded doubtful. "It might be boring for you. Before we tour the hospital, they're going to teach all the husbands how to diaper a baby and give them a lesson on burping."

Doug laughed. "That might come in handy. If you need me to babysit, I'll be prepared."

"Then you wouldn't mind changing a diaper?"

"Of course not. Isn't the whole object to keep them warm and dry—and full of milk and happy?"

Jill's laugh was like sunshine in his ear. She sounded absolutely delighted. "That's it, Doug. You can babysit for me anytime you want. You'd be absolutely terrific!"

Doug was grinning as he hung up. He hoped Jill was serious and she'd really let him babysit for her. He was going to love her baby. He knew that already. And maybe, once in a while, he could pretend that he was the baby's father and Jill was his wife.

There was a grim expression on Connie's face as she pulled in to park. She'd overheard Neil's plans on the extension phone in her room, so she knew who he was meeting. Lisa, his former teaching assistant, was coming to his office at seven.

"Maybe I should kill her, too!" Connie's eyes glittered as she fingered the knife she'd taken from Willy Rossini.

No, Connie. You can't kill her. That would be murder. And we're not murderers.

"Alan!" Connie drew in her breath sharply. "Darling! I've missed you so much!"

I'm always with you, Connie. Alan's voice was clear. *And I'm stronger now that you're about to reclaim what was taken from me.*

Connie smiled. "I'm so glad you're with me, darling. But . . . I don't understand. Why wasn't it murder when we killed the others?"

Because they would have died without my gifts of life. You simply took them back and let nature have its way.

Connie didn't want to argue with Alan, but she wasn't sure she understood. "I guess that's true. Willy and Mark would have died without your kidneys, and the reverend's heart disease would have killed him. But how about Neil? He would have gone blind without your gift, but he'd still be alive."

You're wrong, Connie. I'm in a place where I can see what would have happened. Without the gift of my eyes, his depression would have driven him to suicide. I saved his life, Connie, and you are entitled to take it from him. It's not murder; it's a question of justice.

Connie nodded. "I see. But I'm not entitled to take Lisa's life?"

That's correct. Leave her alone, Connie. Lisa will suffer her own fate, but not at our hands. You must wait until she's gone before you take my gift of life from the professor.

"All right." Connie settled back to wait. She'd parked in a perfect position to see the entrance of Neil's office building. As she watched, a woman approached it, glanced at her watch, and then sat down on one of the benches to wait.

"That must be Lisa." Connie tried her best to see the woman's face, but it was in deep shadow. Then she noticed the lights of an approaching taxi. "He's coming, Alan! And he's right on time."

He must be hot to trot. Right, Connie?

Connie gasped at the phrase Alan had used. "Alan! I've never heard you say that before!"

I've learned a few things, Connie. That was a favorite expression of Turner's, if memory serves me correctly. Now watch. He'll kiss her, and they'll go up to his office.

Connie watched as Neil kissed the woman, and they climbed the steps. He unlocked the door and they went in, locking it again behind them.

"I have a key. I could—"

No, Connie. You must be patient and wait until she leaves. We'll spend our time talking about the baby and how we'll all be together soon.

"Yes, Alan." Connie smiled and rolled down the window, letting in the cool night breeze. The rain they'd had that afternoon had freshened the air, and the scent of the flowers in the planters outside was very pleasant.

"Do you ever miss it, Alan?" There was an expression of dismay on Connie's face as she considered Alan's plight. "I mean . . . the flowers and the sun and just being alive to see it all."

When Alan answered his voice was soft, so soft and caring Connie had to strain to hear it. *No, darling Connie. I don't miss the things of the world because I still have them.*

"But . . . how can that be?" Connie's voice was shaking with emotion.

Our love has joined us for all eternity. I feel your pain, and I know the sacrifices you've made for me. Soon, my darling . . . very soon now . . . I'll feel your joy as you hold our baby.

* * *

"Do you want a ride, Neil?" Lisa smiled as he unlocked the outside door. "It's still early. We could go back to my place and pick up my car."

Neil shook his head. "I'd better call a cab. She could be home early, and I don't want to take any chances."

"You've never been this worried before." Lisa began to frown. "Don't tell me she's finally got you running scared!"

"Not really. But I don't want to do anything to upset her. She's been a trooper for the past ten months, and I owe her something for sticking it out."

Lisa nodded. "I guess that's true. You sure as hell couldn't have been easy to live with! So what are you telling me, Neil? Are you going to be a faithful husband from now on?"

"I don't owe her *that* much!" Neil laughed. "I'm just being more careful, that's all."

"We can keep on seeing each other?" Lisa reached out to hug him.

"Yes, if you're careful, too. Once she has the baby she'll be so busy, she won't even notice whether I'm there or not."

"How long does she have to go?" Lisa stood on her tiptoes to kiss Neil.

"She's due seven weeks from now, but you can never tell with first babies. The doctor said it could be as early as the end of August or as late as the end of September."

"Maybe she'll go in on Labor Day." Lisa started to giggle. "That'd be perfect, wouldn't it?"

Neil laughed at her joke, and then he looked thoughtful. "It'd be perfect in more ways than one. If she's in the hospital, we could spend a couple of nights at the house."

"Great!" Lisa kissed him again, but then she drew back. "Wait a second. I thought you said you had a live-in house-keeper."

"We do, but she's very dedicated to Jill. If I suggest it, she'll sleep over at the hospital to keep Jill company. They'll have Jill so drugged up, she won't even know whether I'm there or not."

"Sounds like a plan." Lisa snuggled up close and began to unbutton his shirt.

"Hey, cut that out." Neil pushed her away, a playful grin on his face. "If you keep that up, I'll never get home tonight."

"That was the general idea." Lisa gave him a last hug. "But you're right, Neil. We don't want to make her suspicious now. It's just like you said. Once she has the kid, she'll forget all about checking up on you."

Neil grinned as Lisa walked away. It was great having two women who were both dying to sleep with him. Between Connie and Lisa, he was spending more time in the sack than out of it. Two women were manageable, but there might just be a real drain. Thank goodness Jill hadn't been interested in sex for the past two months!

He'd played things just right with her. At the end of May, when things had started to heat up with Connie, he'd told Jill that he was concerned about her comfort. He'd offered to move into the guest room across the hall, just to give her more room to stretch out. Jill had objected at first, but he had convinced her that her comfort was more important to him than anything else. They could visit back and forth, whenever she wanted, but he could live without sex until the baby was born. He'd told her that even though the doctor had said it was perfectly all right, he was concerned about hurting her or the baby.

After she'd gotten used to the idea, Jill had seemed pleased with the new arrangement. She hadn't knocked on his door, and he hadn't knocked on hers. She went to bed early most nights, and she slept straight through until it was time to get up. That suited Neil just fine. He usually spent the night in Connie's room, but he always woke Jill in the morning. What she didn't know wouldn't hurt her a bit, and he was having more fun than he'd ever had before.

And there was Lisa. Neil grinned as he went back to his office. She was even hotter than Connie, and she'd moved into a new apartment, right across the street from the men's gym. Connie thought he went to the weight room before lunch, to keep in shape. She'd never guessed that his only workout consisted of a roll in the sack with Lisa while her roommate was at work.

Neil called a cab, then chuckled as he went back downstairs to wait. He was the luckiest man alive. He had two beautiful, sexy mistresses and a pregnant wife who thought he was the most considerate man in the world. How much better could life get?

At the sound of approaching footsteps, he turned to see who it was. "Connie! What do you want?"

"I want you."

Neil started to grin. Lisa had just left, and now Connie was here. He was one popular guy! "I just called a cab, but now that you're here, I can save the fare. You can give me a ride home. I guess it's fate . . . right, Connie?"

Connie nodded, but there was a strange expression on her face. She didn't look angry. That wasn't it. She just looked very determined. "Is something wrong?" Neil asked.

"No, nothing's wrong." Connie's hand came up to expose the knife, its sharp blade glittering in the moonlight. "It's like you said, Neil. It's fate."

CHAPTER 32

Doug pulled the tape up and fastened it to the other side of the diaper. Then he picked up the life-size, rubber baby doll and handed it to Jill's matronly instructor, "Okay, ma'am. I'm ready."

"Very good!" The instructor smiled. "And very fast, too. Have you done this before?"

"No, ma'am. I've never had the pleasure. But it's a lot easier than roping steers."

The instructor smiled, but she had the last word. "That may be true. However, we'll wait until you actually have something *in* that diaper, and then we'll see how you feel about it."

The whole class cracked up, including Doug. Jill laughed the hardest of all. She'd never had so much fun in class before, and she knew it was because Doug was there.

The instructor glanced at her watch. "It's time for our tour. Follow me and I'll show you around the maternity wing."

Doug took Jill's arm as they rode up in the elevator. After they got off at the fifth floor, the instructor led them past the labor rooms and Jill was surprised at how beautifully they were decorated. The rooms were private, with only one bed, and each was furnished with a full-size sofa, a table with two comfortable chairs, and a console television set.

The instructor led them into a vacant labor room, and Doug raised his eyebrows. "This is nicer than my apartment. I thought it would look like a hospital room."

"That's exactly what we *don't* want." The instructor smiled at him. "We find our mothers-to-be are much more comfortable in a setting that looks like home."

One young wife looked very nervous, and she gripped her husband's hand tightly. "How long will I be here?"

"That's a good question. I'm afraid I can't give you a definite answer." The instructor smiled at her kindly. "It varies with each woman. First babies usually take a while. That's why we want the labor rooms to be as attractive as possible."

Another young woman spoke up. "My doctor told me to stay home until the contractions were twenty minutes apart. He said I'd spend less time in the hospital if I didn't come in too early."

"That's usually good advice, especially if you live close to the hospital. But if you're anxious about getting here on time, you should feel free to come in any time after labor has started."

"But then you're stuck here." An older woman, who was having her first child, spoke up. "When you come in, you have to stay in bed . . . don't you?"

The instructor shook her head. "Not anymore. Things have changed in the past few years. When you arrive, a doctor will check to see how far your labor has progressed. If you're in the early stages, you have quite a few options. You can go down to the courtyard to walk around, talk to the other couples in the reception area, or play cards in the game room. You're also welcome to stay here and watch television or read, but we encourage you to stay on your feet for as long as you can. It speeds up the process."

A tour of one of the delivery rooms was next, and Jill noticed that several of her classmates looked visibly nervous.

"You won't be in here for long." The instructor smiled at them. "You won't be brought in until you're ready to give birth, and the average delivery takes less than fifteen minutes."

"Where do we go when we get out of here?" The older woman was curious.

"You'll be taken to a regular room on this floor, and your baby will be carried to the nursery. Follow me. I'll show you."

The regular room was nice, too, and Jill noticed a bassinet by the bed. "That's for mothers who choose rooming in?"

"That's right." The instructor nodded.

"I wanted to room-in with my baby." One of the young women looked very disappointed. "But when I checked with our insurance company, they said they'd pay for only one night. It seemed kind of silly to choose rooming-in when the baby and I have to leave in the morning."

The instructor nodded. "Most insurance companies pay for only one night in the hospital. But our doctors are convinced that mothers and babies are much healthier and have fewer medical problems if they stay for two full nights."

"But that extra night is expensive, isn't it?" One of the husbands looked worried.

"Not at all. You'll have to fill out a questionnaire every month for the first year, but it won't cost you a penny. We're fighting to change the insurance coverage. We're hoping our statistics will convince them that allowing two nights in the hospital will save them money in the long run."

The young woman who'd looked so disappointed only moments before was smiling now. "Is it too late to change my mind and choose rooming-in?"

"It's not too late." The instructor smiled back at her. Then she motioned for them to follow and headed down the hallway. "And now . . . the place you've been waiting for all night. Let's take a quick peek at the nursery."

The nursery was at the end of the corridor, behind a huge plate-glass window. When they arrived, one nurse was seated in a rocking chair, feeding a newborn infant. Jill watched her for a moment and then her eyes traveled to the rows of bassinets. Two baby boys, wrapped in blue receiving blankets, were sleeping peacefully. A little girl, wrapped in a pink blanket, was yawning in preparation for waking up, and the baby boy in the next bassinet was trying to eat his fist.

Jill smiled as she watched the baby boy try to capture his fist with his mouth. He wasn't having much luck, and his mouth opened in a wail. Almost immediately, another nurse walked over to pick him up. She was smiling as she held him up to her shoulder and patted him softly.

"I never knew they'd be so little." Doug turned to Jill in amazement. "Look at the one she's holding. I've caught bigger trout that that."

Jill laughed and nodded. "They really are tiny, aren't they? It makes you wonder how something that small can be that perfect."

Everyone was silent, staring at the babies for a long moment. Jill became lost in her private thoughts, her innermost worries. Her doctor had told her that her pregnancy was normal, that the baby appeared to be healthy and thriving. But what if he had made a mistake and something was terribly wrong?

Doug seemed to know what she was thinking because he reached out to take her hand. "Don't worry, Jill. Your baby will be perfect, too."

"It's time to go back to the classroom." The instructor motioned to them. "Since tonight is our last meeting, we're having cake and punch."

With the other members of the class, Jill and Doug followed the instructor down the corridor. When they got back to the classroom, Doug was still holding her hand and Jill pulled away reluctantly.

"Hi, Jill." A couple in the class came up to them. The woman smiled at Doug and shook his hand. "I'm so glad you could make it tonight, Mr. Bradley. I'm Jean Olsen, and this is my husband, Fred. It's a real pleasure to see you're just as excited about the baby as Jill is."

Jill opened her mouth to explain that Doug wasn't her husband, but he was already shaking the woman's hand. "I'm glad to meet you, but I'm not Jill's husband. He couldn't be here tonight. I'm standing in for him."

"Oh, I see." Jean looked very flustered. "You seem to care about each other so much. I guess I just . . . Well . . . it's really nice of you to come with Jill."

"Thank you. It's been a real education for . . ." Doug stopped and reached for his pager. He glanced at the number displayed on the screen, then began to frown.

"Is it an emergency?" When Doug nodded, Jill's heartbeat quickened. The last time his beeper had gone off, the serial killer had struck again. She reached in her purse for her cell phone and handed it to him. "Here, Doug. You can step out in the hall if you want privacy."

"Thanks." Doug turned to Jean and Fred. "I'm sorry, but I've got to call in. It was nice meeting both of you."

After he had left, Jean pulled Jill to the side of the room. "Your friend is certainly handsome! What does he do?"

"He's a detective." Jill smiled. "We've worked together a lot in the past. Doug's a good friend, and he's my contact with the police department."

Jean nodded. "That's right. I'd forgotten that you were with the DA's office. Is he married?"

"No. He's single."

"Good!" Jean looked delighted. "Do you think he'd like

to meet a friend of mine? She's single. She wants to get married, but she just hasn't found the right man. If I tell you all about her, will you give him her number?"

"Well . . . uh . . . sure. I can do that."

Jill's heart sank as Jean told her all about her beautiful, talented, and successful friend. She had to admit that the woman sounded perfect for Doug.

"Well? What do you think?"

Jean looked anxious, and Jill nodded. "You're right. They sound perfect for each other."

"Then you'll give him her number?" Jill nodded again, and Jean scribbled a telephone number on a business card. "Her work number's on the front of the card, and I wrote her home phone on the back. Wouldn't it be wonderful if we were the ones to get them together?"

"Yes, I guess it would."

Jill tucked the card in the outside pocket of her purse, but she was frowning as Jean went off to rejoin her husband. She didn't like playing matchmaker. It was pushy and almost rude to assume that they could pick out the right woman for Doug. They would be meddling in his private life. He might resent it And if she gave Doug the card, she might very well lose the best friend she had!

There was a wastebasket by the instructor's desk. Jill's fingers went to the card. She had half a notion to drop it in the trash and never mention it to Doug. He'd never know. His chances of running into Jean or Fred again were very slight. She could do it now, while no one was looking, and pretend that Jean had never given it to her.

"Jill?" There was a hand on her arm, and Jill whirled around guiltily. It was Doug. He looked grim and sorry and horribly upset.

"What's wrong?" Jill's heart started to pound, and she leaned close so the others couldn't hear her. Doug looked very strange, as if he were fighting back tears. "Is it the serial killer?"

He nodded and took her arm, guiding her to the door. "We have to leave."

"Of course. You have to go to the crime scene." Jill hurried down the hallway with him, and they went out the main door. It wasn't raining any longer; it had turned into a beautiful night. "I'll go with you, Doug. I really don't mind, and maybe I can help. When you get enough extra officers on the scene, someone can drive me home."

"No, Jill. You can't come with me."

Doug's voice was shaking, and Jill stopped at the edge of the curb to stare at him. "What's the matter? Did you get in trouble for taking me to the last crime scene?"

"No, Jill. That's not it."

His voice was soft, and his arms were trembling as he stepped close to hug her. He held her for a long moment, and Jill began to feel very uneasy. Doug seemed to be trying to comfort her, and she wasn't sure why.

"Jill, honey . . . let's go to the car." Doug hugged her once more, then took her arm. "I'm afraid there's something I have to tell you."

She didn't utter a word on the drive home, and Doug glanced at her anxiously in the lights from the dashboard. She was staring straight ahead, lost in a place her shocked mind had provided, a refuge without pain or tears or awareness. Doug was silent, too. He didn't want to disturb her, to remind her of the present and the horrible event that had happened. It was best to let her escape for as long as she could so she might gather her strength for the ordeal ahead.

Doug's mind was racing as he drove silently to her house. Would Jill turn to him, now that Neil was dead? Or was it wrong to even hope that might happen, at least this soon after her husband's murder? He toyed with these questions all the way to her house, and when he pulled into the driveway, he'd made up his mind. Jill would need time to get over her loss. It would be unfair to press her or try to influence her when she was this vulnerable. He'd be her good friend, nothing more, until she came to him . . . if she did.

"Jill? We're here." He spoke very softly so he wouldn't startle her.

"Yes. Thank you, Doug." Jill blinked, and she seemed to become aware of her surroundings. Then she looked frightened. "Do you have to leave right away?"

"No. I won't go until someone comes to stay with you. Don't worry, Jill. I won't leave you alone."

When Doug took Jill's keys and started to unlock the door, someone opened it from the inside. She was an attractive young woman with glasses and dark blond hair, and Jill rushed straight into her arms. Doug knew immediately it was Connie, but he was puzzled because she looked familiar. He had the feeling he'd seen her somewhere before, though perhaps that was because Jill had described her so accurately.

"Jill!" Connie looked completely baffled. "What's wrong?"

"He . . . He . . . Oh, it's awful!"

Connie turned to him, puzzled, and Doug began to explain. "I'm Doug Lake. We just got word that Jill's husband is dead."

"Oh, my God!" Connie was clearly shocked, but she recovered quickly and then became just as efficient as Jill had told him she was. "Thank you for bringing her home. Would you help me get her to the couch?"

It didn't take long to get Jill settled with a pillow and a blanket. Connie murmured comforting words while she stroked her forehead. When Jill seemed to fall into a light sleep, Connie stood up and led Doug over to a chair on the opposite side of the room. "Tell me what happened. Was it a traffic accident?"

Doug explained as quickly as he could, and when he'd finished, Connie shook her head.

"I just can't believe it. He was such a vital person, and now he's . . . gone. Poor Jill! I'm so glad you were with her, Detective Lake."

"It's Doug. And I'm glad I was with her, too. Do you think she'll be all right?"

"I'll make sure she is." Connie looked very determined. "I'll call her doctor and ask him to come out. Don't worry. I'll take good care of her. Jill's like . . . well . . . she's like the big sister I never had."

"I know she thinks a lot of you." Doug stood up and shook Connie's hand. "I have to go now. They called me in, and they're waiting for me."

Doug was at the door when Jill called out his name.

"Yes, Jill." He turned to look at her. Although her face was pale and drawn, she was very beautiful.

"I know you have to leave." Jill's voice was trembling. "When are you coming back?"

"I'll be here in the morning. Try to sleep. It'll help."

As he drove to the crime scene, Doug's heart was beating fast. Jill needed him. That much was very clear. Even though Connie was there to take care of her, she had wanted to know when he was coming back.

CHAPTER 33

The voices seemed to come from a long distance away, but Jill heard them clearly. Doug and Connie. And they were talking about her.

Her doctor said she's fine so far, but there's always the chance this could bring on premature labor. If she can get through the next twelve hours, she'll be all right.

There was a pause and then another voice spoke, a deeper voice . . . Doug's. *I'm really glad you were home, Connie. I had to get to the crime scene, and I couldn't have left her here all alone.*

"Why couldn't I be alone?" Jill tried to speak the words, but no sound came from her lips. She opened her eyes and saw the sun streaming across the ceiling of the living room. What was she doing in the living room? And why were Connie and Doug talking so softly?

She turned her head slightly and saw Connie and Doug, seated in the swivel rockers her mother and father had used to watch television. But why was she on the couch, covered with a blanked? Had she fallen? Was she ill? What was going on?

Suddenly Jill remembered, and she drew in her breath

sharply. Neil had been murdered outside his office building. Her husband, the man who'd married her and fathered her baby, was dead. She'd never see Neil again.

Jill swallowed hard and turned her face toward the back of the couch. Neil's couch. She'd never liked it, but he'd insisted it was perfect for the living room. Now the green and tan tweed material seemed to admonish her. They'd fought bitterly over the couch until she'd finally caved in and agreed that they could buy it. There were gold flecks in the tweed. She'd never noticed them before. They were like the gold flecks in Neil's eyes, and Jill stared at them for a moment. Shouldn't she be crying? Or screaming? Or exhibiting some powerful emotion? Her husband had just been brutally murdered, yet she was staring at the couch with perfectly dry eyes.

Last night, when Neil had left in the taxi, she hadn't even said good-bye. She should have kissed him and told him that she loved him before he left. That's what a good wife would have done. And she *had* loved him once, even though it was no longer true. It would have cost her nothing to send him off with a kiss, but she hadn't. Now it was too late.

Guilt, bitter and strong, washed over Jill in a powerful wave. Was honesty really that important? Wouldn't it have been better if she'd played the role of an adoring wife? Things certainly had been much easier between them after they'd hired Connie. And Neil had been trying. He'd been so considerate, he'd even moved across the hall so she could have the whole bed.

Jill sighed. Her husband was dead, someone should tell his family. Connie didn't know them, and the call should come from her. His brother and sister-in-law had to be notified. Someone had to tell his friends. And his students. They should know what had happened. His colleagues in the department—they should know, too.

Thank God for Connie! Jill gave a sigh of relief. Connie knew Neil's students and the other members of the department. She'd send her to the college today, to deliver the sad news.

There would have to be a funeral. It was up to her to arrange for that. And a memorial service on campus. Norma could plan the campus service. She'd want to do it, and everyone needed some type of closure to lessen their grief.

But Jill wasn't grieving. Her forehead furrowed in a frown. Why wasn't she grieving when her husband was dead? What kind of monster was she?

Perhaps it just hadn't sunk in yet. When it did, she'd start to grieve. Or perhaps it was because she'd come so close to divorcing Neil, once when she'd first found him in bed with Lisa and again right after Christmas party.

She'd have to pretend at the funeral. Everyone would expect her to be devastated. Neil's pregnant wife would have to cry or everyone would think she hadn't cared.

Was that true? Jill thought about it for a moment. Then she shook her head slightly. She *had* cared. She'd wanted the best for Neil and the baby. That's why she'd stayed with him and tried so hard to make their marriage work. She'd desperately wanted her baby to have a father.

The thought of the fatherless child in her womb made tears well up in Jill's eyes. That was better. She could cry for the baby who'd never know a father, though she had trouble crying for Neil. No one would know the difference. All they'd notice were her tears.

Poor Neil. She hoped he hadn't suffered. It was a terrible tragedy for the whole campus, a professor struck down in the prime of life, right outside his office.

"But what was Neil doing at his office?" Jill didn't realize she'd spoken aloud until they turned to her. She sat up to face them and repeated her question again. "Why was Neil at his office?"

Connie jumped up and rushed over to soothe her. "It's all right, Jill. I know everything's confusing, but just try to relax. Maybe it's better if you don't think about it."

"But I *have* to think about it!" Jill declared. "That's what I was trained to do. And I know Neil wasn't supposed to be anywhere near his office last night."

"Are you sure?"

Doug pulled out his notepad, and Jill released a sigh of relief. At least someone was taking her seriously. "I'm sure, Doug. His meeting was at the administration building, and that's on the East Campus. Neil's office is across the bridge on the West Campus."

Connie perched on the arm of the sofa and put her arm around Jill's shoulders. "Don't worry about it, Jill. He probably went back to his office after the meeting was over."

"But how did he get there? He went to the campus by taxi. I know because I called for the cab. Neil wouldn't walk across the bridge in the dark. His eyesight isn't . . ." Jill stopped and took a deep breath. She had to remember to use the past tense. "His eyesight wasn't that good. And if somebody gave him a ride, they may have seen something."

Doug nodded. "Good point. I'll ask the other people who were at the meeting."

"Norma Jenkins was probably there. She has an office in Neil's building." Jill turned to Connie. "There's a faculty telephone book on the shelf in the library. Would you please get it and give it to Doug?"

Connie nodded. "Of course. But, Jill . . . you should be resting. I don't want you to get upset. It's not good for the baby."

"I'm not upset." Jill reached out to give Connie a hug. "But you've got to understand. It helps me to think about catching Neil's killer. I want to be a part of the investigation. It's less painful for me that way."

Connie still looked concerned, but she nodded. "Whatever you think is best, Jill. I don't understand, but that's okay. My only concern is for you and the baby."

"I think I understand." Doug waited until Connie had gone to get the telephone book, then he smiled at Jill. "If you can think about something logically, it makes it less personal. Less personal is less painful. Right?"

"Exactly!"

"You said Neil took a cab. Do you know which cab company came?"

"Yes. It was CityWide. I saw it when it drove up—number seventy-three. The driver was an older woman, heavyset with dark hair."

"Good." Doug wrote it all down. "What time was that?"

"Seven thirty-six. I was in the bedroom, getting dressed for my baby class. I glanced at the clock when the cab pulled up, and I remember thinking Neil would just make it in time for the meeting."

"His meeting was scheduled for eight?" Jill nodded and Doug wrote that down. "You're sure it was being held at the Administration Building?"

"Positive. It was a budget meeting, and they're always held in the board room."

Doug glanced down at his notebook. "What was Neil wearing when he left the house?"

"A white shirt with a button-down collar, a dark gray tie, and his gray blazer. And jeans. Neil always wore jeans. He said poets and writers shouldn't dress in suits. It made them too conventional."

Doug nodded. "How about a watch? Or jewelry?"

"No jewelry. Neil said it was too ostentatious. But he did wear a Rolex. He bought it right after he got his first royalty check." Jill frowned slightly. "I told him it was an invitation to a mugging, but he insisted on wearing it. It's not missing, is it?"

"No. It's with his personal effects. I'll get those to you in a couple of days. His wallet's there, too, with forty-three dollars inside. How many credit cards did he usually carry?"

Jill thought for a moment, then answered, "Two. American Express and Visa. And a Triple-A card."

"Then nothing's missing."

"You thought there would be?" Jill raised her eyebrows.

"Not really, but it rules out a mugging."

Jill looked surprised. "I thought you said it was another serial killing?"

"That's what we think. We won't know for sure until the lab results come in."

"When is the autopsy?"

Connie came back just in time to hear Jill's question. "Jill! You're not going to . . . I mean . . . You wouldn't actually—"

"Of course she wouldn't." Doug shook his head. "I know this sounds strange, Connie, but these are actually routine questions."

Connie drew a shaky breath before turning to Jill. "Okay, if you say so. Is there anything else I can do for you?"

"Yes, dear." Jill reached out for her hand. "Just tell me if this is asking too much of you—I know you're upset, too— but do you think you could drive to the college and tell Neil's students what's happened?"

Connie nodded. "Of course. I know most of them and they might take it better if they hear it from me. But how about you, Jill? I don't want to leave you alone."

"I'll be fine. I have to call Neil's brother, and I'd better notify his publisher in New York. Then there's the obit for the paper and the arrangements for his funeral. There's plenty to do. I'd better get started right . . ."

Jill's voice trailed off as a rush of hot tears filled her eyes.

And then she was sobbing, crying like a baby as she realized that Neil was actually dead.

Time must have passed, but Jill wasn't aware of it. She was so cold, as cold as the morgue where they'd taken her husband. There was a buzzing in her ears, like the sound of the chainsaw her father had used to cut up the dead tree in the backyard. The chain saw massacre. Bloody. Horrible. But Neil had been killed with a knife. Why were they being so ridiculously strict about gun legislation? Knives were every bit as lethal, and you could buy them in any store. There was no waiting period, no registration, and for all they knew the serial killer had probably ordered it from a catalog and had it delivered to her house!

Someone was screaming, a high thin noise that sounded like a kitten in distress. Was it her? Then there was a sting in her arm and her doctor's face appeared, pale and bobbing like a balloon on a string, going in and out of focus.

She was warm again, covered with a blanket, as a blessed numbness took control of her mind. But she could still hear the voices, three of them this time.

I gave her a mild sedative. She'll sleep for at least four hours. How about the baby? So far, so good. Keep your eye on her. She tried to say no, she didn't need an eye. What she needed was a husband, alive and warm, holding her tenderly because he loved her. Only her. No one else. And then there was a light kiss on her forehead, lips brushing her softly like a butterfly's wing. *I've got to go, Jill. They just paged me. But I'll be back tonight.*

In this unreal place, events seemed to mark the time as minutes marked the face of a clock. There was the sound of a door opening, and she heard what sounded like Norma's voice. *I'm so glad you called, Connie. I'll sit with her until you get back.*

The doctor says she'll be all right, but here's his number. He can be here in less than ten minutes if she needs him.

And then there was nothing, just the lingering memory of Doug's warm lips on her forehead. It made her feel warm and loved. He would be back tonight. He'd promised. And the one thing Jill had learned about Doug Lake was that he always kept his promises.

CHAPTER 34

A month had passed, and Jill was back at work. Connie hadn't wanted her to go back this soon, but Jill had insisted. She'd packed up Neil's things and put them in storage, but the house still reminded her of him.

Doug had been very gentle when he'd told her what he'd uncovered in his investigation. That had helped, but it was still painful. Neil hadn't gone to the campus for a meeting. There wasn't any meeting. He'd gone to meet Lisa Hyland. That was why he'd been at his office.

Lisa had confessed everything to Doug. She'd come back to town to resume her affair with Neil, and she'd been sleeping with him for the past two months. He hadn't moved out of Jill's bedroom because he was being considerate; he'd done it because he was exhausted. Even worse, Lisa had told Doug she suspected Neil was cheating on her with a second woman.

Although she hadn't told Connie, that was the reason Jill had gone back to work so early. It took her mind off what Doug had uncovered in his investigation. And work would have helped, if everyone in the office hadn't been so terribly careful.

It had happened again this morning, when Jill had wandered into the coffee room. Her secretary, Mary, had been talking to several other secretaries who had gathered to share a break.

"It's going to be great!" Mary had been saying. "His parents are taking the kids for a week, and we're going to the Bahamas. It'll be like a second honeymoon. With the kids and all, I haven't been alone with my hus—"

Mary had broken off in the middle of a word and had put on a bright smile for Jill. "I was just telling them about my vacation. Have you ever been to the Bahamas, Jill?"

"Yes. Neil and I went there on our honeymoon. It's lovely, I'm sure you'll have a good time."

An uneasy silence had set in while Jill had poured her coffee. And then Mary had spoken up again. "Sorry, Jill. I forgot all about that. I really hope I didn't upset you."

"Not at all." Jill had smiled and left with her coffee. She wished Mary wouldn't be quite so sensitive. It almost bordered on the paranoid, and she was getting tired of being treated as if she'd break down in tears at hearing the word "husband."

But Mary wasn't the only one. It seemed all of her coworkers were walking on eggshells. They never spoke about their spouses in front of her, and they avoided all references to the serial killings. It would be much easier if they said whatever was on their minds and let her cope with it.

"Hi, Jill." Doug stuck his head in the door. "Do you have time to talk?"

"Only if you make sure to use the words 'husband' and 'dead' and 'murder.' I'm sick up people pussyfooting around me!"

It took Doug a second, but then he laughed. "What's the matter? Everybody being a little too considerate?"

"You said it!" Jill sighed deeply. "You're the only one who doesn't handle me with kid gloves;"

"That's because I know you."

His voice was soft, and Jill frowned slightly. She wanted to ask what he meant, but she wasn't sure she could cope with his answer. "That's not it, Doug. Connie knows me, and she still does it. I don't think she's mentioned Neil since he died."

"Then maybe I understand you better than anyone else. They don't realize how strong you are. You've never shied away from the truth for as long as I've known you. You're a survivor, Jill. And you don't spend much time feeling sorry for yourself."

"Oh-oh." Jill raised her eyebrows. "Don't tell me you found the other woman Neil was seeing!"

"No. We don't have a clue. But I do have some good news about the investigation."

"Why didn't you say so?" Jill grinned at him. "What is it? Did you get a lead?"

"A big one. Rossini and Turner had kidney transplants. And Woodard got a new heart."

Jill's eyebrows shot up. "University Hospital?"

"Bingo! Why don't you quit this lawyer stuff and come to work for me? You catch on faster than any of the guys on my team."

"Thanks." Jill smiled at him. "That's four out of four, Doug. It's a positive connection. How about other transplant recipients?"

"I don't know. We haven't been able to check that out. We're trying to get Judge Donnely to give us an order to unseal the hospital records, but there's a lot of red tape involved."

Jill nodded. The patient-doctor confidentiality issue was a stickler. "Do you know if they had the same donor?"

"No, but Judge Donnely's scheduled a hearing. We should have access by the end of next week."

Jill looked thoughtful. "Maybe it's the donor, but there are other possibilities. It could be someone who works at the hospital. Or a relative of a patient who's on the list and *didn't* get a transplant."

"I'm working on that, too. I just thought you'd want to know we had a minor breakthrough."

Jill shook her head. "It's a *major* breakthrough. You've finally found a connection between the victims. Now all you have to do is chase it down. Congratulations, Doug. You're getting close."

"Thanks." He looked pleased. "We're going to get her, Jill. You can make book on that."

Connie frowned as Jill picked at her salad. "You seem really distracted. Can I help?"

Jill debated for a few moments. Doug hadn't specifically asked her not to mention the breakthrough, but she knew it was supposed to be confidential.

"Can you keep a secret?" Jill smiled as Connie nodded. Connie was practically family, and she deserved to know what Doug had learned. "The police got a lead, and Doug thinks it's only a matter of time before they catch Neil's killer."

Connie's eyes widened in surprise. "Really? That's wonderful, Jill! Tell me all about it . . ."

Connie wished she'd bought a car with air conditioning as she rolled down her windows and let in the hot, muggy air. It was the middle of August, and it was a sweltering day. She was driving to Northern Minnesota to rent a cabin. It had taken some persuading, but she'd convinced Jill to take a long weekend, starting on Friday and extending to the middle of the next week.

"I won't forget, Alan." Connie tipped her head and listened

to the voice in her ear. "I'll make sure the cabin is isolated and the owner doesn't live in the area."

She's going to go with you willingly?

"Of course." Connie smiled in the direction of his voice. "I told her I needed to get away, and she agreed to come with me. She's getting close, Alan. She's due in three weeks."

That's perfect timing, Connie. Alan's voice was joyful. *Soon we'll have our baby.*

"I know." Connie was so happy she laughed out loud. Thank God for Alan! She'd told him what Jill had said about the investigation, and he'd warned her to move immediately. It was just as Jill had said, only a matter of time until the police caught the serial killer. There was another factor that worried both Alan and Connie, and that factor had a name. Doug Lake. He was the lead detective, and he was good. It was best to move Jill now and not take any chances.

"I think we're here, Alan." Connie checked the address on the mailbox. "Yes, this is it. The rental agent said it had a river-rock wall by the driveway."

Connie turned down the winding drive and smiled as a cool breeze blew in through the window. It would be pleasant to spend the next three weeks at the lake.

The moment she stopped the car, the rental agent came out of the cabin to greet her. The agent was a thin woman with dark hair pulled back in a bun, and she looked very eager. "Hi! You're right on time. I'm Marsha Hopkins."

"Cynthia Woods." Connie gave the same name she'd used when she'd spoken to the agent by phone.

"I'm glad to meet you, Cynthia. Come in and take a look around. From what you told me over the phone, I think it'll fit your needs perfectly."

Connie climbed up the steps and walked into the cabin. It was much larger than she had anticipated, more like a lodge than a lake cabin. She let the rental agent lead her through the rooms, a kitchen, half-bath, and a huge living room on the ground floor, four bedrooms upstairs. The bedrooms all had balconies overlooking the lake, and Connie was glad to see that there was no outside staircase. Once she'd locked Jill in one of the bedrooms, there would be no way for her to get out.

"Lovely, isn't it?" The rental agent drew a lease out of her purse. "What do you think? Is it right for you?"

Connie nodded. "It looks perfect, but I do have a couple of questions. How about the other cabins? Are the neighbors quiet?"

"Absolutely." The rental agent laughed. "It's the end of the season. The cabin to the north is closed up for the winter, and the place to the south is in escrow. There's only one place that's still occupied, and they're leaving today."

"Then you can almost guarantee I won't be disturbed?"

The rental agent nodded. "The only company you're going to have will be the squirrels and the birds."

"Wonderful. It seems to be exactly what I'm looking for. You did a fine job, finding it for me."

The agent looked pleased with herself. "Thank you. When you said you needed solitude to finish your book, I thought of this place right away."

"But how about the owner?" Connie frowned slightly. "He won't drop by every day, will he?"

"Heavens no! Mr. Marvin's in Spain. He won't be back until the first of the year. He bought this place two years ago, and he hasn't been here since. It's strictly an investment property."

"It certainly seems perfect." Connie smiled as she drew out her wallet. "I'd like to rent it for two months, with an option for a third if I need it. I'll pay you in advance."

The agent's eyes widened as she saw the money in Connie's wallet. "You're paying in cash?"

"Yes, I stopped at the bank so you wouldn't have to bother with an out-of-town check."

"That was very nice of you." The rental agent glanced at the money again, then lowered her eyes. "There's only a slight problem. When I spoke to Mr. Marvin last night, he wasn't quite satisfied with the rent. I hope this doesn't change your mind, but he wants five hundred instead of the four I quoted you?"

Connie almost laughed out loud. She knew the agent would pocket the extra hundred a month, but she managed to look perfectly serious as she nodded her assent. "That's fine. It's still a bargain for a place that's so isolated, and I do need my solitude. I have a December first deadline, and it's impossible to work in the city."

"I understand." The agent took the money Connie handed her and counted it quickly. "What did you say your book was about?"

Connie was stymied for a moment, but Alan whispered the answer in her ear. "It's a textbook on genetics. I'm compiling the results of several independent studies. I'd tell you more, but I'm afraid it's quite technical."

"I imagine it is." The agent looked impressed. "Well, you'll have plenty of peace and quiet here."

"You said utilities were included?"

"Yes." The rental agent nodded. "The owner pays water and electricity, and I can arrange for your telephone service."

"Thank you, but I won't need a phone." Connie shook her head. "It disturbs me when I'm trying to concentrate."

The agent nodded quickly. "I can understand that. There's a phone at Tony's Market. That's the little grocery store about five miles back at the turnoff. He closes down the first of September, but the pay phone's outside on the porch."

After Connie signed her assumed name on the lease, she

said good-bye and headed out to her car. As she headed back down the driveway, she heard Alan's voice again.

Good job, Connie. You picked a perfect place. And you're sure there won't be a problem getting Jill to come here with you?

Connie shook her head. "She'll come. And once I get her here, I'll make sure she stays until our baby is born."

CHAPTER 35

The phone rang three times, but no one answered. Doug had hoped to share his good news with Jill. Judge Donnely had ordered the hospital to release the records, and it had been done at eight that morning. The name of the donor was the same for all of the murder victims, just as Jill had suspected, and Doug had spent the past four hours interviewing the other patients who had received transplants from the same donor.

He had found Shelly Devore in her kindergarten classroom, had asked her a series of questions, and had assigned an officer to protect her. Miss Devore hadn't noticed anyone following her, but she had received a strange visit when she'd come home from the hospital. The visitor had been a very nice woman, in her late twenties with red hair. She'd brought Shelly flowers, but when Shelly had called to thank the hospital for sending out such a nice volunteer, they'd told her they hadn't sent out anyone.

With his fingers crossed, Doug had asked if she remembered the woman's name. Shelly had nodded. She'd said it was Charlotte West, she had remembered because one of her coworkers was named Charlotte.

The next name on Doug's list had been Kathy Miller.

He had driven to her home in North Minneapolis, where he'd learned that Kathy had died, shortly before Christmas. But her sister had remembered a strange incident. Flowers had been delivered for Kathy, a huge bouquet without a card. The woman who'd delivered them, a pretty redhead in her late twenties who'd said her name was Chloe White, had told them the flowers were from Kathy's friend, Alan. They were still puzzling over the mystery bouquet. Kathy had never mentioned a friend named Alan.

Ian Perkins was next on Doug's list, and he'd gone to Ian's sixth-grade classroom. Ian, a bright eleven-year-old, had been very cooperative. He'd remembered a woman who had come to visit when he was in the convalescent center. She'd said her name was Camille Ward, and she had been very beautiful. He was sure she'd been older than his sister, a senior in high school, but a lot younger than his mother.

Why had she visited him? Ian had smiled proudly. She'd told him that she was a volunteer from the hospital, but she had another connection to him. She'd sworn him to secrecy and he couldn't tell, but it was a wonderful secret.

It had taken a while, but Doug had persuaded Ian to confide in him. Camille had said he had her boyfriend's liver. She'd told him all about the man named Alan, and he'd sounded like a really cool guy.

Doug had assigned protection for Ian, and then he'd gone over the descriptions. It was clear that the same person had visited all the survivors, although the name had been different. Camille Ward, Chloe White, and Charlotte West. The initials were all C.W. That was too much of a coincidence. It was clear the woman had used her real initials.

While Greg had driven back to the office, Doug had glanced down at his notebook. Shortly before Willy Rossini had been murdered, he'd eaten dinner with a woman named Cherie White. Another C.W. The second victim, Mark Turner, had also known a woman with the initials C.W. His landlady had told them that Cheryl Walton, the woman who had moved into Mark's former apartment had moved again, shortly after his death. The landlady was a bit of a busy-body, and she'd suspected that Mark and Cheryl had been much more than neighbors. And then there was the mystery woman that Reverend Woodard had baptized. All they had was a first name, but Crystal fit the first initial.

How did this fit in with Neil's murder? Doug frowned as he listened to Jill's phone ringing. There had been only one student in Neil's class with the initials C.W. He was a male graduate student, and Doug was sure that Chuck Waxter didn't have a place in the picture. The only other candidate was one of the staff, a temporary secretary named Cindy Wyatt. Cindy fit the description, but she had an alibi. Her boyfriend swore she'd been with him all evening.

Another piece of the puzzle was worrying Doug. The serial killer, the woman who had brutally murdered four people, had spared Shelly Devore and Ian Perkins. She'd killed only grown men, but Doug wasn't sure if that was a factor.

"Damn!" Doug glared at the phone. Jill had told him that she and Connie were leaving today, and they must have hit the road early. Now he'd have to wait to tell her about his progress until she came back on Wednesday.

He had mixed emotions about what Jill had described as her mini vacation. He really hadn't wanted her to leave, but he'd known that a change of scene might help. She'd been complaining about the heat and how uncomfortable it made her, so Connie was taking her to a bed-and-breakfast lodge on a Northern Minnesota lake. The fresh air and cooler temperatures would be a relief for Jill, but Doug wished he knew exactly where she'd gone. When he'd asked, she hadn't known the name of the lake, but she'd promised to call.

There was a knock on Doug's door and Greg came in, wiping his forehead with a handkerchief. "Jesus! It's hot out there!"

"I know, but maybe that's good. It's too hot for street crime!" Greg looked surprised and Doug explained. "Look at the stats. Street crime drops way below normal twice a year. In the hottest month of the summer and the coldest month of the winter."

"Okay. I believe you. And I can understand about the winter. Nobody wants to hang around outside when it's twenty degrees below zero."

"Right." Doug nodded. "Hot weather's just the reverse. If all you can think about is cooling off, you're going to stay home in front of the fan. It's even too hot for fights. People just don't have the energy."

Greg dropped into a chair and fanned his face. "You can say that again! I'm bushed and it's only ten in the morning. Do we really have to wear ties?"

"I'm afraid so." Doug picked up his jacket and slipped it on. "The donor's family is in the social register, and the maid won't let us in the front door if we don't."

"I just don't understand why I'm so tired." Jill yawned again. "I can barely keep my eyes open."

Connie nodded. "That's because we're out of the city and you're starting to relax. Why don't you take a little nap? I'll wake you up when we get there."

"Maybe I will."

Connie smiled as Jill leaned back in the seat and closed her eyes. She'd added one of Jill's sedatives to her orange juice that morning, and it was working perfectly. The doctor had prescribed them to help Jill sleep, but after the first two nights, she had decided not to take them. There had been twenty-eight left in the bottle and a refill on the prescription. Now Connie had fifty-eight pills in her purse. She planned to use them to keep Jill sedated until the baby was born.

Are you sure they won't hurt the baby?

There was concern in Alan's voice, and Connie shook her head. She glanced over at Jill, who was sleeping soundly, and then she replied softly. "No. They're fine. Her obstetrician prescribed them."

Very good.

Alan seemed satisfied, and Connie smiled. He should have known that she wouldn't take any chances with their baby. She drove in silence for a few more miles. Then Alan spoke again.

The detective is bound to start looking for her when she doesn't come back to town. Are you sure you didn't leave any clues?

"I'm positive. It's going to work out perfectly, Alan. I've got everything under control."

But he knows you're going to a lake. She told him that.

"That's true." Connie gave a soft giggle. "But this is Minnesota. Remember what it says on the license plates?"

The Land of Ten Thousand Lakes. Alan laughed, and Connie joined in. *That's very funny, Connie.*

Connie grinned as she nodded. "Thank you, darling. Even if he checked over a hundred lakes a day, he couldn't cover them all in a year. We're safe, Alan. And our baby's safe, too."

"Constance Wilson?" Doug jotted it down in his notebook. "And she was engaged to marry your son?"

Mrs. Stanford nodded. "I'm afraid so. She was totally unsuitable, but Alan was completely infatuated with her."

"Could you please describe her?"

"I'm afraid I can't." Mrs. Stanford turned to her daughter. "I never met her, but Beth did."

Beth nodded. "Alan introduced us. She was about my

height with brown hair and green eyes. She was on the thin side, but she had a very good figure."

"Any identifying features? Birthmarks? Moles?"

Beth shook her head. "Not that I remember."

"How about glasses? Did she wear them?"

"No. Would it help to see a picture of her? There might be one in storage."

Doug nodded. "I'd appreciate it, Miss Stanford."

"We put all our dear son's things in storage after his death." Mrs. Stanford rang the buzzer by her chair. "There were several framed photographs, and if I remember correctly, Miss Wilson was the subject of one. If you can wait for just a moment, Detective Lake, I'll have my butler take you to them."

"We're here, Jill."

Jill opened her eyes to see Connie smiling at her. "How long did I sleep?"

"The whole way. What do you think? Isn't it beautiful?"

Jill sat up and peered out the window at the lake cottage. It looked like a log cabin except it was much larger. There were green shutters on the windows and a series of rustic balconies on the second floor. "It's gorgeous! But . . . where are the other cars?"

"That's my surprise." Connie got out of the car and opened Jill's door. "We're the only guests, Jill. Since it's the off-season, I rented the whole place."

At first Jill was a bit disconcerted, but as she stepped into the lovely cabin, she was glad that she and Connie were alone. "It's perfect, Connie. And you're a darling for thinking of it. If I weren't so sleepy, I'd explore the whole place right now."

Connie laughed. "There's all the time in the world, Jill.

We can explore it later. Right now, I want to show you your room and let you finish your nap."

Connie led her up the staircase and opened the door on the left, revealing a gorgeous bedroom with walls of knotty pine, a built-in dresser, and a king-sized bed.

"It's so beautiful!" Jill glanced out the balcony doors. The lake was sparkling in the sun, and a light breeze was rustling through the tall stately pines that lined the shore. She wanted to go down to the shore to gather some of the huge pinecones scattered beneath the trees. They'd make wonderful Christmas decorations for next year. But she was simply too tired to do anything at all. "Maybe you're right, Connie. I'm sorry I'm such rotten company, but I can barely keep my eyes open."

Connie nodded and patted the bed. "Just stretch out and get comfortable, Jill. I brought your preggie pillow. I'll open the balcony doors so you'll have a nice breeze."

"Thank you." Jill glanced at her watch as she stretched out on the bed. The trip had taken two hours. Even though she'd slept for most of the way, she was still tired. "I can't understand why I'm so sleepy. I must have been much more exhausted than I realized."

Connie nodded and opened the balcony doors. "Just sleep, Jill. You need the rest. I'll take care of all the unpacking, and then I'll make something to eat. You'll be hungry when you wake up."

"Yes. I suppose I will." Jill closed her eyes and snuggled under the light blanket Connie had given her. The bed was comfortable, the breeze was delicious. She'd never felt so relaxed. Connie was right. She'd needed a vacation, and this was wonderful. She only wished that Doug were here to enjoy it with her.

* * *

"Are you sure this is Connie Wilson?" Doug blinked as he stared at the silver-framed picture.

"I'm sure." Beth nodded. "That's exactly the way she looked when I met her at Alan's condo."

Doug swallowed hard as he stared at the familiar face. Connie Wilson was the deranged woman who'd broken into the University Hospital Morgue to see her boyfriend's body. "Miss Stanford, I'm sorry if this brings back painful memories, but do you know whether your brother's body was held in the University Hospital Morgue?"

"Yes. They kept him on life support until they could . . ." Beth blinked several times and took a deep breath. ". . . harvest his organs. Then he was taken to the morgue."

"Here's another picture." The butler handed Beth a snapshot. "I'm not sure it's Miss Wilson, though."

Beth glanced down at the snapshot and then nodded. "It's Connie. Alan showed me this picture. It was taken right after he met her, before she let her hair go back to its natural color. She looks like a different person as a blonde, doesn't she, Detective?"

"Yes, she does." Doug's hands started to tremble as he examined the snapshot. Her hair was a lighter shade of blond and she wasn't wearing glasses, but she was clearly recognizable. It was another C.W., one he'd missed, one who was linked to Neil. This was a picture of Connie Walters, Jill's housekeeper!

"Are you all right, Detective?" The chauffeur looked very concerned.

"Yeah. I'm okay." Doug took a deep breath and steadied himself. There was no doubt in his mind. Connie Walters was the serial killer, and Jill had gone off on a vacation with her!

CHAPTER 36

When Jill woke up, it was after four. She'd slept almost the entire day! She dressed in maternity jeans and a short-sleeved top and went down the stairs to find Connie.

"Hi." Connie looked up as she came into the kitchen. "Did you have a good nap?"

Jill nodded. "I guess! I practically slept the whole day away."

"You probably needed the rest." Connie opened the oven and a delicious aroma filled the room. "I'm baking bread. When that comes out, I've got a pie all ready to go in. We're going to have a Waldorf salad, home-baked bread, and blueberry pie for dessert."

"That sounds wonderful! When will it be ready?"

"In about an hour." Connie closed the oven and turned to smile at Jill. "You haven't eaten since breakfast. Are you hungry?"

Jill nodded. "I'm starved!"

"Good. There's a bowl of fruit on the table. Grab an apple or a banana to tide you over, and I'll unpack your suit-case."

"But I can do that. You shouldn't work so hard, Connie."

"Nonsense." Connie smiled at her. "There's an old-fashioned porch swing that faces the lake, right outside the back door. Why don't you try it out and enjoy the view?"

Jill nodded. "Okay . . . if you're sure I can't help you."

"I'm sure. There's a pile of magazines next to the swing if you get bored. I'll call you in when dinner is ready."

Jill wandered out to the back porch and sighed in contentment as she settled down on the swing. It was a luxury, not having anything to do for five whole days. She tucked her feet up on the cushion and positioned a pillow behind her back. The swing moved gently, and she felt like a child rocked in her mother's arms. The view was just as wonderful as Connie had said. Jill smiled as she glanced at the shoreline.

The lake wasn't large, and she could see the cabins on the opposite shore. A large A-frame, directly across the water, caught Jill's eye. It was bigger than all the other cabins, and it had a huge lawn that was a lovely emerald green color. Jill counted the number of windows in the place and realized that it was too big to belong to a single family. It had to be a lodge or a country club or maybe even a restaurant. Her curiosity aroused, Jill decided to drive over for a closer look.

Her car keys were on the table. She had noticed them when she'd come down from her room. She went back inside to get them and walked quickly to her car.

But it wouldn't start! The engine refused to turn over. Jill frowned and tried it again, but her effort resulted in nothing but a click and then silence. This could be very bad. What if she went into labor and they were stuck here with a car that wouldn't start?

She hurried back to the cabin and raced upstairs. "Connie, I was going to take a drive around the lake, but my car won't start!"

"I know." Connie nodded. "I was going to park it under the car port, and it wouldn't start for me, either."

"But what if the baby comes early?" Jill was in a near panic state.

"Don't worry." Connie smiled at her. "I've already called for someone to fix it."

Jill drew in a deep sigh of relief. "I should have known! You take such good care of me."

"I try." Connie seemed pleased by the compliment. "There is a slight problem though. The mechanic doesn't work on weekends, and he can't get out here until Monday."

"But—"

Connie interrupted her. "Relax, Jill. I talked to the local paramedics. They can be here in less than five minutes. The fire station is just up the road, and there's always at least one paramedic on duty."

Jill nodded. "You've got all the bases covered. Forget I even asked, okay?"

"Okay." Connie laughed. "Since you're here, what do you want me to do with your briefcase? You promised me you wouldn't work while we were here."

"Is there a top shelf in the closet?"

Connie nodded. "Yes."

"Perfect. Throw it up there and I won't be tempted."

"Great idea!" Connie turned on the light in the closet and tossed Jill's briefcase on the top shelf. "Congratulations," she said. "Now that your work's out of reach, you have nothing to do but enjoy yourself."

They'd searched Jill's house, but they hadn't found a clue to the place where Connie had taken her. Doug had gone home, hoping that Jill would keep her promise to call, but he knew that was unlikely. His team was busy calling every bed-and-breakfast in Northern Minnesota, but Doug doubted they'd be successful. It was foolish to assume that Connie had told Jill the truth about where they were going.

Connie could have taken her anywhere, even out of state. The reverse was also true. They could be holed up in a motel on the edge of town, and Doug would never find them. Only one thing gave Doug hope. Connie had killed only adult male transplant recipients. Jill was female, and she hadn't had a transplant. Connie would have no reason to kill her.

The phone rang and Doug reached out to grab it. It was a woman's voice, but it wasn't Jill.

"Detective Lake? This is Beth Stanford. You told me to call you if I thought of anything I hadn't told you about Connie."

"Yes, Beth?" Doug's heart beat a rapid tattoo in his chest.

"Connie was pregnant. Alan told us on Thanksgiving Day. That's why they wanted to get married right away."

Doug frowned. Was it possible that he was wrong? Connie had started to work for Neil and Jill in May, and she certainly hadn't been pregnant!

"She had a miscarriage when they told her Alan was dead." Beth sighed deeply. "While she was in the hospital, my father had the movers pack up the condo. He put Connie's things in the manager's office, and he changed the locks so she couldn't get in."

Doug couldn't help flinching. Mr. Stanford sounded like a real bastard.

"I can't help feeling sorry for her, Detective. Connie lost the home she shared with Alan. And she lost all of his things, even the photographs of him. She even lost his baby, the only part of him that was left alive."

Except for the transplants! Doug's eyes widened as he thought of it. "Just one more thing, Beth. Do you think Connie knew about Alan's donor card?"

"I know she did. Our lawyer told her. He thought it might

help to make her feel better, knowing that a part of Alan lived on."

"Thank you. You've been very helpful." Doug hung up, a thoughtful expression on his face. The pieces were starting to fall into place. Now he knew Connie's motive.

Jill sighed and reached out to turn on the light. It was no use. She couldn't sleep. She'd slept so much earlier that she simply couldn't sleep any longer.

The cup of hot chocolate Connie had made was still on her bedside table. Jill carried it to the connecting bathroom and dumped it down the drain. She hadn't wanted to hurt Connie's feelings, and she'd pretended to enjoy it, but it was the worst hot chocolate she'd ever had. It must have been the sweetener Connie used, but it was slightly bitter with an unpleasant aftertaste.

Jill opened the French doors and shivered slightly. The night was much colder than the day had been. There were two chaise longues, side by side on the balcony. Jill could imagine sitting out there with Doug, holding hands and watching the stars glitter above them. He knew how to be companionably silent, something that Neil had never learned. To Neil, silence had been nothing but a void waiting to be filled by the sound of his own voice.

Thinking about Neil made Jill feel sad. He hadn't been the right husband for her, but no one deserved to die the way he had. Although Doug had spared her the details, she did not doubt that her husband had suffered a fate similar to the other victims'. Doug should have the name of the donor by now, and he'd be interviewing the other transplant recipients. For all she knew, he could be arresting the killer right now, and when she got back, the case would be solved.

Jill picked up the phone on her dresser. She was anxious to find out how much Doug had learned from the hospital records, whether he had the killer in custody. It was almost midnight, but Doug had told her to call him at any time.

There was no dial tone. Jill hung up and tried again. The line was completely dead. The phone had been working earlier in the day. Connie had said she'd called the garage, and she had also spoken to the paramedics. This must be a temporary problem. They'd probably fix it tomorrow. Jill wasn't worried. Even in the worst-case scenario, Connie could walk to the fire station for help.

She was disappointed, though. She'd been looking forward to hearing Doug's voice. She couldn't sleep, and she didn't feel like reading. What could she do to fill the time?

The moment she thought of it, Jill grabbed a warm sweater. She'd sit out on the balcony and watch the silvery path the moon cast on the surface of the lake. It would be peaceful, and she would enjoy a little solitude. She hadn't really had any time to herself since she'd hired Connie.

As she put on her sweater, the top button popped off and rolled under her bed. When Jill got down on her hands and knees to retrieve it, she saw that someone had stored several large boxes under her mattress. They certainly weren't hers. She'd brought only one suitcase, a tote bag, and her briefcase. A former guest must have left them here.

Although she knew she had no right to invade someone else's privacy, Jill's curiosity got the better of her. She pulled out one of the boxes and read the stamp on the side. The box was from Susie's Babyland, a shop in the mall only a mile from her house. And the picture on the front panel showed that it contained a bassinet.

"What on earth . . . ?" Jill pulled out another box. This one had already been opened, and Jill glanced inside. It held a complete layette and a box of disposable diapers, newborn size. Jill didn't bother to pull out the third box. Its contents were written plainly on the side. Starter Kit—Enfamil. Complete Bottles and Liners Included.

Jill sat back on her heels and frowned deeply. Had Connie planned a surprise baby shower for her? Or was there another, more sinister explanation. Although Connie had said they'd only stay for five days, this room was all ready to be set up as a nursery. And she was stuck here with a phone that was dead and a car that wouldn't start.

There was no way all this could be a coincidence, and Jill was aware that panic was setting in. Was Connie planning on keeping her here until she had the baby?

Jill got up and raced to the door. She had to confront Connie, find out what was going on! But when she tried to open the door, she discovered that it was locked from the outside.

This wasn't the time to panic. She had to think clearly. It would do her no good to give way to her fear. She forced herself to tiptoe back and sit on the edge of her bed. She wasn't sure why, but Connie had brought her here and had locked her in. No one, not even Doug, knew where she was.

It took several minutes, but Jill managed to calm herself. So far, she was safe. Connie didn't know she'd found the nursery things. She thought Jill was sleeping. Of course the hot chocolate had tasted bitter. It must have been laced with a sedative. Connie probably planned on keeping her sedated until the baby was born.

She wouldn't eat any of the food Connie prepared. Or swallow the drinks she made. If she was drugged, she couldn't escape. The first thing she had to do was get word to Doug, and she had her cell phone in her purse.

Jill scowled as she pulled out the cell phone. The battery was low. She'd forgotten to recharge it. The charger was at home, plugged into the kitchen outlet, but there might be enough power for one short call. She had to make every second count. That meant she'd better plan what to say.

There was a small memo pad in her purse, and Jill pulled it out to make notes. She couldn't tell Doug the name of the lake. She didn't know it. And since she'd slept all the way here, she had no idea which turn-off they'd taken. The best she could do was say that it was a two-hour trip and describe any distinguishing features of the lake.

Jill slipped out onto the balcony to take a look. There was a small island with one tree in the center. She'd tell Doug about that. And she'd describe the large A-frame with the flagpole in front and the beautifully green lawn. If the phone was still functioning after all that, she'd tell Doug about their cabin, four bedrooms with balconies overlooking the lake and a driveway with a river-rock wall. She'd also mention that there was a dock in front with a bright blue rowboat beached on the sand.

After she'd made her notes, Jill stepped inside her closet and shut the door. She didn't want Connie to hear her talking, and this put one more wall between Connie's room and hers. Her fingers were shaking as she punched out Doug's number and she groaned as his answering machine picked up. Thank God he had a short message, but it seemed to take forever before she heard the beep.

"Doug. It's Jill. Connie's keeping me a prisoner until I have the baby; I don't know why. We're on a lake, two hours from my house. It's got a small island in the middle with one tree on it. There's a large A-frame directly across the lake with a flagpole, no flag, and a huge green lawn. It's big enough to be a hotel or a country club. Our driveway has a river-rock wall, and we have four balconies, overlook— Oh, damn!" Jill's cell phone had beeped and then disconnected. The battery was dead, and she had no way to recharge it. She just hoped she'd given Doug enough of a description for him to find her!

She slipped her cell phone into a pair of hiking boots she'd brought along on a whim, then tiptoed back out of the closet. That was when she heard it, the sound of a door banging open. Connie must have heard her voice!

Jill didn't think. She just dived into bed and pulled the covers up tightly. She started mumbling, as if she were talking in her sleep. Would Connie believe that she was having a nightmare? Jill said a little prayer and then mumbled even louder as Connie unlocked the door.

CHAPTER 37

He'd missed her call! Doug was so angry, he felt like hurling his answering machine across the room. Of course he didn't. The tape contained Jill's voice, and he listened to it over and over, transcribing every word. Finding her would be very tough, but it was possible. Doug picked up the phone and put in a call to Jill's cellular phone carrier.

It took him more than an hour, but at last he had the information he needed. They hadn't been able to give him an exact location, but it had narrowed the field. The call had originated from the two-one-eight area, and it had been transmitted through four satellite receivers to reach him. By drawing the path of the call on a map, Doug had come up with an area roughly fifty miles in diameter. Within that circle there were over five hundred lakes. Sixty-three of them had islands in the center. Doug knew he had his work cut out for him.

It was useless to hope for another call. A cellular phone technician had listened to the tape and given Doug the bad news. The beep he'd heard at the end of Jill's message meant that her battery had run out of power. She hadn't taken the charger with her. When they'd searched her house, Doug had noticed it next to the coffeepot on the kitchen counter.

But why was Connie keeping Jill prisoner? It just didn't make sense. Thank God he had three weeks to find her . . . didn't he?

Doug's fingers were trembling as he picked up the phone. Jill had told him that Connie had called her doctor to make sure it was safe for her to travel. The doctor wouldn't have given his permission if he'd had any doubts.

Jill's obstetrician sounded sleepy, but Doug identified himself and asked his questions, hardly daring to breathe while he waited for the answers. No, Jill's housekeeper hadn't called to find out if Jill could take a vacation. If she had, the doctor would never have agreed. Due dates were only educated guesses, and Jill could go into labor at any time.

After he'd thanked the doctor and hung up the phone, Doug slammed his fist into the table. His hand was throbbing as he put on his jacket and headed out to his car, but Doug didn't even feel it. He was too worried about Jill and the baby he'd come to think of as his.

It was difficult, but Jill had managed to pretend that nothing was wrong when Connie had come to wake her. Her nightmare act had worked. Connie hadn't suspected a thing. Now Connie was making breakfast and Jill was seated at the kitchen table. She kept a cheerful smile on her face and watched Connie's every move.

The eggs were safe. She'd seen Connie break them into an empty frying pan. The jam was suspect, though. Connie could have laced it with a sedative when she'd opened the jar.

"You don't want jam on your toast?" Connie looked surprised when Jill declined. "But, Jill, it's blueberry and that's your favorite."

Jill thought fast. "I know, but I'm saving up calories so

I can have another cup of hot chocolate tonight. It was so delicious, Connie. After I drank it, I slept like a baby all night through."

Somehow Jill managed to keep a pleasant expression on her face during breakfast, and after Connie had cleared the dishes, she turned to her with a question. "What do you want to do today?"

"I don't know." Jill's answer was perfectly candid. "Did you have anything in mind?"

"I thought we'd just relax and enjoy ourselves. It's a real relief to get away from live television. I don't miss it at all, do you?"

"Not really." Jill shook her head, although she suspected that Connie had broken the set deliberately. When she'd flicked it on that morning, she'd received nothing but static.

"We can still play movies on the VCR. I brought along some of your favorites." Connie pointed to the stack of tapes she'd piled on top of the set. "Do you want me to put one on?"

Jill shook her head. If Connie put on a movie, she'd probably sit down and watch it with her, and she really wanted to be alone so she could think about how to escape. "Not now. I think I'd like to sit on the porch and enjoy the sunshine."

"Good idea." Connie nodded. "Go ahead. I'll join you in just a minute."

Jill had no sooner settled down on the porch swing than Connie came out the door. "Let's talk, Jill. We're usually so busy we don't have time. This is a perfect opportunity for us to get to know each other better."

"Okay." Jill nodded, even though she'd much rather have been alone. "What do you want to talk about?"

"I thought I'd tell you about my boyfriend. He died last Thanksgiving."

"That's too bad. I'm sorry." Jill was careful not to react. What Connie had just said directly contradicted the story she'd told about being gay.

"It was awful." Connie sighed deeply. "I loved him. He was a wonderful man."

Jill nodded. "I'm sure he was, if you loved him. Tell me about him, Connie."

"He was handsome, and intelligent, and we were going to be married. The only problem was his parents."

Jill nodded again. She was learning a new side of Connie, and that might be helpful. "His parents didn't want him to marry?"

"It wasn't that. They wanted him to marry, but they didn't want him to marry me. They're very rich, and they've got social connections. They didn't think I was suitable."

"That's terrible!" Jill pretended to be very sympathetic. "You're such a nice person. I can't imagine anyone who wouldn't welcome you into their family."

Connie sighed. "Thank you. Part of it was, they didn't give me a chance. They wouldn't even agree to meet me!"

"They sound like awful people." Jill managed to look outraged for Connie. "You said they were rich?"

Connie gave a bitter little laugh. "Richer than God! That's what Alan used to say. They've got a big fancy estate, with a whole houseful of servants to wait on them hand and foot."

"Sometimes I wonder how people can possibly make that much money!" Jill was doing her best to keep Connie talking. She wanted all the information she could get. Connie might let something slip and give her a clue as to why she was holding Jill prisoner.

"They didn't make their money, they inherited it. Alan

told me all about it. His grandfather was some kind of stock market genius. When the market crashed, he was the only one who made money instead of losing it."

"So Alan's parents don't have to work?" Jill looked surprised.

"Of course not. His father owns a huge corporation, but all he does is sit in his office and watch the money come in."

Connie appeared very upset, and Jill led the conversation down another path. "How about Alan's mother? What does she do?"

"Charity things!" Connie fairly spit out the words. "You know how it is, Jill. People like Alan's mother don't do anything. They don't even raise their own children. They hire a nanny to do it for them."

Jill nodded. "I've heard of people like that, but I've never actually met them. Maybe it's a good thing. Alan's parents sound like horrible people."

"They are." Connie stood up and headed for the door. "Just talking about them makes me so upset I'm going to take a couple of aspirin. You said it all, Jill. The Stanfords are truly horrible people!"

Jill's mouth dropped open in surprise, and she was glad Connie wasn't there to see her reaction. There had been a chart on the nurses' desk the night Neil had gone in for his transplant. Jill had noticed the name on it—Alan Stanford. She'd wondered if that was the name of the donor, but when the doctor had told her that it was strictly confidential, she hadn't asked.

Jill's mind raced through the possibilities. If Alan Stanford had been the donor, Connie could be the serial killer. She could be sitting here calmly discussing life and love with her husband's killer!

* * *

"Are you sure, Doc?" Doug stared at the police psychiatrist in shock. When he'd described his crazy theory about how Connie Wilson had lost her baby and had then attempted to get pregnant by the men who'd received part of her boyfriend's body, Dr. Emmerson had said that Doug was probably right.

"It's a reasonable theory." Emmerson nodded. "Why are you so surprised?"

"Because the last part doesn't fit in. She's kidnapped Jill Bradley, the wife of the last victim, and I think she's holding her hostage until Bradley's baby is born."

Dr. Emmerson raised his eyebrows. "It *could* fit in with your theory. When did Mrs. Bradley conceive?"

"She's due in three weeks." Doug did the math quickly. "It had to be sometime in December."

"And when was her husband's transplant?"

"The day after Thanksgiving. But . . ." Doug stopped in mid sentence as the awful realization sank in. "Oh, my God, Doc! Jill got pregnant *after* her husband's transplant. And now Connie wants her baby!"

Dr. Emmerson nodded. "It fits with your original theory."

"Doc?" Doug's face was pale as he asked his final question. "What do you think she'll do to Jill, after the baby is born?"

Emmerson winced and glanced down at the table. When he looked up again, he couldn't quite meet Doug's eyes. "I'm sorry, Doug. Your serial killer has a single purpose that drives her. She wants a baby fathered by one of the transplant recipients. Once that baby is born, there's no reason to think she'll leave the natural mother alive."

When afternoon had rolled around, Jill had told Connie that she was sleepy. Connie had tucked her in bed for a nap and then had gone back downstairs. But the moment Jill had heard the lock click, she'd tiptoed to the closet, climbed up on a suitcase, and taken her mini cassette recorder out of her briefcase.

Now she was sitting on the edge of the bed, making a recording of everything Connie had told her. When she was finished, she planned to hide it under the floorboard she'd loosened at the back of the closet. If something happened to her, Doug would search the room thoroughly. He'd find the tape, and then he'd know everything that Connie had told her.

"The things she told me reminded me of something. Check with Dave Kramer at my office. He had a case, right after Thanksgiving, a woman who broke into a morgue to see her dead boyfriend's body. I can't remember all the details, but I remember that the boyfriend's parents locked her out of the place where they'd lived and she went a little crazy. Her lawyer pleaded extenuating circumstances, and we didn't prosecute. I'm not sure it was Connie, but part of it seems to fit."

Jill shivered slightly. There was something else Dave had said, something very important. She wished she could remember, but she couldn't seem to think straight.

"She seems to want to confide in me, and I'm sure I can get more information. I'm going to encourage her to drink and see what happens. When we got here, the rental agent had left a basket of fruit and a case of white wine. The doctor told me I could have a glass of wine with dinner, and I'm going to tell her that. I'll have more to tell you tonight, I'm almost sure of it. She seems to want to unburden herself, and I'm the only one here to listen."

Jill pushed the stop button, then tiptoed to the closet to hide the recorder. When she was back in bed again, she took a deep breath and let it out in a shuddering sigh.

"Find me, Doug." The whisper was like a prayer. "I'm scared, and I don't know how much longer I can keep up this charade. I'll escape to the woods if I can, but right now she's watching me too closely. Please, Doug . . . hurry!"

CHAPTER 38

"But I thought alcohol was bad for the baby." Connie frowned at Jill.

"It is, but only in excess." Jill kept her expression perfectly neutral. "Remember those sedatives the doctor gave me when I was having trouble sleeping?"

"Of course." Connie nodded. "He told me they were perfectly safe."

"They are, and so is one glass of wine. I'd certainly rather have wine than a pill . . . wouldn't you?"

Connie considered for a moment, and then she nodded again. "You're right, Jill. We're having chicken breasts stuffed with mushrooms tonight, and a glass of white wine would be nice. But I didn't think you could drink, so I didn't bother to bring any."

"Didn't you say the rental agent left us a case of white wine?"

"That's right!" Connie smiled. "I'll put a bottle in the refrigerator, and we'll have a glass for dinner."

Jill laughed. "Go ahead. Put in two bottles. I'm restricted to one glass, but you can have all you want. You've been working so hard, and this is supposed to be your vacation, too."

"Well . . . all right." Connie headed for the kitchen, but she stopped at the doorway and turned around. "No more than one glass, Jill. We have to think of our baby."

"That's right." Jill smiled, but after Connie had left her expression became anxious. Connie had said *our* baby, not the baby or your baby. Perhaps she'd used the same phrase before, Jill didn't remember, but this time it sounded very ominous.

"Thank you for your help, Sheriff." Doug was frowning as he got back into his car. He'd checked ten of the lakes that matched Jill's description, but none of them had a rental cabin with a river-rock wall near the driveway.

As he put the car in gear and started for the next location on his list, Doug felt helplessness wash over him in waves. He knew Jill was out there somewhere, but he was getting nowhere.

He had plenty of help. That wasn't the problem. Five two-man teams were scouring the area he'd drawn on the map. But driving around the lakes in the area was tedious and difficult to do at night. Although Doug had a handheld spotlight, it was difficult to see.

There had to be an easier way. He pulled off the road and parked in front of a rustic café. Coffee might help him to think, and he needed food. He'd talk to a couple of the locals and see if they had any ideas. He'd never been in the northern part of Minnesota before. They knew the area.

The waitress, a thin woman who must have been pretty when she was younger, was friendly when she brought his coffee. And when she found out that he came from Minneapolis, she told him all about the trip her daughter's class had taken to the Minnesota Zoo.

"So what are you doing up here?" She stood poised with her order pad.

"It's police business. I'm looking for two women who rented a cabin at one of the lakes."

"Which lake?" The waitress looked interested.

"I don't know. All I have is a description. It's small, and it has an island in the center with a single tree. The cabin has a river-rock wall by the driveway, and there's a big cabin, directly across the lake from theirs, with a huge green lawn and a flagpole."

"I don't think there's any lake like that around here." The waitress frowned. "But if there is, Speedy would know."

Doug leaned forward. "Speedy?"

"Speedy Harmon." The waitress nodded. "That's him in the checkered shirt at the end of the counter. Speedy drives around the lakes every day. He's our RFD man."

"Excuse me?" Doug was puzzled.

"RFD That's Rural Free Delivery, but they don't call it that anymore. The post office changed the name. Now it's a Star Route."

"The post office!" Doug was so excited, he almost jumped up to hug her. He handed her two twenties instead, then slid out of the booth. "Do you think you could get me a couple of sandwiches to go? I don't care what kind. And keep the change. I'm going to talk to Speedy."

It didn't take long before Doug was back in his car. In less than a minute, Speedy had eliminated the four lakes on his route and had given him the location of the neighboring Star Route delivery zone. Doug's spirits were high as he drove to the next sheriff's substation. Driving around four lakes would have taken him until dawn, yet he'd accomplished the check in minutes. And the only thing he'd had to do was buy Speedy Harmon a beer.

* * *

"What's the matter, Jill? Are you all right?"

"I'm fine." Jill smiled, though she felt like wincing. "I'm just a little tired. I think I'd better call it a night."

Connie glanced at her watch. "You're right. It's past midnight. Sleep well. I'll come up in a minute to tuck you in."

Jill climbed up the stairs and shivered as she opened the door to her room. Connie would lock her in again, and this time it would be for keeps. What she'd hoped was a touch of indigestion had turned out to be her worst nightmare. If she wanted to live to see her baby grow up, she couldn't let Connie know that she was in labor.

They'd set up a checkpoint at the Bemidgi Station, and Doug was on the phone. Two deputies were helping him, tying up all but one line.

"Detective?" One of the deputies waved him over. "I've got Red Spiers on the line. He delivers to Lady Lake, Elbow Lake, Beaver Lake, and Big Buck Lake. I read him you description, and he says there's a couple of driveways walled with river rock on his route."

Doug's hands were shaking as he took the phone. "Mr. Spiers? How about a big log cabin with a flagpole and a big green lawn?"

"Yup." Red Spiers sounded eager to help. "That'd be the Twin Pines Golf Club. It's right across the lake from the old Sherman place, and that's been a rental since Sherm moved to Florida and sold it."

"Does the Sherman place have a river-rock wall by the driveway?" Doug held his breath as he awaited the answer.

"Yup. It's got river rock. You can go with me in the morning, if you want to see it."

Doug felt like whooping with joy, but he took a deep breath instead. "I have to see it now, Mr. Spiers. I'm working on a kidnapping case, and I think they could be holed up there."

"Why didn't you say so in the first place?" Red Spiers was clearly excited. "Sit tight, sonny. I'll throw on some clothes and be there in a flash."

"Doug? I'm in labor. She doesn't know, but I can't keep it from her for much longer." Jill's voice was shaking as she recorded her message. "I got her drunk, and she told me everything."

Jill took a deep breath as another contraction hit, then let it out in a shuddering sigh. "She was pregnant, and she lost her baby when her boyfriend died. His name was Alan Stanford. He donated organs to Rossini, Turner, Woodard, and Neil. She's got this crazy idea that Alan will live on if she gets pregnant by a man who received a part of him. Rossini wouldn't cooperate. When he called her crazy and threatened to turn her over to the police, she killed him. Turner was next. She rented an apartment in his complex and seduced him. After two months, she found out he'd had a vasectomy, and she murdered him, too."

"She went on to Reverend Woodard." Jill took a deep breath and hoped her stomach would settle down. She wasn't sure if it was because she was in labor or if the sick feeling was caused by the awful things Connie had told her. "She said she tried to seduce him when she was being baptized, but he resisted her. He was praying for guidance when she murdered him. And she asked me if I didn't think it was a nice touch that she killed him on an altar."

Jill took another deep breath. Her hands were shaking, but she knew she couldn't panic. She had to make sure Doug caught Connie, and this tape would help. "She's sick, Doug. You've got to get her. She's like a loaded cannon, ready to fire, and I . . . I know I'm next. She's going to take my baby,

Doug. And she's going to kill me. She said it would only hurt for a second and then . . . then I'd be dead."

"Doug?" Jill was silent for a long moment. "I know this isn't the time, and it isn't the place, either . . . but I just want you to know that I love you. I've loved you for a long time and . . . Oh, Doug, I hope it's not too late for us!"

Jill wiped away a tear with the back of her hand and forced herself to calm down. If she got upset, the baby might come more quickly. The longer she could stay in labor without letting Connie know, the more time Doug would have to find her.

"She told me about Neil. She was his mistress, Doug. Connie was the other woman. She killed him after she went to the doctor and found out she couldn't have any more babies. It all makes sense, Doug. I got pregnant after Neil's transplant. That's why she wants my baby!"

Jill clicked off the recorder and hid it under the floorboard. After taking a deep breath for courage, she timed her contractions. They were forty-five minutes apart. Her baby was coming, and she couldn't wait much longer. The last contraction had been strong. Soon they would become more frequent. Now was the time to try to save the baby. If she delayed, she wouldn't be able to escape.

Red Spiers was a man in his sixties with a red beard streaked with gray. He arrived with a double-barreled shotgun under his arm, and he shook his head when Doug suggested he leave it at the station.

"Now look here, sonny." Red patted his shotgun. "I'm a pretty good shot, if I don't say so myself. You said this was a kidnapping case, and you might need some backup."

Doug nodded. "Okay. Let me drive and you ride . . . uh . . . shotgun."

"That's the spirit, sonny!" Red threw back his head and

laughed. "I like a man with a good sense of humor. Time's wasting so let's get going. Lady Lake's eleven miles to the south."

Jill's hands were shaking as she climbed over the balcony rail and grabbed her makeshift rope. She'd knotted her sheets together and secured them to a balcony post, and she'd changed into a dark sweatshirt so she'd be less easy to spot.

Could she climb down the rope when she was so unwieldy? What would happen if she had another contraction and lost her grip? She took a deep breath for courage, grabbed the first knot on the rope, and let herself swing down into space.

The post creaked, and Jill drew her breath in sharply. She didn't dare think about what would happen if it gave way. She just concentrated on letting herself down, one knot at a time, praying that Connie wouldn't hear her.

There were ten knots in the sheets, and Jill had gone past four when something ripped. Her sweatshirt had caught on a nail. She reached up with one hand to pull it free. Her heart was in her throat as she climbed down another knot and then another. Only four more knots to go and she'd be on the ground.

Just as Jill's feet touched solid ground, the lights went on in Connie's room. Connie had heard her. She had to get away!

Jill ducked around the side of the house and headed for the woods at an awkward run, her heart pounding in fear. She was only a few feet from the safety of the trees when she heard an almost inhuman scream.

"My baby!" Connie's voice was a raging howl. "I see you, Jill! You can't escape me! I'm going to find you and cut my baby out of you!"

CHAPTER 39

Connie was coming! Jill could hear her crashing through the bushes, and she clamped her hand over her mouth to stifle a gasp. She was having another contraction and she couldn't let Connie hear her. Jill had found a woodpile by the edge of the driveway and she'd ducked down to hide behind it. She could see the beam of Connie's flashlight and all she could do was pray that Connie wouldn't see her.

The beam of light was coming closer and Jill swallowed hard. If Connie's light swept over the woodpile, would she see her hiding there? Jill pulled the hood of her dark sweatshirt up, over her face, and curled into a fetal position. Doug was on his way. Jill was sure of it. But until he got here, she had to save her baby from Connie.

A light rain was falling and Jill shivered from a combination of cold and fear. She'd been out here for what seemed like hours and she was drenched to the skin. She'd managed to elude Connie by hiding behind trees and shrubs, but Jill's goal was to get to the road and she knew she hadn't made much progress.

Connie was coming closer! Jill could hear her voice now, and the words Connie was shouting made Jill's face turn pale with fright.

"Talk to me Alan! A part of you is inside her and you know where she is! Please, Alan! You've got to help me find our baby!"

Jill shuddered. Alan Stanford had been dead for almost ten months, but Connie still thought he was alive. She was insane. That was very clear. And she was also a killer. If Connie found her, her knife would slash down and Jill's life would be borne away in a wash of her own blood. She'd suffer the same fate as Willy Rossini, Mark Turner, Reverend Woodard, and Neil.

The shouting stopped. The night was perfectly quiet and for one brief, hopeful moment, Jill thought that Connie had given up. But then she heard Connie shout again and Jill realized that she was only a few feet away.

"What was that, Alan? Our baby is close to me? But where? Tell me where, darling! You've got to tell me where!"

Jill's heart was pounding so loudly, she was afraid that Connie might hear. The beam of light swept closer and closer, and then it was directly in her face.

"I told you not to hide from me!" Connie's voice was a shriek of pure rage. "You tried to run away with my baby!"

Jill knew she couldn't fight Connie physically, not in her weakened condition. For the space of a heartbeat, she gave way to overwhelming panic. It was over. Connie had found her. And she was going to die.

But some instinct for survival lifted Jill out of her panic. It made her mind start to work again, searching for ways she could throw Connie off balance. Connie believed that Alan was still alive. And she believed that Jill's baby had been fathered by a part of Alan.

"Thank God you found me!" Jill managed a weak smile. "Alan told me you'd come. I'm in labor, Connie. I'm having your baby and you've got to help me!"

Connie stepped back, startled. For the first time since Jill had met her, she looked confused and unsure of herself. "Alan told you I'd find you?"

"Yes." Jill nodded. "He was afraid I'd lose your baby, out here all alone in the woods. And I couldn't call out for you because I was having a contraction."

Connie's knife lowered slightly and there was a puzzled expression on her face. "Alan really talked to you?"

"He's wonderful." Jill nodded again. "I can see why you love him, Connie. He's very caring and he loves his baby. He told me he's inside me because he's a part of the baby."

All the rage left Connie's face and she sat down on a log next to Jill. "What else did Alan say?"

"He told me to stay here and wait for you." Jill managed to look perfectly sincere. "But I'm so cold and Alan said that's not good for the baby. What should we do, Connie?"

"We have to get you warm. Stand up, Jill. I'll help you back to the cabin."

"No, Connie." Jill shook her head and pretended to be listening to a voice deep within her. "Alan says I shouldn't move. Your baby's too close to being born and I might hurt him. I wouldn't want to do anything to hurt your baby, Connie."

Connie reached out to stroke Jill's hair and Jill tried not to shudder. Her touch was gentle, but the knife was still in her hand.

"Alan says you have to build a fire, Connie. It's the only way to save your baby." Jill pretended to listen again, and then she nodded. "He told me that if my body temperature drops too low, your baby could die of exposure."

Connie began to frown. "But I can't start a fire. I don't have any matches."

"Then go back to the cabin and get some. Bring some dry firewood, too. You have to keep your baby warm."

Connie's eyes narrowed. "I'm not going to leave you, Jill, You'll try to run away with my baby again!"

"No, Connie." Jill paused, and then she took a big chance. "Alan says . . . no, I can't tell you what he said."

"Tell me! What did Alan say?"

Jill winced, as if she didn't want to repeat it. But then she nodded. "All right, I'll tell you. But don't get mad at me."

"I won't. What did he say, Jill?"

Jill took a deep breath and then she blurted it out. "Alan's disappointed because you don't trust him!"

"What do you mean?" Connie's mouth dropped open. "Of course I trust Alan! He's the father of my baby and I love him!"

"I know that. And you know that. But Alan's not convinced. He says he's a lot stronger now that the baby's getting ready to be born. You have to trust him to stay with me while you go after the matches."

Connie nodded, but she still didn't look completely convinced. "I still think this could be a trick. How can I be sure that Alan's really talking to you?"

"Alan says he can prove it." Jill thought fast. "He says he'll tell me something that only you would know."

Connie nodded. "All right. What is it?"

"It's about the tapes." Jill remembered what Doug had told her about the Turner case. "Alan says he helped you find your tapes and take them away from Mark Turner's apartment. He told you to leave the other tapes to confuse anyone who searched the place."

Connie nodded. "That's true. Tell him I need more proof, Jill. I want to believe you, but I'm still not sure."

"He's going to tell me about a lawyer." Jill did her best to recall everything that Dave Kramer had told her about Connie's arraignment. "This lawyer helped you when you were in Judge Swensen's court. And his name was . . . Green. Harvey Green."

"That's right!"

Connie was beginning to look convinced and Jill decided to force a decision. If she was wrong, it would be all over. But if she was right, Connie would leave her to go back to the cabin.

"Alan says to stop wasting time, Connie. You've got to get those matches right now. If your baby dies, you'll never see him again!"

"Noooo!" Connie looked absolutely horrified and she reached out to stroke Jill's stomach. "I'm sorry, Alan. I was a fool not to trust you. I'll hurry right back with the matches, darling. I promise!"

Jill managed to stay perfectly still as Connie jumped to her feet. A moment later, Connie was running through the woods, her knife in one hand and her flashlight in the other.

How much time would she have? Jill shivered and sat up. Ten minutes? Twenty minutes? She watched until the beam from Connie's flashlight had faded into the distance, and them she pushed herself awkwardly to her feet. Jill knew she had to start now and go as far and as fast as she could. She'd bought herself precious minutes, but her ruse wouldn't work a second time. She had to get out to the road and flag down a car before Connie came back and discovered she was gone.

Jill forced her shaking legs to move, one foot in front of the other. As she brushed past trees and made her way deeper into the woods, there was only one thought in her mind. Doug was coming. He was a good detective and he would put all the pieces together. He'd find the lake and the cabin, and he'd be here any minute. She just had to keep moving, no matter what, until she was safely back in Doug's arms.

The drive seemed to take forever, but it was actually only ten minutes by the clock on the dash. Doug took the turn-off to the lake and shouted out a question. "How much farther?"

"Two, three miles." Red reached up to grab the roll bar in Doug's Explorer. "Careful, sonny . . . Some of these curves are steep. You're not going to do anybody any good if you wind up in the ditch."

Doug took a deep breath and slowed down. Red was right. But his heart was in his throat as he drove around the curves.

"Okay, sonny. It's right up here on your left. Cut your lights. You don't want 'em to see us coming, and the moon's bright tonight."

Doug didn't take time to consider whether Red was right or not. He flicked off his lights and blinked several times until he could see the faint outline of the driveway.

"It's straight for about thirty yards. Then there's a curve to the right. I'll tell you when we get to the curve. I've been down this driveway so many times, I could drive it in pitch black night."

Doug kept the wheel straight and turned when Red told him to. They'd just come out of the curve when both of them heard a crashing in the bushes.

"Stop, sonny! Now!" Red's voice was hoarse with emotion, and Doug tromped on the brakes. A second later, a figure dressed in dark clothing broke from the bushes, running straight toward them.

"Jill!" Doug jumped out of the car and caught her. "Are you all right?!"

"Yes . . . I mean, no! She's after me, Doug. And she's got a knife!"

Before Doug could do anything but thrust Jill behind him, another figure hurtled out of the bushes. It was Connie, and her knife was raised high.

"I'll kill you!" Her scream was so loud, the words seemed

to echo off the trees. "You can't take my baby away from me again!"

She was almost on top of them when a shot rang out, exploding the stillness of the night. Connie crumpled and the knife skittered across the gravel, coming to rest by Red's feet.

Red shrugged and put down his gun. "Hope you don't mind, sonny. I know you're the cop, but she almost got both of you."

"No . . . I don't mind." Doug sounded dazed. "Get in the car, Jill. Now."

Red helped Jill into the backseat. Then he joined Doug who was kneeling at Connie's side. "Is she dead, sonny?"

"Yes." Doug nodded. "I'd better call it in."

"No need, sonny. I can hear 'em coming at the end of the driveway. You just get yourself over to the county hospital. It's on the main road, about twenty miles to the north. You can't miss it."

"The hospital?" Doug gave his head a little shake to clear it. "But I told you before. She's dead."

"Not for her. For that other little lady in the car. I've got seven of my own, and I can tell you, you don't have any time to waste."

EPILOGUE

Jill had told him about the tape on the way to the hospital. One of the deputies had retrieved it. He'd brought it straight to the hospital, and Doug had played it while Jill was being examined by the doctor. There were still tears in Doug's eyes. She had been so courageous, yet so terribly frightened. Doug's tears had turned to happy tears when Jill had said that she loved him and she hoped it wasn't too late.

He had gone into action immediately, eliciting the aid of the whole sheriff's department. It had taken some frantic phone calls, but the sheriff had persuaded a friendly judge to cut through the red tape. Now Doug was grinning as he walked down the hospital corridor, carrying a big bouquet of flowers from the hospital gift shop. He was dressed in a tuxedo one of the deputies had borrowed from the local dry cleaner, the sleeves only an inch too short. The pants were short, too, but the sheriff's wife had come up with a pair of black socks and one of the doctors had contributed a white dress shirt.

"Doesn't she look beautiful?" The nurses were gathered around Jill's bed, and they were all smiling. One of them had rushed home to search through her closet, so Jill was wearing a white organdy blouse with delicate Irish lace at the collar and cuffs.

"Jill always looks beautiful." Doug smiled at her. "And your hair, with all those flowers and ribbons. Jill, honey . . . you look like a princess!"

Jill laughed and pulled the blankets a little higher. "You wouldn't say that if you saw the rest of me. Doug? Are you really sure you want to do this right now?"

Doug nodded.

"If you're going to do it, you'd better do it now." The head nurse gave Doug a gentle shove toward the bed. "We don't have much time. Her contractions are only three minutes apart."

"Okay." Doug took Jill's hand. "I'm ready if you are, Jill." Jill nodded. "I am."

The sheriff motioned for the judge, who took his place at the foot of the bed. He opened a book and cleared his throat, and then he looked very serious.

"We don't have much time so we're going to skip part of this and get down to the basics. Douglas Edward Lake, do you take this woman to be your lawfully wedded wife?"

"I do." Doug smile at Jill.

"Jill Marie Bradley? Do you take this man to be your lawfully wedded husband?"

"I . . . do!" Jill let out a groan and grasped Doug's hand. "Are we married yet?"

The judge shook his head. "Not quite. By the power vested in me by the State of Minnesota, I hereby pronounce you man and wife. Doug? You may kiss your bride."

"Thank you, Judge." Doug leaned over and placed a kiss on Jill's forehead.

"You're legal now." The judge closed his book and smiled at Doug. "And I suggest you get your wife straight to the delivery room. You're about to become a father."

* * *

The baby was lovely, with sandy hair and every one of his fingers and toes. Jill held the bottle to his lips and smiled as he gulped it eagerly. "Look, Doug. He knows exactly what he wants."

"I can see that." Doug reached down to stroke the baby's head. "He's just like me, Jill."

Jill laughed and then she was silent for a moment, watching their baby eat. When she looked up at Doug, she asked the question that had been on her mind ever since she'd arrived at the hospital. "Is she dead, Doug?"

"Yes." He took her hand. "It's over, Jill. Everything's over, and we can start a new life."

Jill looked up at him and blinked back a tear. "Thank God! I love you."

"I love you, too." Doug hugged her, but he didn't quite meet his new bride's eyes. It was true that Connie had died at the scene, but the paramedics had managed to restart her heart and hook her to life support for the trip to the hospital. Her brain waves were flat, but her body, still functioning with the aid of machines, awaited the arrival of a special team of doctors. There was only one reason the hospital was taking such heroic measures for a patient who was legally dead. Connie Wilson had filled out a donor card.

A KILLER RIVALRY . . .

When Eve Carrington is chosen to participate
in an exclusive writers workshop, she knows it's
a once-in-a-lifetime opportunity.
For one month, she will live, write, and share her work
with nine other aspiring authors.
The top three will get a chance to be published.
But when the building they're staying in isn't ready and
Eve sees the old mansion they'll be moved into,
she starts having second thoughts. Not only is the
mansion isolated but the deadlines are tight,
the pressure intense, and the competition incredibly
fierce. Her biggest rival, Angela, is writing a murder
mystery based on the workshop and its participants.
It's a brilliant idea. Until life begins to imitate art—
and death begins to knock out the competition . . .

**Please turn the page for an exciting sneak peek of
Joanne Fluke's**

WICKED

**coming in August 2016
wherever print and e-books are sold!**

PROLOGUE

It was over a hundred degrees in the shade and Eve Carrington was too hot to even smile at the handsome truck driver who pulled up beside her at the stoplight. One glance in the rearview mirror told her that he probably wouldn't have reacted anyway. The heat had ruined her expensive new hairstyle, her makeup was streaked by beads of perspiration, and the cream-color linen blouse she'd bought especially for today was impossibly wrinkled.

The stoplight was a long one and while she was waiting, Eve did her best to repair the damage. She brushed her midnight black hair, touched up her makeup, and applied new lip gloss. There wasn't a thing she could do about her wrinkled blouse, but she'd brought four suitcases of clothing with her and she'd change just as soon as she arrived.

The light turned green and Eve sighed as she stepped on the gas. Instead of broiling in this horrible heat wave, she could have been enjoying the private beach at Hampton Cove. All her friends had left for the beach last night and this was the first year she hadn't gone with them. At this very moment, she could be sipping an ice cold drink and reclining on a chaise longue under a striped umbrella, while handsome waiters hovered, just waiting for her to beckon for a refill. Why had she ever signed up for this stupid writers' workshop when it was bound to be the hottest, most boring month of her life?!

Eve frowned and reached out to check the air-conditioning vent. Cool air was pouring out, but the noon sun was so hot, it warmed the frigid air the moment it came out of the vent. The interior of her car felt like a sauna, and it was all Ryan's fault that she was so uncomfortable!

They'd planned to spend the entire month of August at the beach, but Eve's boyfriend, Ryan Young, had signed up for a workshop in creative writing. He'd told Eve that he was sorry he couldn't go to Hampton Cove with her, but he didn't want to pass up the opportunity of a lifetime.

The opportunity of a lifetime? Eve had lifted one perfectly shaped eyebrow. Exactly what was that? And Ryan had explained that this particular writing workshop was being led by Professor Hellman who had connections to several large publishing firms in New York.

Eve had shrugged. So? What good would Professor Hellman's connections do for Ryan?

Ryan had laughed and told her she couldn't possibly be so dense. She knew he wanted to write historical fiction. He'd told her all about it. This workshop was important because Professor Hellman had promised to take the best three workshop projects and submit them to his publisher friends.

Eve had listened as Ryan had described the workshop. They'd live in the Sutler Mansion on the edge of campus for four weeks. Professor Hellman would come in every Friday to critique their work and give them advice. Only ten students were being accepted, five guys and five women. That meant there was better than a thirty percent chance that the professor would choose Ryan's manuscript and send it to New York.

Normally, Eve wouldn't have batted an eyelash. There were plenty of handsome guys at Hampton Cove, and she could have had a pleasant vacation without Ryan. But one thing about the workshop worried Eve. Ryan would be spending his vacation with five other women, and he'd be with them day and night. It sounded like a recipe for romance to her, and she wasn't about to let another woman pick up on her handsome boyfriend.

Eve had called her father and asked if he could pull some strings. As a distinguished college alumnus who contributed heavily to various college funds, one word from him had done the trick. Ryan had been delighted when she'd told him that she'd been accepted at the workshop, but he'd also been puzzled. He'd had no idea that Eve was interested in creative writing.

Eve wasn't interested in creative writing, but here she was, dripping sweat, driving across campus to the Sutler Mansion. And to make matters worse, she wouldn't have the foggiest notion what her project would be. It would have to be good. Ryan thought she was as dedicated as he was, and she certainly didn't want to make a fool of herself.

She checked her map and drove around the corner, and there it was, the Sutler Mansion. Eve gave a groan of dismay as she parked in front. It looked like something straight out of a horror movie with its wavy glass windows and dark shutters. Ryan had told her that they were renovating it for faculty offices, but it was clear they hadn't started yet. The Sutler Mansion looked as if it might fall down around their ears.

Two girls barged out of the front door as she started to get out of her car. Eve smiled as she recognized them, Cheryl Frazier and Tracie Simmons, two of her sorority sisters.

"Hi, Eve." Cheryl, a pretty redhead with her hair in a ponytail, rushed up. "You're late."

"I know. I had to stop on the way to pick up some things."

"We'll help you unload." Tracie brushed her curly brown

hair out of her eyes and grabbed one of Eve's suitcases. "Everybody's already staked out their rooms, but Cheryl and I saved the best one for you."

It was no less than she had expected. She had the best room in the sorority house, too. It was only right. Since her money paid for most of the parties, and her father had arranged to have the whole place redecorated, it wasn't surprising that all Eve's sorority sisters treated her like a queen.

Eve let Cheryl and Tracie carry everything up the front steps. "I can hardly wait to get inside and cool off in front of the air-conditioning."

"Bad news, Eve." Cheryl shook her head. "We don't have air-conditioning . . . just fans, and they don't work very well in this kind of heat."

Eve gave a little sigh. This was turning from bad to worse. She followed them into the house and sighed again. It was slightly cooler inside, but not much.

"The brochure said there wasn't a pool, but I had no idea we'd be living in a place without air-conditioning!"

Tracie nodded. "Look on the bright side, Eve. It's supposed to cool off tonight and you've got the only room on the girls' floor with a balcony."

"The girls' floor?"

"That's right." Cheryl nodded. "The guys are on the second floor and we're on the third. The fourth used to be servant quarters and those rooms are off limits."

"Why?" Eve was curious.

"Because they haven't started fixing them up yet. There could be loose boards and weak spots in the floor."

"We've got a surprise for you, Eve." Tracie started to grin. "Your room's right above Ryan's. He's got the second-floor balcony and I thought it might be romantic, like Romeo and Juliet."

Eve sighed. Tracie was always trying to be romantic.

"Romance like that I don't need! Did you forget that Romeo and Juliet killed themselves in the end?'"

"I never thought about that!" Tracie was clearly shocked. "You're not mad at me, are you, Eve?"

"Of course not." Eve smiled at her. "I'm glad I have a balcony. I can leave the door open and maybe I'll get a breeze. Who else is on our floor, Tracie?"

"Beth Masters. She's got the room next to you."

"I'm sure you've seen her around campus." Cheryl noticed Eve's totally blank look and she went into detail."

"Beth's got light brown hair and she wears glasses. She's had a couple of her poems published in the *College Chronicle*."

Eve shrugged. "I probably know her. It just doesn't ring a bell. Tell me about the guys, Tracie."

"There's Ryan, of course. And Jeremy Lowe's here. I'm sure you remember him!"

Eve winced. She remembered Jeremy very well. She still couldn't believe that he'd actually had the nerve to ask her for a date. "Unfortunately, I do. He's the frat guy who put the dead lobster in our pool."

"That's Jeremy." Cheryl sighed. "I just hope he doesn't play any of his dumb practical jokes on us. And then there's Scott Logan. He does those in-depth things for the *Chronicle*."

"I've met Scott. Who else?"

"Marc Costello." Tracie frowned slightly. "His father does the Channel Seven sports and I went out with him once. Marc's cute, but he doesn't have a romantic bone in his body."

Eve nodded. Tracie was always looking for romance, but the kind of man she wanted was only found in books.

"Dean Isacs is here." Cheryl went on. "I know you've seen him around campus. He's a music major, really tall and skinny with long black hair."

"The guy who always carries his guitar?"

"That's him. Dean wants to write a rock musical."

"That's mildly interesting." Eve sighed. With the exception of Ryan, the rest of the guys didn't interest her at all. "I thought there were supposed to be five girls. Who's the other one?"

Tracie looked a little puzzled. "Somebody named Angela Adams. But she's not here yet."

"Angela Adams?" Eve repeated the name. "I don't think I know her."

Tracie nodded. "We don't know her, either. She's a new freshman and she's enrolling in the fall."

"A new freshman?" Eve was surprised. "I thought this workshop was only for current students."

"So did we," Cheryl said. "I don't know why they made an exception, but I guess we'll find out when she gets here."

"We have to finish fifty pages a week?" Eve stared at Ryan in shock. "But that's a lot of work!"

"Of course it is. This workshop is intensive. You didn't think we were going to sit around and play games, did you?"

"Of course not." Eve shook her head. "But I didn't realize we had to do quite that much. How about this computer keyboard and screen? How does it work?"

"It's exactly the same as a personal computer. We're all hooked into a network. The main CPU's up in the fourth floor hallway, along with the high-speed printer. When you want to print out you just send it up there and the pages print out."

Eve frowned at the small student desk with its secretarial chair. She wasn't looking forward to spending long hours, alone in her room, working on a project that didn't interest her. "How about food? Is it being catered?"

"Catered?" Ryan laughed. "That's a good one, Eve. If I didn't know you better, I'd swear you were serious."

Eve laughed, too, but she hadn't been joking. "Then we have a cook that comes in?"

"No caterer, no cook." Ryan shook his head. "We're roughing it, Eve. We're all going to take turns in the kitchen. The schedule's up on the bulletin board."

This was even worse than Eve had thought. "Then I guess we don't have maid service, either."

"No way. It's up to us to keep the place clean. We've got a dishwasher in the kitchen and a laundry room right next to the back door."

"I guess that's . . . handy." There was no way she'd wash her own clothes. Most of her things had to be dry cleaned anyway. She'd just stuff them all in a laundry bag and drive them out to the cleaner.

"You'd better hurry up, Eve." Ryan glanced at his watch. "'Get into your grubbies and meet me in the ground floor library. We've got a meeting at four.'"

"A meeting?"

"With Professor Hellman." Ryan headed for the door. "We're going to discuss our writing projects with him before we start."

"Wonderful. Thanks, Ryan." Eve waited until Ryan had left and then she glanced at her reflection in the mirror. She thought she looked very fashionable in her red sleeveless dress. She'd put on heels and she was wearing her ruby earrings, but perhaps that was too dressy for the crowd here.

Eve thought about it for a moment, and then she went to her closet to see what else she could find. Cheryl and Tracie had been wearing shorts and T-shirts when they'd come out to help her with her luggage, but if that was the way they were supposed to dress for the workshop, she was out of luck.

Why hadn't she stopped at the store to buy some designer

shorts and tops? Eve frowned as she surveyed the contents of her closet. She finally settled for a pair of tan slacks that had been especially tailored for her, and a forest green silk shell that hugged her figure and almost matched the color of her eyes.

Eve chose a pair of hand-sewn moccasins and slipped them on her feet. She looked casual, but elegant, and that was fine with her. Let the rest of them wear jeans, and shorts, and wrinkled tank tops. She had her standards and even if Angela Adams was dressed to the teeth, Eve knew she could stand her own.

She was about to leave her room when she heard a creaking sound. Eve stopped, her hand on the doorknob, and shivered slightly. It sounded as if someone were walking softly, on the floor above her. But that was impossible. The fourth floor was deserted and they weren't supposed to be up there.

Old houses creaked. Eve knew that. It was probably nothing but a floorboard expanding in the heat, or a cat or a squirrel running across the roof. Eve glanced up, her heart pounding hard, but there was no way she wanted to go up there and look for the source of the noise. She just pulled open the door and hurried out, into the hallway.

The third floor was deserted and Eve shivered. It gave her a slightly creepy feeling to be up here alone and she felt like glancing around to make sure no one was following her as she rushed to the door that led to the stairs.

Eve arrived at the library, breathless. But no one noticed that she was out of breath. Everyone in the library was gathered around the newcomer. Angela Adams had arrived.

Angela was gorgeous, with long blond hair and a peaches and cream complexion. Her lips were full, her teeth were even and white, and her smile was perfectly lovely. She was holding court in the center of the room and she was dressed in immaculate white shorts and a lavender-colored stretch top that left absolutely nothing to the imagination. She was tanned to perfection and her legs and arms were golden from hours in the sun. Angela Adams looked like a model for a designer line of expensive beachwear.

Eve watched intently as Angela spoke. She was too far away to hear what Angela was saying, but everyone else was paying rapt attention. She was telling a story with such graceful gestures, she looked almost as if she were dancing.

As Eve stood there staring, Angela laughed. It was a full-throated laugh, an infectious, happy laugh. Within the space of a second, she had everyone else laughing with her.

That was when Eve saw something that made her frown.

Angela reached out and put her hand on Ryan's arm. It was a possessive gesture, intimate and warm, and Eve felt her temper flare. Instead of pulling away, as Eve expected Ryan to do, he just smiled at Angela and put his hand over hers.

Eve clamped her lips shut tightly and stood there glaring, unable to tear her eyes away. Ryan was gazing at Angela with an expression that Eve knew well. It was a deeply personal, private look that she'd thought was for her alone. Ryan was gazing at Angela the same way he gazed at Eve, right before he kissed her good night . . .

The lines were drawn. The battle was on. Eve glared at her rival with undisguised malice. No one tried to steal Eve Carrington's boyfriend and lived to tell about it. It just wasn't done. Angela Adams was her enemy and Eve would make her pay . . .